TAKE ME
BACK

TAKE ME BACK

Paradise, Idaho: Book Four

ROSALIND JAMES

Published by Montlake Romance, Seattle

www.apub.com

Amazon, the Amazon logo, and Montlake Romance are trademarks of Amazon.com, Inc., or its affiliates.

ISBN-13: 9781503940789
ISBN-10: 1503940780

Cover design by Eileen Carey

Printed in the United States of America

Take what you want and pay for it, says God.

—*Proverb*

LAST ROUND

Henry Cavanaugh was winning, because that was what he did. Right up until he didn't.

He fixed his visitor with the cold blue stare that had proven effective for sixty-seven years now and wasn't getting any less so. His third most powerful weapon, after his razor-sharp mind and lack of sentiment.

"You going to tell on me?" he asked. "I'm shaking."

He turned his back on his visitor and headed to the bar that made up one entire wall of the enormous den. Outside, the heat lingered. The sun was setting, but the recently harvested wheat fields of Paradise, Idaho, having baked all day in a late-August heat wave, hadn't gotten the message yet. Inside the big house on the hill, though, where the town's wealthiest developer looked down on everybody below, it was cool and comfortable. Henry had a powerful thirst all the same. Getting into it with somebody always did that to him. He opened the little refrigerator, scooped out some ice cubes, and tossed them into a heavy tumbler, then twisted the top off a bottle and splashed a generous measure of Jim Beam over the ice. He didn't offer his visitor anything. He wasn't looking for company.

"How exactly do you see that playing out?" he asked, taking that best first swallow. The bourbon burned a path down his throat, as welcome as a young woman in a short dress and a tight spot.

"I'll mess you up if it gets out," his visitor said. Desperate, and not hiding it well enough. "I'll . . . I'll make sure I do."

"Really? Because I'd say that I'd be more likely to mess *you* up." Henry started to laugh. "Hell, I'd do it just for the entertainment value. Know what? I think I *will* do it. Thanks for the idea."

Fear was the best motivator there was. Nothing like a dose of good ol' terror to get your way. He dropped onto the couch, still laughing, and swung his booted feet up onto the huge reclaimed-wood-and-rebar coffee table the decorator had put in here, like wood from a barn was a hot thing. She'd had lousy taste, but a great ass.

He leaned back against the heavy distressed leather of the oversized couch and tipped the drink up again. The ice clinked, and a cube slipped against its neighbor, slid out, and shot down his windpipe. He coughed spasmodically in surprise, sending a fine spray of bourbon into the air that splattered in amber droplets onto blue jeans and pale wood. He tried to draw air into his lungs, and failed.

Damn ice cube. He was choking.

You were supposed to grab your throat. To signal. He was doing it with one hand, his glass falling onto the couch beside him. The cold liquid soaked his jeans, but he barely noticed as he stabbed a finger toward his Adam's apple.

Choking. Dammit. Choking, he signaled. His eyes were bulging, his mouth wide, but it wasn't working. Nothing was coming in. The ice should be melting, but it wasn't.

His visitor did nothing but stare at him. *Idiot.*

Henry was canted too far back on the couch to lean forward and cough up the cube. He swung his legs down from the table, but his feet tangled along the way, the high heel of a cowboy boot getting caught in the scroll of ironwork that made up the base.

Stupid bitch of a decorator, he thought as he lunged toward vertical and stood, finally getting his boot untangled. The movement shoved the coffee table forward, rucking up the Navajo rug beneath it. He wobbled, and finally—*finally*—he was dimly aware of the visitor behind him, putting a hand on his back.

His vision was fading, his hands jerking, but he could tell that wasn't the right way. You were supposed to grab the person around the middle, under the ribs. *Fool.*

When the shove came on both shoulder blades, he wasn't prepared for it. He lurched, tried to catch himself, tripped on the rug, and fell forward.

He saw the black metal at the edge of the coffee table coming toward him. Then his forehead met it, and he didn't see anything at all.

◆ ◆ ◆

The visitor stepped back hastily, heart racing, breath audible in the silent room, then scrambled around the table, half expecting Henry to clamber to his feet again.

There'd been no choice. *I think I* will *do it,* Henry had said. *Thanks for the idea.* He would, too. Just for fun. Henry had about as much mercy as a rattlesnake.

If he came to and remembered who'd been here and hadn't helped him . . . and then that other thing. The push.

He'd been so out of it, though. Choking, gagging. *Would* he remember? Or would he think that his visitor had screwed up the Heimlich maneuver?

That was it. An accident. The Heimlich didn't always work, and Henry was tall and big, hard to grab around the waist. It almost *had* happened that way, really. It had been a slip. Just a slip.

Everything would blow up if Henry talked. Reputation, home, future, *everything.*

Unless he was actually dead right now. Impossible to tell without touching him, and that wasn't happening.

A few anxious seconds, then, mind racing, heart pounding, thinking about how to make sure of it. Suppose Henry had left his car running. The garage was just outside the den. Henry had turned the car on, maybe, had come back inside for a drink and fallen while his house had filled with carbon monoxide.

No. Stupid. Nobody would believe that. Too risky anyway, leaving traces in the car. It was on all the cop shows. Fingerprints. Fibers. And that would be one too many accidents.

Forget it. Just get out before somebody sees you.

Night was falling outside the big house on Arcadia Ridge, and it felt as if curious eyes were peering in through the picture window that was starting to reflect the room: The giant moose head on one wall and the gleaming rows of bottles and mahogany bar opposite it. The huge leather couch and matching recliners, and the big-screen TV.

And the still form lying facedown across the coffee table, a dark patch staining one leg of his jeans where the bourbon had spilled, his bristles of gray hair sticking up aggressively on his lean head, the wrinkles etched into a neck tanned to leather by the years spent squinting at construction sites, shouting at foremen. Shouting at everybody.

Henry wasn't moving. Was he breathing? It didn't look like it.

Get out of here.

Fingerprints. The thought came with a hand an inch from the doorknob leading to the garage.

A careful backtrack, touching nothing. A tissue pulled from the box on the end table, then a twist of the doorknob into the garage. Using the tissue on the knob on the other side, because nobody would leave the door to the garage open. Certainly not Henry. Turning in the dark, then, toward the tiny yellow-lit square of the garage door opener. A shuffle through the inky blackness, and the visitor jumped as something fell over and landed with a clatter on the hood of Henry's truck.

Focus. Calm. A push with the tissue-covered hand against the garage door opener, then another push just as the massive door finished rumbling open, so it reversed direction. Darting fast, before it closed again, between the massive extended-cab truck and Henry's brand-new Cadillac, their black paintwork gleaming dully in the faint light from outside. Finally, the visitor was ducking underneath the rumbling garage door and walking along the driveway and down the road for a horribly visible three hundred yards to where the car sat tucked in between an RV and a boat. Outside Henry's neighbor's house, which had no lights on, because nobody was home.

Henry hadn't noticed the car on his way home tonight, and nobody else would have, either. Nobody would know.

Coming here tonight had been an impulsive decision. Almost disastrous. Maybe miraculous.

Then there was the drive home through the quiet dusk with hands that trembled stupidly on the wheel.

You didn't do a single thing wrong. Failing to succeed at rescuing somebody, not calling for help—that wasn't a crime. Practically a public service, in this case.

And whatever had happened to Henry . . . the son of a bitch deserved it.

LEADING CITIZEN

Jim Lawson was patrolling out by Ithaca, coming back in from the county line. He'd taken a slow, deliberate cruise through the mobile home park, aka Methtown, noting the group of guys sitting outside on a concrete patio despite the late-morning hour. He made some mental notes, returning the hostile stares with a bland gaze. On the way back to Paradise, he pulled over a battered Grand Am with an out-of-state plate for a broken taillight, asked a couple questions of the two young guys in it, ran the plate and registration, and let them go on when they didn't trip any of his switches. That was about the high point.

Not much going on, not on this sleepy Thursday morning in late August. The students were back in school, and the truckers knew better than to go over the limit.

"I swear, not a thing ever happens in this county," the department's new big-city detective, Tony DeMarco, had complained the previous week as the two of them had been working out at the university gym. "I thought I was slowing down. Good for my stress levels, the doc said. Good for my marriage, the wife said. Didn't realize I'd be watching TV just to see some police action."

"Seems to me an exciting thing or two has happened here recently." Jim eased the weights onto the barbell, then shifted around to the bench press. "Spot me, will you?"

"Recently?" DeMarco said. "I guess in Idaho time. It was all over months ago." He positioned his hands obligingly under the heavy bar as Jim pushed it slowly overhead and paused at the top for an excruciating two seconds, then brought it back down with control. "And it doesn't exactly require 'detection' when some lowlife comes home from the bar and starts smacking his girlfriend around."

Jim finished his set, then sat up and wiped his head down with a towel. "See, that's the difference between you and me," he finally said. "If you were from here, you'd realize that 'boring' just means that nobody you know is having an especially rough time right now. Not exactly a bad thing."

"Not itching to get into that SWAT uniform and make the bad people dead?" DeMarco said. "Hard to believe. No point in a specialty if you never get to use it."

"Put it that I already bagged my limit," Jim said. Nine years as an Army Ranger would do that to you. "Plus, maybe I'm lazy, you think of that?"

"Only every day," DeMarco said. Which was a lie, but made Jim grin. "Get your ass off that bench and give me a shot. My wife likes a good set of pecs."

"So where's she looking at those?" Jim asked, and stood up. "You talk too much, Chicago."

Now he smiled, remembering the conversation, then slowed for the Paradise city limits before heading south on 95 toward Union City. Which was why he was close when the call came through. An injury, possible death, at Cavanaugh's place. He put on the siren and took off.

The ambulance wasn't there yet when he arrived, but a young woman was. She was sitting on the fender of a ratty old Corolla, wearing red shorts and a gray T-shirt. Jim didn't know her. Thirtyish, thin, her brown hair in a ponytail. She stood up, wrapped her arms around herself, and walked in an agitated circle as Jim's white Explorer rolled up the blacktopped driveway. A surprising level of upset, considering whose house this was. But then, most people weren't used to coming across dead people, if somebody *was* dead.

On that thought, Jim grabbed his Smokey hat from the seat beside him and climbed down fast. "Ma'am," he said. "You put in a call?"

"He's . . ." She stopped and took a ragged breath. Pretty enough, but no makeup at all, and the ponytail was messy. "Henry. Mr. Cavanaugh. He's dead. At least, I'm pretty sure he's dead. He's not . . ." She swallowed. "Not moving. He looks . . . stiff."

"Where is he?" Jim headed for the house, and she followed behind.

"Downstairs. Den."

"What's your name?"

"Eileen. Eileen Hendricks. I'm the cleaner. That's all. I just came to clean. I'd done the whole upstairs already." The pitch of her voice was rising, becoming nearly hysterical. "While he was down there. All the *time.*"

Jim said, "Come with me, please, ma'am. Show me."

One of the oversized, ornately carved double doors was standing open as if Eileen had come flying out of it, which she probably had. Jim went on in with her following behind and took a quick look around the soaring entryway and the two-story-high wall opposite that was lined with river rock interspersed with Henry's proofs of manliness.

Nothing as insignificant as a deer had been allowed to pollute the trophy wall. A couple of elk, an antelope, a bighorn sheep, a mountain goat. On the floor, facing the door, an enormous black bear reared up on its hind legs, its heavy-clawed paws out in front of it, its mouth stretched wide in a snarl, showing all its teeth. Hell of a welcome mat.

Everything looked neat, nothing out of place. But then, Eileen had been through here already.

"Downstairs," she said, indicating the wide stairway.

"Don't touch the banister, please," Jim said on the way down, although if she already had, it wouldn't matter much. An open corridor stretched out before them with a few doors leading off it. Only one of them open, at the back of the house. Jim stepped into the den, and there he was.

Henry Cavanaugh, the least popular man in Paradise. Dead as a doornail.

◆ ◆ ◆

"It was all locked up," Eileen insisted fifteen minutes later. She was still shaky. Jim had told her to get herself a glass of water, but it was sitting untouched on the blocky marble coffee table.

The two of them were upstairs again, sitting on the living-room couch, under a giant window that looked out onto an endless landscape of rolling hills, an ever-changing scene more picturesque than any painting, all dusty golds and browns now with harvest complete.

The couch was white and pristine, and Jim would have bet that nobody'd sat on it in years. Eileen had vacuumed it already, she'd said, and all the upstairs carpet, too, as well as taking Lemon Pledge to every surface. If there had been evidence up here—not that evidence was going to be needed, if Henry's had been a natural death—it was gone.

The ambulance had left without Henry, because Jim had sent it away and called in the crime scene team and the doctor. Because of who Henry was. Because the TV hadn't been on. Because of all sorts of things.

The body was in full-blown rigor mortis, which meant Henry had died the previous night at the earliest. He was always at his office until after five, keeping an eye on his staff to make sure nobody took off early. If he hadn't been there the day before, Jim would find out soon enough. And it was at least fifty-fifty that he would have turned on the TV as soon as he'd entered his den, even before pouring himself a drink and sitting down. The baseball season was winding up, and Henry was the kind of guy who, when he went into a bar, made the bartender turn on the TV right away even if nobody else wanted to watch.

It was probably a heart attack. A stroke. Something like that. He'd been drinking something, though—bourbon, by the smell of it—and he'd keeled over and died. A guy without known health problems, who'd bragged about how his doctor called him "a bull," with one of those looks that let you know what he was talking about. Now, he was lying dead with a huge lump on his forehead.

They sure as hell needed an autopsy.

"Every door locked? You sure?" Jim pressed Eileen now. They had been when Jim had checked. Unusual for around here. "Front door, too? Anything out of place when you came in?"

She bobbed her head emphatically. "Yes. No. I mean, nothing out of place. It was all locked, always. He barely wanted *me* to have a key."

"How about the burglar alarm? Were you the one who switched it off?"

"He didn't turn it on, at least the days I came. I don't think he wanted me to have the code."

"When was the last time you saw him?"

Her hands were twisting in her purse straps. "I don't know. I just cleaned, that's all. He paid me with one of those bank things. The check came to my house. From the bank. I just cleaned."

Too much protesting. "Uh-huh." Jim scratched the back of his head and looked at her, keeping his gaze neutral. "How often did you come out here?"

"Thursdays." That answer came fast. "Like today. Every Thursday."

"How long did you spend out here?"

The hands were twisting again. "Hours. He made you clean everything, even if he didn't use it. Even though the only room he ever really used was the kitchen. He never did the dishes."

"Hours." Jim kept looking at her, and her eyes dropped. She hadn't mentioned Henry's bedroom or bathroom. Huh. "Did he ever come home while you were here?"

Her mouth opened, then closed. Her eyes met his, shifted away. "I don't know. Sometimes, maybe."

"What did he do when he came home?"

She wasn't answering. She was just staring at him like a deer in the headlights. The way Henry had probably shot those trophies. He'd been the kind of guy who'd shoot from his truck, who liked his prey helpless.

"I can't . . ." she whispered. "I needed this job. My kids . . . I've got kids."

"Did Henry ask you to do more than clean?"

Her mouth twisted in a grimace. "He didn't *ask*. And I'm a single mom."

"You couldn't afford to lose this house," he guessed.

"It's my best house." Her brown eyes begged him to understand, and Jim looked at her again. No makeup, old clothes, unflattering hair. Looking as unattractive as she could when she came here, but that hadn't discouraged Henry. "I got other houses out here because I cleaned his. And he told me he'd say something to the others if I didn't do it. That I'd stolen something." She was pleading now, and Jim didn't think it had anything to do with being a possible suspect. He didn't think she'd even realized she might be one.

Jim got the rest out of her, little by little, and what a sordid tale it was. "And that's been going on for almost a year?" he asked. "Did you think about calling us?"

The bitterness twisted her mouth again. "Who would've believed me? I clean houses. He's *rich*. And he paid me extra. You're going to find that out anyway. I know how you guys work. He paid me with a check, with the 'bonus' listed in the line at the bottom, you know, so there'd be a record. He said . . ." She closed her eyes, then opened them again. "That he could even write off his whores. But I'm *not*. I didn't ask him to pay me. I didn't want to get . . . money. I just wanted to feed my kids. I just wanted to do my *job*." She was crying now, the red blotching her thin cheeks. "I didn't want to use the money at all, but I had to, some of it. My son got sick, and I . . . I . . ."

"How did you spend the last couple days?" Jim asked. "Tuesday and Wednesday?" In case this was anything, he'd ask her now, while she was shaken up, scared. You couldn't be a nice guy and do this job.

She was scared, all right. In fact, she looked terrified. "Uh . . . during the day, I was doing houses. Then . . . umm, night before last—I was home. With my kids. Watching TV. Last night, I was home with my kids for dinner, of course, and I took them to Bible study at First Methodist. To day care there, you know, while I was at the class. Do you mean . . . I need an alibi? But he didn't—did somebody kill him?"

"We don't know what happened yet," Jim said. "I'm getting information, that's all. We'll be asking lots of questions. Hang on a minute and I'll write out a statement, have you sign it."

"I don't have to say about that, do I?" she asked. "Is everybody going to know? Please don't tell anybody what I did. I'll lose all my jobs. I'll . . . I'll . . ."

Jim was already writing. "The statement's about what happened today. About finding him, what you did today when you came out here, and when the last time was that you saw him. If I need more, I'll come ask you for it. None of the rest of it will come out unless it has to. If you didn't do anything wrong, you've got nothing to be scared of."

"That's not how it works," she said, and he wished he didn't know that was true.

He had her sign the brief statement, then reached into his pocket for the card case and pulled one out. "Here," he told her. "Give these folks a call. They can help."

She stared down at it. *Rape Crisis Center of the Palouse.* "But I wasn't . . ."

"Did you want to have sex with him?"

Her thin shoulders shook as she shuddered. "No," she said with the most energy she'd showed today. "No."

"If he made you do it, it's sexual assault. Doesn't have to be force. Coercion counts. Threats count."

"I'd be so ashamed, though. How could I tell anybody? How could I stand them to know what I . . . what he did?" The hand holding the card was shaking, the nails cut brutally short. Her whole persona said, "Don't look at me. Erase me."

"I'm guessing that's something they'll talk to you about," Jim said. "That you aren't the one who needs to be ashamed. Call them. They'll say it so you can hear it."

He walked her out to her car afterward. She climbed inside, then looked up at him through the open window and said, "If somebody else gets the house—maybe they'll need a cleaner. Do you think it would be soon?"

"Maybe," he said. "I don't know."

She drove off, passing the van with the crime scene guys coming the other way up the driveway. And Jim stood there and waited for them and thought, *Son of a bitch is dead.*

It was a good feeling.

DOORKNOBS AND
BROOMSTICKS

Jim was in the den, watching the doctor stripping off her gloves and two guys bagging the body, when DeMarco walked in.

"Ask and ye shall receive, huh?" the detective asked. "What have we got?"

"Not much," Jim said. "Unknown causes. Died between seven thirty and eight thirty last night." He glanced at the doctor.

"Nine at the very outside," she said. "But more like eight thirty. Air-conditioned in here, temps were constant."

"Hmm." DeMarco gazed at the body, face-up now, the mouth stretched wide, the eyes open and staring. "That bump on the head enough to do it?" It was a red swelling the size of a half dollar, rising high on one side of Henry's forehead.

The doctor said, "Can't say until they do the post. I didn't feel an obvious depressed fracture. No mushiness, to use the technical term. No bleeding from the nose or eyes. He fell and hit his head. That's all I can say at this point."

"Huh," DeMarco said. "Could be heart attack or something, then the fall. Older guy like that, with a gut." The zipper closed over Henry and the two techs took off up the stairs with the bag, and DeMarco glanced at the fingerprint tech, dusting along the bar now. "So why all this? Why the crime scene tape?"

Jim went to the door leading to the garage, standing open now, its knob gray with fingerprint powder. "Just a feeling at first. But take a look. His rig's there. He drove home and parked, came inside, right?"

"Yeah. So?"

"So take a look at this doorknob."

"Huh," DeMarco said again. "Smudged."

"Yep. He came in from the garage, presumably. Vanessa—" Jim nodded back in the direction of the den, toward the fingerprint tech. "She got some partials where you'd expect them, down low on the knob. Inside and outside of this door. And full sets on the knobs on the door to the den, so he opened that one." He twisted a curled hand as if he were opening a door. Fingers, thumb.

Vanessa had come to join them in the hallway. "But this smudge that's overlying his prints on *these* knobs," she said, "that's different. Could be somebody in gloves, or . . ." She pulled the sleeve of her coveralls over one hand and flapped the white material at them. "Covering their prints. *After* the last time Cavanaugh's bare fingers touched it."

"Work gloves?" DeMarco suggested.

"Ninety degrees out yesterday," Jim said. "Even at night, who'd have gloves on while he drove? Besides, his prints are there on the steering wheel of his rig, and on the driver's side door handle, too. No smudges. No gloves. And here, we've got smudges. On the garage door switch, too," he said, flipping on the garage light and showing DeMarco the glowing switch on the wall. "They cover their hand to get out, punch the garage door opener with that same covered hand, punch it again when it starts opening so it starts to close again, duck under it, and they're gone. And then there's this." He indicated the broom handle that had fallen across the hood of Henry's truck.

"A broom," DeMarco said flatly. "Yeah, that's damn suspicious. What, the person poked him in the head from across the room with the end of a broom handle? Book 'em, Danno. Does it have smudges on it, too, at least? Dare I hope for prints?"

"No," Jim said. "Not other than Henry's. Not even the cleaner's. She didn't do the garage, she said." He led the way back into the den again with DeMarco following. The fingerprint tech was back at the bar again, working on the liquor bottles. "But the broom falling across his rig like that? It's out of character. Somebody let their cart bang into his door in the parking lot at Walmart once and he went ballistic, took up two spaces every time from then on. He wouldn't have knocked it over in the first place, and he wouldn't have left it there if he had. Somebody was leaving, and they knocked it over."

"So that's what you've got," DeMarco said. "Smudges and a broom."

"And the kind of guy he was."

"Enemies?"

"Only everyone who knew him. What do you say, Doc?"

"Not a popular man," Dr. Marilyn Wright agreed, zipping up her bag.

"He was drinking," Jim said. "Sitting on the couch. Something happens, something sudden, and he spills his drink, stands up, then falls over and hits his head."

"Get the glass and body checked for toxins," DeMarco said. He looked at Dr. Wright. "What works that fast?"

She shrugged. "Plenty of things. Most of them you'd taste, though. And fast-acting poisons aren't something you can buy off the shelf."

"Would you taste it in bourbon?" DeMarco asked.

"Maybe not," she conceded. "Not if it was neat bourbon, anyway. If something's there, though, it should turn up when we run the toxicology screen. There aren't actually as many undetectable poisons of the Amazon rainforest as people seem to think."

"I know it sounds like a stretch," Jim said, "but I keep thinking he could've been pushed down onto the table, too. Hitting right at the corner like that, right on that rivet . . . maybe that was finishing him off. And the TV . . ." He explained about the TV not being on, then ended with, "Maybe he was even having, I don't know, some kind of survivable episode, and somebody gave him an extra shove to make sure he didn't survive it." He glanced at the doctor again.

She sighed. "I'm not psychic, guys. This is why we put him on the table, you know? And if that's it, I'm going. I have alive people who need me."

The fingerprint tech took off, too. She'd tried doing some dusting upstairs without any success. The cleaner, Eileen, had been right. She'd wiped every surface down thoroughly. Too thoroughly? The only prints had been hers, and there weren't many of them. Front door, light switches. That was about it.

"Who found him?" DeMarco asked when everyone else had left.

Jim explained about Eileen, and DeMarco whistled and said, "Bible study's a pretty good alibi, though."

"Bible study at First Methodist is over at eight," Jim answered. "Assuming she took the kids home first, it'd take her at least ten, fifteen more minutes to drive out here. The timing would be tight, if she stayed at the church for the whole thing, but it's an outside shot."

"He sounds like a piece of work," DeMarco said. "Maybe the hand of God just caught up with him."

"I don't know," Jim said. "Maybe."

"Why are you so hot to think it could be murder?" DeMarco asked. "If he's sitting down here with somebody, drinking, and he's not a guy with many friends, he must have known the person pretty well. Burglar alarm didn't go off. Doors weren't forced. With a rich guy like this, you're thinking money, right? So who inherits? He got family?"

"One brother. Younger. Worked for him."

"Promising. No kids?"

"Just one," Jim said. "A daughter in Seattle. Hallie."

◆ ◆ ◆

Jim was back at the office on Monday evening, dropping off some paperwork and about ready to head out, when DeMarco stuck his head in the squad-room door.

"Hey," he said. "The ME's report on Cavanaugh finally came in."

They went into the conference room, sat down, and DeMarco handed it over. "Idaho," the detective said. "How can reports take this long? Weekends off, that's why."

"You're not in Kansas anymore, Toto," Jim said absently. He flipped through the report, scanning, then reading more closely.

"Huh," he finally said. "That's weird. Haven't heard that one before. Traces of bourbon in his larynx. But only traces. How would that kill you?"

"But then the skull fracture," DeMarco said. "Possibly not enough to kill him under normal circumstances, either, but enough to keep his body from dealing with the asphyxiation. A perfect storm."

"Choked on a tiny bit of bourbon?" Jim said. "And *died?* How could that happen?"

"Ice cube," DeMarco said, reaching over and flipping a page. "That's what the doc thinks. Some microtrauma in his larynx, and clear signs of asphyxiation."

"You telling me he drowned on an ice cube," Jim said.

"I'm not telling you. The ME is."

"And the fall?"

"No bruising on his back, but a shove wouldn't necessarily leave bruising, of course. Looks like he choked, staggered around some, tripped on the rug, fell, hit his head, and died. And if anybody was there . . . well, being there isn't a crime. Could be that cleaner after all. She's the only other person in the house that we found evidence of. Fingerprints, and two hairs in the sheets that *she'd* taken off the bed. Fluids, too, I'll bet." None of which had been tested yet. They'd been waiting for the ME's report.

Jim considered. "Could be her, of course. The sheets and towels were in the laundry basket, though, left in the hallway. She was about to put them in the washer, but she looked in the den and saw the body. That's what she said. If she'd been the one there when he died, and she'd had the presence of mind not to leave fingerprints? All she'd have had to do was to turn the washer on the next day, then 'find' him and call us, and those hairs and fluids would have been gone. Wiping the fingerprints, but not washing the sheets, and then telling me about what he was doing to her, setting herself up to be suspected? No. And anyway—no. I'm not buying it. Even if the times worked, she'd have had to leave her kids alone to do it, or brought them with her. And *that,* I'm not buying. They're four and six. I don't care what he was holding over her head, she wouldn't have done that."

"You're a romantic," DeMarco said.

"No," Jim said. "I'm sure not. Women are capable of anything. *That* woman—I'd buy her killing for her kids, but not leaving them alone at night. Let alone the other inconsistencies."

"Probably not the brightest bulb in the chandelier," DeMarco said. "A cleaning lady."

"My cousin Luke's married to a cleaning lady."

"Oh." DeMarco had the grace to look discomfited. "Kayla? I thought she was a waitress."

"She wasn't always. But this whole thing . . ." Jim sighed, tapped the pages of the report together, and handed it back to DeMarco. "Feels hinky to me."

"Might be hinky," DeMarco said, "but there's no good evidence of a crime. The DA wouldn't waste time prosecuting even if we had a suspect, and you know it. The guy goes to work like normal. Secretary leaves at five fifteen, and he bitches at her like normal. He leaves his office at six fifteen like normal, goes to dinner at Ruby's like normal, reads the paper, doesn't talk. Leaves at seven fifteen like normal and gets in the truck alone. His prints in there, both doors. His prints at home, and nobody else's. No evidence but a smudged doorknob and a broom that fell over. So—what? Tell a jury that somebody made a guy choke on an ice cube? They'd laugh. There's no case. This is coming in as accidental death. Release the body to the grieving family, take the tape off the scene. We're done."

"He fell mighty hard onto that table, though," Jim said, not sure why he didn't want to let it go. "And I'm betting that somebody stood and watched him die, at the least. Who doesn't have a clue about the Heimlich maneuver, enough to at least give it a shot? Didn't help, didn't *call* for help, didn't report it? Watched him die, then covered up their presence at the scene? I'm not saying he didn't deserve to die, but that's cold."

"It might be cold," DeMarco said, "but it's not murder." He gathered the papers and stood up. "Another potentially interesting opportunity for detection bites the dust. So to speak."

LICENSE AND REGISTRATION

Hallie Cavanaugh looked at the clock on the dash again, like that would help.

Friday afternoon, 2:03 p.m. Great. She was still ten minutes from Paradise, and from her father's funeral, too. The hills ahead were hiding the town from view, but she knew exactly where she was, even though she hadn't been back for more than five years. Living in the same place for the first eighteen years of your life could do that to you. You never really left it behind.

She wasn't that person anymore, though. She wasn't a passive-aggressive teenager who could only defy her father by being late or forgetting to do something. Except that she'd delayed her departure from Seattle past any reasonable point, had forgotten to get gas the night before, had remembered at the last minute that she had to pay her rent and iron her skirt. And it had just gone on from there.

Fat lot of good the ironing had done her. The AC had been out in her car all summer. She'd taken it into the shop, heard the estimate, and promptly decided she could live without it. She liked driving with the windows down anyway unless she was on the freeway, so all she had to do was avoid the freeway when it was hot, right? Easy.

Driving through a North Idaho heat wave, though, was something else. When she'd looked into the mirror at the last rest stop—a stop that had probably been another delaying tactic—she'd seen her red hair curling into tight corkscrews, her pale skin glistening, her eyeliner a thing of the past, and her skirt wrinkled into accordion pleats. Linen had been a terrible choice, but it was the only respectable dark-colored skirt outfit she had. She didn't think showing up in canary yellow would have gone over big.

She was one hot mess. Literally. And she was already three—five— minutes late for her father's funeral.

Well, they could start without her. And her father wasn't going to be there to disapprove. That was kind of the point of the event.

Unfortunately, it seemed that an RSVP with regrets to your father's funeral wasn't allowed. At least not according to his lawyer.

"I'm sorry," Hallie had told her Uncle Dale when he'd called on Tuesday night to tell her that her father's body had been released by the police and the service scheduled for Friday. "I don't think I can make it. I teach, you know."

It was the lamest of excuses, one she'd already made when Dale had called the previous week to tell her that her father had died. Her uncle had sounded so shocked, so saddened, and all Hallie had felt was numb. Her procrastination today was classic avoidance. She didn't want to feel, because she was afraid of what would come up when she did. Knowing the reason for it didn't help much, though.

The excuse hadn't sounded any better an hour later when she'd made it to her father's attorney, Bob Jenkins. But how could you say, "My father was a miserable person, and the idea of going to his funeral and listening to people talk about him makes me hyperventilate and want to run away?" Not to mention going home at all. Back to the ghost of Henry Cavanaugh, and the ghost of the pathetic person she'd once been.

"I'm afraid it's not a choice," Bob had replied. "The will is specific about that. You're required to attend."

That had taken her aback. "I'm *required* to attend? Or what?"

"Or . . ." Bob had sighed. "You fail to inherit."

"Inherit what? He told me he was cutting me out." Something she'd long since made her peace with. If the price of inheritance was blind obedience, she'd chosen disinheritance. Or she'd thought she had.

When Bob had told her that she'd inherited her father's house, she'd been—well, "shocked" didn't begin to cover it. "The rest requires explanation that I can't do on the phone," he'd said. "I'll set up a meeting for Saturday to go over it. Assuming you're coming. Saturday morning at ten, if that suits you. There will be a number of others present."

"Saturday?" she'd asked, eager to focus on something else—anything else. "You work on the weekend? But I have to get back. If I can come at all."

"I think you'd better ask for a day off, if necessary," he'd answered. "As I said, there are others to consider as well."

After she'd hung up, she'd thought, *Others? Multiple others? Who?* And then, *I should have insisted.* Why couldn't she have made him talk to her today? But as usual, she managed to be tough only in her own mind, and after the fact. She was always a slow reactor, coming up with the perfect retort an hour too late to make it. But one Friday with a substitute wouldn't do her students any harm, and a death in the immediate family carried three days' bereavement leave.

She'd almost called back to say no all the same. She didn't want anything from her father, including his house, and she hated the thought of him pulling her strings from beyond the grave.

But when she'd told her mother that in her next phone conversation, Elaine had had another opinion.

"You're not going for him," her mother had said. "You're going for yourself. For closure. You deserve to be able to go home again, and to do that, you need to be able to look into that box. Then you can choose to put it away."

"It had better be a closed casket," Hallie had said. "I'm not looking in there."

Her mother had sighed. "You know what I mean. Closure. Trust me on this."

Hallie had done her best to rally. "Maybe you should come for it, then. It could be a closure party. A closure fest. We could serve margaritas."

Her mom had laughed, sounding as serene as always, as centered as Hallie almost never managed to be. "Nice try, baby. I got all the closure I needed a long time ago. Nothing says 'done' like 'Decree of Divorce.' I haven't been back to Paradise for fourteen years, and I'm not starting now. I'll be there in spirit, how's that? Call me and tell me everything."

"Over-under bet? Say, ten mourners?" Hallie had suggested, because what she'd wanted to say was, "Please, Mom. Please come. Please help me get through this."

"Nope," Elaine had answered. "I know the answer, and so do you. Can't bet unless you've got a sucker on the other end. Call me after. You can do this. You're a strong, determined, capable woman. And remember—in spirit."

She still wished her mother had come, but maybe it was too much to ask. Anyway, once you were an adult, your parents probably weren't required to go that far out of their way to give you moral support. If Hallie thought she'd do it differently herself—well, it didn't look like she was going to get the chance to find out. Another depressing thought for a woman of thirty-one with a total remaining family unit of one sometimes-distant mother and one *very* distant uncle.

Which was fine. It was *fine*. She was a full-grown adult. "You're going to be fine," she said aloud.

If she didn't want to be here, though, why was her foot pressing the gas pedal harder as she wound her way through the final curves and over the last hills hiding Paradise? Because she was late, and she hated being late, hated feeling breathless and guilty, the person she was trying so hard not to be anymore. She had to be here, so she just wanted to get it over with.

Strong. Capable. Determined. Yeah. That.

The white SUV flashed past in her peripheral vision before she registered it. Sitting just off the highway, nose pointed out, lettering on its side, light bars on top. She took a look at her speedometer. Sixty-eight. *Whoops.* She eased her foot up off the gas and told her heart to slow down, too. She was fine. Eight miles over the limit. Fine.

Fine in Washington. Where she wasn't.

She heard the siren first, a faint wail. Then it got louder, and the flashing lights appeared around the curve in her rearview mirror. An impatient blip on the siren let her know that he wasn't just looking to pass.

She muttered something she'd never say in a classroom, turned on her blinker, and slowed down. A final curve, and the Super 8 motel appeared on the right, with the town of Paradise stretching out below it. Where she was supposed to be right now. She pulled into the motel parking lot, laid her hands flat on the steering wheel, and told herself, *Breathe.*

Now that she was stopped, the full force of the September heat hit her through her open windows, together with the sound of ticking metal from her hood and the faint chirp of crickets. She heard a car door slam heavily behind her and watched in the rearview mirror as the deputy walked toward her, his gray-clad shoulders broad in his short-sleeved uniform shirt, his big dark-gray hat and aviator sunglasses shading his face. His gait was confident. Not strutting, just solid and sure.

He stopped outside her window, put a big hand on the frame, giving her a close-up view of a whole lot of corded forearm muscle, and bent to peer inside. "Ma'am," he began.

She said, "You have got to be kidding me."

She still couldn't see all of his face, but she didn't have to. She'd have known that walk anywhere.

His hand was still there on the window frame, and he didn't move. One second. Two. Then he said, "May I see your driver's license, registration, and proof of insurance, please?"

The first words he'd spoken to her in more than fourteen years.

Her day had lacked only Jim Lawson giving her a ticket. All he had to do was breathalyze her now to make the humiliation complete. She stabbed at the glove compartment with a forefinger and yanked out the envelope. It took her a while to find the right documents, and then she had to search for her license in her wallet, because it was buried, too. She should have organized her purse before she'd left this morning. Then she'd have been late enough to miss this whole thing. Just kiss that inheritance good-bye, and good riddance.

Closure was *way* overrated.

She handed the documents over, and Jim took them and said, "Would you step out of the vehicle, please?" His voice was deeper than ever, and completely impersonal.

No hope for it. She shoved the door open and got out.

She'd spent way, way too many hours imagining this moment. Somehow, though, she'd always been rich and famous when it happened. A Hollywood actress, first, paying a visit to her hometown to dedicate a new wing of the high school. And then, because the actress idea had been manifestly stupid, a high-tech start-up whiz doing the same thing. By the time she'd been a high school teacher who would never be dedicating so much as a restroom block, she hadn't needed the daydream anymore. Maybe once in a while she marveled that she'd ever cared that much, but that was it.

Honestly.

She might have chosen not to be a sticky, sweaty mess for it, though. And not to have been pulled over for speeding, too.

If you can't make it, fake it. She crossed her arms, put one strappy-sandaled ankle over the other, leaned back against the baking-hot car door, and said, "Deputy Lawson, I presume."

Jim was still holding her documents, but he wasn't looking at them.

"Hallie." His face had gone hard, the way it always had when he'd been under stress. Like he was closing down and hunkering behind the barricades.

"In the flesh. And late. So hustle up." She couldn't believe she'd managed that. She was doing fine. *Keep going.*

That perfectly chiseled mouth tightened. The mouth that had gone to work on her own, once upon a time. "You don't get to tell me that."

"And yet I just did." She gestured at the documents. "Give me a ticket. Go on. I've got this funeral to attend." *Better and better.*

"I'm surprised you bothered."

"Believe me, so am I. I could've gone another ten years easy without coming back here. And, yeah, I was speeding. Not even going to argue. So go on, Jim. Do it."

His head came up fast, and she would have grabbed the words back if she could.

"Go on. Do it. Please, Jim. Do it."

She'd breathed the words that night, had begged him as she'd looked up at him standing over her. When she'd been stretched out on the hood of his car, because he'd pushed her down onto it. After he'd perched her up there and taken off her clothes, and she'd pulled at his T-shirt and run her hands over his chest, touching a man for the first time and loving it. On that night when he'd kissed her so deeply he'd stolen every bit of her breath and her will, and then had taken her lower lip between his teeth and given it a nip that had made her whimper and the heat flood. The night when his mouth and teeth and hands and tongue and every other aggressive, demanding part of him had let her know that this was for real.

Until she'd found out that it wasn't real at all. That it hadn't mattered, he didn't care, and he could dump her again without a word, without a backward glance, when she'd needed him most.

He shoved her documents back at her. "I'm not giving you a ticket. You can't yank my chain anymore. Get on out of here."

He turned and walked back to his car. His shoulders were even broader than before. He'd always been built, but now, he was so much more.

Because he'd been a soldier, that was why, and now was a cop. Hard, physical training for a hard, physical job.

People changed. Jim had been through all kinds of trouble, the sorts of things she wouldn't have wished on anyone. He'd been a soldier, and a husband, and a father, and then a widower. He wasn't the brooding, intense twelve-year-old who'd made her ten-year-old knees helplessly weak, or the nineteen-year-old bad boy who'd broken her heart. And she wasn't that girl anymore, either.

It didn't matter anyway. It was over. Water under the bridge. A wave in the rearview mirror.

So why could seeing him still hurt her? Why had she resorted to a pretend toughness that she couldn't maintain for five minutes? Because she was weak, that was why.

She got back in the car, shoved everything back into the glove compartment, and took off with a squeal of tires.

Give me a ticket for that, Deputy.

◆　◆　◆

Jim sat in the car and watched her drive off without the ticket he should've given her.

Who cared that she still looked sweet as strawberry wine and had a voice that curled right down inside him and went where it had no business being? You put the distractions away and did the job. And he hadn't.

This hadn't been his plan at all for how their first meeting would go. He was supposed to see her tomorrow at the lawyer's office. *That* was the plan. Wearing a fresh haircut, a white button-down, black jeans, and his good boots. If he'd picked his clothes out already, so what? You suited up for the job. In this case, the job was to be cool and strong and calm, showing her how he'd moved on. He wasn't that nineteen-year-old kid with no future and nothing to show for himself but a tool belt, spending the hot summer days pounding nails into another one of her dad's crappy houses. He wasn't the hormone-crazed teenager swinging down for "supplies" when the boss's daughter came onto the work site in her little shorts and her strawberry-blonde corkscrew curls and her snug pink T-shirt. He wasn't the rough trade who'd had to settle for watching those big eyes sliding on over to him, checking out his arms and his abs, while he'd wanted his lips on hers, his hand in her hair, and her whole sweet self backed up hard against the wall. And had known it would be more than his job was worth to make a move. Which had turned out to be exactly right, and then some.

He wasn't that guy anymore, though, that kid with no prospects and nowhere to turn after she and her father had thrown him to the wolves. He had a good life, thank you very much. A house and a kid and respectability, right back here in the town where her dad had tried to take it all away.

And what had he done? He'd told her she couldn't yank his chain. Which was clear-as-hell manspeak for, "You're yanking my chain right this very minute." He put his head back against the headrest and swore.

When she'd leaned up against her car, crossed her pretty legs, and stared up at him, though . . .

She hadn't been cool—she'd been sweaty and messy and wild—but she'd been in control of the situation, and he hadn't. The V-neck of her blouse had showed him that her skin was still pale and unmarked by freckles, and her arms had been firm and shapely under the tiny sleeves. And that blouse . . . it had clung to her in the heat, and that hadn't done him any favors at all.

Go on, Jim. Do it.

No. He turned the key, slammed the rig into gear with unnecessary force, and put his blinker on. He wasn't going to think about her stretched out on the hood of his car, or the way her skin had gleamed in the moonlight, or the way she'd shivered and moaned when he'd touched her. He wasn't going to remember how it had felt to give sweet, sexy little Hallie her first time.

On the hood of a car. Yeah, Mr. Romance.

He shook his head and turned back onto the highway.

Tomorrow. You didn't always get second chances, but tomorrow would be his.

Cool. Calm. In control.

Hopefully.

MY CONDOLENCES

Hallie walked up the brick steps of Schalk's Funeral Chapel and into the hushed lobby, wiping her sweaty hands on her skirt and swallowing her queasiness. The air-conditioning was turned to a temperature so low that you couldn't help but imagine it being for the benefit of better corpse preservation, and the scent of lilies hung sickly sweet in the air. Discreet floral carpeting muffled her steps as she advanced down the hallway to the spot where a sober-faced young man stood, dressed in a black suit, hair cut ruthlessly short and parted on one side, hands clasped before him.

She hoped he got completely toasted on Friday nights and cut loose, because his expression was sadder than she'd bet anybody else here would be able to manage, and that kind of acting had to be stressful.

"Henry Cavanaugh," she said.

"The Lemhi Room," he answered.

Hallie followed the direction of his gaze into a hushed chamber playing piped-in organ music. She found padded chairs set in rows, walls hung with heavy deep-blue curtains, and risers in the front boasting a huge mahogany casket covered by a giant spray of flowers that she'd bet money had either been sent by the lawyer, the bank, or Cavanaugh Development. Behind the casket stood a lectern with a chair beside it, where a man she didn't know sat with his head bowed over a folder. This had to be the smallest room Schalk's had—it couldn't have held more than forty people at the most—but it wasn't exactly standing room only.

Everybody turned to look as she walked in, and she avoided eye contact, set up an invisible force shield around the gleaming casket—its lid blessedly closed—that held the man whose DNA she shared, and made a beeline for the only person here she truly wanted to see. Anthea Gray, her best friend since the seventh grade. Anthea sat in the next-to-back row wearing a black suit, her brown hair twisted into a neat coil, her entire appearance infinitely more appropriately funeral than Hallie's.

"Hi," Hallie whispered, slipping into a chair beside Anthea and nodding past her friend at Bob Jenkins, the senior partner in Anthea's firm—and Henry's attorney.

Anthea gave her a hug, then made a face and wiped her hands on Hallie's wrinkled skirt, which made Hallie take a surreptitious slap at her arm.

"Some people take the shower with their clothes off," Anthea said. "It's a concept."

"Long story. I was running late."

"Hey," Anthea said, dropping her voice even further so Bob couldn't hear, "we don't care. We're billing by the quarter hour. I'd bet you anything that Henry's foremen are on the clock, too. You could be paying for just about everybody's time here."

Hallie snorted, then turned it into a cough as heads turned. Her Uncle Dale gave her a little wave and a sorrowful smile from the front row, his wife, Faye, touched an eye with an actual white handkerchief, and the man up front stood, moved behind the lectern, cleared his throat, and said, "I think we'll begin."

"Let 'er rip. Story hour," Anthea muttered, and Hallie had to cough again.

The guy did his best, Hallie supposed. Another job that couldn't be easy. He recited Henry's resume, making a big deal of the way he'd built his business up from a hardscrabble beginning, building spec houses down in Boise and living rough in each while he finished them during every waking hour outside his day job. Settling on Paradise for his empire and never wavering in his determination to succeed. Sinking all his capital into his first development project, powering equally hard through every setback and triumph, never altering his routine or changing his nature, even as he became one of the wealthiest and most powerful men in Paradise.

"He was at heart a simple man," the hired minister intoned. "Hard work was his mantra, and hunting was his passion."

"Not hardly," Anthea said in Hallie's ear. "Screwing people over was his passion."

"He didn't suffer fools gladly," the minister continued, "but he built his name by never settling for less than anyone's best."

"If his name was 'asshole.'" That was Anthea again, and Hallie dug her elbow into her friend's side and hissed, *"Stop."* Nothing could be less appropriate than getting the giggles at your own father's funeral, and it felt way too close to happening. When she'd wanted to feel something, "hysteria" hadn't been on her list.

The service took less than fifteen minutes, and then the minister asked if anybody wanted to speak. There was a long pause, then Hallie's Uncle Dale got up, walked to the lectern, and said, "My brother wasn't a perfect man." And it all started again.

"He was my brother, and I'll miss him," Dale said at the end of it. His voice broke a little. Maybe it was true. Dale had worked beside his brother for forty years. What would he do now? Run the company, presumably, without Henry there telling him what an idiot he was every day. Not something Hallie would personally have missed, but then, people were nuts.

Her thoughts were interrupted when Dale asked, "Hallie? Would you like to speak?"

"No," she blurted out, then added, "No, thank you."

Dale stood for another moment, irresolute, then moved away, and the minister stepped up again and put a merciful end to things. "There will be no graveside service," he intoned, and Hallie thought, *Good thing, too, because we would've been down to, what, five?* Maybe it would have been healthy—more closure, and all that—but everything inside her shrank from the idea.

"Well, that was awkward," Anthea interrupted her thoughts to say, gathering her purse from the floor. "You, I mean."

"See, now, if it had been *you*," Hallie retorted, "you'd have gone up there and said, 'Why do you think I haven't been home for five years?'"

"Well, why not?" Anthea said with a shrug. "Everybody would've loved it except Dale. Given people something to talk about, anyway."

"I cannot believe you're an attorney," Hallie said. "You are the least tactful person I know. I'd think every client would fire you on day one."

"I think it and don't say it, that's how," Anthea said. "Until I go home to Ben and let loose. When you do family law, trust me, snark is self-preservation."

Bob Jenkins was turning now, though, saying, "Hallie. It's good to see you," and she had to accept condolences she didn't want. From Bob, from Aldon Cranfield, the president of the bank, then from two middle-aged men she didn't know, one lean and one bulky, who introduced themselves as Henry's foremen and made a beeline for the door immediately afterward. And from Uncle Dale and his wife, Faye.

Eight mourners, counting her. If she'd gotten her mother to take the bet, Hallie would totally have won.

Right now, though, Dale was pulling Hallie into a tight hug and saying, "It's so good to see you. I can't tell you," and Hallie was doing her best to reciprocate.

In fact, Uncle Dale had never been a huge part of her life, so she didn't know why seeing her would be anything special. But then, she was the closest blood relation he had left, so maybe that counted. Maybe it should count to her, too. Her mother felt like family, of course. Anthea and her kids felt like family, and so did a couple of her friends in Seattle. The family she'd chosen.

Faye did some air-kissing next, her cheek smooth and powdery against Hallie's. She must be forty-five now, but she looked barely thirty-two, any wrinkles held firmly at bay.

The twenty-year gap in age between husband and wife had never been more apparent, because if Faye hadn't aged, Dale certainly had. He looked gaunt, almost haunted, and Faye tucked her arm protectively through his and asked Hallie, "Where are you staying, honey? We'd love to have you at the house."

"Oh," Hallie said. "At Dad's. At least, Bob said it was . . . that I could. It's just for the night."

She should be having some emotions, especially now, with that huge gleaming mahogany casket taking up her peripheral vision despite all her attempts not to see it. Regret, anger, sadness. *Something.* Henry had been her *father.* Instead, all she'd felt since she'd heard the news was a sort of blank, hollow . . . space. Well, that and, once she'd set out today, the overwhelming urge to turn around again. The same way she felt right now, looking at Faye and Dale and reminding them that her father's million-dollar-plus property belonged to her, seeing the look in their eyes when she did. A look that asked, "Where does the rest of the money go?" *Awkward* didn't begin to cover it.

Faye looked momentarily taken aback at Hallie's refusal to stay with them. "Oh. I didn't realize you'd be allowed . . . that you'd be in the house." She glanced at her husband, got nothing but a shake of his head, and waved a manicured hand. "Never mind. Won't you be scared and lonesome out there all by yourself, though? It's so isolated up there, and with your dad—you know . . . Wouldn't you rather come and be cozy with us?"

Cozy didn't quite describe her uncle's house, at least the last time Hallie had been there. On the ridge a half mile from her dad's, it wasn't as big or as remote as the larger one to the east, but unless Faye had redecorated since Hallie had last been there, the whole place was terrifyingly white and cream. Hallie had sat down once with jam on her sleeve, and the living room had looked like a crime scene afterward.

"If she gets scared, she'll come stay with me," Anthea said. She hadn't left Hallie's side, to her relief. "I already invited her."

"I'd have to sleep in a bunk bed," Hallie said. She knew what Faye had meant: that Hallie would be uncomfortable, or worse, in the house where her father had died. But people died at home all the time. If nobody could live there afterward, half the houses in the world would be empty.

She'd hold that thought.

Anthea said, "Hey. You'd get the top bunk. Got *Frozen* sheets on there, too. You know you love Elsa."

Dale smiled. "You two girls. Always so perky."

Anthea just looked at him. "Well, not the exact word I'd have used, but OK." She turned to Hallie. "About ready?"

When the two of them were headed across the parking lot, Hallie asked, "How do you do that? I always hang around awkwardly and wait for somebody else to break up the party."

"Got to take up your own space in the world," Anthea said. "I keep telling you. Stand your ground. Say good-bye first. Make the plans. Kiss the boy while he's still thinking about how to make his move. Let *them* feel awkward, if somebody has to. But really, they'll just be relieved that somebody's made a decision. Come on," she added. "I took the afternoon off. Let's go have a drink. You look like you could use one."

Hallie sighed. "You just did it again."

"You bet," Anthea said. "Watch and learn. Follow me, Princess Hallie. Daiquiris await."

"That's just what I told my mom," Hallie said in surprise. "Closure party. Except I said margaritas."

"See?" Anthea said. "You have great ideas. Next time, put it on out there. Announce it, and I'll follow *you*. All it takes is guts."

SECRETS AND LIES

The killer looked at the clock on the dash. Four o'clock. Henry's body would be going into the ground right now, and taking all its secrets with it.

It had been a nervous week. You could say that. Starting with the first part—waiting for the body to be discovered. Jumping at every phone call all evening and through all of that long, dragging next morning, expecting a knock on the door at any second, all the while trying desperately to disguise the fear. Trying to forget waking drenched in cold sweat from a dream of Henry standing up from the coffee table, blood streaming down a terrible, grinning face, and pointing an accusing finger at his killer. A dream that had come every night since, no matter how many times you repeated the words.

You didn't kill him. You didn't do anything. You tried to do the Heimlich, and he slipped. He choked, and he fell.

Maybe it would have been better to make it look like a burglary. That was the thought that had had the killer swinging out of bed that first night, after the dream. Maybe it would be better to go back to the house, break in, and trash the place. In gloves. The killer had made it all the way out of the bedroom before realizing how stupid the idea was and suffering another sickening stab of fear at coming so close to doing something that crazy.

Why would somebody choke and fall right when they were being bur-glarized? That would be so much more suspicious. Plus, you'd have about ten minutes before the cops got there, if the alarm's on. Stay cool. There's nothing linking you to it.

Hearing the news that the body had been discovered had been the biggest relief of the killer's life, had caused some more sweaty palms and weak knees despite every pep talk. After that, though, the crime scene tape had gone up, and if the killer thought the first wait had been nerve-wracking—the hours and days that followed were worse. Going over and over the events of the evening, trying to see how anybody could draw a link, rehearsing the story just in case they did. *He choked. You tried to save him. He fell. You saw he was dead, and you got scared and ran. There was no point in calling for help, because he was already dead.*

And what link could there be? The killer had never intended to do anything but talk to Henry. All right, to confront him, to make sure he wasn't going to talk about . . . the thing. But nothing more than that. Not parking in Henry's driveway hadn't been for any evil purpose. It had just been to make sure Henry would let his visitor in. He'd been so unpredictable. Downright nasty, at times. That was the reason the killer had waited around the corner from the garage and then walked through the open door when Henry's truck had rolled in. Just to talk, that was all.

There had been nothing left behind. No clues. No fingerprints, because Henry had gone through every door first. Because Henry *always* went first, like he had the divine right.

No. There could be nothing. No proof. Unless somebody had seen the car.

That was the thought that had kept the killer's palms sweaty, the thoughts circling and nagging and tormenting until the crime scene tape had come down and the funeral had been announced in the paper, together with the cause of death.

Accidental.

Which was what it had been.

Now, Henry was in the ground, and it was all over. Except for the reading of the will.

Tomorrow.

FAMILY TIME

When Jim walked through the back door into his mother's kitchen a few hours after seeing Hallie, his daughter, Mac, looked up from the paper and colored pencils spread around her on the table and said, "You're late."

"Yep." Jim went over and dropped a kiss on top of her shining dark head. Her French braid still looked great, he saw with satisfaction. "What're you working on?"

"World Geography homework. A map of the Middle East. Two maps, actually. Past and present. You wouldn't believe how much the boundaries have changed in the past hundred years, Dad. It's really interesting."

"Mm." He'd believe it, actually. His boots had pounded a whole lot of desert sand among those shifting boundaries, going after one warlord or another. Which had only brought in another warlord to fill the power vacuum, but then, policy hadn't been his job. "Where's Grandma?"

"Bunco night." Mac began to slot her colored pencils neatly into their box. "I ate dinner already. Your shift was over at four. What happened?"

She always knew. Mackenzie might only be eleven, but she kept a copy of his shift schedule in her notebook, and barely needed it. Mac's brain was a filing cabinet all its own.

"Wrapping up the paperwork on a case," he said.

"Was it that old guy who died?"

"How do you know about that?"

She sighed. "I read the news, Dad. It was online. Plus, kids were talking about it. They said it was a murder, like a mystery, because there was police tape around the house. I said there's *always* police tape if they're not sure how somebody died. That doesn't make it a murder."

"Well, you were right. No mystery, and no murder. Just a guy who died." He didn't want to talk about Henry Cavanaugh. The man and his death stuck in his craw like a chicken bone. Or an ice cube. "Let's go home. I'm hungry."

Before they could do it, though, his half brother, Cole, wandered into the kitchen. When he saw Jim, he stopped, pulled his earphones hastily out from under his shaggy blond hair, opened the refrigerator door, and bent to study the contents.

"What are you listening to?" Jim asked.

"Nothing."

Jim yanked the phone out of the back pocket of Cole's skinny jeans, and Cole whirled to face him. "You're pirating again. We've had this talk too many times." When Jim had found over two thousand songs on his brother's computer that he hadn't paid for, for example.

"That's bullshit," Cole said, a faint flush appearing on his cheeks. "It was bullshit last time, and it's bullshit now. And you're not in charge of me." He looked a little scared that he'd said it, and rushed on to say, "Anyway, art should be free."

Jim didn't say anything. He just got still and looked at his brother until Cole dropped his gaze. Jim didn't have a chance to continue, though, because Mac had somehow gotten between him and Cole with a hand on her hip, her dark eyes flashing. Looking exactly like her mom, just that tiny and fierce, and Jim's heart both hurt and swelled to see it. Like always.

"Don't talk to him like that," she told Cole. "Show some respect."

Cole said, "He's not my dad. He's just my half brother. And I'm your uncle. *You* show some respect."

Jim put a hand on his daughter's shoulder. "Hang on, partner," he told her, and then said to Cole, keeping his voice even, "First, don't use that language in front of Mac again. Got that?"

Cole scowled, but he muttered, "Yeah."

"Second," Jim said, "it's illegal, it's theft, and it's wrong. If you like those bands so much, support them."

"I can't afford it."

"Then don't listen. I'd like a brand-new, tricked-out, crew-cab F-150, myself. Black. Got that sucker all picked out. I'd like a whole lot of things I don't have. And I already said this, but I'm going to say it again. The one they'd come after would be Mom. You want that?" It was the last thing their mother needed, and it wasn't going to happen. But helping to raise a resentful, fifteen-year-old half brother, Jim had long since found out, was a whole lot different than raising your own child. Especially when that fifteen-year-old could have been you seventeen years ago, lousy attitude and all, and you'd left home when he'd been all of two years old.

"I told you," Cole said, "nobody's going to come after her. Or me, either. Everybody torrents."

"I don't care who else does it. Everybody else in the whole wide world can do it. Except you. If I find it again, the phone's gone, and so is the computer."

"Hoo-ah, Sarge," Cole muttered.

Jim felt Mac tensing under his hand. He gave her shoulder a squeeze and said, "Yep. I'm all that. Everything you're thinking. But I'm also the guy who'll take that phone and toss it without giving it a second thought if that's what I've got to do to finally stop this. Twenty-four hours, and your computer and phone had better be wiped of anything you haven't paid for. I'll check."

Cole shot him a sidelong look, muttered, "Fine," and left the room, and Jim sighed and scratched the back of his head.

"That went well," he told Mac.

She headed back over to the table and grabbed her backpack. "Why does he have to be such a jerk?"

"Because he's fifteen. It's a rule. Give it another three or four years, and you'll be rolling your eyes at me yourself like somebody flipped a switch. Let me tell you, I can wait for that." He took the pack from her and hefted it over one shoulder. "Let's go home, partner."

FACING THE GHOSTS

As a closure party, Hallie thought, it hadn't been much. One drink with Anthea in the blessed cool of Señor Fred's, during which she tried hard not to notice that she was home for the first time in five years or to think about the reason, and Anthea obligingly talked about other things, and then back to Anthea's.

Another place she hadn't been for five years. No matter the obstacles, though, some relationships were forever, and they weren't always romantic ones.

"Thanks, hon," Anthea said when her husband came inside with a platter of barbecued meat and set it on the kitchen table. "Too hot to turn the oven on."

"Here's my question," Hallie said, snitching a slice of jicama from the salad bowl. "What's the deal with barbecuing? Why does it seem like a good idea to stand over a burning fire in ninety degrees?"

"Shh," Anthea said. "Ben hasn't figured that out yet."

"Men love fire," Ben said. "It's in the DNA." A math professor at the university, he wasn't exactly good-looking, with his solid build and his glasses. But he had laughing eyes that still got a little goofy when he looked at his wife. Anthea had some gene that had flat-out missed

Hallie. The "find a good man and keep him" gene. Not to mention the "stay in the hometown" gene.

"I like fire!" Tyson, their four-year-old, piped up. "I'm going to be a fireman when I grow up."

"Firefighter," Anthea corrected automatically.

"Fire *man*," Tyson said stoutly. "Because I'm a boy. Or I'm going to be DeeDee's dog."

"Umm . . ." Hallie said. "DeeDee" was Deirdre, Anthea and Ben's seven-year-old, who was sitting beside Hallie.

"I *told* you, Ty," Deirdre said with a sigh. "You can't be my dog. Boys can't be *dogs*."

"Yes they can," Tyson said. "If they're boy dogs."

"It's the Twilight Zone," Hallie said. "I'm back in town for four hours, and I'm in the Twilight Zone."

It had been a joke. But when they'd finished the dishes and she'd refused another offer to stay and was driving out to the Ridge, it was hard not to feel like it was true. Anthea was Hallie's best friend, but on nights like tonight, the gulf between them loomed like an unbridgeable chasm. Anthea was going to bed with her husband after putting her kids to bed, and Hallie was going . . . here.

At seven thirty, with the sky turning pink over Paradise Mountain to the east and the light soft and low, she drove to the end of the road and up the long blacktopped driveway toward the two soaring stories of wood and stone. The security lights outside came on as she approached, but all of the house's giant windows were as dark and blank as missing teeth in a skeleton's smile.

Hallie sat in the car, turned the key, and swallowed. *Home.* The house where she'd spent her childhood. The one her mother had left when Hallie had been fourteen. And after that? It had been three more years of having to leave her mom in town and spend weekends and summers two miles out of town, in this cold, barren house. Just her and her dad. Without her mother's presence it had been a lonely spot, a place where Hallie had always come up short. She'd spent most of her time in her downstairs bedroom, with her TV and her computer and her books. Hiding. And that was before that last horrible summer, when her mother had moved to Arizona, and there had been no escape.

So why was she back here?

Because this was where the ghosts were, and she was tired of running from her ghosts. Because if she were going to that meeting tomorrow with Bob Jenkins and whoever the "others" were, she had to be ready for it. She had to face this, and it was too easy to lean on Anthea. When she'd made it through to the other side, she'd be stronger, better able to face whatever came next. She knew that for sure.

She shoved the car door open, popped the trunk, and hauled out her little suitcase. *One night.*

It was almost over before it started, the moment she opened the front door with the key Bob had given her, together with the news that he'd had the burglar alarm reset by the company, and the number to call for the new code. Hallie slapped the hallway light on, shrieked, jumped back, tripped over her suitcase, and fell on her butt.

The bear was new.

She crawled to her feet, hastily punched the numbers into the burglar alarm, picked up her suitcase, and muttered, "That goes. First thing."

She rolled the suitcase over the hardwood floor, then on second thought, turned to the lunging, snarling beast and said, "Sorry, buddy. You got the raw end of the deal."

She turned on the hallway light and hefted the little suitcase down the stairs. The air smelled stale and somehow metallic, and she tried not to think of it as the smell of death, wishing with every cowardly cell in her body that she'd accepted Anthea's offer to come out here with her. She wasn't going to be feeble and call now, though. Instead, she turned down the hall to her old bedroom and lifted the suitcase onto the quilted spread.

It looked just as it had five years ago. As it had fifteen years ago, for that matter, when the decorator had redone it. Pale-blue, flowered bedspread, darker blue curtains, white walls, beige carpeting, a mirror, and a framed picture of flowers on the wall, all chosen by a decorator. Bland as a hotel room, as if its occupant hadn't dared to impose her personality in even the smallest way. Which was about right.

"OK," Hallie said aloud. "OK." She opened a couple windows to air out the room, then unzipped her suitcase, removed her bag of toiletries, headed into the bathroom across the hall, and pulled out her toothbrush and toothpaste, grimacing at the wild-haired apparition in the mirror.

Geez. Things hadn't gotten any better despite her hasty repairs in Señor Fred's ladies' room.

This situation definitely called for alcohol. Her uncle Dale had told her that her dad had died in his den. That was where the drinks were, too.

Face the ghosts, she told herself. And went to do it.

WELCOME HOME

Hallie stepped out of the light and into the darkness of her father's den, flipped the light switch, and froze.

There was some kind of gray dust on every surface. Table. Bar. Leather couch and chairs. The coffee table was pushed forward on one side, canted wildly in a way her father would never have allowed, the rug beneath it crumpled. But that wasn't the worst. That would be the white shape drawn onto the coffee table. An outline of a thick torso, its left arm flung out across the pine table, the shape of the right arm ending where it would have hung off the edge.

And the head. An oval of white, bisected by the diagonal iron band that extended across the table's wooden surface. And a thick black rivet just to one side of center of the head's outline, up near the top.

"He fell and hit his head," her uncle Dale had said. Hallie hadn't expected to see the evidence of it, to be able to imagine it so vividly. It was as if he were still there. Still lying dead. The metallic smell was stronger, too. *Copper. Blood.*

She wrenched her gaze away from the table and glanced wildly around the room. What was the gray dust? It was *everywhere,* like the house was an archaeological site covered by the sands of time. She felt the faint grittiness under her fingers, looked down, and snatched her hand away as if the doorknob had been red-hot, wiping her fingers hastily on her abused skirt, and swallowing back the sickness.

Fingerprints. It was fingerprint dust, and the smears and marks in the gray were prints. Her dad's—and maybe other people's. But it had been an accident, Dale had said. Her father had tripped and fallen.

She was retreating without even realizing it, backing up, then turning and nearly running down the hall. Into her bedroom, noticing with horror for the first time the gray dust on that knob, too. She fumbled in her purse for her phone, then gave it up and snatched the whole bag, took the stairs up at a run, hit the light switch for the living room, and saw more gray dust.

It covered the whole house. Every room. Everywhere.

Panic. She was shaking, gasping, heading outside, whimpering as her hand landed on the gray smears covering the doorknob of the front door, then hurried down the driveway to a boulder set in a curve of the road. The flat rock where she'd sat on so many evenings as a teenager, looking over the hills and longing to be gone. Especially during that last long, hot summer after graduation, after Jim, after everything, when she'd longed for escape and feared it would never come.

But it had. It *had.*

She sat on the gray stone, tucked her heels into the narrow ledge, rocked back and forth, and told herself, *Breathe.* How many times had she reminded herself today? The drive. The ticket. The funeral chapel. The casket. And now this. The worst.

Phone. Call somebody.

Who did she call, though? What did she say? "Help?" "Rescue me from the devil dust?"

In the end, she called Anthea.

"So—yeah," she told her friend. "It's like *CSI* down there. Only no cute detectives. Just me, a whole lot of gray smears, and a . . ." She swallowed. "Chalk outline."

"Any blood?" Anthea asked practically.

"I didn't . . ." Hallie put a hand to her head. "Yeah. I think so." *Oh, God. Blood.* The dark stain on one corner of the table. His head had been smashed in. That had to be it.

Henry on the table, facedown. Dead.

The staring glass eyes of the dead moose above the dead man. The hunter and the hunted. Making her think of Henry's body in the casket, as butchered as the moose had been. Because there'd been an autopsy.

The panic and nausea rose again at the thought, and she forced both of them back and focused on her friend's voice.

"OK, that's gross," Anthea was saying. "But other than that, it's just dust and chalk. Windex and paper towels, right? Any rubber gloves out there? Then you don't even have to touch anything until you've wiped it clean. I'll come over and help you. It's not like your father's the one who left the dust there. It was the sheriff's department, not Henry. Well, nothing but the blood. It's just the investigation." Which all sounded completely reasonable, completely rational.

"But wait," Hallie said. "Why wouldn't they have cleaned it up? The cops? Who leaves this kind of mess for the . . . the next of kin? That can't be normal. And why didn't Bob tell me?"

"I don't know," Anthea said slowly. "I don't do criminal. I never thought about it. I don't know what they do. Bob may not have known, either."

"I'm finding out." Suddenly, Hallie wasn't shaken and horrified. She was *mad.* "Right now."

"I'm getting dressed," Anthea said. "Be out to help you clean it in twenty minutes."

"No," Hallie decided.

Anthea's sigh came over the line. "There's such a thing as being too independent, you know? I mean, good for you that you're coping, but what are friends for?"

"I just . . . I can't explain. But it's mine to deal with. I have to. My house. My ghosts."

"Not *alone*."

"Yeah," Hallie said. "Alone. I have to go. Thanks for talking."

It was almost dark now, but being out here in the dark didn't scare her. The air was fresh and cool, the crickets chirped as they always had, and a few pale stars had begun to wink through the darkening sky. A sliver of moon gleamed over Paradise Mountain, a silver-white fingernail. Hallie sat in the darkness, a breath of wind ruffling the hem of her skirt, and scrolled and tapped her phone, finally pressing the screen and hearing the ringing start.

"Sheriff's department," a woman's voice said.

"Yes," Hallie said. "I'd like to speak to the person in charge of the investigation into Henry Cavanaugh's death."

"That'd be Jim Lawson," the woman said. "He's not on duty tonight, though. Can I take a message?"

"No," Hallie said slowly. "No message. Thanks." She hung up, thought a minute, then dialed again.

"Hey," Anthea said on the other end. "Change your mind? Want me to come out? Or better yet—forget it for now and come on back here. Princess Elsa's waiting for you on that top bunk. We'll take care of it tomorrow, in the daylight. Much better."

Hallie didn't answer any of that. "Can I have Jim's number?"

Silence on the other end, then finally, "Why?"

"He investigated my dad's death." Hallie's hand was shaking, and she shoved it under her leg and told herself furiously, *Deal.* "He left the house like this. For me to see. On purpose."

"I'm sure he didn't," Anthea said. "He wouldn't."

"He *did*."

"Then there's a reason."

"Look." Hallie closed her eyes, then opened them, because it didn't do any good. The pictures in her memory weren't anything she wanted to see. "I know he's your brother. I've never tested your loyalty, have I? I've always known where it would be, and I know why."

"What? Of course I'm loyal to him. He's my twin. I know you're weird about him, but I can't give you his number, not without checking with him first. Don't ask me."

Hallie had to swallow again. Her deepest secrets, her darkest shame, remained her own, still and always, because there was nobody to share them with. Because Anthea wouldn't want to know. An invisible barrier that had stood between them for years despite their friendship, and still stood today.

He's my twin.

"Right," Hallie said. "I'll call him tomorrow."

"Come over," Anthea said. "You know I love you. Come over and let me help."

"No. Thanks, but no. I'll do it myself. See you tomorrow."

"Right. Tomorrow." Anthea hesitated as if she wanted to say more, then added, "But if you change your mind—"

"I won't change my mind." Hallie was already climbing off the rock. "Bye." She shoved the phone back into her purse and headed back up through the dark, the security lights winking on again as she approached. She went inside, forcing herself to grab the doorknob normally, went into the kitchen, and pulled out Windex, a roll of paper towels, and a pair of yellow rubber gloves.

She didn't do the whole thing. She couldn't. Not in the dark, with the ghosts hovering. But she did some of it, starting with wiping down the taps and edges on the shower and sink in the upstairs guest bathroom. Nothing but gray dust there, not even a fingerprint, because her father wouldn't have gone into either place.

Henry's ghost wasn't there. Or in the living room, either, which she tackled next. Henry hadn't liked that room, with its formal furnishings and soaring spaces. "Like a funeral parlor," he'd always said. Oddly enough, it was the one place that *didn't* feel like a funeral parlor now, where she didn't feel his presence so acutely.

She braved her bedroom once more for her suitcase and her toothbrush, ran upstairs with them as if her father's spirit really were after her, and finally took a shower in that pristine "guest" bath that probably hadn't seen a guest for fifteen years. No hair dryer up here, and she couldn't bring herself to care, not tonight. She'd be a mess tomorrow, and so what? She'd been a mess today already. She changed into a pair of yellow shortie pj's, grabbed a blanket and pillow from the linen closet, lay down on the white couch with a paperback that was as close as she'd come to romance in quite some time, and thought, *You're doing it. One night. The worst is over.*

And then she thought, *Hallie Jane Cavanaugh. Welcome home.*

◆ ◆ ◆

Jim didn't see the text from Anthea until he got home.

Hallie's upset. Call me.

After ten. Too late to call Anthea back tonight. His relief felt a whole lot like cowardice, but he'd see his sister in the morning anyway. Time enough to find out what it was all about then.

He'd see Hallie, too. Not that his presence would help with the "upset." Even if it were about her dad's death. *Especially* if it were about her dad's death. He wasn't exactly going to be commiserating.

He wandered into the kitchen, opened the fridge, and stared inside the same way Cole had a few days earlier, and for the same reason. Because when guys didn't have anything better to do, they stared into the fridge, like there might be a TV on in there.

He contemplated a beer, then abandoned the idea and swung the door shut. He'd had one already tonight, and he had a feeling that "one more" was going to turn into, "Mac's not home, so why the hell not?" And there was no cure for loneliness or frustration at the bottom of a bottle. He ought to know.

He pulled his T-shirt over his head and dropped it into the washing machine on the way to the bedroom, unsnapping his jeans en route. He stripped down the rest of the way, tossed the rest of his dirty clothes into the hamper, stepped into the shower and started soaping up, and thought about how stupid he'd been.

He should totally have gone for it.

His Friday night hadn't started out all that exciting, but it had ended with a lot more promise. He'd driven Mac and her friends Crystal and Alexandra to their first JV volleyball game, then had sat in the bleachers and yelled every time Mac had scored. Five kills, which was pretty damn good. She was small, but she was quick and aggressive and fearless, and she had the same kind of hand-eye coordination Jim did himself. The kind that made you good at sports, and a good shot, too.

The girls had lost, but Mac had fought hard to the end, and Jim had clapped and whistled and thought, *Look at that, babe. Your girl's a fighter. Just like you.*

It was moments like that, oddly enough, when he missed Maya most. The good times, the sweet times, because she wasn't there to share them.

Which could explain why he'd been extra susceptible after he'd taken the girls out for pizza and then over to Crystal's house for their sleepover. And why he'd stayed for that beer when Crystal's mom, Danielle, had offered it. Although that was probably giving himself too much credit. More like pure, hundred-proof, haven't-had-it-in-way-too-long horndog.

Danielle Delgado, new in town. Even her name was sexy. She'd been working it a little tonight, too. Blonde hair loose and tousled, falling over one eye. Sitting in a kitchen chair with one foot tucked under her, wearing a tiny white T-shirt and satin pants that looked like pj bottoms and clung to her curves, tied with a bow in front and hanging low on her belly, so that when she stretched her arms overhead, she'd showed an inch of taut brown stomach and a very nice flash of oval belly button, complete with a winking silver stud.

They'd talked, and he'd looked, and finally, she'd put a light hand on his forearm and said, "It must get lonesome over there with just Mac to keep you company. I know I feel that way, and I've got two kids. But it's not the same thing, is it?"

Jim had looked down at his beer bottle and peeled the corner of the label back. "Sure isn't."

"More than two years, I heard." Her hand was still on his arm. Now, her fingers moved, tracing the line of muscle, and damn, but that felt good. "I was sorry to hear about your wife."

"Thanks." It never got that much easier to hear.

"It's a long time to be alone," she said, peering at him from under her lashes.

"It is. But I'm not really looking for a relationship right now." Best to be up front. He might be feeling a little desperate, but he wasn't a total asshole.

"I get that." She hadn't moved her hand. "Marriage sounded real good once. Not anymore. Live and learn. I don't need anyone telling me what to do. I sure could use the company sometimes, though. A good-looking, decent guy, one who knows how to treat a woman right? Yeah." She sighed, let go of him, and pushed her curtain of hair back with one hand. "That'd be real nice. I'm pretty sure the girls are asleep. Maybe I'll just go double-check that, huh?"

It was one of those times when you froze, because your body and your mind were telling you two exactly opposite things. His body said, *Hell, yeah, baby. Let's go.* And his mind went, *With the girls right here?*

He'd ended up taking a final swallow of his beer, standing up, and saying, "Yeah. You're right. It's late. I'd better take off." When he totally should have said, "You know what? I'll take a rain check on that. How about tomorrow night? My babysitter. My . . . treat." And given her a good hard look of his own, and a good hard kiss at the door, too. Down payment.

But he hadn't said that, or done it, either. Which was why he was in the shower alone. And horny as hell.

None of which had anything to do with Hallie Cavanaugh.

NEWS OF THE DAY

"You going to tell me why we're here?" Jim asked his mother again on Saturday morning as he held open the front door of the converted frame house on Pine Street that housed his sister's law offices. Cole trailed behind with Anthea, the cool air welcoming them.

Vicki Lawson's tension was evident even under her carefully applied makeup. "I already did. To hear about Henry Cavanaugh's will. That's all I know."

Jim's mother was a little heavier at fifty-one than she had been when Jim had been growing up, but that hadn't stopped her from attracting the usual second look from a passing man when she'd climbed down from Jim's rig onto the sidewalk. She'd never tried to hide her generous figure or blonde hair—in fact, she still wore it in waves past her shoulders, defying anyone to call her trashy. She'd never acted ashamed of herself despite her children's absolutely fatherless status, her patched-together network of jobs, or their lack of funds.

"A hard-working woman deserves respect," she'd always told her kids, "and it doesn't matter one bit what that work is." Waitress, cleaner, cashier, bartender—Vicki had done it all at one time or another. Once Anthea's kids had been born, the jobs had been reduced to child care and some bartending. Less bartending in the past three years, once Jim had brought his little family home and added Mac and Maya to the caretaking list. And then just Mac.

Jim knew without discussing it that his twin felt the same way he did. Nobody would love their kids as much as their grandmother did, or take better care of them. They'd both had to pay somebody anyway, and they'd rather pay their mom, take some of the burden off her in a way she'd accept. But he worried about what would happen once Deirdre and Ty got a little older and didn't need the care. Mac was just about grown out of it already.

But now . . . Henry Cavanaugh had left something to Vicki in his will? Not possible, not with the way Henry had felt about Jim. Unless . . . but no. His mom had hardly ever mentioned Henry's name, especially since Jim had come home from the Army. The few times she had, it had been with thinned lips.

So why were they all here? Only one possible answer. Half of his mind said no, and the other half said, *You know it's true. Face it.*

Anthea led the little group down a narrow hallway and into a former bedroom that now featured a narrow oval conference table and eight chairs. The window looked out onto a back garden planted with soothing flower beds, a fountain bubbling in the middle. Civil law, Paradise style.

Three of the chairs were occupied. Bob Jenkins, her father's lawyer and Anthea's senior partner, sat at the head of the table, urbane, distinguished, and giving nothing away. Then Henry's brother, Dale, at Bob's left hand, looking stringy, gray, and anxious. His wife Faye beside him, polished, perfect, and a little supercilious, glancing at Jim's mother in surprise, then at the rest of them with some dismay.

"I didn't realize there'd be so many attendees," Faye said to Bob.

"Henry stipulated that the details be kept to myself until the meeting," Bob said. "I'll explain everything as soon as we're all gathered."

"Mom, why don't you sit here," Anthea instructed, settling her mother halfway down the table, which unfortunately put her straight across from Faye, who was still looking at all of them as if they were something the cat had dragged in. Anthea sat between Bob and her mother, and Jim took the seat on Vicki's other side. Cole slid reluctantly into a chair at the foot of the table, as far away from everybody as he could get.

The kid was still in the baggy shorts and black Smashing Pumpkins T-shirt he'd worn that morning. Not exactly formal wear, but the scowl on Cole's face had kept Jim from saying anything. You picked your battles, and Jim didn't much care what Cole wore.

Cole hadn't wanted to come, but their mother had asked all her children to come with her. She was going to need their support, and Jim intended to give it. She sure had never held back her own, and he was in her corner till the end.

Faye glanced ostentatiously at the clock mounted beside the door. "I thought you said ten, Bob," she murmured. If the Botox had allowed it, she would have been frowning. As it was, she wore her usual perpetually surprised look, only a faint twist of her mouth showing her displeasure. She was in a purple suit today. Apparently the period of deep mourning was over.

The sound of a door opening came from outside the room, and Anthea got up, but Bob was there first, rising and heading out of the conference room.

Jim forced himself to breathe evenly. He'd known she'd be here. Time to man up and take it.

Then she *was* there. Hallie. Looking about a hundred percent more polished than the day before, her hair parted on the side, the curls tamed but still looking sassy-good. She was wearing makeup, too, and he found himself staring at her mouth for a second too long even as he stood. Her lips were lush and pink, just like always, and she didn't need any lipstick to make them that way.

And the green eyes above that mouth, shining emerald-clear today, her gaze meeting his with none of the uncertainty he'd seen in the past. Instead, her eyes snapped with what looked like temper, the same kind of temper she'd showed him yesterday, and damned if he knew why. He'd forgotten to ask Anthea about the "upset" this morning. The truth? He'd been a wuss.

Yesterday had been a surprise, that was all. But it had all happened long ago, and his life had turned out fine—well, except the worst parts— so what did it matter how he'd once felt about her, or how her mouth or her hair looked now? If he still remembered how surprisingly soft those curls had felt when his hands had been shoved through them, or how sweet her mouth had tasted under his, that didn't mean a thing. He tried not to glance down her body, because he didn't need to remember that, either. She was wearing a pale blue sheath dress cut just below her collarbones that left her shoulders and arms bare, skimmed her curves, and ended just above her knees, along with strappy, heeled sandals that made her legs look long and lean. She looked appropriate, he guessed. If he thought she looked sexy as hell, with her dress saying *prim* and *buttoned up* and *Daddy's princess,* and her curls saying *wild as you want it*—

No. He wasn't going there.

He needed that girlfriend his buddies kept telling him to find. One who wasn't a redhead, that was for damn sure. He needed to call Danielle Delgado right back up and make that date.

It took him a long second to realize that Cole hadn't stood. He kicked his brother's chair under the table, and Cole rose reluctantly to his feet. Meanwhile, Jim tried hard to remember all the rest of it. All the reasons why Hallie's hair and eyes and mouth and skin were off-limits to him. All the reasons why she was bad news.

"If you'd like to have a seat, Hallie," Bob said, "we can begin."

She walked around the table and sat opposite Jim, one seat down from her aunt. And then she told Jim, "I'd like to talk to you afterwards, if I may," as the men sat.

"Uh . . . sure," he said. Something about the investigation, probably. But then why was she looking at him like she was contemplating the various forms of torture, and trying to pick one?

Then he stopped doing any wondering at all, because Bob started talking.

◆　◆　◆

Hallie had gone for a run all the way down to the university campus and back up the Ridge that morning, then had wiped down the rest of the upstairs, getting rid of the dust. The taint. Everything but her father's bedroom and bath, that is. She hadn't managed to make it in there, or back downstairs, either.

She hadn't needed to do any of it, because she was leaving today, but she'd wanted to know she could. Then she'd spent too much time on her hair and her face, loaded her suitcase into the car again, and driven into town.

Already halfway gone.

Why was Anthea's family here? Anthea was Bob's partner. Her presence wasn't any kind of a surprise. Anthea had told her about it the day before. Why hadn't she mentioned the rest of her family being invited?

Well, Hallie guessed she'd find out. She'd listen to what Bob said, tell Jim what she thought of his games in a cool, calm, *adult* manner, talk over whatever she heard today with Anthea, get a referral to a Realtor to unload the house and its contents, and drive on down the road. One step at a time.

Now, Bob was talking, so she quit glancing out of the corner of her eye at Jim and noticing all the ways he'd changed. She stopped looking at the dark hair that didn't fall that defiant, shaggy bad-boy inch beneath his collar anymore, but was instead cut ruthlessly short and neat. At the new lines she could see at the corners of his eyes and around his mouth, lines carved by desert sun and pain and too many deaths. At the faint white tracing of battle scars on his forehead, the edge of his chin, and, horrifyingly, extending a full three inches down the right side of his face, there beside his ear. At the way he sat so still, without any of the restless energy she remembered, only his watchful brown eyes betraying his tension. At the way he filled out that white dress shirt, and the way he'd filled out his jeans when he'd stood up as she'd entered the room.

This was why she liked living in the big city. You were never trying not to look at a guy's muscular thighs, let alone his crotch, in a conference room and remembering how he'd looked in his swim trunks at seventeen. Or, worse, in a clearing among the moonlit cedars at nineteen—the first time you'd explored a man—and how he'd sucked in his breath at your tentative touch. You never had to remember how he'd whispered, "This might hurt a little, baby. We'll go slow." You never had to remember the difference between his hot, sweet kisses, the way he'd touched you like you were something precious and wonderful, and the eyes that had stared into yours so coldly a week later, and then looked away. You never had to remember the way he'd left you to deal with everything. The way he'd left you alone.

She didn't want to think about any of it, so instead, she listened to Bob talking legalese. And after a while, she forgot about Jim.

The first part was about her, and she already knew it.

I give all my residences, blah blah blah, *with their contents, including all vehicles on the property, to my daughter, Hallie Jane Cavanaugh, for her use absolutely.*

No restrictions. She'd worried some about that after Bob had told her the house was hers. She wouldn't have put it past her dad to make her live in it.

Also, it meant she could dump the bear.

I give my brother, Dale Marion Cavanaugh, the sum of five hundred thousand dollars, in the hopes that he can keep some of it from his wife.

Faye uttered a ladylike gasp and said, *"What?"*

"I'll ask you to hold your comments until I've finished reading," Bob said calmly. "At which point, I'll do my best to answer your questions."

I give my illegitimate son, Cole Ryan Lawson, the sum of one million dollars to be paid immediately upon my death, this sum to remain in trust until he reaches the age of twenty-five.

Silence for a long second, and then Cole blurted out, "You're shitting me."

Hallie's gaze flew to Anthea's, and she saw the same shock in her friend that she was feeling herself. She glanced at Jim, but his face was a mask. Frozen hard. She didn't dare look at Vicki. She couldn't.

"I give the remainder of my estate," Bob continued to read, "including the full value of my shares in Cavanaugh Development, to my brother, Dale Marion Cavanaugh, and my two children, Hallie Jane Cavanaugh and Cole Ryan Lawson, to be divided six months after my death as follows. To Dale Marion Cavanaugh, ten percent. To Hallie Jane Cavanaugh and Cole Ryan Lawson, forty-five percent apiece, with the following provisos. Cole Ryan Lawson's portion will remain in trust until the age of twenty-five. Hallie Jane Cavanaugh will receive her portion outright under the following conditions. That she live in Paradise, in the residence hereby bequeathed her, if such a residence exists at the time of my death, for six months consecutively after my death, with no more than one absence per month for no more than three consecutive days during that period except in an extreme emergency, the validity of such emergency to be defined by my trustees, and that she not have a sexual relationship with Jim Lawson during said six months after my death. If she fails to meet these conditions, I give her share of my estate, except the house and its contents, to be divided as follows. Seventy-five percent to Cole Ryan Lawson, and twenty-five percent to Dale Marion Cavanaugh. If either of my children is not living after said six-month period beginning at the date of my death, their share passes in a proportion of seventy-five percent to the other living child, and twenty-five percent to Dale Marion Cavanaugh, if living. In the event that Dale Marion Cavanaugh is not living at the end of six months and Hallie Jane Cavanaugh has not fulfilled these conditions, the estate passes in its entirety to Cole Ryan Lawson, in trust until the age of twenty-five."

"Wait," Cole said again. "I get the whole *thing?*" Which wasn't the part Hallie had focused on.

Bob held up a hand and kept reading.

"During said six-month period, Hallie Jane Cavanaugh will receive the following sums as living expenses. One month after my death, ten thousand dollars. Upon reaching three months after my death, thirty thousand dollars. Upon reaching four months, five months, and six months, further sums of ten thousand dollars per month."

Bob read a few additional paragraphs that didn't tell Hallie anything other than that the trustees were Bob himself and Aldon Cranfield, the president of local branch of the Bank of Idaho—Henry's banker, in other words. Then he set the document down, removed his glasses, folded them neatly and set them in precise alignment to the edge of the paper, and said, "Now. I welcome your questions."

Hallie opened her mouth, not sure what she could possibly have said, but Faye, who hadn't even been named in the will, got the first licks in. "You're telling me Dale doesn't get anything?"

"No," Bob said, "I'm not telling you that. He receives five hundred thousand dollars. And ten percent of the residue of the estate after six months."

"Five hundred thousand," Faye said. "And ten percent? Ten *percent?*"

"Honey," Dale said. "It's all right. I've got my own stock, you know, and we already have plenty. Henry didn't owe me anything. I was just his brother."

"No," Faye said. "No. It's *not* all right. You *slaved* for him for twenty years, and now there's *another* kid? After he said he'd—" She glanced at Hallie, then broke off.

"That he'd disinherited me," Hallie said. She was still numb. No, not numb. Reeling. "Yeah. He told me that, too. Can I get a copy of all that, please?" she asked Bob. "The part that's about what I'd have to do, if I decided to?"

She heard the faint huff from Faye and ignored it. And she didn't look at Jim at all.

"Of course," Bob said. "And to answer your question," he told Faye, "the amount in question, outside of the corporation, is somewhere in the neighborhood of four million in investments, at its current valuation, after the stated sums are paid out to the legatees. Keep in mind that value can fluctuate significantly, so in even six months—who knows what it will be. Most of Henry's net worth was in the corporation."

"Which is worth what?" Faye asked.

Bob hummed. "Difficult to say. The face value of the shares in a closely held corporation is, of course, meaningless. Some millions. I wouldn't want to commit beyond that."

Some millions.

"You're shitting me," Cole said again.

Jim looked at him and snapped, "Try again."

"I mean," Cole said, "I'm his *kid?* And I get the same as Hallie?"

"Yes," Bob said.

Nobody was looking at Vicki. Well, Hallie realized with a glance to her right, nobody but Faye. Faye opened her mouth, and Hallie jumped into the breach, because Vicki didn't deserve to hear what Faye would have to say. "Can you explain my part again, please?" she asked Bob.

"Of course," he said. "You get living expenses of roughly ten thousand dollars a month, and then nearly half of the residue of the estate, after Cole's and Dale's shares are paid out, after six months. That date will be reached on February twenty-eighth of next year, which is actually"—he consulted some notes—"about five and a half months from now. *If* you live in Henry's house for all of that time and don't have a—" He gave a dry little cough that could only have come from a lawyer. "A sexual relationship with Jim, here."

Hallie felt the sticky strings of her father's web tightening around her. She didn't dare look at Jim, but she'd already seen his face. She'd call that look *stony.* "And if I leave, I get the house, and that's it."

"Yes. If you're gone for more than three days a month, or violate the . . . other provisions, your share is divided between Cole and Dale."

Hallie glanced down the table at the boy, and he dropped his gaze. "I'll need to think about it," she said.

Bob raised both hands flat above the table. "Of course. Entirely your choice."

She couldn't process it. But she wasn't the one who'd had the biggest shock here. She could see the expression on Anthea's face, too. On Cole's and Vicki's. And, she was sure, on Jim's if she dared look at him again. It was too hard on all of them, having this secret spilled in front of everyone. She was betting that it *had* been a secret to all of them. To everyone but Vicki. To Vicki, she was suddenly sure that it had been more like shame. That would have been why it was a secret. Her father hadn't been an honorable man. There must have been something all wrong about it, and she'd bet it was bad.

For once, she took action. She stood up and said, "I think we're done, then, right? At least I am. If you'll e-mail me that copy, Bob, I'd appreciate it."

Jim was up as fast as she was, a hand under his mother's elbow. "She's right," he said. "We're done." He looked at Bob. "We'd like a copy, too, please. We'll call you if we have questions."

Hallie left the room first, not checking to see who was behind her. She didn't stick around, either. She hit the front door, headed out into the heat, and thought, *Car. Suitcase. Leaving. Or not.* Which was when she hesitated.

Anthea came up beside her, looking distracted. "Hey," she said. "You OK?"

Hallie shook her head. "Yes. No. I don't know. Did you know what it said? Couldn't you have warned your mom? That was too hard. That wasn't fair."

"No," Anthea said. "I didn't know. It would have been a breach of confidentiality for Bob to tell me." She glanced over her shoulder. "I didn't guess. I should have, but I didn't. Or I did, but I didn't want to.

I hate to leave you, but I need to go be with my mom. Call you later? You want to come to dinner?"

Hallie shook her head. "I don't know. I can't tell. I'm just . . ." She ran a hand through her carefully arranged curls, not caring how much she messed them up. "I can't decide. I'll talk to you later."

Anthea nodded, hesitated, and left, and Hallie thought, *Guess I'll go home*. And remembered.

She turned and went after Jim, who was standing with his family. "May I talk to you a minute?" she asked him.

He stared at her, looking even more shut down than the day before, then glanced at Anthea. "Go on and take Mom home, would you? I'll be right there."

"I'm not an invalid," Vicki snapped. Her own look at Hallie wasn't one bit friendly. "I don't need to be watched over."

"Maybe I think family'd be good right now," Jim said. "But whatever you want." His expression, his voice were calm. Almost wooden. But he couldn't be feeling that way. Not possible.

"No," Vicki said. "Come home." Another sharp glance at Hallie. "Seems to me you could wait, whatever it is. Show some respect."

Hallie swallowed, folded her arms, then unfolded them. She wanted to apologize. For herself, for her father, for everything. She wanted to run. She was still groping for something to say when Anthea said, "Come on, Mom. Maybe Hallie deserves some respect, too. She just lost her dad. She just got her own news. How do you imagine she feels about Cole?"

It hit Hallie like a punch in the stomach. She looked at Cole, saw him staring back at her, his face white under the mop of blond hair. Maybe searching for the same thing she was.

A likeness.

He's my brother.

DISCLOSURES

"I . . ." Hallie started to shake. It was so hot out here. She needed a drink of water. "I don't—"

Anthea said, "Hallie!" But the voice came from down a dark tunnel, and it was Jim who grabbed her, Jim who put an arm around her and said, "Come on." He told the others, "Go on home. I'll be right there," and then he was leading Hallie back toward the law office.

She shied away from the door like a horse at the scene of a kill. "No," she said. "Not in there. And don't try being nice to me now. It's not going to work anyway. For, oh, *millions* of reasons."

If that was bitter, sue her.

"I'm not being nice," he said. "I want to dump you on your butt and walk away. I'm doing my job. Come on."

She shrugged his arm off and walked down the street and across Main with him to Brewster's. He went with her, even though all she wanted was to be alone, and when they were in the air-conditioning, he said, "Go sit down. What do you want?"

"Beer. And plenty of it. But I'm going to get an iced latte."

"No. I am. Go sit. You're pale as a ghost."

"I'm always pale."

A muscle twitched at the corner of his mouth. "Paler than ever. Sit down. I'll bring you a water."

A few minutes later, he was back with their drinks, then kicking out a chair and sitting down himself. She said, "I don't know what to think now. Not the part about you and me," she hurried to add. "I mean the rest of it."

He sighed and scratched the back of his head, not messing up his hair. It was too short for that. "Man, neither do I. My mom and your dad. Wow."

"Do you think it was consensual?" she asked quietly. "Or fully consensual?"

His hand stopped at the back of his neck, and his hard eyes met hers. "I don't know. What do you think?"

"He wasn't a good man. He had the power. And she was out there every week, cleaning his house."

His head snapped back. "I'd forgotten that."

"No, you hadn't." She wasn't that girl who ran away anymore. She was a woman who faced facts, at least with herself. "It was all wrapped up in how you felt about me. Why you slept with me out of nowhere, and why you dumped me afterwards. Why you had to hurt me."

His expression was so rigid that his mouth barely moved when he said, "That's not true."

She started to answer, then stopped herself and sighed. "I don't care. It doesn't matter. It's done. Your brother is my brother. That's what matters. He's going to be hurting, and excited, and confused, and mad. He's going to be all mixed up, and it's going to be hard. For your mom, too."

"And you would know. And care." His voice was flat.

It was cool in here, but she was burning. "I'm aware of what my father was." She tried to keep her tone as level as his, but it didn't work. "I'm aware of how he used people, how he hurt people. That's one reason I hadn't spoken to him in five years. And I teach high school.

I know teenagers. I even like them. So don't you tell me that I don't know or don't care about how your brother—*my* brother—might feel."

"It takes more than biology to make family."

Her hand was trembling on the latte glass. "I know that. You bet I do. Sometimes even biology doesn't do it. I know that, too."

"What?"

She shook her head violently. *Calm down. Forget it. It's all over.* "Never mind. No. Look, we aren't going to get anywhere. There's no point. Go talk to your mom. Go be with your brother."

"You wanted to tell me something," he said. "Or ask me something. What?"

Breathe. Calm. "When I went to the house last night," she said, "it was a mess. Fingerprint dust." She took a gulp of her latte in an effort to hold the sickness back, swallowed wrong, and coughed. Then kept coughing for a full minute, gasping for air, grabbing a napkin and holding it to her mouth, her eyes streaming with tears.

This is how Dad died. Choking. The thought was trying to panic her.

Jim had jumped up, was patting her on the back. Thumping her. She wanted to tell him to stop, but she couldn't speak.

Finally, she got herself back under control. "Sorry," she said weakly, mopping her eyes one more time, dabbing at the table where she'd, humiliatingly, sprayed coffee. "Right." If she'd had to choose a way *not* to be during this encounter, this would be it.

Jim sat down again, and she said, trying for businesslike, for unemotional, "There was gray stuff all over the house. Fingerprint dust, I suppose. And his chalk outline on the coffee table. And blood." She met Jim's gaze squarely this time. "I can't believe you normally leave a house like that for somebody to find. Did you do it because it was me? So it would upset me? If you did, it worked. It upset me."

He didn't look stony now. His mouth actually opened a couple times before he said, "No. Of course I didn't do that. Who would clean it up? We don't have any kind of crew for that. Or any budget, either."

"When there's a wreck on the highway," she insisted, "somebody sweeps up the glass and takes away the pieces. They're not just *left* there. I can't believe you'd leave somebody's . . . somebody's *blood* for their family to clean up. For them to find, after the funeral." She was shivering, remembering. She'd thought she'd come through on the other side, but it seemed she still had so much further to go.

"I'm sorry," Jim said. "But that's how it is. Bob will have known, though. Maybe I didn't tell him, but I assumed he'd know." He shook his head. "Can't remember. But he should've had it cleaned, or at least told you."

All the fight went out of her, and too much of her spirit along with it. Of course Jim wouldn't have done it on purpose. He didn't care. She knew that. "Never mind. I'll . . ." She raised a hand, dropped it again. "Clean it, I guess. I'll deal. Sorry. Jumped to conclusions. It was a shock, that's all."

"Somebody could help you with that."

"Yeah. Anthea already offered. Awkward, under the circumstances, for her to be in my father's house, wouldn't you say?"

Would she lose her best friend if she decided to stay? Could their friendship survive this kind of divided loyalty? Anthea's best friend versus her own family. Hallie didn't want to put it to the test. She wanted to leave town now, to walk away from the money and the past. It wasn't worth it.

"I wasn't thinking about Anthea," Jim said, not addressing the rest of what she'd said. "I was thinking about your father's cleaner, Eileen. She asked me about it. She'd like to keep on with the job. She needs the work. Got little kids." He pulled a notebook out of the back pocket of his jeans and turned it around so Hallie could see the number. "She's the one who found the body, though, so I'm not too sure about the blood. She was pretty shook up herself. Nice woman, but she's had a hard time. And an extra hard time out there. Go easy on her."

Hallie looked at the notebook, then back at Jim. "You're kidding. No."

71

"No what?"

"He wasn't sleeping with her, too."

"I can't discuss this with you, Hallie." Which told her it was true, and it was bad. "If you want her number, take it."

She tapped the name and number into her phone with fingers that insisted on shaking despite all her attempts to control them.

He asked, "You OK?"

She nodded, not looking up, and he stood and said, "I'm going to go, then. My mom. Cole." He hesitated, though, beside the table. "Call Anthea," he said. "No matter how Cole or my mom feel about her doing it, you have to know that she'll help you anyway. She'll clean up that blood, too. It'd take more than a little blood to spook my sister."

◆ ◆ ◆

Jim headed back up the street, moving fast despite the heat, and thought, *That went well. Not.*

He had to go talk to his mom and to Cole. But first, he had to pick up Mac.

He set the memory of Hallie's white, stricken face aside and drove to Danielle's, where he stood in her kitchen, made small talk, and waited for his daughter, letting the professional mask fall down over his face and seeing Danielle draw back as if he'd slapped her. He wanted to tell her not to take it personally, but he didn't, because he didn't know how. Seemed it was his day to upset women.

Finally, though, Mac came out, and he said good-bye to Danielle with relief, tossed Mac's bag in the back of the rig, and waited for her to fasten her seatbelt before he took off.

"Good time?" he asked her.

"Yeah."

"What did you do?"

"Talked."

"What else?"

She sighed. "*Dad. Nothing* else. It was a sleepover. We talked and did hair and stuff."

"Oh." He tried to imagine sitting around with a bunch of guys when he'd been eleven—hell, now—and just talking, but he couldn't. Playing basketball, sure. *Watching* basketball, even. But talking? Nope.

"Hair looks good," he said, glancing across at her. It was in a high ponytail, sectioned off all the way down with white-flowered bands that contrasted with its darkness. "You do that?"

"No. Crystal did." She fingered the ends. "Not as good as yours, though."

"That's loyal."

"No. It's true. Yours are the best. Everybody says so."

"Thanks."

It had started out of desperation, the first morning Maya had been too sick and weak to sit up in bed and do Mac's hair before school. Mac had started to throw a weeping, hysterical fit, and Jim had been furious.

"You don't talk to your mom like that," he'd thundered over his nine-year-old daughter's sobs. "Do you think she doesn't want to take care of you? How can you be that selfish? Can't you see how much it hurts her that she can't?"

"Honey." Maya had turned her pale face toward him on the pillow, her own dark hair lying lank against the white cotton. "No." She'd reached a hand out to her weeping daughter. "Go to your room, baby. Daddy will come talk to you in a minute."

Mac had run out, her feet pounding down the hall. "No," Jim had said as soon as he'd heard her sobs fade, her door slam. "She doesn't get to do that. Not OK."

Maya had patted the mattress, and Jim had sat down beside her, wanting to bury his head in his hands and sob himself. Too much. Last straw.

"Everything's changing for her," Maya had said, her hand on her husband's uniform sleeve. Such a fragile grasp to have so much hold on his heart. Such a weak touch to be able to bring him to his knees. "She's so scared, babe. She's as scared as you are, and she doesn't have your strength, not yet. She can't hide her fear like you can. She's trying, but it's coming out all the same, because she can't hold it back anymore. She's lost. You've got to help her find her way."

"Babe . . ." Jim had had to swallow, and he'd felt himself tearing up anyway.

"I know," Maya had said. "I know. But you have to do it. You have to help her find her strength. For both of us. For all of us." She'd taken his hand, put it on the mound of her belly, held it there over the ripple that was their son moving inside her, and smiled at him.

He'd broken down some then, and she'd held on to him, had held strong, and he'd thought, *I do not deserve this woman. And I'm not going to get to keep her.*

And then he'd gone down the hall and done his daughter's hair.

His efforts hadn't turned out well that first time, but he'd kept doing it, because he'd had no choice. And he'd improved, eventually.

Now, Mac looked across the truck at him, interrupting his memories. "What?"

"What?" he asked in return.

"What happened?" she asked. "How come you're all weird?"

"Me? I'm not weird. I need you to stay at Aunt Anthea's for a while, though." He turned onto the east end of A Street, the outer fringes of the good part of town. "I need to go over to Grandma's for a little bit."

"Uh-huh," Mac said. "I live with you, Dad. I know when you're being weird. Did somebody else get killed?"

"Just—" he said in exasperation. "I'll talk to you later, OK? Go on and terrorize your cousins."

"I do not terrorize," she said with dignity. "I lead."

"Yeah, right," he said, cracking a smile at last. "Go do that."

UNDESERVING

All right, the killer thought again and again. *It's all right. It's going to work out. Henry's dead, you're not suspected, and the money's right there.*

It could have been so much better, though. Everyone knew that Hallie hadn't been home for five years, and that Henry had said he'd disinherited her.

The only problem was, he'd said that too long ago. The will had been dated only six months previously. If only Henry had died sooner.

It had been so easy, really, hadn't it? Just a little nudge to help fate along, because Henry had deserved to die. Just like Hallie didn't deserve to inherit all that money for doing nothing but live in town rent free for six months with a ridiculous amount of money to spend. She'd always been closed off and secretive. Uncaring. All these years without a single visit. Selfish. Like father, like daughter.

If she didn't stay, she didn't inherit. Simple as that. And all the money would go . . . elsewhere. What had she said when the will had been read? "I'll need to think about it." Who needed to "think" about whether they wanted millions of dollars?

She didn't even want it. She sure didn't deserve it. And she already had the house, set on four prime hilltop lots, not to mention all Henry's possessions. That was worth a million, easy. A million dollars for somebody who hadn't even cared enough about her father to go see him once in five years or be on time to his funeral? A million was more than enough.

It really wasn't fair.

FAMILY PARTY

When Jim walked into his mother's kitchen, all hell had already broken loose.

"Why didn't you tell me?" Cole was standing smack in the middle of the room, facing away from Jim as he came through the door, but you could hardly miss the way the boy's fists were clenched at his sides, or the tone of his voice. "How come I had to find out who my dad is in front of everybody? That it's *him?* What right did you have to keep that from me?"

"Whoa," Jim said, and his brother whirled to face him, his mouth tight, two spots of red flaring on his pale cheeks. "Whoa," Jim said again. "Settle down. Sit down."

"I won't sit down!"

"Yeah," Jim said calmly. "You will. You'll sit down and remember that that's your mother."

Cole was still scowling as he stalked across the room, pulled out a chair with unnecessary force, and dropped into it across from his mother and next to Anthea. Vicki was sitting up stiffly, posed like a doll, as if she might break if she moved. Tense, the same way she'd been for the past week. And now Jim knew why.

Jim sat beside his brother, his movements deliberate and controlled. *De-escalating the situation,* it was called, and it had never come harder.

"So, hey," Anthea said into the silence. "At least we know why you're good at math, Cole."

Cole glared at her. "You think this is funny?"

"Nope," she said. "Well, maybe a little. In a cosmic kind of way. Sort of a best-case/worst-case scenario, wouldn't you say? I mean, you've basically won the lottery here. Let's be real."

"But everybody's going to say that Mom—" Cole began, then stopped at a look from Jim.

"This would be the 'worst-case' part of it," Vicki said. Her head was high, but her neck muscles were taut. Anthea put a hand out and gripped hers, and Vicki turned her own hand over to clasp her daughter's. "He wasn't a good man," Vicki told Cole. "That's about all I'm going to say about him. I can't change the fact that he was your father, or that you'll have to deal with it. But you aren't him. You're the same person you were this morning before you knew. A good student, a good son, a good friend. You care about people. You aren't him."

"That's right," Anthea said. "Plus, you're thinking about what everybody's going to say. They're going to say, 'Dude, you've got a million bucks! Party's at your house!' And you're going to say, 'Excuse me, but I think you're forgetting my superlative discipline and focus on my academic career. Also, I'm in Math Club.'"

Cole actually smiled a little, and Jim said, "Anthea's right." He hesitated, then went ahead and said it. "I know how you feel, because I felt exactly the same. I realize you think I'm this, ah—"

"Tight-ass," Cole muttered. "Hard-ass."

"Well, yeah," Jim said. "Although I prefer 'disciplined.' I was mad that we were poor, and that I didn't have a dad and everybody knew it." He didn't look at his mother. "Jealous, too, so I guess that's different. Especially of the Jackson boys, because they were my cousins, but they had all that stuff I didn't. A dad. A farm. Money. Respect. I carried a whole sack of attitude around with me until the Army and Maya shaped me up. Know how much good that attitude did me?" He held up a hand and made a circle with finger and thumb. "Zip. And, yeah, people are going to wonder. They're going to gossip, and they're going to make comments, or maybe just shut up when you come into the room. For a while, until something more interesting happens. They're going to be jealous, too. But so what? That's always true. People will always say what they want and think what they want. Anybody worth knowing, though, is going to keep judging you the same way as always. On who you are."

It was a lot of talking for him. Practically a commencement speech. He hoped it worked.

"That sounds good." Cole had his thin arms wrapped across his chest now. "But it isn't that easy."

"Nope," Jim said. "I didn't say it was going to be easy. It's going to be hard sometimes, especially the next few weeks. But you've got at least three houses full of people you can talk to about it. People who feel exactly the same way about you as they always have."

"That you're a moron," Anthea put in helpfully, and Cole laughed, a quick, startled sound. "But cute," Anthea added, reaching out her hand and messing up his hair. "Good news. Chicks like cute, shaggy-haired blond guys, especially when they've got a little jingle in their jeans."

"Which you won't see much of at all until you're eighteen and start college," Vicki put in. "By the way. That's what the trust says."

Cole's expression was almost comical. "What?"

Jim laughed. "Oh, man. Busted. What kind of rig was it?"

Cole grinned sheepishly. "Jeep. Black."

Jim shook his head. "Unreliable vehicle, the Jeep."

"Not if it's new," Cole said. "Warranty."

"Now, see," Jim said, "there's that brainpower. That's on the plus side of the deal." He glanced at his twin. "They got something in that trust about cars?"

"At the discretion of the trustees," Anthea said. "Mom and I took a quick look. We'll go over it," she told Cole. "It has to do with getting accepted to college, not getting kicked out or put on probation, summer jobs, maintaining your GPA, and a lot of other depressing things that pretty much rule out Brazilian supermodels in Jell-O-filled hot tubs. Just as one example," she added at a frown from her mother.

Cole sighed. "Man, that's depressing. Do you think people will know by school on Monday?"

Anthea considered. "Mm . . . depends. I won't talk about it, and Hallie won't, either. Bet your life. Neither will Bob, of course. Client information is privileged. But I'm guessing it'll get around anyway, eventually."

Cole said, "That guy, you mean. He's my uncle, I guess. And she's my aunt."

"Yep," Anthea said. "Dale and Faye Cavanaugh. He's all right. She's not. But you know what they say. You can pick your nose, and you can pick your friends, but you can't pick your family. Alas." She smiled ruefully at her younger brother. "If you could, there'd have been times I'd have chosen a different twin. Somebody I could've shared clothes with. But you know what I'd do?" she went on more seriously. "I'd get proactive. Talk to your buddies. Put it out there. Tell them about it, let it get around town right away. Then you're not all tense, waiting for it to come out. *You* put it out there, and you have the power. Always better to be in the driver's seat."

Cole glanced at Jim, and he nodded. "Yep. Good idea." And tried not to think about Hallie. Sitting over there alone, trying to digest all this. Wiping the fingerprint dust off the surfaces of her father's chilly, trophy-filled house, trying to get up the guts to tackle the blood in the den. *You can't pick your family.*

As if Jim's thoughts had conjured her up, Cole said, "That girl's my sister. My half sister."

Anthea said, "Yep. And she's my best friend. You got lucky there. Hallie's great."

"How come I've never met her?" Cole asked.

"Because she didn't like her dad," Anthea said. "*Your* dad."

The words hung there. *Your dad.*

"Wow," Cole said. Overwhelmed.

Jim knew the feeling. "You know what I'd do right now if I were you?" he asked. "I'd ride my bike over to Aaron Clayborn's house and play some video games. Casually drop the subject of your millions into the conversation, if you want, like Anthea says, to start the ball rolling. But get out of here and go do something else. Your life's still the same, even if it doesn't feel like it. You're still the same guy. Same family. Same friends. Same house. Same lousy wardrobe."

Cole stood up. "Yeah. OK. I will."

Vicki hadn't said anything for ages, Jim realized. Now she stood, her movements slow. As if she'd grown older, somehow, in these past hours. She came around the table, took hold of her son, and wrapped him in a fierce hug. He stood stiff for a moment, and then his arms went around her.

She stood back at last, her hands on his shoulders, and said, "So you know. I've always been glad I had you. From the moment you were born, I've wanted you, and I'll never stop loving you for who you are. Which is my son. Nothing that happened or could happen would ever change that."

Cole nodded, but didn't look at her. "Yeah," he said, turning away. His voice came out choked. "OK. I'll just—I'm going."

The back door banged, and he was gone.

"OK," Anthea said. Vicki sat down again, but Anthea got up. "I feel like we need tea," she said. "Anybody else want tea?"

Jim stared at her. *Tea?* "It's hot," he pointed out, just as his mother said, "I would."

"No tea," Jim said. "I'll take a glass of water, though, since you're up. I'd take a beer or three, actually, if I wasn't a better person than that. But I'd sure take a sandwich."

Anthea stood at the sink, filling the kettle. "Better get up off your lazy butt and make it then. I'm not your servant."

Jim sighed and stood up. "Ben's a poor, unfortunate soul."

"Isn't he, though?" his twin said amiably. She was older by fifteen minutes, and she'd never let Jim forget it.

Jim was slapping mayo onto bread and opening a couple cans of tuna fish when Anthea said, "So. Mom. Tell me our dad was a secret billionaire, will you, and that Jimbo and I don't inherit until we're thirty-five. Make my day. I can cope with the public disapproval."

Jim shot a look at his sister, but she was pouring hot water into cups like her life depended on it.

"You know who your dad was," their mother said. "Rusty Calhoun, ranch hand and bum." She'd sat Jim and Anthea down on their sixteenth birthday, handed them their birth certificates, and told them about him. Now, she was telling them more. "If he was a thousandaire, it was a good month. He was still better than Henry Cavanaugh, even if he did run out on me when I was pregnant with you two and never amount to a hill of beans afterwards. I never did too good in the man department." She murmured a "thanks" as her daughter set the cup of tea in front of her, then said, "Good thing that isn't an inherited trait. Ben's a good man."

"By the way," Jim told his sister, "I dumped Mac on him."

"Yeah," Anthea said. "I figured." She sat down beside her mom, and Jim brought over the sandwiches and some carrot sticks he'd tossed into a bowl, then went back for plates.

"You're waiting for me to tell you about Henry," Vicki said. "And I know I have to. I was going to tell Cole some, too, but I was going to wait until he was eighteen." She picked up half a sandwich, then set it down again. "I knew it would be rough. You were so mature, Anthea, when I told you two, and your dad wasn't right here in town, and he wasn't a horrible person with a legitimate child he actually gave a damn about."

"And I *wasn't* mature," Jim put in, "but I had a sister to talk to."

"Yes," Vicki said. "You did." She was still looking down at the table, but now, she faced the two of them, but didn't start talking. She was always feisty, always quick with a comeback, but not today.

Jim said, "I think I should tell you that Henry's house cleaner told me he was more than inappropriate with her. And that goes nowhere. Her business. But I think you might need to know, Mom."

Vicki closed her eyes for a moment. "Oh. Poor woman."

"She has kids," Jim said. "She needed the job."

Vicki nodded, her face bleak. "I should tell you two," she said. "But it sounds like you already know. Not a whole lot you can do when the sheriff's in the guy's back pocket."

"Not anymore," Jim said. Everything in him was curled up hard and tight. In the past, he could have taken that motivation into combat with him and put it to use. Now, that option wasn't available.

"No," Vicki said. "Not anymore. And he paid me off. Child support. Eight hundred a month if I'd leave his name off the birth certificate. Which I did, because I was stupid."

Jim thought back to all the night shifts his mom had worked, all the peanut butter sandwiches they'd eaten. "But . . ." he began.

"I saved most of it," Vicki said. "I was always afraid he'd decide to cut it off, and I wanted to save it for Cole, anyway. It was his."

"But you could have taken him to court," Anthea said. "Requested a DNA test, and then the support would have been court ordered, and it would have been a whole lot more than eight hundred a month."

Vicki looked at her daughter, the weariness evident in her blue eyes. "And had Cole find out? Have had to tell him the story of what his dad was, and what he did? Anyway, Henry could've fought that forever. He could've broken me. And Cole."

"Or you could've broken him," Jim said slowly. "Hurt him bad, anyway. No statute of limitations on rape, if that's what we're talking about."

"Let's say it wasn't my choice," Vicki said, meeting his gaze with her head high. "And don't you dare tell Cole."

"Don't worry," Jim said. "Not happening." Yeah, that wouldn't mess the kid up much.

"Besides," Vicki continued, "it would've been his word against mine. One guess how that would go. Impossible to prove."

Jim set the rage aside for later. It wouldn't do any good now. And if he wished with all his heart that Henry were still alive so he could beat him half to death, and the hell with the job? Well, he wished lots of things. "That's why he didn't give me a hard time when I came back, though, isn't it? Why I got the deputy job? I thought I'd have to work over in Washington. That he'd have blackballed me in Idaho."

"Yes," his mother said. "That was why. Because I heard he was putting some pressure on, down at the sheriff's. And I told him to back off. I didn't know what he had against you. Now I'm guessing I do. That you did something with Hallie—*to* Hallie—that you didn't tell me about." She didn't look one bit happy about it, either.

Anthea said, "Wait. Henry tried to blackball you, Jimbo? And let's go over the terms of that will, please. Because I'm not getting your part of it."

Jim said, "You don't know?"

"Don't know *what?*" she asked. "This is way too many secrets. Just tell me, all right? Let's get it out there."

Jim said, "Not just my story to tell. If you don't know, I guess we'll leave it there."

PAST IMPERFECT

Hallie was all the way up on Arcadia Ridge before she realized that she should have bought groceries on the way. Or stopped for a sandwich, maybe, since her stomach rebelled at the thought of eating in her father's house, especially after everything she'd learned today. She pulled a U-turn and headed back again, ending up with a chicken salad from Taco Bell at the Eastside Mall, which she ate sitting in a plastic booth that looked across the parking lot toward Safeway. A family walked by, mom and dad swinging their toddler daughter between them before the dad lifted the little girl up to put her in the seat of a grocery cart. Nice if you could get it.

She should be thinking about everything that had happened, but once again, she was blank. Empty. Overwhelmed. So instead, she set it aside, chewed her way determinedly through half the salad, tossed the rest, and headed out.

When she rolled her suitcase through the front door of the big house for the second time, it actually didn't feel quite as bad. The air still had a metallic taint, but nothing was a surprise anymore, not even the bear. Not even the will. Not even her . . . brother.

She hadn't locked up or bothered to reset the alarm. Somebody could clean out the whole damn place as far as she was concerned. They were welcome.

She started to dump her purse on the hall table, then avoided it at the last second and dropped it on the floor instead, because the table was still gray with dust.

Change. Clean. Maybe groceries, she told herself. *Oh, duh. Kitchen.* She went in there to check it out, found a stash of energy bars in a cupboard, and opened the wrapper on one, munching as she checked out the fridge.

Not much. Some spoiled milk, moldy American cheese, and a carton of eggs with a sell-by date that suggested they'd been sitting on the shelf for a month. Half a case worth of Rainier in cans, which she wouldn't be drinking. She could live the whole rest of her life without drinking bad beer.

The freezer was more of the same. Stouffer's frozen dinners and store-brand ice cream. There had better be some garbage bags under the sink.

She hesitated with her hand on the open freezer door. It was Saturday. If she were going to turn her back on the money, on the past, on all of . . . this, she needed to go. She had to be in her classroom on Monday, which meant she had to leave tomorrow. No need to shop, or to clean, either, especially if she called that woman. Eileen. If Eileen could handle it, that is. But whatever she decided about the money, she had to go home, even if it were just for those three allotted days. All she really had to do was pick up something to eat tonight, grab breakfast on the way out of town in the morning, and she'd be done.

She slammed the freezer door shut, got herself a glass of water, drank it all down, then tore another chunk off the hard-as-rock energy bar with her teeth, grimaced, and tossed the rest into the garbage under the sink, recoiling at the smell of a week's worth of kitchen waste.

You don't have to decide now. You don't even have to think now. Action would be good, though. Cleaning, whether or not she stayed. A metaphorical thing. Cleaning house. Not to mention emptying the garbage. She could figure out what to do about Eileen later. And everything else, too.

She headed back to the entryway for her suitcase, then hesitated. She didn't want to go downstairs yet. *Change first, then.* A quick detour into the bathroom to brush her teeth, and she was bringing her suitcase into the living room and tossing it onto the stone coffee table, toeing off her sandals, unzipping the blue dress, and then . . . well. Then she rummaged in the suitcase for an outfit that would hopefully magically materialize, like a ten-dollar bill you'd forgotten you'd put in your jacket pocket.

It didn't, of course. She'd planned to drive straight back from the lawyer's today, and she hadn't packed much extra, which meant that it was going to be the little yellow shorts from her pj's and a white T-shirt that was the only other thing she'd tossed in.

Well, it was Paradise, and it was hot. She held up the thin cotton shorts and tried to tell herself that they didn't *necessarily* look like sleepwear.

The peal of the doorbell startled her so badly, she dropped the shorts. Then she heard the door open and Anthea call out, "Hey, Hallie."

"In here," Hallie yelled back. She bent down to retrieve the shorts, then came up with them and said, "I'm just—"

She squeaked and jumped back, then held the shorts to her crotch.

Anthea. And Jim. Who should have jumped back himself, and then left. Instead, he was standing there and staring at her. Not at her face, either.

No. She wasn't cowering. She dropped the shorts again and lifted her arms away from her body. "What?" she asked. "You waiting for me to strip for you? You've seen it all before."

Anthea said, "What?"

Hallie looked at her, ignoring Jim, even as she felt his gaze on her as if it were his hands touching her skin. "You didn't know? I figured you just didn't want to talk to me about it."

But really? Anthea hadn't known about her and Jim? There'd been way too much new information today. She couldn't handle any more.

Jim cleared his throat, but he was still looking, she saw with a quick glance. "I'll just—" he said, and waved a hand backward, in the direction of the entryway. "Give you a . . . sec."

He'd changed clothes, too, Hallie realized. He was wearing pale-blue Levi's and a black T-shirt, both of them faded and thin from washing. He looked good.

Finally, he turned around and headed out of the room, and Hallie stood in her underwear and watched him go.

She was mad. Frustrated, too, with herself as much as anybody. Ready to be done with this, to talk it over and put it behind her. It was nothing but old baggage, it was getting in her way, and it was unnecessary.

Time to clean house.

But she still noticed his shoulders, straining that black T-shirt. And his butt, high and tight in those faded Levi's.

Damn it.

◆ ◆ ◆

Jim stood in the entryway and tried to figure out how long he was supposed to give her.

He was doing his best to think about it, anyway, but it was tough. Most of his brain space was being used up by the retinal imprint of Hallie in a dark blue lace bra that scooped down low, covering barely half her breasts and pushing them up some, too, so they swelled over the tops of the cups. And then there was the very tiny pair of matching underwear, cut in a thin, dangerous V. When she'd been bent over and he'd seen that they barely covered anything in back, either . . .

Oh, yeah. That was another image that wasn't going to be fading anytime soon.

He remembered red-gold curls under his fingers. Those weren't there anymore, because he'd have seen evidence. It was all smooth, pale skin. Shoulders and arms and belly. And breasts. And thighs. And ass. And . . . man.

When she'd lifted her arms from her sides and spoken, it had taken about five seconds for his brain to register what she'd said. Then he'd heard the thing about stripping and thought, *Yeah, I want that. Do that.* It was only when his sister had started talking that he'd come back to himself, had realized that he wasn't supposed to be looking at Hallie half naked, that she was waiting for him to leave. That she'd been getting dressed, and he'd walked in on her.

Now, Anthea called out, "You can quit hiding now, Jimbo. She's semi-decent."

He muttered, "Hoo-ah."

Cool, he reminded himself. *Calm. In control.*

He took a deep breath and went into the living room again. Hallie had the suitcase zipped up and put away, and was standing beside the couch with Anthea. At Jim's entrance, Hallie raised a hand to her hair, tucked a curl behind her ear, and caught the corner of her bottom lip between her teeth. The same way she'd used to do in chemistry class, when she'd had the table next to him and he'd almost flunked.

"So," Anthea said. She had her arms folded across her chest, her brown eyes narrowed, and was looking between the two of them. "Somebody want to explain this to me?"

"This isn't your cross-examination," Hallie said.

"Nope," Anthea said. "It's just my twin brother and my best friend. Two of the people I'd have *said* I was closer to than anybody in the world. Until today, when I find out that they've apparently both kept a giant secret from me for—what? How many years are we talking here?"

"Fourteen," Hallie said, just as Jim said, "Fifteen."

Hallie glared at him. "You don't even remember."

"I remember," he said. "I remember everything."

"Whoa, whoa, whoa," Anthea said. "Start at the beginning." She pointed at Hallie. "You."

"First," Hallie said, folding her own arms, "why are you here? Why is *he* here?"

Jim tried not to notice that she was wearing some very short, flimsy shorts, and that he could see the blue lace of her bra right through the white T-shirt. Or that the T-shirt had a scoop neck that revealed the top edge of her breasts, as well as some shadowed cleavage, especially with her arms folded like that.

"You're staring at my boobs again," Hallie informed him, and he jerked his head back up.

"Sorry," he said. "What was the question?"

She narrowed her eyes exactly like Anthea. "I'm not that good-looking."

He blinked. "Says who?"

"I never tan."

"Nope."

"I'm not that thin."

"That, too," he agreed.

"I have red hair."

He gave up. "And all that adds up to what? That I shouldn't think you're hot as hell and always have? Or is that the wrong answer? If it is, I'll try again."

"You always have?"

He didn't try to hide his exasperation. "Well, yeah. I thought I'd made that pretty clear at one point. What part of it wasn't convincing?" He didn't add the next part. *Tell me, and I'll do it again until I get it right.*

"Then why did you leave without saying good-bye?" she asked. "And never try to get hold of me again? Why wouldn't you even look at me?"

His mouth opened and shut. He had the feeling he looked like a trout. "You know why," he finally managed to say.

"I do know why." She stood there, then, and told him. "Because you hated my dad. You wanted to screw Henry Cavanaugh's virgin daughter before you left for the Army. One last thing, so you could win. You wanted to beat him, because you worked for him and you hated working for anybody, and you did. You won." Her voice was shaking now. "Or maybe because of your mom. Maybe you . . . maybe you knew. Of course you'd be furious about that. How could I blame you? But did you have to use me? What did I ever do to you? I was a *person*. I wasn't just his daughter. I was seventeen, and stupid, and I loved you, or I thought I did, and I . . ." She sank down onto the couch. "Never mind. It doesn't matter. It's all so long ago, and I know you're not that person anymore. I'm not, either. It's the past."

Jim couldn't stop himself. He sat down next to her, took her hand and held it when she'd have tugged it away, and said, "Hallie. No." He could tell she was about to cry, and he was about half sick.

Anthea was looking from one to the other of them in astonishment. "So you're telling me," she said, her finger pointing from one of them to the other, "that you two did the deed, and you took off, Jim, and you never talked about it? OK, you didn't tell me, and you should have, because I'd have . . . well, I'd have done something, I'll tell you that. But holy cow, Jimbo. We'd known her *forever*. How could you do that to her?"

He glared at her. "Because I was nineteen! Because I'd been hot for her since she was about fifteen. Because she was so pretty, and she was in my car, and I was yelling at her, and then I stopped, and she looked at me with those big eyes, and I kissed her, and . . ." He stopped. "You really want me to tell you this? It gets a little graphic."

"No," Anthea said. "Ick. Stop."

"Well, I figured." He looked at Hallie again. She wasn't crying, and she'd pulled her hand from his. "Hey," he said softly. "That wasn't what it was about. That was never what it was about."

She nodded, short and jerky, and didn't look at him. "Sure."

He sighed. "Well, damn. You really don't know." He looked at Anthea again. "You want to give us a moment?"

"No," Anthea said. "But I will. I'll go wipe fingerprint dust."

"Leave the den for me," Jim said, and Hallie looked like she was going to say something, but Anthea was already gone.

MOONLIGHT ON CEDARS

Jim sat next to Hallie on the couch and tried to think of how to start. With her this close, he could feel the warmth of her body, could smell something floral—her shampoo, or her perfume, he didn't know which—and it distracted him.

Just like it had that night.

They'd been in classes together since the sixth grade, since middle school. She'd been a top achiever, always, just like Anthea, even though Hallie was at least a year younger than everybody else, because she'd skipped first grade. Everybody knew that. She was also the only girl in town to be given a brand-new red Jeep on her sixteenth birthday. Everybody knew *that*, too. Meanwhile, Jim had sat in the back of every room, been a badass, and watched her raise her hand and talk, so smart and serious. When she'd come over to the house, he'd pretend he didn't notice her, and then he'd shoot hoops for an hour in the driveway and hope she was watching.

That was the way it had been when he was sixteen, seventeen, anyway. He'd told her and Anthea that he'd had a thing for her since she'd been fifteen. In truth, it was fourteen, but he didn't like to say it. The year she and Anthea had hung out all summer at the city pool, and

Hallie had gotten her first bikini. It had had orange and yellow flowers on it. As he recalled.

By the time they'd graduated, the gulf between them had been too wide to bridge. Anthea, on the other hand, had kept right up with Hallie. Hallie had been headed to the University of Washington, Anthea had been headed to the University of the Palouse with the aid of scholarships and loans, and Jim had been headed nowhere.

He'd been headed that way faster than usual on that Friday night. He'd driven up to a party on Paradise Mountain around nine thirty with a couple of buddies and a case of beer in the trunk, had sat around an illicit campfire in a clearing and popped the top on a can, eyed the girls, and exchanged some glances with Amber Sanderson, sitting with a friend on a log to his right. He'd been about to head on over there when a glob of pitch in the fire had flared up bright, and he'd seen somebody sitting on the other side of the clearing. Somebody with two guys standing over her.

He set down his beer, edged past the girls on the log with a last regretful look at Amber, and drifted over there.

Something was making his antennae twitch. He'd just check, that was all.

He got away from the fire and closer to the little group, waited until his eyes adjusted to the dark, and listened.

"It's hot," a tall figure he recognized as Kyle Roundtree was saying. Good-looking, and mean as a snake. He was standing a little too close to the girl on the rock, and Jim watched as she pulled a knee up against her chest and hugged it to her.

"Yeah," she said, because of course it was Hallie. Who had absolutely no business being at a kegger on Paradise Mountain, especially by herself. "I'm hot, too. I think I'd better go home."

Jim breathed a sigh of relief. He wasn't going to have to do anything.

"I've got a better idea," Kyle said. "I'm going for a swim. I think you should come."

"I didn't bring a towel," she said. "Or a suit."

"You can dry off on my shirt," Kyle said. "And you don't need a suit. It's dark. And we won't peek, will we, Mitch?"

"Hell, no," Mitch Goodman said from Hallie's other side. He put out his hand and twined one of Hallie's red curls around his finger. Her hair was falling down her back tonight, not pulled back the way she usually wore it at school. Mitch tugged, and Hallie uttered a startled "Ouch!"

Both guys laughed. "Come on," Kyle said. He grabbed the hand around Hallie's knee and pulled her to her feet, even as she tried to hang back. "I think she needs to get tossed in, don't you, Mitch?"

"No," Hallie said. "I don't want to. Please."

Mitch was already reaching for the other arm, but he didn't get hold of it, because Jim was there, grabbing him none too gently by the front of his T-shirt and shoving him off.

"Hey!" Mitch said in outrage.

"Well, hey, Mitch," Jim said, looking at him in feigned surprise. "Sorry, didn't realize that was you. That's lucky. Thought I was going to have to kick somebody's ass." He looked at Mitch a little harder, and Mitch, who was about five inches shorter and thirty pounds lighter, backed off a step. "You ready to go?" Jim asked Hallie. "Sorry I'm late."

"Oh," she said. "Uh—"

Jim shifted his attention to Kyle, who was unfortunately made of different stuff. The leader, not the follower.

"Hey," Jim told him. "I've got this."

"She's with me," Kyle said.

"I don't think so." Jim let some of the good nature go. "I think you'll find that she's with me, and she's leaving. Right now."

"Oh, yeah?" Kyle said. "I'd like to see you try." He still had hold of Hallie's arm, too.

"Man," Jim sighed. "Here I told my mom I wasn't going to get in any more trouble."

Kyle started to laugh and said, "Your mo—"

That was when Jim hit him.

Not too hard. But right in the gut, so he doubled over, staggered around, and started to retch. Jim picked him up by the back of the belt and stuffed his head and shoulders into a huckleberry bush for good measure, then told Hallie, "Let's go."

"My purse," she said.

Mitch was saying, "Hey!" and looking like he longed to take a swing at Jim but was trying to work up the courage, and Jim thought about how much trouble girls were, and how little they knew about getting out of the fight before the other guy's buddies jumped you.

She finally found her purse, and he had her hand and was edging around the fire just as heads were turning, voices rising.

They headed over the hill toward the road, Hallie stumbling against him in the dark. "How much did you drink?" Jim asked.

"Two beers. And part of another one. Only a little bit, though."

"I'm going to ask why you came, but I'm going to wait until we're out of here."

"You don't get to ask why."

"Yeah," he said, "I do."

"My car's over here," she said when they got to the road, heading to the left.

Jim pulled her back by the arm. "Oh, no, you don't. I'll come back with you for your car in the morning. You're not driving with three beers in you."

"Two. And part of one."

"Come on." He dragged her down the road to his car, opened the driver's side door, because the passenger's side was all the way against the bushes, and said, "Get in."

She stood still and said, "Why should I go with you when I wouldn't go with them?"

"Give me a break." There were voices coming from up the hill, an angry shout, an answering one. "Unless you want to see a fight," he told her, "get in the damn car."

She climbed in, slid across the seat, and he jumped in after her, hit the locks, and started to maneuver his way out of the tight spot.

He'd just pulled out when Kyle's older brother, Charlie, came running up and slammed a fist into the hood. Jim gunned the engine, Charlie jumped back, and Jim did a fast K-turn on the narrow, rutted dirt road while three more guys ran up. One of them kicked the bumper hard, making the car lurch forward, and Hallie shrieked.

"Now see what you made me do?" Jim said, gunning it again and leaving the group behind. "Probably get jumped tomorrow night. You better come visit me in the hospital."

"My dad's going to kill me," she said. "About leaving the car."

"*That's* what you're worried about? Do you realize what kind of trouble you were in back there?"

He was driving fast, swinging around the curves at the bare edge of control, but he wouldn't put it past those Roundtree boys to come after him.

"I could have taken care of myself," she said.

"No. You couldn't. Where's Anthea? You don't go to a kegger alone! Don't you know anything?"

"Well, how would I know that? Larry Dixon invited me."

Jim stared across the car at her for a split second, then turned his attention back to the road. "Because he wanted to get you drunk and get in your pants. Larry Dixon might be on the football team, but he's an asshole. I wouldn't let him within ten feet of my sister. And where was he?"

"He said he'd meet me. I was waiting for him." Before Jim could even start to tell her what was wrong with that, she asked, "And why does everybody go, then, if it's so dangerous? There were other girls there."

"Because they know the rules! You take your girlfriend. You watch out for each other. Or you go with your boyfriend."

"If guys can't control themselves," she said, "that's not girls' fault. Girls shouldn't have to change their behavior because guys are criminals. You act like girls are the ones who are wrong!"

"No," he said grimly. "I act like girls are the ones who are raped." He was going faster than ever, headed around the mountain, the tires threatening to spin out in the gravel as he came to an intersection and headed up another road on the other side.

"Watch out!" she said. "What are you *doing?*"

"Waiting them out." He bumped off the road into a cedar clearing, shoved the car into park, and exhaled.

"Oh." Her voice had lost some of the fight. "Back there. Do you really think they were going to . . ."

"Maybe not. But I don't think it would've been fun." He tried not to think about what would've happened if he hadn't come tonight. He almost hadn't. Friday-night keggers had started to feel like never-ending high school, like a dead end.

"I just wanted to . . ." she said. "Be normal. I mean, once. I didn't think . . . I thought he liked me. Larry."

"You shouldn't even be let out of the house by yourself," he said, frustrated beyond belief. "What are you going to do when you go to college?"

"I can take care of myself!" She flared right back up with the red-headed temper she hardly ever showed. "I'm not an idiot, and I'm not ten years old. OK, you told me. Now I know. Thank you very much."

"Have you ever had sex?"

She gasped. "You do *not* get to ask me that!"

He ignored that, and did his best to ignore the faint scent of her, too. Flowers and fruit, sweet and spicy. *Perfume,* he told himself. *It's just perfume.* "I'm guessing no," he said. "And I'm guessing your dad hasn't told you a damn thing about guys, either. You're too pretty, and you give off this . . ." He shoved a frustrated hand through his hair. "This vulnerability vibe. Like you don't know. Like it'd be easy. You have to stop doing that."

"I do not do that. And I'm not that pretty, and you know it. Why would you even say that? How would you know what . . . *vibe* I give off? You don't even like me!"

She was sitting there, half turned in her seat, glaring at him across the console, her chest heaving under a V-necked, sleeveless yellow blouse that was just a tiny bit too tight and a tiny bit too low. "I know because I'm a guy," he growled at her. "I know because I want to kiss you right now."

"You do not."

He was all out of patience. He reached for her, got an arm around her shoulders and another one behind her head, hauled her over, and took her mouth.

Just like that, he was lost. His fingers were tangled in all those silky red curls, his head filled with the sweet smell of flowers. Her lips were much too soft, and the second he'd touched them with his own, she gasped. *Gasped.* Her mouth opened, and that was it. He was halfway across the console, his hip digging painfully into the emergency brake, and he didn't care. Her hand came up to grab his shoulder, and she was making some noises. Little whimpers, tiny moans. She was killing him.

He kissed her for a minute, or for an hour. His tongue was in her mouth, and she started touching it tentatively with her own, and he thought he was going to explode right there. He quit grabbing her shoulder, because she was doing a damn good job of hanging on all by herself, and let his hand go where it needed to be. Around the edge of her sleeveless shirt, and then cupping her breast, claiming the soft, sweet flesh that was surely the most perfect thing ever created for a man to hold.

"Oh, God *damn,*" he finally broke the kiss enough to say. "Are you even wearing a bra?"

"It's a . . ." Her breath hitched, because his thumb had found a hardened peak, was teasing it. "Uh . . . soft one."

It was soft, all right. And she had her head back against the seat now, was breathing hard. His mouth was working again, had moved down to the side of her neck, and she turned her head to give him access and made that whimpering noise again.

Somewhere in the dim back of his brain, a tiny voice was trying to tell him that this was Hallie Cavanaugh, and he shouldn't—he *couldn't*—touch her. But the message had absolutely no hope of making it to the surface, not when she was moaning like that and shifting under his hand. Especially not once his hand went inside her blouse and found that the bra wasn't just soft. It was so skimpy, it almost wasn't there. Her nipple was diamond hard, she was whimpering every time he squeezed it through the gossamer-thin fabric, and he was about to die.

He moved again, trying to get closer, hit the seatbelt anchor with a part of him that he could've pounded nails with by now, and jerked back with a yelp.

"What?" Hallie struggled to sit, her hand going to her hair. "What happened?"

He was still sucking air through his teeth. "Never mind," he gritted out. "Just . . . ah . . . got uncomfortable there. I can't kiss you like I need to in here."

"Maybe we should . . ." she began, then stopped.

"What?" he managed to ask. *Give her a chance to tell you to take her home,* the back of his brain said. Which was pretty damn noble of him, considering that every other bit of him was telling him to keep right on going until he was inside her.

"Maybe we could . . . go somewhere else?" she asked in a small voice. "Where you could kiss me better?"

Which punted Noble Brain all the way down the field.

"Out of the car," he said.

Her eyes opened wide—he could see their whites in the moonlight—and she said, "What?" But he was already out himself and around to her side in about three steps.

When he pulled her door open, she said, "Are you kicking me out?"

"What?" he said. "Oh, no, baby. No way I'm kicking you out." He took her hand and pulled her out, and she came straight up and into his arms.

He was going to put her in the backseat. That was the plan. But he didn't make it. His arms were around her again, her hand was in his hair, and he had her pulled up tight against him, all the way up on her toes, backed up against the car, so he could feel her body pressed against his. The moon was full, and he could see her out here, and he wanted to keep looking. So instead of putting her in the back, he walked her backward to the front of the car, lifted her around the waist, and set her on the hood.

"Oh," she said, and jumped a little. Cold metal against bare skin, he realized. But she didn't get off.

He put a hand on one of her bare knees and shoved it gently away from the other, then stepped between her legs, and if there were a better spot on earth to be than between Hallie Cavanaugh's legs, he couldn't think where it would be. He kissed her some more, drowning in her soft mouth, felt her tongue getting bolder, tangling with his, and lost a few more brain cells.

When his hand started unfastening the buttons on that yellow blouse like it had a mind of its own, she wasn't exactly protesting. In fact, she had her own hands under his T-shirt now, was running them over his abs, up to his chest. And when he shoved the edges of her blouse apart, stepped back, and finally got his hands on those soft, round breasts, she moaned.

After that, he had no choice but to take off her blouse. But when his hand found the clasp at the back of her bra and unhooked it, her eyes flew open.

"Let me see," he said, somehow managing to form words. "Please." He pulled the straps over her arms, and there she was. Her skin pale in the moonlight, soft as silk under his hands, especially where he was holding her. She'd never been touched like this before, he could tell, and knowing it was a rush he could hardly stand. He palmed both those luscious young breasts, then bent and took a strawberry-pink nipple in his mouth, and she was making those noises again.

When he pushed her down on the hood of the car, she went. Her feet were on the bumper, her arms were wrapped around his neck, one hand was tangled in his hair, and he was eating her up. Greedy. Feasting on her silky skin. Her neck, her throat, those gorgeous breasts. Her hips rose and fell, but he didn't need any urging. He was already there. Already gone.

After that, unzipping her shorts was inevitable, because he was kissing a path down her belly and those shorts were in his way. He wrestled them down her legs together with her underwear, and she let him do it, let him pull them over the little sandals she still wore, and then let him put a hand on each knee, spread her legs apart, and prop her feet on the bumper again.

He ate her out right there on the hood of his car while he knelt in the dirt, and she curled her fingers into his hair, moaned and yelped and cried out, and came like a rocket, like a redhead, all soft screams and pumping hips and sweet moisture. She was so wet he almost drowned, and he would've been happy to go.

"Going to . . ." he managed to say while she was still shuddering. He stood up, his shaking hand went to his jeans, and he got them unzipped with some trouble, because it felt like he'd grown a couple sizes. He ached with an absolutely physical pain. He had to come, or it was going to kill him.

Her eyes had opened, and now she struggled to her elbows and looked at him. At his face, and then . . . not. She sat up, put a hand out, and then her gaze flew to his again as she asked, "Can I . . . can I touch it?"

"If you don't," he told her, "I'm going to die." He meant it, too.

She looked startled at that, and then her hand was on him, exploring so tentatively, and he closed his own hand over hers, was showing her how to stroke him.

"I want to be inside you," he managed to tell her. "I want it now."

Her eyes widened, and he thought she was going to say no. He should let her say no. He should ask her if she was sure. He was working up the effort to do it when she asked, "What do I do?"

"You lie down. If you want it . . . you lie down."

She lay down.

She was on her elbows again, and then on her back. And it was true. Hallie Cavanaugh was spread out naked for him on the hood of his car, her white body nearly glowing in the moonlight, and his finger was exploring the sweetest, tightest spot you could ever imagine.

"This could hurt a little, baby," he whispered. The only way he could possibly have taken his finger out of her would be for this. "We'll go slow."

She didn't answer, just moaned, her breath hitching.

"You good?" he asked, because he had to.

"Go on," she said. "Do it. Please, Jim. Do it." Which was pretty much the best thing anybody had ever said to him. And then, while she sucked in her breath, he was finally easing inside her.

He was as careful as he could manage. He went slow, even though all he wanted to do was to pump into her hard until he exploded. He did his best for as long as he could. But finally, when she was moaning again, her hips were rising and falling, and her arms were flung out behind her on the hood, he lost it.

He didn't care that it was her first time. He didn't care that he shouldn't be doing this at all. He didn't care that the whole thing was wrong. He had her hips in his hands, he was hearing her cry out with every thrust, and he was pounding it home.

When he got his thumb on that button and started pressing it in little circles, she went straight up again, but this time, he got to feel her do it. The spasms of her orgasm squeezed him hard and worked him over until there wasn't a single thing he could have done about it, because he was past thinking and past caring and almost past knowing.

When the headlights came around the corner, he saw them. When they lit the car up, and himself and Hallie with it, he knew what was happening. But he could no more have stopped himself coming than a rocket could have stopped its launch. He heard the thud of the car door, he heard the man's voice shouting something urgent, and he didn't care. All he saw was Hallie's body, all he heard was her gasping breath, all he smelled was the spicy scent of cedars and the sweet flowers of her perfume. And absolutely all he felt was the climax that ripped him from the earth and shot him straight to the moon.

FACING THE MUSIC

Hallie sat beside Jim on the couch, trying to tell herself she wasn't aware of his shoulder pressing against hers, and not able to fool herself one bit. He wasn't holding her hand anymore, and she wanted his hand back, and she didn't. He was all her worst memories, and only one of her best ones. He was nothing but trouble.

She hadn't even been aware of what was happening that night until the man had been upon them. His flashlight had played over them, and Jim, who had still been gasping as hard as she was, had grabbed her under the shoulders, pulled her up, and stepped in front of her while she'd sat on the hood and tried without much success to cover her breasts and her crotch with her hands and arms.

"Jim Lawson," the deputy said, because that was who'd come to join them. "What a surprise. Who have you got back there?"

"None of your business," Jim said, yanking his underwear and his zipper up. That probably wasn't the best answer, because the deputy shot an arm out, shoved Jim aside, and played the light over Hallie again while she shrank back, wanting to shield her eyes from the brightness, but unwilling to move one of her hands to do it.

"Hey!" Jim said as the deputy took his time. "Knock it off. Give her a chance to get dressed."

The deputy spun again, put his hand on the butt of his gun, and said, "You. Hands on the hood. And keep them there."

Jim stood still for a moment more, and the deputy took a fast step around him and said, "Right now, asshole. Or I'll pull you in for resisting arrest."

Jim glared a second more, then turned slowly around, bent over, and put his hands on the hood. The deputy kicked his feet apart for good measure and patted him down.

This was crazy. What was going on?

Hallie said, "No, wait. Stop. He didn't do anything," which the deputy didn't even seem to hear.

Where were her clothes? She couldn't get off the car and search for them, not naked, not in front of everybody. Jim's palm was right beside her thigh, and he had his head turned and was looking at her, his expression harder than she'd ever seen it. And she was *naked*.

"He didn't do anything? Not how it looked to me," the deputy said. "Looked to me like he did pretty much the whole deal. You're Hallie Cavanaugh. Bet your dad doesn't know you're out here. Did you consent to that?"

"What?" she said. "Of course I did. I need my clothes, and you need to let Jim up and go away. We didn't do anything wrong." She tried to make it sound like her dad would say it, but her voice came out quavery and high, not right at all.

"How old are you?" the deputy asked.

"S-seventeen."

"Right." The deputy pulled out a pair of handcuffs, grabbed one of Jim's wrists, and began to fasten his hands behind his back, and nothing Hallie could say stopped him doing it.

The rest of it was a nightmare. Groping for her clothes on the ground, getting dressed under the deputy's eyes, his flashlight on her, while Jim stood, his hands cuffed behind his back, and glared.

"You bring her up here to do this?" the deputy asked Jim, whose jeans still weren't all the way zipped. Hallie wanted to zip them for him, but it was too personal. She couldn't. "How'd you get her into your car?"

"He didn't!" Hallie said. "He took me out of a . . . out of a party, because I was in trouble."

The deputy ignored her. "Get in the car," he told her when she finally got her blouse buttoned again. "Front seat." He had the back door of his patrol car open, his hand on the top of Jim's head, and was shoving him, still handcuffed, into the back.

"No," Hallie said. "If he has to be back there, I'm riding back there, too. He didn't do anything more than I did."

The deputy had already shut the back door, though, so Hallie had no choice but to ride in the front.

"Take us home," Hallie said when they got to the city limits sign. "Jim first. We didn't do anything wrong. Take us home."

"Nope," the deputy said. "Not how it's going to be." Jim didn't say anything at all from his spot behind the grille in the backseat, and the deputy kept driving until he pulled up in front of the sheriff's department off Main, and Hallie thought, *This is really happening. I'm getting arrested.* It didn't seem real, and it felt much too real. The dread was a cold lump in the pit of her stomach. They were going to call her father.

"You start screwing around," he'd told her more than once, "and you just watch how fast you're out of my life. Nobody's going to be saying my daughter's a slut. You keep your legs together if you want that free ride."

College, she'd thought every time. *Seattle. Just a little bit longer, and my life is going to start.* She had a postcard with the University of Washington logo pinned to the bulletin board over her desk, and every night, she marked an *X* on the calendar page, traced that *W* with a finger, and said the name of the city out loud. *Seattle*. Where her father wouldn't see what she did, and wouldn't know. She might have to major in business, but she didn't have to be a geek anymore, not if she could get the guts not to be.

"Take us home," she said again when the deputy pulled up outside the low brick building, and he didn't even answer. Instead, he made her walk in ahead of him while he led Jim inside with a hand on his arm, and then she was put into a bare little room with a table, four chairs, white walls, and a mirror, and was left there.

Walk out, she told herself. *Just leave. Go see if the door's locked. Leave.* But she couldn't leave, even if they'd let her, if they still had Jim. If they were—what? Arresting him? But why? It wasn't a crime to have sex, and it couldn't be a crime to have sex in the woods. People did it all the time.

She thought about it for half an hour, her thoughts circling endlessly as she longed to get up off the chair, stayed on it instead, and knew she was doing it because she was a coward. And then a different deputy, a woman, opened the door to the little room, and her father walked in, and she knew why she'd kept her thoughts circling. Because she hadn't wanted to think about this.

"Let's go," her father snapped at the deputy, barely looking at Hallie.

Another ride, then, in another police car to the hospital, in the backseat this time beside her silent father, and then she was being examined and questioned by a doctor and the deputy while her father stood outside the curtain and she tried not to think about him hearing her answers. And every time she asked about Jim, they cut her off.

By the time she was driving home with her dad, she felt bruised and humiliated, violated in a way she hadn't with Jim. Her father treated her to the icy silence he specialized in, until finally, as they approached the house, she said, "Did they arrest Jim? Tell me, Dad. I'm not going to get out of the car unless you tell me."

Her father drove fast up the driveway and into the garage, jerking the car to a stop in a way that banged her back against the seat. "You'll get out of the car," he said. "You'll get out if I have to pull you out, drag you to your bedroom, and lock you in there. He told them you asked for it. He said you begged him to do it. And you didn't say anything different, did you?"

The hot flood of shame rose together with the nausea, and she had to swallow. "He wouldn't . . . he wouldn't say that," she managed.

Why not, though? It was true.

"No? He said you were always coming around the job site, trying to talk to him, throwing yourself at him. And that tonight you were at some party, drunk, and you asked him to take you out of there, told him to park in that clearing, then begged him to pop your cherry. And with you saying the same thing, what could they do?"

Hallie winced, and her father saw it and said, "If you're going to behave like trash, you're going to get treated like trash."

It was true, but it wasn't. But at least Jim hadn't been charged with anything. Whatever he'd said—he'd had to say it, surely. She'd made him say it, practically. And she *had* asked him to do it. She *had* begged him. So she stumbled out of the car and through the door into the house, and was heading back to her room when her father said, "Come into the den."

"I want to . . ." she said, gulping in a breath. "Take a shower."

"In the den," he said. "Stand there." So she stood in the middle of the floor, disheveled and sticky and sore inside, while he went to the bar and fixed himself a bourbon on the rocks.

"If you feel dirty," he finally said, looking her up and down with so much contempt, she shriveled, "that's because you acted like a whore tonight. You told me you were spending the night at Anthea's. You were lying. You went out drinking, and then you spread your legs for that loser. On the hood of his *car*. In public. You think that makes me proud? Because it doesn't make me proud to get a call from the sheriff to come down and pick up my daughter, because she's been whoring around on Paradise Mountain, getting screwed by trailer trash out in the open where anybody could see her. So you tell me, why should I send you to college if you're going to behave like a tramp? What kind of decent man do you imagine is going to want a woman who throws herself at a lowlife like Jim Lawson? You think he's in love with you? He's not. He thinks you were an easy piece of tail. He got to screw the boss's daughter on his goddamned car, and he didn't even have to buy her a drink first. He's laughing at you right now, and so is every deputy in the county. Everybody else will hear about it soon enough, and they'll be laughing at you, too. Which is what you deserve, because what you did was pathetic. But they'll also be laughing at *me*." He slammed his glass down on the bar, and Hallie jumped.

"I didn't—" she started to say. "I didn't—" But she couldn't go on. She knew her father thought tears were weak and manipulative. He'd told her so often enough. She could see the disdain on his face as she wept, but she couldn't help it. She'd fought the tears back all night while she'd sat in the station, then later at the hospital, while she'd lain on a gurney, being probed and swabbed and asked all those humiliating questions. She hadn't cried then, but she cried now. She was all out of resistance.

She wanted to take a shower and scrub it all away. She wanted to crawl into bed, put her head under the pillow, and never come out. She wanted her mother. But her mother was on a silent meditation retreat, and she'd told Hallie not to break in, "unless it's life and death, baby. I need this." This wasn't life and death, and Hallie knew it. It only felt like it.

She couldn't call Anthea, either, because Anthea would be so mad at her for getting Jim arrested. Besides, how could she tell? She'd be so embarrassed. So ashamed. It was all her fault. She knew it. She'd gone to the party, and she'd asked Jim to do it.

She stood there under the harsh overhead light and the glassy stare of the moose on the wall, the hot tears trickling down her cheeks, her breath hitching with sobs she tried in vain to hold back, while her father told her that she was grounded for three weeks, until it was time to leave for college. That was if he decided she could still go.

It had been a good night, and then it had been such a bad night.

"That night," she said now to Jim. She didn't want to ask this, and she needed to, with fourteen years' worth of pent-up urgency. "Why did you do it? Tell me the truth." The truth might hurt, but she had to know.

He sighed. "Man . . . why? Because I was half crazy about you. Or more than half. I wanted to get you out of that kegger, and then, when I started kissing you . . ." One broad shoulder lifted. "I was nineteen. Say that my impulse control wasn't everything it could've been. You were so sweet, and so sexy, and so . . ." He put a hand to the back of his head in that gesture she remembered so well and took a deep breath. "Yeah. I was caught in that whirlpool, you know. All those teenage hormones, which is no excuse. Sucked down."

"No," she said, "I think that was me. As I recall."

He turned his head and looked at her, startled.

Nothing had changed, or maybe it had, because somehow, she was saying this. "You kind of messed me up in one way, you know. I thought that was how sex would be. It was ages before I found out I had to ask for what I wanted, and got the guts to ask. Before it was any good."

He was looking warier than ever. "I told you, I was nineteen. Sorry. I was pretty selfish. I just wanted to do it."

"That wasn't what I meant. Never mind." She was back to "humiliated" again. He didn't even remember. He'd been her shameful fantasy material for years. He still was, if the truth were known, despite everything that had happened later. It was as if she could see herself, the metal cold against her naked back, the breeze playing across her heated skin, while Jim's mouth and hands drove her relentlessly into an orgasm unlike anything she'd ever felt. Before he'd given her another one.

If it had never been that way again . . . well, nobody was seventeen forever.

She finally processed what he'd said. "But wait. If you were crazy about me, if you wanted to do it so much . . . why didn't you ever call me again? You were leaving, and you didn't even tell me. And what you told the cops . . ." She swallowed. "Why did you do that?"

"What?" he asked. "Huh?"

"That I . . ." She couldn't look at him. It was fourteen years ago, and the shame burned as if it had been yesterday. "That I came on to you," she finally said. "That I begged you to do it."

"I didn't say that. I said we both wanted it, but I never said that. I wouldn't have said that. I was the one pushing it, and we both know it. I knew I shouldn't do it, and I did it anyway."

She searched his face. Hard, urgent, strong. Could he be lying?

It doesn't matter, she told herself. *It's over.* But it wasn't over, and it did matter.

"And you don't know why I left," he said. "You really don't know."

"No." She was shaking now, and she pulled her bare feet up onto the couch and wrapped her arms around her knees for warmth. This house was too cold, she thought irrelevantly. She was always freezing in here. But it was hers now. She could turn the air-conditioning right off if she wanted. "It sounds like I'm not going to like what I hear."

"The age of consent in Idaho is eighteen. I was nineteen, and you were seventeen. Technically, that's statutory rape."

She couldn't breathe. "No."

"Yes. They breathalyzed me, too. And I'd been drinking."

"But you weren't even driving when he found us!"

His mouth twisted. "Think that matters? Sheriff came to see me in my cell after about four long hours. Because, yeah," he said when she looked at him in horror, "I was in a cell. He told me that you'd given a statement that I'd coerced you. That your father would be going for a charge of sexual assault on a minor, and pushing for that DUI, too—which was the least of my worries. That I was going to prison unless I got out of town and didn't come back."

"But I would never have said that." It wasn't only her body shaking now. Her voice was shaking, too. "Never. I'd never have done that. I told them over and *over* that you didn't. I told my dad. But he said—"

"Sounds to me like he said a lot of things. And I couldn't think what to do. Couldn't tell my mom, my sister. How could I have told them what the charge was? What was I going to do, ask my mom to put up bail money she didn't have for a rape charge?"

"Anthea would have stood by you. Always." She didn't know about his mother, but she'd bet the same thing was true. Vicki Lawson had always been cool and remote when Hallie had seen her. Now that Hallie knew what had happened to Vicki, she couldn't believe Anthea's mom had let her into her house at all. It said something about her that she hadn't lumped Hallie together with her father.

"I couldn't tell them," Jim repeated. "Anthea would've been bad enough, but Mom . . . I knew I couldn't. I know that even more now."

"But she's going to figure it out," Hallie said. "The thing in the will about the sexual relationship? She's going to guess."

"She might guess," Jim said, "but she's not going to know, because I'm not going to tell her."

"You can tell her. You don't need to protect me anymore. I don't want to get in your way."

Jim laughed, and she was so startled, she jumped. "You've always been in my way," he said. "No hope for it."

She wanted to ask what he meant, but she didn't. "So what did you do?" she asked, instead. "Then? You were going into the Army anyway."

The laughter was gone. "No, I wasn't. That was my can't-think-of-another-answer solution. I told the sheriff I'd leave, and then I drove up to the Army recruiting office in Spokane and enlisted. I didn't have any money or any connections. I worked for your dad. Think anybody would've helped me out?"

"And when I saw you—" she said, her voice almost a whisper.

It had been at the grocery store. She'd been with her dad, because he'd carried through on his threat. She hadn't gone anywhere for the next weeks that he hadn't taken her, and that day had been one of the worst.

She'd been in the meat aisle, listlessly picking out burgers and steaks, when she'd turned to toss the packages into her cart and had seen Jim. She'd stopped with the steaks still in her hand and stared at him, hardly daring to breathe.

He'd looked right through her, his eyes as cold, dark, and bleak as a pond in winter. And then he'd turned around and walked in the other direction.

She'd known, then, that her father had been right. That all Jim had wanted was to take advantage of her, and to score on her father. That she'd let him treat her like trash, and now she was trash to him.

"I was home again, waiting to ship out for basic," he said now. "Keeping my nose clean, terrified the whole time that your dad would change his mind and I'd be in jail, wishing I could leave but with no place to go. And, yeah, I blamed you, but not as much as I blamed myself. I guess we both thought the wrong thing, because he made sure of it. Did he give you a hard time?"

"Yeah. You could say that. But at least I didn't have to join the Army."

"Turned out all right. He did me a favor, if you want to look at it that way. I know that's what I've thought. But I don't think he did you one."

"No," she said. "Or yes." She dropped her feet to the floor and ran both hands through her hair, blowing out a breath and trying to let the tension go with it. It was all so long ago. It was over. "Maybe. Who knows. I might not have had the courage to go my own way if I hadn't seen just how horrible he could be."

Anthea came back into the room with a bottle of Windex and a roll of paper towels in her hands, looked at the two of them, and propped her hands on her hips. "All right, you guys. I've had enough. Somebody needs to, *A,* help me out with this disgusting job, and *B,* tell me what the hell happened. Right now."

Hallie laughed in surprise, sneaked a look at Jim to see his serious expression lightening and a smile twitching at the corner of his mouth, and set the rest of this history lesson gratefully aside.

That was enough. Not everything needed to be out there. Not if there was no point. Not if it was over.

TACKLING THE BEAR

Jim was rattled. No doubt about it. He looked at Hallie and said, "What do you think?"

He knew what he thought. He thought he wanted to keep talking to her. He wanted to tell her how good it had felt to be her first, and how bad it had felt when that deputy had been shining his light all over her, looking at her body and loving her embarrassment, while Jim had stood there in handcuffs and burned to beat him blind. He wanted to sit here with a bottle of wine and two glasses, have Hallie curl up next to him, put his arm around her to keep her warm, and kill the past along with the bottle. He wanted to watch her run her hands through her hair again and mess up her curls. He wanted to look down that white shirt. And then he wanted to take it off of her, lay her down, and do it all again. Do it right.

But he didn't, of course, because she didn't want that. For millions of very good reasons, and because they had too much history, and too much of it was bad.

Anthea must have seen how distracted he was, because she sighed in exasperation. "You're hopeless, Jimbo. Ever hear of the twin bond?" Before Jim could tell her what she could do with her twin bond, she was telling Hallie, "And here Jim told me he wanted to come over to help you clean up, and to talk this over. The family stuff. Hah."

"Oh," Hallie said. "Family stuff."

"Yep," Anthea said. "We're sort of all part of the same one, looks like, which makes your obvious previous encounter even *more* awkward, if that were possible."

"Oh, no," Jim said. "Hell, no. Do not be telling her that. Don't be using that word."

"What word?" Hallie asked.

Anthea sighed. "He means 'sister.' And if you're thinking you'll get in her pants again," she told her brother, "even imagining you could keep it secret, which is a pretty big stretch all by itself—you'd have your work cut out for you." She ignored Hallie's gasp of protest. "I'm just saying. She's hopelessly shut down."

"I am not," Hallie said. "I have relationships."

Anthea huffed. "Yeah. With dickless wonders. And then you can't figure out why they don't work. Not that Jim's been doing any better lately. At least *you* go out."

Hallie straightened up and gave Anthea a pretty good glare while Jim was still groping for a response. "Stop," Hallie said. "Just stop. I mean, thank you for coming over to help me clean up, but—"

Jim stood up and said, "Den. Give me that stuff." He grabbed the Windex and paper towels out of Anthea's hands.

Anthea said, "Excuse me? Wasn't somebody going to tell me the story?"

Jim said, "Well, it wasn't going to be me."

"You don't have to clean it," Hallie said. "I'll do it. I need to face it."

"Nope," Jim said. Time to take this situation right back. "I'm doing the den." And when Hallie opened her mouth, he said, "I'm two seconds away from telling you to shut up. I'm doing the den. Not you. Not my sister. Me. It's not going to bother me one bit to do it, it'd bother me like hell to watch you do it, and that's it."

"I didn't ask you to watch me do it," she said. "I didn't ask you to come over at all and start bossing me around, or either of you to talk about who's getting in my pants. I've had a *really bad day*, all right? And I know you both have, too, but . . . stop. Please. Just stop."

She was looking shaky again, and Jim was swearing at himself. "I'm going," he said. "Den." And he went.

◆ ◆ ◆

"Right," Anthea said as Hallie listened to the sound of Jim's feet retreating down the stairs. "Let's hear it, sister." She stopped. "Oh, wait. Awkward."

"No," Hallie said, pulling herself back together. "For heaven's sake. Not awkward. I'm not your sister, and I'm sure not Jim's. And all right, obviously, he and I had sex once. *Once.* A very long time ago. We got caught, my dad found out, and there was hell to pay. End of story."

"And that's why Jimbo enlisted," Anthea said slowly. "Holy *shit*. And you didn't tell me."

"How could I have?" This, Hallie knew for sure. "How could I have faced you, after I got him arrested?"

Anthea looked at her, a twisted smile on her face. "Uh . . . yeah. You know what? I've got a feeling I know which one of you initiated that. And it sure wasn't you."

"I'm not telling," Hallie said, feeling about five years old.

"You don't have to. Let me throw out a wild-ass guess here. Your dad banished the man who dared to sully the purity of his daughter. Except that, whoops, turns out he just happened to have raped that man's *mother* and fathered her child, which could've had something to do with wanting to get her *other* son, that annoyingly protective one, out of the way before he started asking questions. Assuming Cole was born then?"

Hallie sat down again, because her legs didn't want to hold her up. "Fourteen years ago. How old is Cole?"

"Fifteen."

Hallie nodded bleakly. "Did your mom tell you that? Did she say it was . . . rape?" She didn't want to hear it, she didn't want to believe it, and she knew it was coming, and that it was true.

"More or less." Anthea sat down beside her, put an arm around her shoulder, and hugged her close for a second. "Man, he was a piece of work, huh? You always said so, and I used to think you were being dramatic. Turns out you were lowballing it. But you know what?" She got to her feet again. "You need to get busy tossing his evil ass out of this house. Where do we start?"

"Oh, man," Hallie said, so grateful not to be talking about it anymore. She was on overload. "I so want to do that. Could we get some Hefty bags and bag it all up? Throw away anything he used, bathroom and all that, but otherwise . . . could I just call Goodwill? What do you think? I'd throw everything away, but somebody could use it."

"You bet," Anthea said. "Start with his bedroom?"

This was why you had a best friend. Because Hallie couldn't even face looking in there. At the collection of bolo ties, complete with their gigantic hunks of turquoise. At the western shirts with their snap fronts, the belts with their silver buckles like Henry had won them riding rank bulls in the rodeo, the cowboy boots in lizard and alligator and kangaroo and ostrich and anything else that cost extra money and came from far away and couldn't be had by just anybody . . .

Whoops. She was losing control again.

"Yeah," she said. "Start there. The thought of some 'bum' who works down at the recycling center, somebody my dad would've thought was dirt, wearing his ostrich boots? That gives my heart a real nice lift."

"It would've upset him, huh?" Anthea said.

"It would've *killed* him. If he wasn't dead already."

"Then I'm going to do it. You do . . ." Anthea made a vague gesture. "Whatever. But I'm doing this."

They found the Hefty bags under the kitchen sink, and Anthea marched off to the bedroom. Hallie emptied the kitchen garbage, tossed everything from the kitchen that she didn't want—which was almost all the food, because her father had had taste that ran to white bread, bologna, and mayo—and then tackled the living room. She began with the bighorn sheep horns on the mantel, stood on a chair to take down an original Remington print of a lean cowboy on a leaner horse, sighting a rifle across the plains, and then got an idea.

She was on her chair again in the entryway, holding the heavy wood plaque in place with one hand while she unfastened the right-hand screw holding up the pronghorn antelope head with the other, and tried not to stare into its beady, accusing glass eyes, when Jim said from somewhere behind her, "You know, you could ask."

She whirled and lost her hold on the antelope, and it swiveled down fast on its lone remaining screw, its wickedly sharp, curving horn raking a path across her chest along the way.

The pain was instant and red-hot. She heard the screwdriver hit the floor and Jim swearing as she cried out, grabbed her chest, and tipped straight off the chair.

Jim caught her in midair. The chair crashed to the flagstones, but his arms were around her, and he was holding her tight, her feet off the ground, her entire body pressed against his. And then he set her down and put her away from him with one hand on her shoulder while his other hand pulled the fabric of her shirt away to check the injury.

"Stop . . ." she hissed, slapping his hand away and stepping back, "sneaking *up* on me!"

"Stop doing things half-assed!" he snapped back at her. "You get a ladder so you're high enough. You get a spotter. You get a damn electric screwdriver!"

Her eyes had filled with tears, because it *hurt*. She looked down to see a thin line of blood welling up along a four-inch slice that ran diagonally down to the top swell of her right breast.

"Oh, damn it to *hell*," Jim said. "I did that wrong. Don't cry. Come on. Where's the first aid kit?"

"*I* don't know," she said, blinking the tears back. "I don't live here, remember? And it doesn't matter. It's just a scratch."

"Hurts, though."

"No, it doesn't." It did, a razor-thin trail of fire, but it wouldn't kill her. "It surprised me, that's all. The Revenge of Bambi. Ambushed by the Antelope." She had her hand over the scratch, could feel the blood welling up beneath her fingers. "If I get this shirt all bloodstained, though, I don't have another one. Shoot. I need those paper towels."

He ripped a few off the roll and handed them to her. "I'll go get a cold washcloth," he said. "That'll help with the pain, too."

"Never mind. I'll do it. It isn't a big deal." He started to object, and she sighed in exasperation. "Jim. You have a Purple Heart. You've got that terrible scar on your face, and some kind of . . ." She gestured in the direction of his midsection. "War wound that I can't see, the one you got rescuing two of your buddies when they were pinned down in the street. Anthea told me all about it in gory detail, because you almost *died*." She didn't share how shaken she'd been to hear it. "You got shot. I scratched my chest."

He opened his mouth, then shut it again, and she looked at him warily and said, "What?"

He looked sheepish. "Never mind."

"What?" She took the paper towel off and checked out her own war wound, tugging down her shirt to do it and exposing a fair amount of bra and a lot of skin, and looked up to find him watching her do it.

"I was going to say something about your chest being more important than my guts," he said. "But then I decided it was a little—"

"Cheesy," she finished. "And you're staring again."

"I'm trying not to. But if you pull your shirt down like that, I'm going to stare. I'm a guy. I'm hardwired." He looked at the wall of trophies. "OK. I'm moving on, because I'm a professional. We ditching the heads?"

"Yes." It was good to be moving on. Of course it was. Definitely. "I hate them. And to answer your earlier and extremely undiplomatic criticism, I was on the chair with the screwdriver because I didn't want to go to the garage, all right? I didn't want to go past the den. And I didn't want to wait. I want them *gone*." She stared at the bear, who snarled back at her. "And I want Smokey gone, too. No offense, Smoke," she told the bear. "Wait. Probably a girl bear."

"Yep," Jim said. "That's a female bear. Size-wise, and equipment-wise. You know that Henry would never have let the taxidermist take those off. I always thought he must have had some size insecurity, personally."

"I feel we're having a bonding moment," she said, and he laughed out loud. The sound rang out against the hard surfaces of the entry hall, and somehow, it chased away some of the darkness.

He was full-on smiling at her now, the skin around his eyes crinkling with amusement in a completely satisfactory grown-man way. If only he weren't so damn *manly*, this would be so much easier. "Let's bond some more," he suggested. "What do you say? I'll go find a ladder and a better screwdriver, and you can give me a hand getting these down so neither of us gets attacked. But while I'm doing that? Go find some antibiotic ointment. No telling where that antelope's been. He was the low-life type, you can tell. And if you want a hand with the, ah, application? The motto is 'Protect and serve,' you know."

"Yeah, right," she said, and he smiled some more and took off down the stairs to the garage. And Hallie didn't look for the antibiotic ointment, because Anthea would probably have thrown it away by now anyway, and besides, she didn't want to use Henry's Neosporin. But she did have a very stern conversation with herself about the unreliability of physical attraction and the terms of wills and the inadvisability of making decisions while in a fragile emotional state.

Not that it did much good.

FUTURE PLANS

A couple hours later, there were at least a dozen big black plastic bags leaning up against the garage door, and Hallie was feeling a little better about things.

"Wonder if I can donate the vehicles, too?" she asked as she and Jim carried the gigantic moose head out between them and laid it down on the driveway with the rest of the trophy heads. Jim had taken most of the weight—she hadn't missed that—but still, she pulled her sleeve down her arm and wiped her forehead with it. She didn't even think about the fact that she was showing her bra again, and that Jim was watching. Well, barely. It was still hot, even in late afternoon.

"Don't see why not," Jim said. "Can't really see you using that snow-mobile, and I don't picture you as a big Jet Ski fan, either. More of the cross-country-ski, kayak type, I'm thinking. Seattle."

"Got something against hippies?" She went for smart-mouthed, because it was easier than thinking about her father, or about Jim, or about . . . anything.

"Nope, I sure don't. Not if they're you," he said, and she tried not to think that that was a pretty good answer. "The car, though, not to mention the pickup . . ." he went on. "Henry had one classy rig. Sure you don't want it, or at least want to sell it?"

"Oh, yeah," Hallie said as Anthea came out with a bag full of empty liquor bottles whose contents Hallie had already poured down the sink, because she'd decided that drinking her father's liquor was another thing she couldn't stomach after all. "I'm sure. But if you want it, be my guest. One dollar bill, and it's yours."

His mouth twisted. "Yeah. No, thanks. And that's something, because that's my dream rig. Black crew-cab F-150 with all the bells and whistles? That's the one. But I sure don't want it."

"You and me both." She looked around her at the trophy heads, the artwork, the garbage bags. "I'll have to call Goodwill on Monday. There's no way that moose is fitting in my car. But what if it rains before they can get out here? I don't want this stuff in the house, but maybe we should at least shove it into the garage." The clouds had billowed and dispersed all afternoon, giant cumulus puffballs that could bring a sudden, violent North Idaho downpour before you knew it. The garage had an overhanging roof, but still.

Jim looked at her a minute more, his face inscrutable, then pulled his phone out of the back pocket of his jeans, and Hallie tried not to look at his biceps, as she'd tried all afternoon. He poked around a little, then held the phone to his ear and waited.

"Hey, Marine," he said after a moment. "Jim Lawson." He listened a minute, then smiled and said, "Nah. Unofficial. So Henry Cavanaugh died, if you heard. You want, oh, about half his possessions? Most of the good stuff? His daughter's cleaning house, and she's feeling charitable." Another pause, and he said, "Then here's what you do. Wherever you've got the truck going on Monday, can it. Bring it up here to Arcadia Ridge, and all of this is yours. Blow it, though, and I'm calling Caring Hearts of the Palouse on Tuesday. So you know."

Another pause, and he said, "You can probably fill up the truck, yeah. Got some furniture for you, I think. Hang on." He held the phone against his chest and asked Hallie, "Furniture in the den? You want it? How about his bedroom?"

"*No.*" The word exploded from her, and he gave a crooked smile and said into the phone, "Yeah. Big-ass leather couch and chairs, bedroom set, all on the high end. That Wheel of Fortune scoreboard just ticked over another few grand. Better send a couple guys, anyway, because he liked the heavy stuff. Oh, and there might be some vehicles in it for you. But it's Monday morning, or it's gone."

He listened a minute more, then said, "Almost forgot. Got a full-grown stuffed and mounted black bear here that's got 'Merry Christmas to the World's Best Mother-in-Law' written all over it." He laughed, said, "Yeah. Thought so. Monday, Marine," and hung up.

"Marine?" Hallie asked, trying not to be impressed that he'd solved her problem just like that.

"Will Harrison," Jim said. "Manager over at Goodwill. Marine."

"What did he say about the bear?" Hallie asked. "Will he take it?"

"Said, 'Dibs on the bear,'" he said, and Hallie laughed, and Anthea did, too. Jim went on, "So what you do is get a stack of paper, some tape, and a marker. Write 'Goodwill' on whatever you want them to take, stick it on there, let them do the hauling. Including the bear."

"Oh. Good." She'd known it would take all three of them to get that huge thing down the stairs, and she'd shrunk from touching its furry . . . shoulders. If that was what you called the front end of a bear. Somehow, the bear had come to symbolize all her discomfort with the house.

"You could keep that TV in the den, maybe," Jim said, "because that's a sweet piece of electronics, and a wall-mounted TV doesn't retain asshole molecules, would you say?"

Hallie considered. "No. Not so much. OK, I'll keep the TV. You know what would be cool to have in there? A pool table. The room's big enough. If I got a pool table, would you guys come over and shoot pool and drink whiskey with me? We could be badasses."

Anthea said, "You couldn't be a badass to save your life."

Jim said, "I'd do that. I'm guessing I could be enough of a badass for both of us." He didn't smile, just looked at her, a little bit dark and a little bit dirty. Or maybe that was her imagination.

She tore her gaze away, made a business of patting her hair back into place, then realized she was touching her hair for a man and stopped. Jim cleared his throat and said, "One other thing in there you're going to have to decide about. Whatever's in that gun safe."

"Oh. Right." She chewed on her lower lip. "Huh."

"You got a key for it?" he asked.

She started to say no, and then realized that she probably did. "Come on." She took the two of them up the stairs to the kitchen, where she picked the heavy ring of keys up off the counter. "It'll be on there, I'm guessing. He'd have kept it with him. He loved his guns."

"Bet he had a weapon in the truck, too," Jim said. "We'll want to check that before you donate it."

They all trooped down to the garage again, where Jim hopped up into the truck after Hallie motioned him to go ahead. She didn't want to sit in there. He dove into the glove compartment and came out with a snub-nosed semiautomatic. He ejected the magazine, then racked the slide and caught the live round in one hand before climbing out of the truck again.

"This thing's a Kimber Ultra," he told her. "Zebrawood grip? Fifteen hundred new, easy."

He started to hand it to her, but she put her hands up and said, "You keep it." He raised his brows, but stuck the magazine and spare round into his pocket and headed into the den again, picked out a heavy-duty, round-barreled key, inserted it into the lock of the matte black cabinet that sat in a purpose-built niche, and swung the heavy door open.

He took a good, long look, then whistled. "Whoa."

"Whoa what?" Anthea asked. "Seven long guns and a few hand-guns? That's practically unarmed by Idaho standards."

"Not if one of them's this." Jim put the small handgun and the ammo onto two of the safe's shelves, then lifted one of the long guns out of its slot, handling it almost reverentially. "This is the prize, right here."

"It's a shotgun, that's all," Hallie said.

"Bite your tongue. This isn't 'a shotgun.' This is a Purdey. This thing'd fetch thirty grand at retail. And the rest of it . . ." He put the shotgun carefully back into its slot and examined the rest of the guns, then frowned some more, and Hallie waited.

Anthea didn't, though. "When you're done praying over the fire-power . . ." she said. "Anytime."

"Adding it up," Jim said, unruffled. "Not everybody's mental pro-cesses work as fast as yours. But I'll bet you could get forty grand easy for all this, Hallie, even wholesale. One of these rifles is a Jarrett, and those don't come cheap." He looked at her, frowning again. "You can't donate guns. Donate the money if you want, but all this has to go to a dealer, assuming you don't want it. A big one. Seattle would be best. I can call a buddy, get a name for you."

"No," she said immediately. "I'd have to carry them all back in my car. No. Isn't there somebody close by?"

"Not for this. Spokane would work, maybe. Won't get as much, though. And you'd still have to get it there."

"Could you . . ." She hesitated. "Could you sell them for me? I'd give you a commission," she hurried to add. "Five . . . ten percent. Whatever."

He shut the door of the safe and turned the key before he said, "I'll do it for you. And I don't want a commission."

His voice and posture were both stiff, and she sighed. "I've offended you. But it's a lot of effort. It's only fair."

"Say I owe you."

"You do not *owe* me. We talked about this!"

"You bet I do." He handed her back the keys and said, "I'll do it. If you trust me. That's a lot of money."

"Do me a favor," she said in disgust. "Like you'd cheat me." She *did* trust him, she realized in some astonishment. Maybe she shouldn't, but she did. She worked the key to the safe off the ring and said, "Here. Take the whole thing. The safe and all."

"I can't do it today. This thing'll weigh a few hundred pounds. I'll get the Jackson boys out here with me, and we'll load it up."

"Be my guest. Whenever."

"You might want to hang on to one of the shotguns," he said. "Not the Purdey. Maybe one of the twenty gauges. That Winchester—that'd be good. If you're going to be living out here on your own, it might be best. As long as you know how to use it."

"I know how to use it. My dad taught me to shoot. Made me practice, too. I know how just fine."

"So you want it, or not?"

"Not," she decided. "If I need a shotgun, which I don't, I'll get my own." She paused as a thought struck her. "Wait. Cole. Would he . . . do you think he might want one of them?"

"They're not his," Anthea pointed out. "You inherited them."

Hallie made an impatient gesture. "Who cares? I don't want them. And Cole was his son. He has a right."

"Most people would care," Jim said.

"I wasn't expecting any of this," Hallie said. "It's like finding money in your coat pocket. If I give something to him, I'm not losing anything." She shook her head. "I can't explain it well enough. But I don't care."

"But," Jim said slowly, "you *are* losing something. Which is why most people don't feel like that. The second they find out something's theirs, it's *theirs*. You find that money in your coat pocket? If you lose it again, you're bummed. If you don't feel that way, all I can say is—maybe you're not thinking about it clearly."

"Or maybe," she said, feeling the temper rise, "I'm thinking about it *exactly* clearly." She didn't usually let the redhead out. A lifetime spent with her father had taught her hard lessons about the consequences of anger. There'd been one person in this house allowed to get angry, and that person hadn't been her. "Maybe I'm not most people. Maybe I understand that everything comes at a price, including money."

"The camel through the eye of the needle thing?" Jim asked. "Rich men don't go to heaven?"

"Plenty of rich men do, I'm sure," Hallie said. "My dad wasn't one of them, and we both know it. What I'm trying to say is more like that proverb, though. 'Take what you want and pay for it, says God.' Because there'll be a price, always. I didn't think the price was worth it before. I didn't think that seeing my father and doing what he wanted was worth the inheritance. And now that I have it after all, I need to make sure the price is one I'm willing to pay."

Jim didn't say anything. He was looking at her, she was looking back, and the tension stretched out between them like a rubber band. Anthea, for once, wasn't saying anything.

Jim finally said, "You're different."

She said, "So are you."

He looked for a minute like he was going to go somewhere with that, but instead, he just said, "Yeah. Well. I guess we've both done some paying. I'll ask Cole and my mom about the guns, if you want me to."

"Please," she said, and tried not to shake. It wasn't cold in here anymore, but she was wound up all the same.

He nodded and said, "OK. Moving on. I don't know how closely you've looked, but I'd have somebody come in, rip up the carpet in here, and lay some new. Won't cost much, not for one room with no furniture. I did my best with the blood, but even if you got a service in to deep clean . . . not sure you'd ever feel really good about that. But you do that, get your pool table, hang some badass girl stuff on the wall, and it'll be a new room. *Your* room."

"Badass girl stuff?" Anthea said.

Jim shrugged. "Biker chick? Sports? Uh . . ." He gave Hallie his half smile and said, "Sorry. I got nothin'. Put you in black leather, and you'd still be sweet."

That one threw Hallie right off balance. She hadn't been sweet just then, and she knew it. It took her a few seconds to recover, and then she cleared her throat and said, "I'll do that. The carpet. Also—Monday. Now that I know about the guns, I can't leave the doors unlocked. I don't care what somebody steals, but I don't want them stealing guns."

"You sure don't," Jim said. "Set that burglar alarm, too. No telling where those would end up, or what somebody'd end up doing with them. You don't want that. And I'll have to wait until my next day off to go up to Spokane and sell them. I'd rather not take them until then, for the same reason. The bed of my truck isn't secure enough."

Hallie looked out the picture window and across the sea of rolling hills to the horizon. She was having a hard time looking at Jim without the treacherous color, the bane of redheads, rising in her cheeks.

Anthea, who'd been watching the two of them all along like they were on Wimbledon's center court, said, "Know what we need now? Pizza and beer. I already snuck the six-pack into the fridge," she told Hallie. "Surprise for you. And after Jimbo calls in the pizza order, we'll go around and stick those labels onto everything you want to give away, and we'll be all done."

"Oh, I'm calling it in?" Jim asked. "Amazing."

"Why amazing?" Hallie asked.

"That I'd get to decide."

"Oh, you're not deciding," Anthea said. "Hallie and I are deciding. You're just calling."

Jim gave that half smile again, and Hallie laughed and thought, *How about that? I laughed. And Henry's stuff is going, going, gone.*

◆ ◆ ◆

They ate the pizza out on the deck. The day had cooled at last, and a light breeze disturbed Hallie's curls. Beams of sunlight were slanting low through the puffy clouds, creating a landscape like a religious painting and making her remember that not everything about Idaho was terrible.

Once again, she was a mess, her hair disheveled, her shirt damp in places, her yellow shorts limp, dusty, and bedraggled, and she didn't care. She'd be sleeping in a tank top and her underwear tonight, and that would be fine. She wasn't going to stay in her childhood bedroom, either. She'd picked an upstairs bedroom that looked north, toward the town and the university. Brand-new accommodation. She'd go into town tomorrow morning and buy something cheap to wear on the drive home. She'd be fine.

The first beer had gone down fast, and she was well into the second now. Anthea was pacing her, but Jim was holding himself to one. "Driver," he'd said. "Plus, I'm high on life." He'd smiled at her across the table, nice and slow, and she'd gotten a flutter low in her belly. And maybe it had moved on down and become a tingle, or maybe the tingle had been there all along. She wasn't telling.

Now, he looked at her, his gaze measured. He was kicked back in his chair, his feet on the lower rail of the deck, the bottle in his hand. "That scratch is looking angry," he said. "You ever put that antibiotic ointment on it?"

She glanced down at the red line across her chest. It still burned some, and it was in no way attractive. But then, 'attractive' had gone out the window sometime back pre-moose. "Huh," she said. "No. I don't have any. I'll get some in the morning, maybe."

He swung his long legs down from the railing and stood. "Be right back." He loped off across the deck and down the stairs, and Hallie took another swallow of beer and said again, "Huh."

"What are you thinking?" Anthea asked.

Hallie thought about not answering, but this was Anthea, who knew her better than anyone. That she was Jim's twin, too—that was confusing and tricky, but it was reality. "How much he's changed, I guess," she finally said.

"Not too surprising," Anthea said. "You have, too, you know."

"I still feel the same inside, though. I'm guessing he doesn't."

"But you're not. Look at what you've done today."

Jim's head and shoulders appeared, and then the rest of him, leaping up the stairs as easily as he'd run down them. He came over, holding a white plastic box, and said, "What did I miss?"

"Just talking about you," Anthea said, and Hallie put a hand up to stop her saying it, then dropped it. "How you've changed. And Hallie, too. And I was starting to say, not too surprising. You've both had a lot of life happen."

"You haven't changed, though," Hallie told Anthea. "You're still exactly the same, isn't she, Jim?"

"Mm," he agreed. "But then, Anthea's more or less in a class by herself." He'd opened his box, was pulling something out of it.

"You have a first aid kit in your truck," Hallie said. "And it's organized. Now, see, that *is* different. Bet you didn't always have that."

"Nope. But I'm a cop, you know." He ripped the top off a packet and unfolded a thin square of antiseptic wipe.

"And a father," Hallie said. "I guess that changes things, too."

His eyes met hers, and he said quietly, "Yeah. That changes everything." Then he said, "I'm going to clean this off. Might sting a little."

"That's all right." She knew she should take it from him and do it herself. But she didn't. She sat still and let him scoot close. He put one hand on her shoulder and dabbed gently at the scratch. It *did* sting, and she sucked in a breath and stiffened at the first touch. He looked up, into her eyes, and asked, "Hurts?"

"No." If she was a little breathless, it was the sting, that was all. He went back to work, then set the cloth aside, squeezed a ribbon of antibiotic ointment onto his finger, and dabbed it carefully down the cut. His touch was nothing but gentle, and all the same, she was having a hard time sitting still under it.

He finished, but kept his hand on her shoulder. "You still grab your lip with your teeth."

He was so close, she could smell the scent of him, all pine soap, warm cotton, and warmer man. She could see the shadow of beard along his jaw, too, and had a sudden, irrational urge to press her lips to the corner of his mouth, there where he was almost smiling. And then to work her way down the side of his strong brown throat while she rubbed the short hair at the nape of his neck and pressed up close to that big body. Sitting in his lap, maybe, with his hands all over her, because if she were there, he'd be feeling her up. And that would be so good.

And Anthea was right there, watching.

Hallie swallowed, and knew they both saw it. "I . . . yeah. I guess."

Jim took his hand off her shoulder and took his time twisting the top back on the tube and repacking the first aid kit. "That used to drive me nuts. The lip."

"I know," she said. "Bad habit. My dad used to grab my cheeks and shake my head when I did it." Anthea made a little protesting noise, and Hallie could feel herself flushing. She was babbling because she was nervous. She hadn't meant to say that. It had been humiliating, and a little scary, too, to have her dad's hard fingers pinching her cheeks, whipping her head back and forth.

"You know, I'm sorry he's dead," Jim said.

"What?" Hallie said.

"Can't tell you how many times today I've wanted to punch him out. That one goes up there near the top of the list, though."

Not at the top, Hallie thought. *That would be your mother.*

"So," Anthea said. "What's your plan, Hal?"

Jim didn't say anything. He just sat still and looked attentive, and Hallie thought again how different he seemed. He'd always had that watchful air, that impression of coiled strength, but the restlessness was gone now. Maybe she'd call it *controlled.* The energy was still there; it was just held in reserve.

"Mm?" she asked, and he kept looking, and she looked back.

Anthea sighed. "You two are so not going to make it six months. That is bad news. But ahem. The will? Your inheritance?"

"Oh." Hallie had avoided thinking about it all day, but the pieces seemed to have been falling into place all the same. "I thought," she said slowly, "earlier today, that there was no way. Now, though, I'm wondering if I could do it."

"Well, of course you could *do* it," Anthea said. "But do you *want* to do it?"

Hallie said, "I don't know. Maybe giving all his stuff away has given me ideas. I hate to think of him pulling my strings, and I know that was the point. To get me to give up my job teaching brown kids and get me back here. But—it's the kind of thing you ask yourself all the time, right? What would you do if you won the lottery? Would you use it to help people, the way you'd like to think? Or would you just spend it? So what would I do? I know one thing. I didn't want to live my life for my father, but I don't want to live it to spite him, either. Maybe that was what it was about at the beginning, when I went off to teach English in Japan instead of getting a job in business. But then it became some-thing else. It started to be about doing something I enjoyed, something that felt worthwhile. Could this be the same thing? Could I actually do some good with the money?" She looked at the clouds, at the hills, and asked the question of them. "Or would I just be fooling myself? Is that an excuse to say why I want millions of dollars?"

"Seems to me," Jim said, his voice as deep and calm as a mountain lake, "that if you were that kind of person, I wouldn't have been making that call to Goodwill."

"Maybe," Hallie said, "I just want to live here on my terms. Maybe I want to say that there's another way to live, right here with his . . . ghost watching. Maybe I want to win."

"Maybe you do," he said. "Nothing wrong with winning. I've always preferred it to losing, personally."

"Well," she said, "that's because if you lost, you died."

A faint smile tugged at the corner of his mouth, and the way the light was hitting him highlighted that scar along the edge of his hairline. "That, too."

She sat back, yanked at her curls, and sighed. "My students, though."

"School year's, what," Anthea said, "four weeks in?"

"Seattle," Hallie said. "We're only going into week three."

Anthea shrugged. "Give some teacher who thought she wasn't getting hired this year a break?"

Hallie chewed on her lip some more. "I'd have to get a job here."

"Yep," Anthea said. "Too bad you're lazy."

Hallie's eyes opened wide, and then she laughed. "You're right. I'm not lazy." She slapped the table with sudden resolve. Maybe it was the beer, maybe it was the bear. Or maybe it was the company. "You know what? I could do it."

THAT GUY

Jim was still thinking about that when Anthea drained her beer bottle and said, "Well, I suppose I should go hang out with my husband."

"Yeah," Jim said. "We should go." He didn't want to. He wanted Anthea to leave, and then he wanted to hang out right here on this deck and split that last beer with Hallie while he watched the setting sun turn her hair to red-gold. But he hadn't been invited, and Mac was still over at Anthea's, so he stood up, gathered the beer bottles for the recycling, and said, "Can't imagine you could get back here by Monday morning, Hallie, even if you decide to stay. I can probably arrange to swing by and let Goodwill in, if you want to give me your key. Do you have my cell, so I can get the key back to you? And what about that alarm?"

"Uh, no. I don't have your cell." She stood up herself and wiped her hands on those tiny shorts, which were quite a bit the worse for wear by now. She was all messed up again. She looked great.

He was still thinking about that when she said, "Hang on," grabbed the pizza box and headed into the house, then came out with her phone and her father's key ring. She typed the number he dictated into the phone, then handed him the keys. "Give them the Jet Ski and the snowmobile, if the keys are on there," she said, "and the trailer to haul them. But not the car and the truck. Let me think about those for a bit."

She'd either come back to stay or she wouldn't. Nothing more he could do about it. Nothing he could say. So he helped her reset the alarm code and typed the number into his phone, touched that she trusted him that much, then waited while Anthea hugged and kissed her good-bye. Finally, he nodded at Hallie, said, "Drive safe tomorrow," led the way down the outdoor stairs, tossed the bottles, and climbed up in the truck to take Anthea home.

He still wasn't sure if he should have told Hallie his suspicions about her father's death. Well, he *was* sure. He shouldn't. It had come in as accidental death, and that was almost certainly what it was. Telling her would just open a can of worms. Besides, Henry's enemies wouldn't be Hallie's, would they?

Still, he wished she'd keep a shotgun in her bedroom, if she knew how to use it safely. Maybe he could suggest that again, give her a refresher course if she needed it. If she came back.

He was still turning it over in his mind as he pulled out of the driveway and onto the road. Anthea said, "So. You could've told me."

"No. I couldn't have."

Another couple minutes of silence, and he asked the question that had been uppermost in his mind all day. "So what does 'sexual relationship' mean, exactly? In a will?"

"What do you think it means?" Anthea said, which was one of those lawyer-type questions Jim hated.

"Well, obviously it would cover, uh, intercourse. But how far could you, um . . ." He trailed to a stop. "I mean, legally."

She was quiet a moment, and he shot a glance at her. It was a disgusting topic to raise with your sister, but who else was he supposed to ask?

"I'm pretty sure oral sex would still be considered a sexual relationship," she finally said, sounding not one bit rattled at the question, and he thought, as always, that Anthea was the one who should've been a Ranger, and more. She was Delta Force material all the way. A mind like a steel trap, a heart like a lion, and blood like ice water.

"Probably manual sex, too," she went on, "if people found out, which would be the real issue. Does it count as sexual if there's no penetration? How about if nobody climaxes? Interesting questions, in a legal sense. I'm guessing the answer would be yes, once you got into contact with anybody's genitals. Needless to say, you wouldn't want to be texting her any pictures of your junk. And I can't believe I just said all that to you," she added, which at least made her human. "I feel all dirty, suddenly. But if you're thinking she'll get a dispensation if you two don't go all the way? Might work in high school. Probably won't fly in a court of law."

"Didn't work all that well in high school, either," Jim said glumly. "I'm not that good at not going all the way. That was kind of the problem."

"You realize that's too much information. Again." She shook her head and sighed. "But, yeah. She's my best friend. Don't break her heart again. I mean it. Looks like you already did enough. I knew *something* had happened, but I thought it was her dad. She was so weird before she went off to college, and she wouldn't tell me why. I thought maybe we weren't going to be friends anymore. And then, at Christmas, she was still so . . . stiff. But finally, eventually, it got back to being the same. It wasn't her dad, though, or not entirely. It was you."

"Yeah." The guilt was right there. "It was me."

She waited a minute, then said, "You going to tell me more? Without any gory details, of course."

"Nope. Just wanted to know about the . . . sexual relationship thing."

His twin didn't get all-the-way serious too often, but she was serious now. He could feel it. She said, "Unless you want to mess up her chance at that money—and that'd be a lousy thing to do, after everything else you apparently did—don't make a move for six months. Period. Which you aren't going to listen to, and neither of you is exactly the sneaky type, which spells 'disaster' to me. But I'm telling you this. If you don't mean it, don't do it. Go find somebody else. You know you're my other half, and I know how long it's been since Maya died. I know you're lonely, and I know Hallie is . . . she's great, and she's pretty, and you like her. That's obvious. And it'd be easy, because she's lonely, too, and she likes you. She always has. I can't believe I didn't see it before. But she's fragile. I know I joke, but . . . she's not good with men. She gets hurt too easily, and by now she thinks she doesn't have what it takes to keep a man happy. It wouldn't take much to knock her right off the ledge, and dammit, Jimbo, she deserves better. You don't want to be that guy."

"No," he said. "I don't want to be that guy."

◆ ◆ ◆

Hallie was drinking the last beer. It was a bad idea, especially since she had to get up in the morning and make the long drive back to Seattle, but she was doing it anyway. And she was calling her mom.

"Hey, baby," Elaine said. "You didn't call me last night. I hope that means it wasn't too bad."

"No," Hallie said. "It was bad. And then it was better. Maybe."

"Tell me," her mother said, so Hallie did.

"Well, that's all a surprise," her mother said at the end.

Hallie huffed out a little laugh. Trust her mother. "Serene" was one thing. "Teflon" was another. "I'd call that the understatement of the year. I thought he'd disinherited me. He said he would. He never forgave me for the teacher thing. But, Mom." She steeled herself. It was time to ask this. If she were going to lay the ghosts to rest—if she were going to come back here—she needed to know. "Why did you marry him? Why did you stay with him? Why didn't you take me away from him?" The questions wanted to run away with her, so she forced herself to stop before she could add the last one. *Why did you let him do all that to me?*

A long silence on the other end, and then her mother said slowly, "I suppose that's a fair question, and that you deserve an answer."

"Yes," Hallie said. "I think I do." She'd never asked before, and her mother had never offered.

"I was young," Elaine said. "I was naïve. I was dreamy, easy to manipulate. All those things. He was so . . . dynamic. Much older. Smarter. Tougher. Richer. Everything. I was a waitress, and he was practically a god down there in Boise. He was in the paper all the time. Rough around more than the edges, but that was sexy. And then he pulled out the big guns. I got off work one day, and he'd bought me a new car. I was Cinderella. I told myself it was love."

"But he changed."

"Yes. He did. Or he showed himself. Once he had me, he didn't have to try anymore. And gradually, I stopped thinking I was worth trying for."

"Did he . . ." Hallie stopped, then forced herself to go on. "Hit you? Hurt you?"

"Nothing that blatant. He belittled me. In little ways at first, then in bigger ones. You saw them." It was true. Or rather, Hallie had heard them. The digs, the offhand comments. The same kind she'd heard about herself. "He made me feel stupid and worthless," her mother went on, "and I just . . . drifted off into my own world. I did what he wanted, kept the peace. I started doing yoga and meditation because they helped me feel calmer, helped me float someplace above it, so I started doing them more, and something happened, eventually. I realized I couldn't keep putting him into a different compartment and floating through my life. I decided that however bad it would be when I left him, it would be worse to stay. And worse for you, of course," she added.

Hallie tried not to notice that she'd come right at the end. "Why didn't you try to get me full-time?" she asked. "Why did you leave me with him during those summers?"

A sigh came down the line. "I can see you want to blame me, and I suppose I can understand that."

The guilt was instant, and sharp. "I didn't say—"

"Yes, sweetheart. You did. Your father was a powerful man. He said if I pushed it, if I made it tough—the divorce, the settlement, the custody—he'd make sure I got nothing, and that he got you. He said he'd go for full custody, and who knows if it would have worked? And he actually did want you. That was a good thing."

Really? Hallie thought. *Sure didn't feel that way to me.* "Did you know about the other women? And that it wasn't always consensual, at the least? He had a *child.* I had a brother. If you knew, if you suspected—why didn't you say anything?"

A long silence at the other end. "I didn't know about any of that."

Or you didn't want to know, Hallie thought.

"You're trying to make this about me, baby," her mother went on. "It's not about me."

"I'm not—" Hallie had to stop. This call had been a bad idea. Her mother had been serenely accepting of Hallie's decision to cut ties with her father, had never pressed her. If she'd always been a little remote, too—she'd just said why that was. Or it was her nature. And there was no changing her.

Her mother spoke again. "It's not all bad, you know."

"Really?" All right, that was too much. Hallie was starting to burn. "Which part of finding out your father is a rapist isn't bad?"

"You don't know that's true."

"Yes. I'm pretty sure I do."

"If he was," her mother went on as if she hadn't spoken, "that's nothing you did or didn't do, and it's nothing I did. Look at it this way.

You're better off for having been his daughter, not even considering the money. He wanted you to go into his business, even though you were a girl. He didn't care that you weren't a son, and that's something. Maybe because you've got all his good qualities. His drive, his independence, his intelligence, his clear thinking, his strength."

"No. I do not."

"Yes. You do. Look at how you're challenging me right now. That's not easy for you. And you're *there,* cleaning out his house, making it yours. You're taking him on. I never took him on. I just ran. You can do that because you've got his strengths in you. But you have something more, too. You have kindness. You have integrity. You have heart. You've got the best of him, and none of the worst."

"Mom," Hallie said, suddenly so weary. "You can't make lemonade out of these lemons."

"No? I'll bet you can, though."

Hallie sat in silence for a moment. The setting sun was lighting the edges of the clouds with an unearthly pink glow, and the air was cooling. It was beautiful. Peaceful. And it was nothing like those things inside her troubled mind.

"You overestimate me," she finally said.

"No, baby," her mother said. "You underestimate yourself."

It was only afterward that Hallie realized the thing her mother had never said.

That she was sorry.

CHEAP TASTES

The killer was glad to discover that Hallie had left town on Sunday and gone back to Seattle. Maybe she wouldn't come back.

She could only be gone three days. Those were the terms of the will. Sunday was one. Monday was two. If she didn't come back by Tuesday night, that would be it.

Monday afternoon arrived, she hadn't showed, and the hope grew. And then came the news that she'd donated half of the contents of her father's house to Goodwill—so much that they couldn't fit it all in the donation center. Including an almost-new Jet Ski and snowmobile that were already sitting on the lot at Don's Recreation and Marine up in Coeur d'Alene.

She'd *donated* them. Them and so much more. There were rumors that she'd hinted she might donate Henry's car and truck. Next, she'd be giving away his guns. Those, the killer hadn't heard a thing about.

Hallie might not have even realized the guns were there, though, tucked into the niche in the den inside their safe. She surely wouldn't know how much they were worth.

The killer took the risk of driving up to the house on Monday evening, just to check it out. Empty houses were vulnerable to burglars, everyone knew that. Even if she'd locked up, how hard was it to break a sliding door?

The vehicles, maybe not. It was too much to hope that she'd have left the keys inside. Anyway, they'd be impossible to sell anonymously. Pink slips, VINs, all that. Impossible. But the guns were so portable, so beautifully salable. Liquid assets of the very best kind. All you'd need was a few strong men to load up the safe. Some boys from down in a bar in Union City, maybe, who wouldn't have known Henry or his house and wouldn't care, not for a hundred bucks apiece. Drive down and pick them up right now. Another five hundred for the use of one of their trucks. Seize the moment. And then you could figure out how to get that safe open. There would be a way. A locksmith a good distance away, safely across state lines, someone willing to do a job with no questions asked? Missoula, maybe. And then the more incurious type of dealer. All of them gone by Tuesday afternoon, and all that cash to take their place that you didn't have to report or account for to anybody. That was yours to spend . . . however.

The house loomed, satisfactorily empty and seemingly unguarded, and for a moment, hope surged. But then the killer saw the red light mounted on the eaves of the garage that winked its message of *Not a hope,* and had to turn around and leave in disgust. No way you could get that safe out and loaded before the cops showed up, once the alarm went off.

Hallie wouldn't really donate anything else big, though, now that she'd made her point. That was an easy hundred grand right there—the truck, the car, and the guns. Nobody would be that stupid or care about money so little that they'd give all that away. Or rather—if she actually *didn't* care more than that, and since she'd already showed that she hated Henry enough to get rid of that many of his possessions without even getting anything for them, she probably wouldn't care about inheriting the money, either. She'd have a million, and she'd figure a million was enough.

She had simple tastes. Call them what they were. *Cheap* tastes. Bad taste. You could tell by her clothes, and her car, and her career. She was her mother's daughter, not Henry's, which had been the whole problem as far as her dad was concerned, hadn't it?

The guns were small change compared to the house. She'd stay gone, she'd sell the house, and it would all be over, the money divided only two ways, and divided right now.

It would be so easy. And much fairer, really.

HIGH SCHOOL DREAM

When Jim got the call from Hallie on Tuesday that she was on her way back, he might have had to take a walk around his patrol car to calm himself down.

Makes no difference to you, bud, he told himself. *No difference at all to your life.*

He answered himself, too. *You lie like a dog.*

"I'll drop the keys with Anthea," he told Hallie with regret. He was on duty until eight. "I'll come get those guns late Friday afternoon, though, if you still want to get rid of them."

"I still want to. Unless Cole wants one of them. Or you could keep it for when he's older if you think he's too young for it."

"I asked. He said no. He doesn't care for hunting much."

Jim's brother had gone deer hunting a few times with Cal Jackson or some friend's dad, but had come back the last time saying, "It's kind of boring. I'll pass." Which could mean anything, Jim knew, from "I'm not actually their son or their brother, and I feel weird being this kid with no dad, tagging along," to an honest "it's kind of boring." Jim had felt the occasional pang of guilt that he hadn't taken his brother out himself, getting in that bonding time. It seemed, though, that he'd lost the taste for it himself. Maybe he'd hunted enough in his life, one way and another.

Cole's reaction to being asked about the guns had been more complicated, though, than Jim had told Hallie. In fact, the boy had stood still a minute, then said, "I guess I should want one, huh, if they're valuable. Why would she give it to me, though? Is she stupid? Or does she expect me to buy it from her, and she wants the money? Or did you maybe not tell her they were worth a lot, so she'd give one to me?"

"Of course I told her." They'd been at Jim's mother's house, where Jim had dragged Cole out to mow the lawn. And to talk about this. "And no, she's not stupid. She was as smart as Anthea, growing up. Maybe smarter. She's just generous."

"I guess," Cole said, leaning on the silent mower. "So she's not, like, a bitch? She seemed kind of stuck up to me. She seemed like she had a stick up her ass that day."

Jim forced himself to breathe and said, "Those are some pretty lousy words to use about a woman. Especially your sister, because that's what she is. It wasn't any easier for her to sit in that room than it was for you. And giving you one of the guns was her idea. She said that you were his son and you had a right. She had no reason in the world to have to say that."

"Did you guys have a thing going on?" Cole asked. "Is that why there was that part—" He stopped, and Jim realized that his face had probably gone hard, in what Mac called his "crazy wild mustang" look.

"Like you're about to run somebody down and stomp them to death with your hooves," she'd said, and he'd said, "Well, that'll never be you, so you don't have to worry." But Jim was showing that face now.

"I like Hallie," he told his brother. "She's a good person. And the rest of it is none of your business."

"Yeah, but did you—" Cole began, and Jim gave him some more of the wild mustang, and Cole finally shut up.

"You might want to come with me to her house on Friday," he suggested to his brother after a minute. "You could help me load up the safe. Get to know her a little bit, maybe. As long as you can be decent to her. She's been nothing but decent about you."

"Maybe," Cole said. "Tom Ingeborg was saying that I should try to keep her from sticking around, because she gets almost half the money if she stays, and I get more than half of her part if she leaves. That I should look out for my self-interest, because otherwise, it's kind of hypocritical. Besides, the invisible hand."

"The *what?*" Jim said, not trying to hide his disgust.

"Adam Smith," Cole said. "We learned about it in European History. It says that the highest social benefit arises when individuals act in their own self-interest."

"Sounds like bullshit to me," Jim said, for once not caring about his language. "Excuse to be an asshole. In my experience, the highest social benefit happens when people act like they actually care about other people, even if they don't."

"They're still teaching about the invisible hand, though," Cole said. "So I guess maybe Adam Smith knew more about economics than you do."

"I suppose you should do the self-interest thing, then," Jim said. "If you're more interested in money than in being a decent human being. Which was Henry Cavanaugh all over, by the way. Congratulations on your inheritance." Which had shut Cole up, but had ended the conversation, too, with a score of Effort: 1, Bonding: 0.

Jim didn't say anything about it to Hallie on the phone, of course. Cole was fifteen. Jim wasn't sure he'd been all that much better at fifteen. Resentful, angry, and hormonal made for a fairly potent cocktail. He just told Hallie that Cole didn't want any of the guns, then said, "See you about five thirty Friday, then? With a moving crew."

"Sounds good."

He hung up, and he *didn't* swing by to check on her on Wednesday, or on Thursday, either, because she hadn't invited him, and there was no point. He waited until Friday. And he did bring Cole. He brought his cousins, too. Cal and Luke Jackson.

"You sure about this?" he asked Hallie when they were in the den. "Still want me to take all of them?"

"Yep." She rubbed her hands over the legs of her khaki shorts, which were, well, *short*, but a little grimy again—and glanced at Cole, who was leaning up against the wall with Cal and Luke, because there was no place to sit down. "Are *you* sure, Cole?" she asked him. "That you don't want a hunting rifle, maybe?"

"How come you don't want them?" Cole asked.

She looked at him for a moment and finally answered, her tone measured, "I didn't like my father very much. I don't like hunting, either, although saying that will probably get me kicked out of Idaho before my year is up. And, yes," she said with a hint of a smile, "that's hypocritical, because I do eat meat. Maybe I just don't want to own something that my father used to kill a living creature. It feels too . . . destructive. I'd say it brings dark energy, but . . ."

"Yeah," Cal said, "that's a little bit Seattle. But I don't think any of us is unfamiliar with dark energy, except that Cole may not have had the pleasure."

"I'll bet you kill insects, though," Cole told Hallie, still sounding sullen but slightly more interested. "How is that less of a living creature than a deer?"

Jim said, "Cole," but Hallie made a patting motion at him with her hand and said, "Good question. Level of sentience, maybe? Should that matter? How much pain does an ant feel? Did you know that followers of Jainism sweep little whisk brooms ahead of them wherever they go so they'll never step on a bug?"

"Really?" Cole said. "Wicked."

"Or not," she said with her sweet smile. "But I know what you mean. I suppose it's just a matter of finding your comfort level. I'm not comfortable with my father's guns, so I'm getting rid of them. But if any of you wants one," she said, taking in all the men with her glance, "please feel free."

"No, thanks," Luke said. "I'm not too big on the dark energy myself."

Everybody else shook their heads as well, and Hallie said, "All right, then. I'll just believe that the dark energy floats away with distance, and toss them out into the void," and gave Cole another little smile. Not pushing it. Casual. She taught high school, Jim remembered. *I know teenagers,* she'd said. *I even like them.* He could tell it was true.

Now, Jim shoved with a booted foot at two dusty rolls of carpet and foam backing that lay against the long wall where the couch had been, under the picture window. "Am I guessing that this is why you're all messed up again?" he asked Hallie. "That you decided to rip this out by yourself?"

Luke muttered, "Smooth, man," Cole snorted, and Jim frowned absently at both of them.

"Yes," Hallie said. "It wasn't that hard. I just finished." She looked down at herself. "I should've cleaned up, though. Whoops." She tugged her blue V-necked T-shirt down, which didn't exactly help much, as far as Jim was concerned; just showed him some more cleavage he wasn't supposed to look at.

"You could've told me," he persisted. "We'd have given you a hand."

"Maybe," Cal drawled. "Or Mountain Man here could've done it all by his lonesome, thrown it into his rig with a mighty heave, and taken all the credit. And what?" he asked at another frown from Jim. "I get that wrong?"

"Well," Jim said, deciding that his safest bet was to ignore his cousins, "I *will* throw it in my rig and haul it to the dump tomorrow. On my way to Spokane with the guns," he added hastily. "No problem. It's on the way." Oh. He'd already said that.

Cal said, "Could we get to the guns sometime this week, do you think? I'm supposed to take Zoe dancing. Got the folks babysitting overnight and everything. No offense, Hallie."

"None taken," she said. "I heard you had a baby."

"Yep. Alice. Just turned one in August." Right on cue, he pulled his phone out of his back pocket and started thumbing down it. "Here you go."

"She's so cute," Hallie said.

Cal scrolled some more and said, "This is her on her Big Wheel. She's already scooting around like crazy. Walked at nine months, and I swear, she was running about a week later, seemed like. She's kind of a terror."

Jim didn't say anything, just grabbed the hand truck, set to work with Cole and Luke to get the safe up onto it, then said, "If you're all done boring Hallie to death, Cal, you could give us a hand."

"Hey," he said, "I'm entertaining her."

"Not so much," Luke said. "I have a feeling she's seen a baby before."

"Not one this cute," Cal said with certainty, and Jim smiled and rolled the cart out the door, and Cal finally put his phone away and helped out.

It took some effort even with the four of them to get nearly four hundred pounds' worth of guns and fire safe hauled up onto the pad lining the bed of Jim's rig, while Hallie hovered around and said, "Should I help?" and Jim said, "No," and Luke shook his head.

They got it in there eventually, and then Jim ran a chain over and around the top of the safe and fastened it to the metal rings at the corners of the truck bed and locked it down. Not the best, because there was nothing to run the chain through on the safe, but as much as he could do. Finally, he spread a mover's blanket over the whole thing.

He'd washed the truck before he'd come over here. He hoped that wasn't too obvious. Or that it was. Whichever was better.

"I hope you're admiring Jim's muscles," Luke told Hallie while Jim finished up. "I swear, I thought he was going to strain something vital there, trying to show you how he benches three hundred."

"I'm admiring all of you," she said, and Jim looked up fast from his chaining to see her smile trying to break out. "This is kind of the high school dream, isn't it? The three of you out here at my house in your Levi's and boots, carrying heavy things? Excuse me, Cole," she added. "Indelicate."

"Those two, maybe," Jim said, snapping the heavy padlock closed with a satisfying snick. "I wasn't anybody's high school dream."

She looked like she wanted to say something, but she didn't. Luke spoke up instead, because Luke always spoke up. "Nah. The bad boys always get the hottest girls. Isn't that right, Hallie?"

She shot a look at Luke, then was looking away again with some color creeping up her chest and making its way into her cheeks. Cole opened his mouth to say something, then shut it again, and Jim realized that Hallie would think he'd talked about her. He said, "Shut up, Luke."

Luke looked startled, but said, "Sure. We'll go get that carpet. Give me a hand, guys."

Jim watched them go, then said to Hallie, "I didn't tell them."

That was all they had time for, because Luke and Cal were back with the roll of dusty carpet and heaving it into the truck bed beside the safe, Cole following behind them with a smaller roll.

"You could keep these in here until you're back from Spokane," Cal suggested. "Make it look like you're hauling a bunch of junk."

"Thanks," Jim said. "Already had that thought."

"Ah, yeah," Cal said. "I'm being bossy again." He told Luke, "Come on, bro. I'll drop you off at your place and go boss somebody who actually likes it."

"She doesn't like it," Luke said.

"Well, she kind of likes it," Cal said. "Depends."

"And on that note," Luke said, "we're taking off. Come on, Cole. We'll drop you off on the way. Good to see you again, Hallie. I guess I should say, 'Welcome home.'"

"Thanks so much, guys," she said. "Really. Thank you, too, Cole."

"No problem," Luke said, and he and Cal sauntered out, followed by Cole. They hopped up in Cal's rig, and took off down the driveway.

"He was being tactful," Hallie said. "Luke, I mean. Taking Cole, too."

"He was," Jim said. "And I didn't tell anybody. At the time, or now. I found out why it didn't get out, too. Turns out the sheriff told the deputies that heads would roll if anybody talked about it. That came from your dad, of course, so you could say that's one good thing he did for you, even if he really did it for himself. I always figured my mom and Anthea would know. Couldn't figure out why they didn't mention it. Now I know. But the will isn't a secret, so sooner or later people are going to talk."

"What about that deputy who . . . found us?" she asked. "Is he still working there?"

"No. He's down in Union City now. I do see him from time to time, though. He said something early on, but not after that." Not after Jim had told him he wasn't a teenager anymore, and that he'd be happy to discuss Hallie with him. Outside.

"It's OK," she said. "It was a long time ago. It doesn't matter."

"Yeah. It does. It mattered then, and it matters now." She seemed to have no expectation that anybody would defend her. That anybody would even stick up for her.

She nodded again, then said, "Thanks for bringing Cole. I guess the first time's the hardest, huh?"

"Hope so." He looked at her, and she looked back at him, then away, bit her lip, then cleared her throat.

"Cal and Luke Jackson," she said at last. "It takes me back."

They were still standing by the truck, and she was leaning up against the tailgate now. Still looking messy. Still looking just fine. Soft pink lips, big green eyes, clear pale skin, pretty curvy body. Just fine.

"I'm guessing you probably had a thing for one of them," he said. "Or both of them. Cal, probably, though." Luke had been in their year, Cal two years older. Captain of the football team, king of the school. Jim had hated both of them with a deep, shameful, burning passion, because he'd thought they had everything he didn't. All those years he'd spent resenting them, and all the time, it had had everything to do with him, and nothing to do with them.

She said, "Cal? Too remote. On another plane."

"Ah. Luke." Another golden boy. Homecoming King, hometown royalty in every way, and now, the principal of that same high school.

"Too clean-cut, I guess," she said. "He was right. It was the bad boy for me. Always."

He was still working out how to answer that when she said, "I should invite you to have a beer out on the deck, to say thanks. But I don't think it would be a good idea."

"It could just be a beer."

Her gaze was level. Steady. "Could it?"

"No," he admitted. "Probably not. Because I want to kiss you again."

Her eyes hadn't been this dark before, surely. She was leaning back a little more, looking at him, her lips parted, her breath coming too fast, and he muttered, "Aw, hell," put his hands on her shoulders, leaned down, and brushed his lips over hers.

Just like that. Just like before. Warm, and soft, and right there for him. He had an arm around her, was hauling her up against him, his other hand was tangling in her curls, and he was kissing her harder. Kissing her better. She was backed against his truck, her sweet mouth opening under his, her body molding to his like it had been made for it, because, God help him, it had.

He kissed her, and then he kissed her some more. There would never be enough of his mouth moving over hers, swallowing her sighs, her little moans. Of feeling her hands coming up to hold his shoulders, like she couldn't help hanging on any more than he could.

Finally, when he couldn't stand not to do it, he licked into her. She tasted sweet and salty and hot, so he did that some more, too. And when his hand went down to grab the curve of her ass in those little shorts, only because he had to do that to haul her closer, and then stayed there, his fingers brushing bare skin and, best of all, that wonderful crease, she gave that little gasp again, and she *wriggled.* She was snuggling closer, and he was holding her tight and eating her up, and he had to keep doing it.

His other hand was still behind her head, so he could hold her where he needed her to be, but her own hand was between their bodies now, and he realized, after too long, that she was shoving him. Shoving him *away.* It took a second, but he dropped the hand that had been holding her up, stepped back, tried to wrestle himself into some kind of control again, and ran his hand over the back of his head. And, finally, managed to look at her again.

If her chest had been heaving some before—now, it was doing a whole lot more than that. She was wearing some kind of barely there bra, just like the first time. He could see those two hard little points, and it was killing him. His hand wanted to go there, to slide right inside and explore that. His hand *had* to go there. Except it couldn't.

"Wait," she said.

"Yeah. I'll just . . ." He gestured toward the truck and wished he didn't have a hard-on the size of a sledgehammer. There was no disguising it, so he didn't even try. "I should get on back. Home, I mean. I should . . ."

He could see the movement of her throat when she swallowed. Her skin was so translucent, it was like he could see straight through it. Her emotions were right there underneath it. He could see them, too.

Confusion—and something else. Desire, maybe. Hurt, for sure. Too much hurt, which was his fault. "Yeah," she said. "Sorry. I should've . . ."

"No," he said. "Not your fault. I did that." He tore his gaze away from those big green eyes, which were surely darker than they had been earlier. Did her eyes change color with her emotions? It seemed like it, but that was impossible. "I'll go," he said. "I'll, uh, call you tomorrow. Tell you what price he's offering."

"Oh," she said after a second. "Yeah. Sure. The guns. Thanks." It seemed like she didn't realize that she was still pressed up against the back of his rig. He saw the moment when it sank in, because she jumped away and said, "No, really. Thanks for everything. I'll talk to you tomorrow, then."

He got in the truck and drove on out of there, told himself to call Danielle Delgado and knew he wouldn't.

Because that wouldn't be fair to Danielle, maybe. Or could be that wasn't it at all. Danielle wouldn't mind one bit. She wanted some uncomplicated, discreet fun, a part-time good time, and Jim could have been that. Once.

That wasn't the real reason. The real reason was that he didn't want Danielle. He wanted Hallie. And he couldn't have her.

ON MY WAY

Hallie watched Jim's brake lights blink on at the bottom of the driveway, his truck turning onto the road, carrying off her father's weapons.

Well, that was stupid, she thought, even as her body continued to hum with arousal. Her mouth still felt swollen and tingly, and so did everything else that he'd been about to get his hands on. He'd have been shoving a hand inside her shirt in another minute, not to mention down her shorts, and she'd been doing nothing but wishing for it. He'd have done her on the truck again. She knew it. And the worst part was, she'd wanted it.

Their first time, she could have blamed him. If she hadn't been honest with herself, that is. This time, there was no way. When he'd said, "I want to kiss you again," all she'd thought was, "Come and get me, then." She'd stopped herself, and him, at the last screaming minute before she would've been begging. Begging for his eyes and his hands and his mouth all over her. Not to mention everything in those tight Levi's that had showed off exactly what he wanted to do to her. Which was exactly what she wanted him to do.

She hadn't changed her clothes after the dirty, sweaty work of tearing out the carpeting, even though she'd known the guys would be coming over in half an hour. She'd told herself that there was no need to dress up for the Jackson brothers, much less for Jim Lawson, because she wasn't in high school anymore, and she didn't need to be attractive to any of them.

Who was she kidding?

She punched the button to close the garage, leaving Jim behind, then went into the den, and looked around. It already felt different. No guns, no carpet, no couch. Nothing but a big-screen TV and the gleaming mahogany bar with the black leather stools she hadn't been able to bear parting with, because they were already perfect. And because her dad had almost never sat in them. He'd always been on the couch, and the couch was gone.

She stood in the middle of the empty room, flung her arms out, and spun. Rotating past the windows, past the bar, past the TV. Henry was gone. This was *hers*, and so was the town. So was her life. Life didn't often give you do-overs, but she was getting one now. That's why she'd come back. To take charge of her life.

She was going to choose how she lived in this world, starting with how she lived in this house. Her past wasn't her present, and it sure as hell wasn't her future.

She'd paint in here. A soft blue-gray, maybe. Pale gray carpeting. And that pool table. When Jim sold the guns, she'd take a few thousand—she had to think how funny that sounded, so casual. *A few thousand.* She'd take it and fix this room up. She'd leave the master bedroom empty, would shut that door and leave it closed. But this room was going to be hers.

She still wondered if she'd done the right thing about the guns. She'd had dinner with her uncle and aunt on Wednesday, her first day back in town, and they'd asked about them.

She'd sat in their fussy dining room, now decorated in pale French provincial shabby-chic straight out of *House Beautiful*, and had eaten a salad consisting of a leaf of iceberg lettuce, a ring of pineapple, and a scoop of cottage cheese, followed by thick slabs of pepper steak, all made from the kind of recipe that should have been thrown out after the nineteen seventies.

"How are you getting on out there?" Dale had asked. "I heard you did some cleaning out. Kinda wished you'd asked me first, because there were a few little things I'd have liked. Mementos, you know."

"Oh." The familiar guilt had made Hallie's stomach sink. "I never even considered. I'm sorry."

"Never mind," he'd said. "It doesn't matter."

"No, honey," Faye had said. "You know it does." She'd put a soft hand on top of her husband's gnarled one and said, "You need to ask her about the guns. Henry meant them to come to you."

"Honey," he'd said, "if it wasn't in the will . . ."

"No. It isn't fair." Faye had looked at Hallie and said, "Henry loved those guns. He called them family heirlooms. Of course, they were just hunting guns, not really anything special except to somebody who'd love them like he did, maybe just because they were so precious to him. Please don't tell me they're all gone, too. That would be a shame, and it would go straight against your father's wishes. You weren't here so you wouldn't know, but I'm sure he meant all of them to be passed along to somebody who would've used them."

"They're not gone," Hallie had said. "But they will be." She'd been willing to give a gun to Cole, and maybe she'd even have offered one to her uncle, but something in her was balking now. Maybe it was the sharpness in Faye's eyes. "If you'd really like them," she'd told her uncle, carefully not looking at Faye, "I can get a quote, then sell them to you instead at the wholesale price. Or any of them that you'd particularly want. But actually, they *are* valuable. I'm surprised you didn't realize that, since you hunted with him. I've been told I could get forty thousand at least for the collection, even at wholesale."

Faye had drawn in a sharp breath. "I can't believe you'd do such a thing. You'd give away your father's things to strangers, but begrudge your uncle his prize possessions, things you don't want that were supposed to come to him anyway? Family's family."

It hadn't been guilt, then, but anger that had made Hallie's stomach clench. *Really?* she'd thought. *Then where were you after my mom left? Why did I feel so much more welcome at Anthea's house than I did at yours growing up? Even after what my father did to her mother?* She'd found herself saying, "I guess if they were supposed to come to him, that would have been in the will. What I've given away so far is some furniture and a few bolo ties, though, not tens of thousands of dollars' worth of guns. But you're right about family. You probably tried to talk him out of disowning me, when he had that plan. I wish I'd known. It would've been nice not to feel so cut off from everybody."

She hadn't missed the sharp glance Faye had shot Dale before Dale had shaken his head and said, "That was a terrible thing. Like Faye says—family's family, but you know what a hard head Henry had. Anyway, you're back now, and I hope we'll be seeing a lot more of you. If you don't see it about the guns—well, I guess you have the right."

Faye's mouth had tightened, and Hallie could almost hear the words that had wanted to come out of her aunt's mouth. *Like hell she does.*

Hallie had called Bob Jenkins the next day just to make sure. She'd had a sickening moment where she'd wondered if she'd violated the terms of the will already by selling off her father's things, then had reminded herself that her feelings about her inheritance had been mixed from the start. She was afraid it was what Jim had said—now that she knew the money was hers, or was going to be hers, it *felt* like hers, and losing it would be a blow.

"Is there any reason I can't sell or give away everything in the house, if I want to?" she'd asked Bob. "I have to tell you, Goodwill will have taken away a bunch of the contents by now."

"No reason," he'd said. "It reads, 'for her use absolutely.' The only stipulation is that you have to live in it for six months, so you wouldn't want to sell the house itself during that time. It didn't say anything about keeping the contents, though."

"I'm surprised it's only six months," she'd said. "I'd have expected him to go for, oh, a year at least."

"He wanted to do that. I don't think there's any problem with me telling you so. He thought, though, that it might push you too far. He wanted to hold you here, to get you back in his house, so he made you an offer you couldn't refuse."

Which had, of course, made her want to refuse it more than ever. What was she doing, dancing to her father's tune again? "Did you know about any promise to my uncle that he'd get my father's guns?" she'd asked, abandoning the other question for now. "Was it in any former will or anything?"

Bob had hesitated, then said, "His former will would be privileged information, so I can't tell you either way. You have a copy of the will that was in place when he died, and that's all that matters."

Not exactly an answer. "Well, I'm selling the guns," she'd said. "Or rather, Jim Lawson is picking them up tomorrow night and taking them to Spokane on Saturday to sell them. So if there's anything I should know, tell me now, because they're on their way out the door."

"What you choose to do from any family obligation is one thing," he'd said, offering up another nice little stab of guilt, "but you have no legal obligation."

Well, it was done. She'd given them to Jim, and she was here. Right or wrong, she'd made her decision.

She'd driven from Seattle on Tuesday afternoon, her car stuffed full of clothes and personal items after the world's hastiest packing job, worn out from supervising the movers who'd taken the rest of her things out of her apartment and into a storage unit. Her heart had plunged at the cost of last-minute packing and hauling services, before she'd reminded herself that she'd be living rent free for the next year.

Not to mention the 10K a month. Yeah. Not to mention that.

If she stayed.

It was already late September, though. All she had to do was make it one more week, and she'd have that first check. She'd take it one step at a time. She could change her mind at any point.

Except, of course, that she no longer had a job. Or tenure. Or an apartment.

Move on. She stood in her new room, pulled out her phone, and dialed a number Jim had showed her in a coffee shop a week—or a lifetime—ago.

"Hi," she said. "Is this Eileen Hendricks? This is Hallie Cavanaugh."

A few sentences later, she'd set it up. She had a cleaner who'd start next Thursday. She'd *never* had a cleaner. Even if she could've afforded one, which she couldn't. She'd never wanted one anyway, not since those teenage years when she'd felt all the awkwardness of having her best friend's mom cleaning her toilet.

That was why she'd called Eileen, though. Because she hadn't wanted to, and because it was the least she could do.

She hung up and thought, *I'm in the house. Everything I hated is gone. I'm on my way. Now all I need is a job.*

VISITORS

Jim never slept all that soundly. Ten years of bedding down with one ear open, because it made it more likely you'd live to wake up, could do that to you. Not to mention the months of lying here beside Maya, waking when she did, doing his meager best to make her more comfortable, watching helplessly as that got harder and harder to do. And then the months and years of lying here without her.

So it wasn't too surprising that the faint rattle woke him. He came awake fast and fully, like always, and lay still for a moment, listening hard.

There it was again. Something metallic. Coming from the driveway, or someplace close to it.

Shit.

He was up, not bothering with shoes or shirt but going right for his service weapon. He pulled the Glock down from the top shelf of the closet, reached into the drawer where he kept his ammo, and shoved a magazine home, then racked the slide. Locked and loaded, in as much time as it would have taken another guy to decide to do it.

He padded quickly down the hallway and into the dark living room, edged a curtain aside, and looked out.

Two dark figures stood in his truck bed, with another rig pulled up close, tail to tail. The men were trying to shove something heavy across to the other truck. Something a whole lot like a gun safe.

Jim was running now. Not out the front door. To the back one. Flipping the outdoor floods on, lighting up the driveway like Christmas, then opening the door and standing in the shelter of the back porch, out of sight, while he shouted, "Police officer! Freeze!"

He heard a scramble and risked a quick look around the corner. The two guys were out of his rig and hauling ass into the passenger side of theirs. The driver gunned the engine, and the truck pulled away. Its tires spun for a long moment, the truck's forward momentum halted by the gun safe that was half in, half out of its bed, and then the horse-power kicked in, and the truck tugged itself free. The night was split by the sound of four hundred pounds of gun safe hitting the concrete driveway, and then the heavy vehicle was turning into the street with a mighty fishtail that had Jim, who'd run into the driveway now, hold-ing his breath for fear that they'd go through somebody's living-room wall. They took off down the road at close to fifty, and Jim lowered his weapon.

No chance of stopping them. He wasn't firing hollow-point rounds in an inhabited area to catch a burglar.

He turned to go back into the house and saw Mac at the front door. The *open* front door.

"Daddy?" she asked. "What happened?"

A window opened on the neighbor's house to the left, and Mrs. Sanchez called out, "Jim? Everything OK over there?"

"Yeah," he said.

George Carstairs, his other next-door neighbor, was on his porch with the light switched on, making Jim painfully aware that he was standing in his driveway in nothing but his briefs, with his weapon in his hand.

"What's going on?" George asked.

"Attempted burglary," Jim said. "Lock your doors, both of you. Just in case."

George was looking at the metal box on the driveway. "That's a gun safe," he said, displaying a blinding grasp of the obvious. "Want me to call the cops?"

"I *am* the cops," Jim said, ignoring the leftover adrenaline racketing around his body with no place to go. "Consider me called."

"You take care," Mrs. Sanchez said.

"Always." Then Jim *did* go into the house, closed and locked the front door, and told Mac, "Go back to bed, partner."

"I want to know what's going on," she said.

"And I'll come tell you. When you're in bed. One minute."

He locked the back door while he called in an attempted burglary to the Paradise PD, then grabbed a pair of sweats and a T-shirt and pulled them on, unloaded his weapon but left it and the ammo on the bedside table where he could get to them fast, then went into Mac's room. He needed to see to that safe, but this came first.

She was sitting up in bed with the light on and her arms folded across her chest.

Oh, boy.

"Hey," he said, coming to sit on the edge of the bed beside her. "Everything's OK."

She studied him through narrowed brown eyes, her nearly black hair mussed in its braid. "That was reckless," she told him. "You've always said that a burglary isn't worth dying over, or killing over."

"And did I die? Or kill anybody?"

"You were in the *driveway*," she informed him. "With no body armor on."

"Yep. And I wasn't there until I knew they were leaving, and that they weren't shooting. I was trying to get a plate."

"Did you?"

"Nope. Tailgate was down."

"Oh. Too bad."

"Yep." He looked at her and got serious, because the moment when he'd seen her standing there hadn't been a good one. "Listen good, now," he told her. "If you ever look out the window again to see me with my weapon drawn? Or anybody else with a weapon drawn? You do *not* open the door. You *lock* all the doors first, call 911 second, and third, you lie down on the floor and wait to hear me or another officer call out to you before you unlock them again. One, two, three. Lock, call, fall. Got it?"

"If I lock the doors," she said, "you can't dive back in for cover."

"I'll take my chances. This isn't an argument, Mackenzie. This is a rule. Lock, call, fall. And the answer is, 'Yes, sir.'"

"You never make me say that anymore."

"I'm making you say it now."

She heaved a martyred sigh. "Yes, sir. Lock, call, fall. Happy?"

He smiled at last and bent to kiss her forehead and smooth the hair back from her face. "Nope. But I'm happier. Go back to sleep."

He turned out her light and closed her door, then called Luke.

"Jim. What?" Luke's voice answered after a single ring.

Jim explained in a few sentences, and Luke said, "Well, shit," and Jim said, "Yeah. That's what I said," and heard a soft female voice on the other end, urgent with alarm.

"Hang on," Luke said, and Jim heard him reassuring Kayla. "Right," he said. "I'm back. What can I do?"

"Need you to come help me put the safe back in my rig, if you don't mind," Jim said. "I'll call Cal, too, but it'll take him a while to get in from the farm, so figure in half an hour. And I know it's three in the morning," he added, "but this feels damn hinky."

"We don't need Cal," Luke said. "I'll get Travis. We'll be there in ten."

Jim hung up and put on his boots, then strapped his shoulder holster on, reloaded his weapon, and shoved it in there. He shrugged into a jacket, checked Mac's room and saw her asleep again, locked the front door behind him, and headed out to survey the damage and wait for the guys to show.

When they came, it wasn't just Luke and Travis Cochran, the not-local boy who'd married Rochelle Marks. It was Rochelle, too. The three of them walked up the driveway, and Jim told Rochelle, "No." He looked at Travis and said, "Absolutely not. She's not helping."

Rochelle said, "Geez. Way to talk to my husband over my head. Maybe I came over to do womanly things, you know? Like brew coffee for the menfolk after they get done with the heavy lifting."

"Or maybe you were just curious," Travis said in his usual slow, amused drawl. "And don't worry," he told Jim. "She's not lifting a damn thing."

Rochelle sighed. "Overprotective much? I'm pregnant, guys. Not incapacitated."

The wedding had been in June, and Rochelle had already been a couple months gone. She must be a good five months along now, though she was tall and full-figured enough not to show it the way a more petite woman would. Like Maya had. She put her hands on her hips and said, "So, hmm. Luke says you guys loaded this thing up tonight, you put it under a blanket, and, what, nine hours later you've got people in your front yard trying to steal it?" She looked around at the rolls of carpeting and the blanket that still littered the driveway. "Under all that. Somebody sure had some inside knowledge. Henry Cavanaugh's guns, though—it's not a secret that they're worth a mint. Best gun collection in town."

She reached a hand out for the bolt cutters in the bed of the truck along with the severed chain, and Jim said sharply, "No. Fingerprints," while registering that Rochelle knew about Henry Cavanaugh's guns. But then, Rochelle knew most things, and most people.

"Oh," she said, drawing her hand back. "Wouldn't they have worn gloves, especially if they knew they were robbing a cop? Who robs a cop?"

"They did wear gloves," Jim said. He'd seen them during that brief flash of light when they'd climbed into their rig. Or rather, he hadn't seen the gleam of pale skin. "But we might find fingerprints from the last time somebody used those cutters. They wouldn't have expected to leave them behind. You going for a new career in law enforcement? You could sure enough do it."

"By which you mean," she said, "nosy and without the good sense to run away." She gestured at the safe. "I guess you guys had better load it up, though."

"You think?" Travis asked, exchanging a grin with Jim. "I guess we'd better, then. Except that Jim may have something he's waiting for. You know, being a trained officer of the law and all."

At that timely moment, a cruiser pulled up to the driveway and Jesse Hartung got out, hitching up his gun belt. "Jim," he said. "You called in?"

"Hey," Jim said. "Yeah. I'll give you the story and some bolt cutters, too." He told it fast, such as it was. "Older model Dodge Ram. Say '05, '06. Dark blue or black. Not a rig I knew, off the bat. Didn't recognize the guys, either, but it was dark. Call them five ten and one sixty—skinny guy—and six one and two twenty—big guy. Wearing feed caps, so no hair color. I'm guessing late twenties to mid-thirties, from how they moved."

"Recognize them again?"

"No," Jim said with regret. "Mainly saw their backs, running away. Didn't get the driver at all."

"Got an idea who did it?" Jesse asked.

"Depends," Jim said. "On who knew this was here. I'll ask around."

Jesse nodded and stuck his notepad back into his pocket. "Do that. That's an odd thing."

"Yep," Jim said. "It is an odd thing." He shoved a boot against the safe. "And this is a heavy thing. Want to give us a hand?"

Once Jesse had tagged and bagged the bolt cutters, he did. It was a job, with the safe flat on the ground and no hand truck to help them out, but they got it done in the end. They were all breathing harder by the time Jim was fastening the shortened chain over the safe again as best he could and snapping the lock back in place.

Jesse said, "I'll take off, then."

"Let me know if you get anything off the cutters," Jim said.

"You bet," Jesse said. "You take care. Don't do anything stupid."

Jim said, "I never do anything stupid."

Jesse said, "Yeah, right. They come around again, with your little girl in the house? I wouldn't take a bet on that. If they do show, give us a call first. *Before* you do anything stupid. You call in an in-progress, and I'll be here in five. Quiet night so far, and the drunks are all in bed by now." He nodded to the others, took the bolt cutters, climbed back into the cruiser, and rolled away.

"Right," Jim said after Luke and Travis had tossed the rolls of carpeting up into the truck again. "Thanks. Sorry to get you all out of bed."

Travis eyed him. "You're not just going to leave this here, though, for them to come take again." It wasn't really a question.

"Well, no," Jim said. "I'm sleeping in the cab for the rest of the night."

"Need help?" Luke asked.

Travis said, "Give me a minute to drop Rochelle back home and pick up a shotgun, and Luke and I'll hang out in the truck in front of the house." Rochelle huffed, and Travis looked at her and said, "What? Would you rather I squeaked, 'Don't shoot me,' and used you as a shield?"

"Well, no," she conceded. "If you put it that way."

"I do put it that way. You might as well get used to it."

"Gosh, you're masterful," she said, and Luke sighed and said, "Guys."

Jim said. "Thanks, but I don't need help." He wasn't bringing civilians to his fight, and if he couldn't handle two clumsy rent-a-lowlifes by himself, he needed to go into another line of work. "I don't really expect them to come back. Just say that I'm . . . annoyed."

Which he was, he thought when they'd left and he was bedded down as best he could in the front seat with a couple blankets, a pillow, and his shoulder holster, and with Mac safely behind a locked door. This was annoying, and it was alarming.

He'd have time tomorrow on the drive to think it through and figure out what to do. For now, he was going to make sure that if anyone showed up again, they came back to a nasty surprise in the form of one seriously pissed-off cop.

His last thought before he fell asleep was Rochelle's voice asking, "Who robs a cop?" Which was a very good question.

DEDUCTIONS

The night passed, and nobody came. It wasn't the best night Jim had ever spent, but it wasn't the worst, either. In the morning, he hauled his stuff back to the house, made Saturday-morning pancakes with Mac and dropped her at Anthea's, and at eight thirty, he was rolling for Spokane and calling his brother.

"Wha . . . ?" Cole, unlike Jim, didn't wake easy.

"I've got a question about last night," Jim said.

"Huh?" Some rustling that was probably Cole sitting up in bed. "What time is it?"

"Almost nine. Time to get up."

"I've got a question myself," Cole said. "Were you ever actually, you know, young?"

"I could be grumpy," Jim conceded. "That tends to happen when you get woken up in the middle of the night by three guys stealing a safe full of guns out of your driveway."

"Huh?" The sleepiness was gone. "They're gone?"

"Nope. That is, the guns aren't gone. The guys are."

"Oh, man." Cole's voice was awed. "You *shot* them?"

"What? No. Of course I didn't shoot them. They ran away."

"Oh."

"I normally only shoot people who give me a really good reason," Jim told him. "Sorry to disappoint you."

"Those were some sweet guns, though. Isn't that a good reason?"

"Nope. They're property. And how do you know they were sweet guns?"

"Uh, you told me."

"No. I didn't. I told you there was a good hunting rifle or a Winchester twelve gauge you might want."

"Well, somebody else must have told me, then."

"Uh-huh." Jim took a curve, noting automatically that most of the farmers up here had their plowing done, and said, "When would that be?"

"I was over at Tom Ingeborg's house last night," Cole said. "Somebody there was mentioning."

"Huh," Jim said. "Exactly who was mentioning? And who was listening?" He'd pushed 'Record' on his phone before making the call, fortunately.

"Um . . ." Cole said. "You don't think somebody from over at Tom's stole them, do you? It was just a bunch of high school guys. I mean, some of them have their licenses, but . . ."

"No," Jim said. "I don't think it was any of them. The guys I saw weren't sixteen, or eighteen, either. But I think it's possible somebody told somebody else. In fact, somebody *had* to have told somebody else. And it wasn't Luke or Cal, because I asked. They didn't mention it to anyone but their wives, obviously. And they're checking, but I seriously doubt that it came up as a topic of conversation for Kayla or Zoe."

"Maybe Hallie did."

"Maybe." Jim held on to his patience. "I'll be asking her, too. This is Police 101, that's all. You find out what the possibilities are, and you go from there. You tell me there were only two guys there with you last night, and I'll be thrilled, because it'll make finding the person who did this a lot easier. But I don't think there were only two guys there. And finding out matters," he went on when his brother was silent. "Unless it's all right with you to have low-life scum in my driveway and Mac on the porch, it matters."

He had to unclench his fingers from the steering wheel. That was the real problem. Mac. And Hallie. Maya had called him on the protectiveness more than once, just as Rochelle had done with Travis the night before, but Jim couldn't help it any more than Travis could. Like he'd told Hallie—he was hardwired.

"Mac was out there?" Cole asked, finally sounding something other than wary.

"Yeah," Jim said grimly. "She was. So come on. Name some names. Give me something to go on."

Cole gave him four or five names and said, "That's who I think was there when we were talking about the guns, but there were other people around."

"Who was most interested?" Jim asked. "Who told you they were sweet guns?" he went on when Cole didn't answer.

"Uh, this friend of Tom's brother," Cole said. "But that doesn't mean he—"

"No, it doesn't," Jim said. "Tom's the invisible-hand guy, huh."

"Yeah," Cole said. "His brother's cool, though. He's a senior. He's probably going to Stanford. And their mom's a professor. I don't know his friend much, but—"

"Lower social class doesn't necessarily correspond to scum level," Jim said.

"Huh?"

"Nothing." Jim thought about asking where Tom Ingeborg's professor mother had been during the evening, but he didn't. He figured he knew the answer, and asking the question would just make Cole clam up again. He was going to have a talk with their own mom, though, and soon. "What time was this?" he asked, instead. "When you were talking about the guns? And did you mention them to anybody before last night?"

"No," Cole said. "I know I didn't say anything before. Because— you know. I didn't want to say about whose they were."

Right, Jim thought. *Awkward.* Until, maybe, you had a beer or two in you, and bragging seemed like a good idea.

"What time . . ." Cole went on. "Probably about ten. We were playing a video game, you know, and talking some. They have a sweet rec room."

Not much time between ten and two thirty for word to get around, and for somebody to round up two buddies, or two hired hands, from some bar. Anyway, Jim didn't believe for a second that some senior at Paradise High School was a budding criminal mastermind, Stanford bound or not. He'd check it out, but his gut told him this wasn't the source.

"Well, thanks," he told Cole. "For telling me. That's helpful."

"Is Mac OK?" Cole asked. "Did she get scared?"

Jim smiled. "In a way. She got mad at me for going after them. But she's at Anthea's today. If you wanted to stop by and check in with her—that'd be good. I won't be back till three or so. You could get her to tell you about it, maybe."

"You think that'd help?" Cole asked. "You think she's got some trauma or something?"

It was actually a pretty sensitive question. Jim said, "You know—I think she could have. I suppose when you've got one parent, you don't like to see him out in the driveway in his underwear with his weapon drawn."

"Seriously?" Cole asked. "You went after them with your gun, in your underwear?"

"Yep. Sure did."

Cole laughed. *"Wicked."*

And Jim hung up, shook his head, and thought that it was too bad that fifteen-year-old boys so rarely thought with their higher powers.

But asking about Mac had been a good sign.

◆ ◆ ◆

It was three hours before he called Hallie.

"Hi, Jim," she said when she picked up, unfortunately sounding not one bit like a woman who wanted to be kissed against his tailgate again. "What does the dealer say? What's he offering?"

"Well, you know what," he said, "I'm all done and on my way home."

"What? I thought you were going to call me."

"Yeah, well, I walked out to do that, you know, like the car salesmen do, checking with my manager, and you didn't pick up, so I just pretended I'd talked to you and went for it. I had him wriggling on the hook, and I wanted to net him."

"Nice image."

"Thanks. I liked it." He was feeling good.

"So what did you get for them?" she asked.

"You know—I'm going to surprise you. Got a money order here for you. I decided that was safest." He'd kept an eye out behind him on the drive and hadn't seen a thing, but even so, he hadn't wanted to walk around with that kind of cash, shoulder holster or no. He sure didn't want to leave Hallie holding it, not after what had happened the night before. "I'm about an hour out," he told her. "Want me to swing by the house?"

A long pause, and she said, "I'm not saying I'm irresistible, but . . . a restaurant might be better. Maybe I could buy you lunch, since you went to all this trouble."

"You're irresistible," he said. "Unfortunately."

"Oh."

There was a long pause on the other end, and he finally said, "But you could buy me lunch."

"Maybe not in town," she said. "In case anybody sees us. Since that's what this is all about. I mean, it's clearly a perception issue."

"A perception issue," he said slowly.

"Well, yes," she said, in what must be her teacher voice. Brisk. Businesslike. "It's not really about what we do. It's what we're perceived to have done. Who's going to determine whether you and I had a sexual relationship? Somebody who sees us leaving each other's house at six in the morning, kissing passionately on the front steps. Or catches us—"

"Having sex on the hood of a Pontiac," he said. "For example." Although he'd take passionate kisses on the front steps. Or both.

"Right," she said, still businesslike. "That would be a no. And so would drinks on Main Street. Or at your house, or at my house. Your truck can't be in my driveway all the time, or it doesn't matter how innocent it is, it's going to look bad. I appreciate your selling the guns, and I'd still like to pay you a commission, but—"

He wasn't feeling good anymore. He was getting downright irritated. "Yeah," he said. "I got it. And I told you. You don't have to pay me off. In any way."

He heard the soft sigh. "I didn't say that, and I didn't mean it."

He said, "Sangria Station, over in Marshall, on the highway. One thirty," and hung up.

Not exactly worth sleeping in the truck for. Except that he hadn't been able to do anything else.

◆ ◆ ◆

He got to the restaurant first, as he'd known he would. Another thing Maya had taught him. He might not be happy with Hallie, but he wasn't going to leave her sitting at the table alone.

The restaurant was across the state line in Washington. A different university, a different crowd, and there was nobody he knew in here. He took a booth in the back, though, just in case.

He had one eye on the door when Hallie came in wearing a white dress with a skinny belt and cowboy boots with blue roses on them, holding a jean jacket in one hand. He was on his feet without knowing how he'd gotten there. Her curls were bouncing, her eyes were flashing, and she was stalking across the floor like a panther. Like anything but Hallie.

She stopped in front of the booth and said, "Why didn't you tell me?"

"Uh . . ." he said. "Tell you what? You look great, by the way."

She made a swatting motion with her hand, and he wished her dress didn't have tiny little sleeves and that sort of heart-shaped neckline. Or that her breasts didn't make a heart shape in it, or whatever was going on there. That there wasn't that heart shape.

She didn't sit. She stood there and hung on to the back of the leatherette booth like she was going to launch off of it and said, "Somebody tried to steal those guns last night, and you were out there with your *own* gun chasing them off, and you didn't *tell* me? I didn't tell you to put yourself in danger for me!"

He didn't lose his temper. He controlled situations, they didn't control him. Except now. "I guess I didn't get my instructions right, then," he said, and if it was a growl, who could blame him? "Instead, I decided to follow my training and prevent a burglary that was happening on my property."

"You *slept* in your *truck*. With your *gun*."

"Yeah. I did."

"Why?"

"Why what?" he asked, so exasperated he could barely talk. Her chest was heaving again, she was all fired up and redhead hot, and he didn't want to yell at her, he wanted to kiss her. Hard. "Why did I protect my property, and your property? Because that's my job. That's my life. And how do you even know about this?"

"Rochelle Marks called me. Half an hour ago. But she's not Rochelle Marks anymore. She's . . . Rochelle something. I'm not up on it."

"Rochelle Cochran. Still got a big mouth, though. What's she telling you that for?"

"She *wanted* to say, welcome back. She just *happened* to tell me how come she *knew* I was back. She was surprised I didn't know. And so was I. Why didn't you call me last night, so I could have . . . I don't know. So *I* could've guarded my property, if somebody had to do it?"

He said, "Well, hell," and ran a hand over the back of his head. "How about we sit down, you buy me a beer, and I tell you why that is the most terrible idea I have ever heard."

She gasped, and he said crossly, "And quit that."

"Quit *what?*"

"That . . . sucking in your breath thing. Next to biting your lip, that's the thing you do that bugs me the most. And you're doing it again," he informed her. "Stop it. Sit down."

She sat down with a thump, her pretty mouth still half open, then said, "I take it back. You haven't changed at all."

"The bad boys always get the hot girls, though," he informed her. He was still mad, but it felt better. "You still buying me a beer? Because one of us is buying me a beer. I earned it."

She waved a hand again, shook her head helplessly, and said, "I'm buying you a beer."

"Good." The waitress was headed their way, too. "You want one? Or something else?"

"Yes," she said. "Beer. Since you're telling me what I want."

"I'm not telling you what you want. I'm telling you what *I* want. Except not." The waitress was there, and he said, "Two Coronas, please. And we'll hang on to the menus for a minute."

She went away again, and Hallie said, "Except what not?"

"Telling you what I want."

"We are not going there," she said. "Tell me what happened."

"Wait. I need my beer first."

She scowled at him. "I liked you better when you were being nice."

"Nah," he said. "You didn't. And for the record, I like you like this a whole lot, even though you've got my pulse rate way up there where it shouldn't be."

"You don't get to choose. Which way I am."

"Nope. And neither do you."

She had her arms crossed over her chest, and he smiled. "You look just like my daughter last night." The waitress showed up with their beers and a couple glasses, and he said, "Thanks," skipped the glass, and waited until Hallie poured hers, then took a sip that tasted pretty good.

"How did your daughter look last night?" Hallie asked.

"Like that. With the arms and all. When I went after those guys trying to steal the guns. Which I did," he added, "carefully and methodically." Well, except for being in his underwear. "I'm a cop. I was a soldier. It's my job."

"I'm not crazy about it."

"Women usually aren't. Unless they're cops or soldiers themselves. Or unless they think cops and soldiers are a little hot," he decided to add.

"The idea of it, maybe," she said.

She took a good sip of beer, then touched her mouth with a napkin, not leaving a mark on it, and he said, "You still don't wear lipstick much."

"I don't like it." She was looking belligerent again. "Too bad."

"Nah. I like your mouth. Always have. How it's so pink and soft and . . . uh . . . naked."

Her pupils were dilating, he could swear it, because her eyes were darker again, and he could see her swallow. "Well, good," she said weakly, and took another drink.

"So tell me about last night."

"Let's order, and then I'll tell you. I'm not shutting you out," Jim added when she would have objected again. "It's a serious deal, and I know it. You distracted me for a little bit there, but I'm ready to get back into it. First, though, I'm going to order some kind of fancy thing with prawns. I've got a millionaire buying."

They did get serious, unfortunately, once they'd ordered. He'd been right. It was a serious deal.

"I have to think," he told her, "that somebody knew about those guns. That was a target of opportunity, sure, but it's not like anybody could have walked by and seen them. I didn't tell anybody I was picking them up, and neither did Cal or Luke or their wives. Cole did, though. Did you?"

"Yes." She was serious, too. "I told my aunt and uncle, and I told Bob Jenkins."

"When?"

"Wednesday for Dale and Faye, Thursday for Bob."

"Anthea says Faye talks."

"Yes," Hallie said drily. "I'd guess she does, since Rochelle knew the terms of the will. *All* the terms. And I don't think that came from you or me or your mom. I'm thinking from under a head of foils at the hairdresser's."

Jim's gaze sharpened, and it was focused on her face this time. "You mean, the part about you and me."

"Yep. But Rochelle didn't know about before. She guessed, because who wouldn't, and she said it's being talked over. So I was right about that. We probably shouldn't even be here."

"Except," Jim said as the waitress came over and set their plates in front of them, "that we're on opposite sides of the table in broad daylight, we're fifteen miles from Paradise, and we're not engaging in carnal conversation. The will didn't say we couldn't *talk* to each other."

"You know what I mean."

"Yeah. I do. But I still think we're good here." They ate for a couple minutes, and Jim thought, and Hallie let him do it. "Bottom line," he finally said, "the fact that I'd be picking up those guns could've been spread around pretty well in two days. If Dale was upset about the guns, he could've shot his mouth off at the office and around the job sites. Plenty of guys there whose ears would perk up, hearing a couple of those brand names. Word would get around quick enough. Get some roofers or drywall guys knowing it . . . notoriously loose in the moral-fiber department, drywall guys."

"You were a drywall guy."

"How do you think I know?"

Hallie smiled a bit. "I'm not sure how upset Dale was. It was more Faye. She went on about it."

She described the scene, and Jim listened, frowned, and said, "Mm. I saw that in Bob's office, too. But just because a guy doesn't make a big noise about it, that doesn't mean he's not feeling plenty."

Her eyes shot straight to him. "Speaking from experience, I take it."

"Speaking as a cop. And from experience. I don't know Dale that well. Her, I'd say I had a better feel for."

"Yeah," Hallie said. "She puts it out there. So what will you do now?"

He raised his eyebrows inquiringly at her, then got a little distracted again at the sight of her eating a prawn, sucking the flesh into her mouth and pulling out the tail.

She didn't seem to notice, fortunately. She wiped her hands on her napkin and said, "About the theft."

"Follow it up," he said. "Not my case, so it's a little tricky. Pass along who knew to the Paradise PD, find out if they got any fingerprints off the bolt cutters the guys left behind, let them do some questioning. But nothing happened, so it's not like it's high priority. Still—" He hesitated.

"What?" she asked after dispatching another prawn.

"I think you should know. I told myself that even if there was something there, it wouldn't spill over to you, but now I'm not so sure." He told her how he'd found her father's body, his suspicions. He hated seeing the light die out of her eyes, the way her body seemed to shrink. "It's probably nothing," he finished. "Probably a coincidence, like we said. A target of opportunity with the guns. But I don't know. Keep that alarm on, OK?"

She nodded jerkily. "Guess I'll stop by North Idaho Sports on the way home and pick up a shotgun of my very own, too."

"Want me to give you a hand with that? You need a refresher, or to go out to the range?"

"No." She was keeping it together a lot better than that scared girl he remembered. If he'd changed, so had she. "There's not a lot to using a shotgun other than safety, and I'm a safety kind of girl. Just point it in the general direction and pull the trigger. I'll get a pump action, keep the ammo in the bedside table, and give myself some practice loading and unloading. After that, I won't be loading it or pointing it if I'm not intending to pull the trigger."

He tried to think of something else to suggest. "You could get a roommate."

"Or a tough boyfriend," she said.

"What?" she asked at his frown, like she didn't know.

Not your business, he told himself, while everything in him shouted, *Like hell.*

"Did you have a present for me?" she asked sweetly. She was doing better than he was here. How had that happened?

"What?" He blanked for a second.

"A check," she prompted.

"Oh. Huh." He shook his head a couple times like he was getting water out of his ears, reached for his wallet, unfolded the money order, and passed it over. "You'll want to get it into the bank as fast as you can. Considering everything."

He had the satisfaction of watching her lose her cool.

"Wow," she said. "Wow. Forty-six thousand dollars. That is a *lot* of zeroes."

"Yep. Course, I had to walk all the way out and get into my truck one time, but . . ."

"I am buying the most badass pool table," she said. "And then doing something good with the rest," she added hastily.

"It's OK to enjoy it, you know. You've been a teacher, what, ten years? Anthea said in a pretty tough school. I'd say you've earned it."

"Nine years." Her fingers traced the numbers on the paper. "It doesn't feel real, that's all. It *isn't* real. Not my real life. Not the life I want. But it's still nice, somehow."

"Pool-table nice," he suggested. "Not new-car nice."

"No. My car's OK," she said absently. She put the check into her purse as if she wanted to get it out of the way, like she wasn't allowed to even look at tempting things. "I'd say thanks, but I'm not sure 'thanks' is enough. Is there anything *you* want?"

Yeah, he thought. *There is.* She must have picked up on it, because she flushed, shoved her curls back with a hand, and said, "Do you want a pool table?"

"Nah. Maybe I could play with you on yours sometime."

That one took her a second to respond to. "After six months. But I won't be here. I could give it to you when I go."

It was a good dose of cold water. "Did you already decide that?"

"I never thought anything else. I can't live here."

"Right."

He'd finished his lunch a while ago, and now she shoved her own plate away and said, "So. Thanks again for the guns, but I know 'thanks' doesn't cover everything you did. I'm glad they're gone, anyway. Maybe that's the end of it after all. There's nothing at the house worth stealing anymore."

She was restless. Nervous, and she wanted to leave. Something he confirmed in the next minute, because she started nibbling at that full pink lip and pulling on her short denim jacket.

And that was the end of lunch. Not the most satisfying meal he'd ever eaten.

If you don't mean it, don't do it, Anthea had said. *She's fragile.* Jim wasn't so sure that Hallie was the one whose heart was most in danger here, though. Because she wanted to leave, and all he wanted to do was stay.

THE GHOST CHASER

It took Hallie a while to talk herself down on Saturday afternoon. Yes, she'd dressed up a little for lunch, but that was because she'd already tried being sloppy around Jim as a way to show herself she didn't care, and it hadn't worked. This time, she'd gone for the thing any woman with sense would have done from the start. Looking her best so she'd have some power in the encounter. And then she'd had the news from Rochelle that had had her coming in hot, and that had felt good, too, in a strange way.

And there Jim had been in another of those annoying T-shirts that showed his biceps, glaring at her like he wanted to spank her. Or eat her up. Or both. Neither of which did anything at all for her peace of mind. Before, that is, he'd switched gears on her and talked about his daughter, and discussed the issue of the guns like he'd wanted her opinion. Not to mention when he'd dropped his suspicions about her dad on her. *That* had been a bombshell.

She'd left the restaurant shaken up more than a little. But she *had* bought a shotgun, and then she'd bought paint and supplies, and she'd gone home and taken out her frustrations and fears on the den and had felt better.

She went to dinner at Anthea's on Saturday night and *didn't* talk about Jim, except to tell Anthea and Ben about the guns after the kids were in bed. Not *all* about the guns. Just about the money. That was all Anthea needed to know. Hallie wasn't going to talk about Jim unless Anthea did.

You compartmentalized, that was what you did. You left the work at work, and you left your personal life at home. And you left completely exasperating, desperately sexy, Levi's-and-boots-wearing deputy sheriffs with hot eyes that looked right through your clothes and big, strong hands that wanted to be all over you—those, you left in your past.

She was stroking paint onto a windowsill on Thursday morning, thinking that she should be on the computer getting ready to start her new job on Monday but wanting to get this done first, when she heard the doorbell ring. She climbed down her stepladder, set her paintbrush in the tray, and made her barefoot way upstairs.

"Uh—hi." The young woman at the door was painfully thin, her hair scraped back into a tight ponytail. "I'm Eileen? The cleaner?"

"Hi," Hallie said, with what she hoped was a reassuring smile, because Eileen looked so nervous. "I'm Hallie." She stuck out her hand, then realized it was covered with white spots. "Whoops. I'm painting." She drew her hand back. Eileen's gaze seemed to be fixed somewhere above Hallie's own, and Hallie snatched the paint-dappled bandanna off her head and said, "As you see. Come on in. I hope it's OK that I'm here while you clean."

"Sure," Eileen said. "Whatever you want. It's your house. Um . . ." She reached into her battered black purse and pulled out a key. "I wasn't sure if you'd changed the locks. I don't think Henry—Mr. Cavanaugh—your dad gave out his key to anybody, but maybe—" She flushed and stopped. "Sorry. I mean, do you want the key?"

"Oh. I never thought about that. I did get the locks changed." As soon as possible once Jim had told her of his suspicions about her father's death. She'd tried not to freak out, but it had seemed . . . prudent. "I'll give you a new key," Hallie said. She went to the kitchen with Eileen following behind and handed her one of the keys on the counter. "Oh, and I reset the alarm code." She gave it to the other woman, who took a notebook from her purse and wrote it down. "Maybe I should show you around. I changed a few things."

"Sure," Eileen said. "And whatever you want me to do. Any instructions."

"I've never had a cleaner," Hallie confessed. "Other than when I lived here as a kid. So maybe you could ask *me* questions. You'll know more than I will. But come on." She took Eileen to the big room in the back over the garage that faced the hills and was totally empty now, only the indentations in the beige carpet marking where furniture had stood. "If you'll vacuum in here and clean the bathroom this time," she said, "that's all I need, and then we'll just shut this door. Really, all I'm using is the other bedroom up here and the guest bath and the kitchen, so . . ." She trailed off, because Eileen, who'd been red before, had gone white. "Are you OK?"

"Sure. I'm fine. So just . . . this one time, and after that, your room. And, uh, kitchen and living room. And I can do your sheets and towels, if you want." Eileen pulled out her notebook and pen again, but her hands were trembling.

"Eileen," Hallie said, and the other woman looked up, her eyes wide and startled. "Are you OK? Can I get you a drink of water?"

"I . . . No. I'm fine."

She didn't look fine, but Hallie led the way out of the master bedroom. "Right, then. Here's the bedroom and bath I'm using, and besides that . . ." She took Eileen downstairs, where the smell of paint was strong. "Like I said on the phone, I'm redoing all this." The den was empty now all the way down to the concrete floor, except for the drop cloths around the edges. Hallie had been repainting the trim an antique white to set off the soft blue-gray walls she'd already finished.

"The carpet guys are coming tomorrow, so just ignore in here until next week. After this first week, I'm guessing the rooms I use will be about what my dad did. Kitchen, bedroom, bath, and this room. Whatever we call it when I'm done. I'm thinking 'family room,' even though I'm not exactly a family." She was babbling, alarmed by the expression on Eileen's face. "But I'll pay you whatever my father was," she hastened to add. "I'm sure you'll be doing about the same things."

Eileen's mouth worked, but nothing came out.

"Hey," Hallie said. "Are you all right?"

Eileen swung around to look at her, but her eyes were unfocused. Blind, like she couldn't bear to look at this room.

Hallie couldn't stand it. She stepped forward and took the other woman in her arms. "Hey, now," she said, feeling Eileen stiffen in shock. "It's OK."

Eileen gasped, reared back, and sobbed once, dry and hard. "I'm sorry," she said. "I'm sorry."

She pulled away, and Hallie said again, "It's OK. Really. Let's go upstairs and sit down for a minute, all right?"

Eileen nodded dumbly and followed her, and Hallie sat her at the kitchen counter and busied herself boiling water and pulling out tea bags.

"I'm sorry," Eileen said after a minute. "It was just seeing it. It hit me. But I'll be fine."

"I'll bet it did. Jim told me it was hard on you, finding him. If you don't want to do the house, I'll understand."

"No!" Eileen said. "I want to do the house! Please. But you don't have to pay me what he was. It'll be more for today, but after that . . . you don't . . . did Deputy Lawson say . . ."

"Eileen." Hallie set the tea in front of her, then came around to sit beside her. "Did my father rape you?"

Eileen's eyes were dark pools in the chalk-white of her face. "I know that's a terrible thing to ask," Hallie told her, her heart aching with pity and rage. "But I know it happened to somebody else, so it wouldn't surprise me a bit to know it happened to you. It would make me furious," she continued at the look of shock in the other woman's eyes. "It would make me glad he's dead. But it wouldn't surprise me. And, no, nobody told me," she added, because it would be one more violation for Eileen to think that Jim had talked. "I guessed."

"Yes." It wasn't a word, just a movement of Eileen's mouth. "The people at the—at a center I went to—they said it was. But he didn't—force me. He said I had to. But I could have said no and just not had the job."

"But you needed the job."

"Yes."

Hallie hadn't known it was possible to feel so much anger. Surely it would make you burn up. Surely it would make your head blow off the top of your body. She shoved it down and forced herself to speak calmly. "Then it's rape."

"That's what the deputy said. But I—"

"Jim," Hallie said, and Eileen nodded miserably. "He said that because he knows. "Look." She sat down beside Eileen and took both of the other woman's freezing hands in hers. "My father was a miserable person, and I know it."

"I'm sorry," Eileen said. She grabbed a Kleenex from her purse and took an angry swipe at her eyes. "I'm so *mad* at myself. I had a whole plan for how I was going to be today. All cool and professional, and I've totally screwed up."

Hallie laughed. She couldn't help it, but Eileen looked up, startled. "Do you know," Hallie said, "that's exactly what I told myself when I came back here. *Exactly.* I was going to be all cool and collected. And then I walked in this house and fell apart. I ended up running down the driveway like his ghost was after me."

Eileen gave a short, sharp laugh. "You're kidding."

"Nope. I wasn't actually screaming, but other than that, it was horror movie time all the way. Henry tended to have that effect on people. But I got over it. His ghost is *gone*. I wiped it out." She squeezed Eileen's hands again. "And if you vacuum up the last traces of him from his bedroom? Wipe him out of the sink? You'll wipe him out, too."

Eileen smiled back at her, even though it was shaky. "Is that why everything's gone? The bear and . . . everything?"

"Ah," Hallie said. "I knew I liked you. Did you hate the bear?"

"*Yes*. My ex liked those, too, but I *hate* those trophy heads. Isn't it enough that you killed the deer and ate it? Do you have to display its head to the whole world to prove you won?"

"I know!" Hallie said with delight. "It's not like you brought it down, *mano a mano*. Or hooves *a mano*. Whatever. You shot it with a gun. Big friggin' deal. Not exactly a fair fight." She became aware, then, of something she realized she'd been hearing for some time. The insistent sound of a dog barking. "I'm sorry, but—do you have a dog?"

"What?" Eileen said. "No. I mean, it's nothing."

The barking was still going on. "There's a dog out there," Hallie said. "And I don't have neighbors. I know this is more important, but—" She went to the door with Eileen following behind, and walked around the side of the house. And then she laughed.

An ancient, battered sedan sat in the driveway. And behind the wheel, its paws on the dashboard, looking for all the world like it was about to take the car down the road, was a big, shaggy golden retriever with a smile on its face.

"I think your dog's planning a road trip," Hallie said.

"Oh, man," Eileen said. "I *knew* he'd blow it."

"No," Hallie said. "Bring him in."

"He's not supposed to—I don't usually bring him," Eileen said.

"No. Bring him in," Hallie insisted. "I want to say hi."

Eileen went around to the car, opened the door, and about eighty pounds of dog leaped joyfully out, pranced around, and then headed straight for the planter at one corner of the garage and lifted his leg.

"Cletus!" Eileen shouted.

"No," Hallie said. "It's fine. Cletus. That's one heck of a country name."

"I picked it. It fit. Cletus and my kids are about the only good things I got from my ex. He didn't want any of them, and they're all *great*. But then, he was an idiot." Cletus had come over to join them now, and Eileen bent down, rubbed his ears, and said, "You're bad. I *told* you to be quiet."

Hallie barely heard her, because Cletus had turned his considerable attentions to her now, was wagging his feathery tail furiously, smiling like a loon, and asking her to scratch behind his ears. So she did.

"What a great dog," she said. Cletus had rolled over now, his tail still going like mad.

"Yeah," Eileen said, but she sounded despondent.

Hallie looked up from where she was crouching, rubbing an ecstatic Cletus's furry belly, and said, "What?"

"I have to get rid of him," Eileen said.

"Oh, no. Why?"

"My landlord. That's why he's in my car, because I have to take him to the . . . the shelter, but I keep putting it off. And my kids are just—" Eileen's thin shoulders sagged. "Crushed. My little boy—he's four—he said this morning, 'You're the meanest mommy in the world.' He doesn't get it, and my daughter—she just cries. I told them Cletus would find a new home, that a new family will want him, but—" She was on her knees, now, rubbing the dog's silky ears again. "Cletus is eight, so I'm worried that the pound will just put him down. He's such a great dog, but I've asked everybody at church, and—he's eight."

"So what?" Hallie said. "So he's eight. So what?"

"Everybody wants a puppy. A young dog. They think it's going to be easier, or that it'll be better, because an older dog will die. Well, of *course* he'll die. If you have a dog, it's going to die. But if you have a *great* dog, you're glad you *had* him. That's the point." She broke off. "Sorry. You don't care about this."

"No," Hallie said. "I do. Oh, your poor kids. Poor you."

"You know what's terrible?" Eileen said. "I know I should feel more horrible about your—about Henry. And I do. Every time I think about it—the whole thing—I'm sick. But what makes me cry is . . ." Her voice broke. "Cletus." The dog looked up at her from his upside-down position, wagged his tail again, and smiled harder, and she buried her face in her shoulder. Her thin shoulders heaved, and after a second she said, "It's my fault, really. The landlord said thirty pounds max when we moved in last year, and I lied, because I couldn't find anyplace else I could afford that would take dogs at all. I told myself that it was OK, because the landlord never comes around, and if he ever saw Cletus by accident, he'd realize he's better than some yappy Chihuahua that's going to *bite* people. He doesn't bark much— I mean, if he's not in the car and worried—and he's quiet, and clean, and friendly, and—but the landlord didn't care," she finished. "Cletus isn't thirty pounds."

"No," Hallie said. "He sure isn't. So are your kids in school?"

"My girl is. First grade. My boy's in day care."

"I've got this crazy thought," Hallie said. It was impulsive, but so was everything else she'd done for the last two weeks. "How would Cletus like to come live with me? And then your kids could come visit. I've got that fenced area off the—the family room." Where her swing set had stood, once upon at a time. Her dad had grumbled about putting up the simple wooden fence, because he said it spoiled the view, but for once, Hallie's mom had insisted. "You could even bring your boy with you," Hallie added in a burst of inspiration. "Let him play with Cletus on Thursdays while you clean. How about that? I'd really, *really* like to have a nice big dog. I'd like *this* dog."

"I don't think he's a guard dog," Eileen said dubiously.

"I don't care." Hallie had another thought, an even crazier one. She was going to go with that, too. Sometimes you didn't have to think things out. Sometimes you didn't have to plan. Sometimes life handed you the answer. "He's perfect. He's a ghost chaser."

COVERING THE BASES

Jim hadn't seen Hallie again all that week and into the next one. All he'd had was a text message from her on Monday.

Deposited the money order. All quiet on the Western Front. Got that shotgun by my bed, though. Don't come around in the middle of the night without calling first, because I'm armed and dangerous. Ordered my pool table, too. Wait till you see my new room.

Which was a pretty interesting message. Either she was all buzzed and happy, or . . . He'd thought a minute, then texted back, *I'll call first, then.* He hadn't heard from her again, so it had probably been a bad idea, but how much temptation could a man take?

His mother hadn't mentioned her, and neither had Cole. His brother seemed to have gone back to living his normal teenage life, which was good. He was probably checking out black Jeeps and red Corvettes online, but what fifteen-year-old boy wouldn't have been? He hadn't dropped out of Math Club, anyway.

The bolt cutters had come back with some fingerprints that hadn't lit anything up on the FBI's database, which was interesting in itself. This had been amateur hour all the way, either local muscle recruited for a job or a few roughnecks from a job site who'd seized on an easy score. Jim would have bet, though, that the amateur muscle hadn't been told they'd be burglarizing a cop's rig. Which left him with the idea of a single brain behind the endeavor, someone who'd brought tools and labor and a plan for the job, knowing how much that safe might weigh and that it would probably be fastened down. Which was a lot of information.

He'd passed along the names Cole had given him to Jesse Hartung, because it wasn't Jim's case and he couldn't go looking up addresses of teenagers in an unofficial capacity. Jesse had uttered a dubious, "We'll check it out. Do our best," that told Jim what he already knew. Nothing had been stolen, the guys Jim had seen hadn't been teenagers, and the Paradise PD had plenty to keep it busy.

"I've got a couple possibilities I know personally," Jim told him, "so I'll do a little more poking around, pass anything I get along to you to follow up."

"No skin off my nose," Jesse said. "Long as you keep it clean."

It wasn't that Jim didn't have enough to keep *him* busy. It was because those lowlifes had been in *his* driveway and inside *his* rig. And because Mac had been on the porch. And because he needed to know whether Hallie was in danger, and whether the tingle he'd felt at the back of his neck in Henry's den had been the air-conditioning or something else. He'd owed his life and the lives of his squad to that tingle too often to ignore it.

Lots of very good reasons.

He stopped by Dale Cavanaugh's place first. Six thirty, Monday night, a calculated time that worked out fine, because Dale came to the door still holding a pink cloth napkin and snapped on the porch light.

"Jim Lawson," Jim said, just in case Dale didn't recognize him out of uniform.

"Of course," Dale said. "What can I do for you? Is something wrong?"

"Nothing's wrong, but I do have a couple questions for you and your wife."

"Come on in, then."

Faye turned in her chair at the dining-room table as the two men approached, asking, "Who was—" Her blue eyes widened at the sight of Jim. "Oh."

"Evening, ma'am," Jim said. "I just have a few questions for you and your husband. Unofficially, as you see."

Faye's eyes sharpened, and she started to say something, but Dale said, "What is this about?"

He didn't invite Jim to sit, and neither did Faye, which was interesting. "Well, it's about those guns of Henry's," Jim said. "Hallie mentioned that she talked to you about them."

"She certainly did," Faye said, but Dale made a faint motion toward her, and she subsided.

"Has she reconsidered, then?" Dale asked. "I'm surprised she wouldn't have discussed that with me. Where do you come into it?"

Jim raised his brows. "I thought she'd mentioned to you that I offered to sell them for her."

"Right," Dale said. "Sorry, I forgot. I was a little preoccupied at the time."

"Call it what it was," Faye said. "You were devastated."

"Honey—" Dale said. "No. Disappointed, maybe, that's all. But that's life. Hallie did what she thought was best."

Faye huffed, and Jim said, "I'm wondering who else you discussed this with. The guns."

Dale paused, his gaze going somewhere beyond Jim, and finally shook his head. "Can't recall that I discussed it with anybody. Like I said—I was disappointed. Didn't want to think about it much. Why do you ask?"

"Bob Jenkins, maybe?" Jim persisted. "If you thought you had a right to them?"

"You know," Dale said, "I never even thought of that. Maybe I should've. Henry always said I didn't have enough of a ruthless streak to make it in business."

"How about you?" Jim asked Faye. "Who have you mentioned the guns to?"

"I asked Bob about them right away," she said. "I did," she told her husband at his hastily muffled exclamation. "I wanted to make sure. He said there was nothing we could do. And I may have said something at the hairdresser's on Friday," she said, confirming Rochelle's earlier suspicions. "And at coffee after my exercise class, now that I think of it. Of course I did," she told her husband, the smooth lines of her face marred by the peevishness around her mouth. "Because you know and I know that those guns should've come to you, whatever Bob said. Hallie didn't even offer you *one* of them, and that wasn't right. You can say anything you like, and I'll still say it. She's ungrateful, and she's selfish."

"Did you mention that I'd be taking them?" Jim asked her, ignoring the rest of it.

She shrugged her shoulders, which caused her carefully maintained breasts in the snug pink wool to move not at all. "Probably. Your name may have come into it, one way or another." She couldn't entirely suppress a knowing smirk, and Jim had a feeling he knew in what way his name would've come into it.

Hallie had been right. Kissing on the front steps was definitely out.

"Well, they're gone," Dale said. "No point worrying about it now, I'd have thought. So what is this all about?"

"*Are* they gone?" Faye asked. Her bright-blue gaze was back on Jim. "I think he's over here to tell us they're not. Hallie's probably reconsidered, maybe because I *did* tell people, and now they're talking, and it's gotten back to her. I'll bet she's decided to give them to you after all, but she's embarrassed to show her face here and tell you. She always was one to run away. So instead, she's . . . *recruited* Jim to do it."

"No," Jim said calmly. "She hasn't recruited me, other than to sell her father's guns, like she said. They *are* gone, I'm afraid. Somebody came to my house to steal them Friday night, not ten hours after I took them from Hallie's, which is what's got me wondering who knew they'd be there."

"Oh, no," Dale said. "Well, that's a real shame. A *real* shame. Seems like Paradise keeps getting more like the big city. We've got an element coming up north . . . but I don't need to tell you about that."

"Up north from Mexico, you mean?" Jim asked.

"I don't like to be prejudiced," Dale said. "But you can't deny that things have changed. Never used to have to lock a door. Now, you've got to watch the job sites like a hawk or tools just walk away."

Faye didn't say anything, but Jim had seen the ladylike gasp and then the smile she'd quickly suppressed. She wasn't exactly brokenhearted.

"Well, good news," Jim said. "I said somebody came to my house. I didn't say he'd left with the guns. I managed to chase him off."

"Oh." Dale shook his head and gave Jim another little smile. "Guess you were just messing with us there. You got me good. Well, if I couldn't have them, it's better that Hallie gets the benefit of them, at least. Family's family, after all. Did you happen to get a look at the burglar at all?"

"We have a few leads we're following up, yes," Jim said.

"That's good, then," Dale said. "Keep me posted, if you don't mind. Let me know if you get any closer. I sure hate to think there's somebody out there ready to pounce on any opportunity like that. Better keep the doors locked, honey," he told Faye. "And set that alarm."

"*I'm* not the one who doesn't set it."

That got another smile from Dale. "Guilty. Like I say—just can't get used to changing times. It's a whole new world."

"It can be," Jim said. "I won't take any more of your time. Thanks for your help."

◆　◆　◆

The next day, he stopped by Bob Jenkins's office. Covering all the bases.

"Hi, Jim," Pam Garrett, the receptionist said. "You looking for Anthea?"

"Nope," Jim said. "For Bob, if he's got a minute."

Bob came out of the back five minutes later with a smile and a handshake and ushered Jim to an office dominated by a huge, old-fashioned wooden desk, with a backdrop of floor-to ceiling bookshelves filled with rows of matching law books. Anthea had told him that attorneys mostly looked things up online these days, "but the clients love the books. Makes the bill look less horrifying."

"Have a seat," Bob said. "I've got a client coming in ten minutes, I'm afraid, but if it's a quick question—something about Cole, I assume? I thought Anthea had it pretty much covered, but whatever I can do." He shook his head of well-barbered gray hair. "Your sister's a crackerjack, that's what she is. A crackerjack."

"You're right," Jim said. "And I think I'm safe leaving all that to her. This is about something else. Hallie Cavanaugh says she told you that I was picking up her dad's guns. I'd like to know who you told about that."

Bob's expression grew more alert. "Is this an official visit?" He eyed Jim's blue button-down and Levi's.

"No," Jim said. "Off duty right now. Just a question. Somebody tried to steal those guns on Friday night."

"Really. Well, that's a terrible thing, but I guess you and I both know that some people just run crooked. You said 'tried,' though."

"That's right. They didn't succeed. But you can see why I'd like to track down who knew I was picking them up."

Bob lifted his hands from the desk, palms down. "I don't generally go around shooting my mouth off about my clients' business. If Hallie already told you she asked me about it, though—yes, I can confirm that. She did."

"Did you discuss the guns with Dale Cavanaugh?" Jim asked. "Or his wife?"

"I think that would fall under the category of 'client privilege,'" Bob said. "As you're talking about the division of estate property, and Dale and Faye are beneficiaries—and clients. Maybe you should ask them."

"I did that. But you didn't discuss the guns with anybody else?"

"Why would I? I can't say they were of great interest to me."

"Really? Not even that Winchester? That'd run you fifteen grand all by itself."

Bob's gaze sharpened. "That was the best gun in the safe?"

"Why? Was there something else?"

Bob laughed. "Well—Henry. He was always talking things up. And I probably wasn't paying much attention, to be frank. I'm more of a golfer, myself. I save my blood lust for legal battles." He looked at his watch. "So if that's all—I've got that client coming." Right on cue, the intercom buzzed on his desk phone. "Ah. There you go."

Jim didn't get up quite yet. "Would that have been when you were drafting his new will? I noticed it was dated in this past year."

"I don't recall whether that was the exact visit. Does it matter?"

"Possibly. I'd like to know what changed in this one, and who knew about those changes."

"And that would be something else I couldn't tell you." Bob was still genial, but he was standing now. "That pesky attorney-client privilege, you know."

"A subpoena could take care of that," Jim said. "Or you could go on and avoid the formalities and tell me now."

"Or I could wait until somebody in uniform comes into my office with a piece of paper signed by a judge. Which I can't imagine any reason for, so I don't think either of us should hold our breath." Bob smiled, and the moment of tension passed. "Hell, Jim. What do you have to worry about? Whoever tried to take those guns—and I can't believe that was anything but chance, or rather, somebody with a loose grasp on the principle of private property seeing a gun safe sitting, nice and tempting, in the bed of a pickup—bottom line is, you stopped them. Meanwhile, your brother's coming out of this thing set for life. Why would you worry about what any other will said? The last thing you want is to get any of the other beneficiaries stirred up and thinking they've got some kind of contestable grounds. You start talking about a court case, and that money gets eaten right up. Of course, I'd be the one eating it up, so I should be advising the opposite, but whatever you're thinking—don't. That won't have a happy outcome. You wouldn't want to put Cole or your mother through DNA testing, for example."

Bob was still looking pleasant, but Jim wasn't. "Are you suggesting that DNA testing might bring back some sort of surprise result?" Jim asked. "That my mother was sleeping around?"

"I'm saying don't rock the boat," Bob said. "Your brother's set, and that's what matters."

MOVING ON

That was as far as Jim had gotten with the investigation. The guns were sold, Hallie had the money, and he had no real answers, only more questions. Meanwhile, a week later, life was back to normal. Work, home, no further word from Hallie, and no interest in anybody else. And on this Thursday in mid-October, open house at the middle school, which meant an early dinner before he dropped Mac at his mom's and headed over there.

They'd made spaghetti squash and tomato sauce with Italian sausage tonight, and he told Mac, "We did good on this."

They were sitting at the old-fashioned yellow dinette table in the kitchen, as usual. "Yeah," Mac agreed. "We should keep this one. I'll add it to the book." Which was their recipe book, maintained by Mac, complete with color-coded dividers. Nothing fancy in there, but then, neither one of them liked fancy much. Jim wasn't always home for dinner—it depended on his shifts—but when he was, the meal was a team effort.

They'd started doing it together when Maya had been sick, and they weren't too bad at this point.

It had been Maya's suggestion. "It'd be good for both of you," she'd said. "Bonding time, like girls usually have with their mothers." She hadn't said that both of them would need that, because Mac wouldn't be growing up with a mother. She hadn't needed to. She'd just set things up so he and Mac would have their best shot at "normal." A new normal.

"So," he said to Mac now. "Open house. Got a schedule for me?"

Mac leaned over, rummaged in her pack, and pulled out a neatly filled-in block schedule with classes and teachers listed.

"Intimidating," Jim said, chewing a chunk of sausage and looking down the list. "Finding my way to all these rooms again. I hope they've changed the desks since I went there. I may have carved some things into a couple of them. That'd be embarrassing."

"Try being me," Mac said. "I'm actually *in* sixth grade, not remembering it. And I think you can find your way. Use your compass."

He had to smile. "That shouldn't be OK with me. Too bad I think you're funny. I kind of miss back-to-school night at the elementary school, though. Looking at your maple-leaf poem and reading your short sto—" He stopped with his finger on the last block. "Who's this last one? World Geography?"

Ms. Cavanaugh, it read. *Room 115.*

"I told you," Mac said, making a business of twirling spaghetti squash around her fork. "That we were going to have a long-term sub, because Ms. Bailey broke her back in that accident. She'll be gone at least until January. I *told* you."

"You did," Jim said. "And I remembered."

It would've been pretty hard to forget, considering that he'd been the first officer on the scene.

It was one of the bad ones, but not the worst. A teenaged driver, crossing the center line and hitting the other car head-on. As always seemed to happen, the kid who'd made the mistake hadn't ended up too bad off. But the other driver, Charlene Bailey, had been screaming with the pain of what had turned out to be a fractured back. And with fear.

"My baby," she'd kept moaning, the thought overriding even her pain. "My baby."

A bald little boy of barely three months, wailing with fear, but blessedly unhurt. Jim had taken the baby over to Charlene once the EMTs had checked him out and said, loud enough to make it through the baby's wails, but keeping it strong and calm, "Your little boy's fine, Charlene. He's just fine. See, here he is."

"Is he OK? Is he OK?" she'd kept saying. "He's crying. Oh, God. It hurts." The EMT had slipped a mask over her face, then, had gotten her breathing oxygen and narcotic painkillers, but her eyes had still been wide and panicked above the plastic.

"He's all good," Jim had said. "Look. I've got him, and he's fine. I'm going to make sure he's safe. Don't you worry."

He'd seen her eyes calm and glaze with the painkiller and his promise, and he'd kept his word and held the boy until his mother had been rushed away. The baby had quieted eventually, maybe because his mother wasn't crying anymore, and Jim had held the surprisingly solid little body close, the baby's head nestled into his neck in that killer way babies had, had felt the tiny bones of his spine under his palm, and had told him, "You're OK, bud. You're fine. And your mom's going to be OK, too. You'll see." Feeling stupid for saying it, but needing to. Then he'd given him to an EMT, who would take him to the hospital, just in case. And to his no-doubt frantic father, who hadn't lost his wife that day. Or his son.

That night, Jim had found himself on his knees beside his bed, his head in his hands. He'd tried to pray, to ask for the strength to make it through. And he'd ended up crying, muffling the tears in his palms so Mac wouldn't hear.

The low points didn't come very often anymore, but they still came, dark and hopeless. And, as usual, he'd ended up talking to Maya instead of God.

I can't do this, babe, he'd tried to tell her. *I can't take it.* While she'd been sick, he'd done everything he could to be her strong place, her steady place. And once she'd been gone, he'd realized how much she'd been that for him.

Like always, he wasn't sure God heard, but he could hear Maya, her voice weak and thready, but so sure in its resolve in those last days.

You're such a good dad, Jim. Such a good man. You're my hero, and you can do this. You're going to keep living hard and working hard and loving hard, and you're going to come out on the other side. You'll see.

All right, maybe the past week hadn't been completely normal. Or maybe it had. Some things he was grateful for, and some things he'd have given anything to change. Some good times and some hard times. His life.

Just like right now, he was holding a schedule that had a name on it he wasn't expecting and telling Mac, "Your long-term substitute is Hallie Cavanaugh."

"She just came on Monday," Mac said, focusing on her dinner again. "And she didn't say her first name. They never do. They just write, 'Ms. Cavanaugh,' like 'Ms.' is their first name. Like I used to think yours was 'Sarge.'"

"You did not. Your mother called me 'Jim.'"

"I thought 'Sarge' was your *other* first name. When I was little."

"Quit trying to change the subject. Why didn't you tell me your long-term sub was Hallie?"

"Maybe because I've never met her, so I didn't recognize her?" Mac said sweetly. "Or because you didn't tell me she was my uncle's sister? That she had the same dad as Cole? Which makes her my aunt."

"No, it doesn't." Why did everybody keep trying to make Hallie a member of Jim's family? "Who told you that?"

"Cole. Well, not exactly," she amended. "I heard him talking on phone about it, so I asked Grandma."

"Why didn't you ask me?"

She shrugged. "I don't know."

"Mackenzie." He gave her a hard look, and she sighed and said, "Well, maybe because . . . Cole said something that sounded weird. About you and her."

"Uh-huh. What?"

"I don't know," she said again.

Great. How did he explain this? About her *teacher?* He said, "I'm guessing he was talking about a strange part of Hallie's father's will. Her father—well, Cole's father, too—knew me growing up, and he didn't like me. I'm guessing Cole probably said something about how I wasn't supposed to . . . spend time with Hallie."

Mac gave him a pretty good side-eye. "That wasn't it."

"Well, what he probably actually said isn't appropriate for me to discuss with you. You don't need to worry about what he said. Hallie—Ms. Cavanaugh—is in town for a few more months, and I guess she'll be your teacher until Christmas. She's good friends with Aunt Anthea, so you'll probably see her around, and so will I. And that is all."

"Do you want a girlfriend?" Mac asked, and Jim about dropped his fork.

"Why?" he asked cautiously.

She shrugged. "I just wondered."

"I might. Would that bother you?"

She got up and took her plate to the sink, scraped it off, then put it in the dishwasher. She wasn't looking at him when she said, "Honor Campbell says that men have to have sex, or they could explode."

A sip of Jim's water went down the wrong way, and he had to do some coughing. He finally said, "Who told Honor Campbell that?"

"Her sister Janice. She's fifteen."

"Well, Janice is wrong. And so is Honor. You can tell her I said so. Men don't *have* to have sex. Teenage boys tell girls that to make them feel guilty for not wanting to have sex. Teenage boys are mostly jerks."

At least Mac was looking at him again. "You weren't a jerk."

"Oh, yeah. I was." He probably shouldn't say that, or maybe he should. He never knew the right answer. "That's how I know. Any boy who tells you he has to have sex, or it'll be painful, or he'll . . . explode, or whatever—there's your red flag that he doesn't really care about you."

Geez. Mac was *eleven*. This talk was supposed to happen when she was . . . fourteen. Or thirty. Not now, anyway.

"Does that mean you're not going to get a girlfriend?"

"Uh . . ." Once again, he wasn't sure of the right answer, so he went for honesty. "No, it doesn't. Your mom's been gone for more than two years. I miss her like crazy and I'll love her forever, but I'll probably get a girlfriend, one of these days. You can love more than one person in your life."

He hadn't thought so at first, no matter what Maya had said. Sometime in the last months, though, he'd started to think it might be possible. And sometime in the last weeks, he'd started to think it could actually happen.

Mac crossed her arms and leaned back against the counter. "Crystal's mom likes you."

"How do you know?"

"Crystal said. Her mom was telling somebody on the phone. That you were so hot. And you had a great butt." She rolled her eyes. "Gross."

Jim wished people in Paradise would make their damn phone calls with the door closed once in a while. "Well, I don't know about that. I think my butt's fairly normal. But sooner or later, I'll go out with a woman."

"To have sex?"

That took Jim a minute. "None of your business," he finally said, which wasn't exactly a parental answer, so he tried again. "Not something I'm going to talk to you about. There'll be somebody I like, and I'll get to know her, and I'll . . . date."

Date. It even *sounded* weird. He hadn't *dated* for a long time. *What do you call that lunch with Hallie?* his mind mocked.

Lunch, he answered, and his mind said, *Ha.* Even his *mind* back-talked him.

"Will you ask me first?" Mac said.

"No," Jim said, going for honesty again. "But I'll let you know."

Mac was giving him the side-eye again. "What if I hate her? What if you get married and I have a stepmother and I hate her?"

"I'm not going to marry somebody you hate."

"But if you're not going to ask me if I like her, how will you know?"

"Trust me, I'll know." He got up and put his own plate in the dishwasher. "I'm going to be late to this thing."

"First period is PE," she said. "I'm good at PE, and it doesn't matter for my future anyway. You can miss it."

BACK TO SCHOOL

World Geography was seventh period, so Jim had all evening to get used to the idea. All the same, when he walked into the classroom at eight thirty, it was still a shock.

He'd had a class in this room himself, he was pretty sure. Hallie had been in it, too.

This Hallie looked a little different. She waited at the front of the room as the parents filed in and sat at those too-small desks, which fortunately *had* been replaced in the past twenty years, so any swear words written or carved into their undersides at least hadn't been put there by Jim.

Luke and Kayla Jackson were up in the front row, and Hallie was perched with one hip on the teacher's desk, chatting to them. Wearing a long, drapey, peacock-blue top over cream-colored leggings and low brown boots, and looking fine.

Well, no, he decided as he sat beside Luke. Looking a little tired. But then, it was the end of the evening.

She glanced his way, smiled, then went on talking to Kayla. Cool, just like in the restaurant. Professional. In her element.

In the next fifteen minutes, she was even more so. She explained what had happened to Charlene Bailey, for those who hadn't heard, gave an update on her progress, and outlined her own background, which was pretty damn impressive.

"Even though I'm filling in here," she told them, "I can promise you that your children won't be losing any learning time. Fortunately, Ms. Bailey left thorough lesson plans, and I'll be supplementing with some ideas of my own. Sixth grade is an exciting time. Your sons and daughters are thinking more critically, and they're ready to share those thoughts, so we'll be having class discussions that I expect to get lively at times. I've been here four days," she said with a wry smile, "and I can tell you that they already have. Our unit now, as you may know, is the Middle East. Our focus will always be on understanding the cultural, economic, and geographic forces that have shaped a region, which may mean that your kids will arrive home with ideas and questions that might startle you. But that's all part of learning to think for themselves."

"You going to be teaching them that terrorism's part of their culture?" asked Charlie Roundtree from the back row. He was a couple years older than Jim, but Jim remembered him just fine. Charlie Roundtree, the brother of Kyle Roundtree, the guy Jim had punched in the stomach on Paradise Mountain a few years back, when he'd grabbed Hallie and tried to pull her into the woods.

Man, small towns could be murder.

"We'll be doing some reading and discussion on the roots of Muslim extremism," Hallie said. If she remembered Charlie, she wasn't letting on. "Our goal in this class is understanding the forces that are shaping the world your sons and daughters will be living in."

"We don't do multiculturalism in Paradise," a thin, intense woman with a head of frizzy brown hair said, to a murmur of agreement.

"Then you may want to talk to Mr. Van Buren about applying for an exemption from this class for your child on the basis of personal beliefs," Hallie said calmly. "Because the Idaho standards for sixth grade

World Geography and Cultures are all about the study of—well, world cultures. I'd be happy to share a copy with you. But I suspect that your children's main complaint is going to be that they have to write too much."

"Already heard that," Luke put in with his patented grin. "And you won't get any complaints from me."

"Of course you'd be on her side," Ms. Frizzy-Hair said. "We all know that teachers stick together, and that the state is telling you to push its agenda."

"Doesn't sound to me like there's a side," Jim said. Enough was enough. "Sounds like Ms. Cavanaugh's got a curriculum she's supposed to follow, and she's following it. Which would be what she's paid to do. It's her fourth day, folks. Maybe give her a break."

"We know why *you're* saying *that*, too," Charlie said.

About half of the room held its breath, with the other half—the parents who were connected to the university and not tuned in to the Paradise gossip network—merely looking confused. Jim swung around in the cramped seat, looked across the rows of parents at Charlie, and said, "If you've got something to say to me, I'm happy to talk to you afterwards. This isn't the time or the place."

Hallie held up a hand and said, "Excuse me," with authority in her voice that Jim had never heard. Jim swung back around, and she said, "The good news is, we'll be moving on to sub-Saharan Africa next. And while that has its own set of fascinating issues, they're less politically charged. In any case, I hope you can see why our class discussions may get lively, and why we'll be stressing courteous discussion that keeps to the topic." She pointed to a poster on the wall headed *Ground Rules for Discussion.* "I have some copies up here that I'd be happy to share." She looked at the back row when she said it, and she didn't get any lip, so Jim assumed Charlie had gotten the message. She looked like she was all ready to send him to the principal's office. She'd probably do it, too.

The bell rang, and she said, "Thank you all for coming. My e-mail address and phone number are on the board if you have further questions."

Jim didn't go outside to talk to Charlie Roundtree. The conversation he wanted to have with him mostly came in the form of a fist, which wouldn't be too helpful. Besides, he kind of wanted to stick around here. So he said good-bye to Luke and Kayla, stayed where he was, tried to think of what to say, and started with, "I didn't realize Eli had this class with Mac."

"Yes," Hallie said. "*I* didn't realize that Eli was Luke's stepson until tonight. He's a nice boy. Sits behind Mac, in fact."

"He bother her?" Jim asked. When Hallie looked surprised, he said, "I was remembering. We had a class in this room, didn't we?"

"Yes," she said. "We did. You didn't sit behind me, though."

"Nope. But somebody else did. Can't remember who anymore. He was always pulling your hair, and you'd turn red and get upset, and everybody would laugh."

She got busy behind the desk, packing up, and Jim realized that she must have been here since early morning. "I remember that."

"I was remembering it, too," he said. "Tonight. Wondering why that was OK with anybody at all. Why a boy would be allowed to put his hands on a girl like that and harass her. If anybody did that to Mac now, I'd be all over it."

"And so would I." She shoved her laptop into a fabric bag. "So would Mac. She's got plenty of confidence. So would Eli, for that matter. He sits behind her, like I said. But, yes. That was Eric somebody, with the hair. Probably in prison now. One day, we had a substitute. Eric did that hair thing, whispered something about my *other* hair, which I didn't even figure out for a couple more years, but . . . man, I'd had it. I was holding a really sharp pencil, and I turned around and stabbed him in the hand. Hard. Bet I punched right through the skin.

He let out this wail and told the teacher, and she said, 'It looked to me like you deserved it.'" She sighed. "That was a *great* day. That was when I first wanted to be a teacher. It was a little thing, but it sure made an impression."

"So did you, tonight." He was smiling. That had been a good story. "Walk you out to your car?"

"Sure." She glanced at him sidelong, the same way Mac had done earlier, and said, "I notice we're gossip material."

"Did you recognize him? Charlie, in the back?"

"No. Should I have?"

Jim told her, and she laughed. "Talk about second chances. I've sent his kid to the principal's office once already, and moved his seat right up by my desk, and we're only on day four. I'll keep hoping to make an impression on him, but meanwhile, at least he's not keeping anybody else from learning, and that's something."

"You really like this," he said, holding the classroom door for her, then waiting while she locked up.

"Only reason anyone would do it," she said. "The hours stink, and it doesn't pay enough. Probably like being a deputy sheriff."

"Probably." They walked down the echoing corridor together, only a few stragglers remaining now, and past the rows of lockers. "So I've got a question for you," he said.

"Just don't make it too hard, because I'm about dead on my feet."

"Yeah. Noticed that. This'll be a quick one. What age are girls when they . . . notice boys?"

"That's your idea of a quick question?"

He gave her a sheepish half smile. "Just give me a hint."

"This is about Mac, I presume?"

"Yep. She was asking me all these questions tonight. No body armor for that."

"Like what?"

He shrugged a shoulder. They were out of the building now, headed to her car. "Like, did I want a girlfriend. Would I be having sex with my girlfriend. I about spit out my drink."

She laughed and shook her head. "I guess being a single dad gets pretty tough."

"Yeah."

"But you haven't—" She hesitated. "I mean, this hasn't come up."

They were at her car now, with good-byes being called around them, the sound of engines turning over in the cool October night. "No," he said. "It hasn't. And now it is."

"Oh." She unlocked the car and put her bags in the back, then said, "When do boys start thinking about it?"

"You asking when I did? I remember right there in sixth grade, noticing your butt, wondering how come I liked to look at it. If that helps."

She gasped, and he said, "You just did that sucking-in-your-breath thing again. I noticed that, too. Bothered me then, just like it does now."

"I was *ten*."

"Yeah, well, what can I say. I was eleven. Twelve. Whatever. When did you notice boys?"

"If we're being honest here," she admitted, "I noticed you. You made me feel all sort of . . . weak. Knee-wise."

"Ah. That's nice."

"So I'd say," she said, going for that brisk professional approach again, "that Mac's probably normal. I can tell you that Eli Chambers likes her just fine, and she likes him, and since they're both nice kids, you don't have too much to worry about. She's got good taste, anyway. Doesn't go for the bad boys."

"Oh. Whoa. You're kidding. I wasn't ready for *that*."

"I'm guessing no dad ever is. But if you're answering her questions calmly—I mean, the ones about you, besides any others that come up—you're doing it right."

"I told her it was none of her business."

"Maybe not quite right," she conceded.

"I'm working on it." She stood there, holding the door, and he wished he could kiss her goodnight. See if he could still make her weak in the knees. He was willing to work on that, too. But there were people all around them, so instead, he just said, "I still like looking at your butt. So you know. I liked you all messed up in those short little shorts both times, and I liked you in that pretty white dress, and I like the way you look tonight. And trying out your pool table with you would be about the finest thing I could imagine. So if you need anything, out there by yourself? You've got my number."

Then he went and got in his rig, let her pull out first, followed her to the first turn, and headed to his mom's to pick up Mac.

Who liked Eli Chambers just fine. He was *definitely* not ready for this.

DISTURBING THE PEACE

Jim's mind had gone straight back to Hallie, and the look on her face when he'd said that last bit, when his attention was caught by the rig in front of him that had turned left at the stop sign just before Jim turned right. A brand-new black Ford F-150 with light bars and a trailer hitch and all the bells and whistles.

Henry Cavanaugh's truck.

Well, shit.

Jim was in his personal vehicle, and he wasn't on duty. He thought about calling it in, then decided just to follow it for a while and see what he saw.

Ten blocks, all the way through town. A right, then another one. All the way down to Frogtown, where the truck pulled over in front of a dingy apartment building Jim recognized.

The driver got out, and Jim had about ten thoughts all at once. That he'd made a stupid assumption, a rookie mistake. That the easy answer was so often the right one. That real life wasn't a mystery novel, and you didn't look for the least probable person, you looked for the one with motive and opportunity. Not to mention the one who had a key.

And that women could have lowlife boyfriends who could be real interested in valuable items in somebody's house, things they could have their girlfriends spot for them.

It was Eileen Hendricks, driving Henry Cavanaugh's truck through town and apparently thinking nobody would notice.

Had Hallie reported it missing? No, or Jim would've heard. Could she not have noticed it was gone, maybe? He could tell she didn't like being in the garage much. Or had she noticed, and suspected, but had some sort of Noble Hallie moment, thinking that you could excuse theft because the person who'd taken your property must have needed it more than you did? That would be exactly like Hallie. Especially if it was *this* person.

He was pulling over on the opposite side of the street, a little ways back, on that thought. He had a moment of indecision, then told himself, *Don't be stupid again,* pulled out his phone, and called it in.

"I'm going to approach the subject," he told the dispatcher.

"I've already dispatched," she said. "Wait for backup."

Jim was watching Eileen, though. She was reaching into the backseat and hauling a sturdy little figure onto the sidewalk, with a taller kid jumping down after them. Then she went for some plastic bags in the truck bed, handing one to the older girl and taking four herself.

"Negative," Jim said. "I'm approaching. She's got her groceries and her kids."

He hung up, stuffed the phone into his pocket, jogged across the street, and came up fast. Eileen whirled, and even when Jim came into the pool of light cast by the street lamp and she recognized him, she still looked tense.

"Oh," she said with a tentative smile. "Hi."

Jim said, "I'd like to know why you're driving Henry Cavanaugh's truck."

She looked shocked. Guilty. "I . . . Hallie . . . Ms. Cavanaugh. She gave it to me."

"She gave it to you," he said flatly. He could hear the siren, approaching fast, and he relaxed a little, but she tensed more.

"Well, actually," she said with a nervous laugh, "she traded it. I mean, she sold it to me."

"Which is it?" Jim asked, doing his best to harden his heart against the wide-eyed little girl who stood, canted to one side by the weight of the grocery bag she was holding in two hands, staring at him in what looked like terror. The same terror he could see in her mother's eyes. The little boy had hold of his mom's pant leg and was staring at Jim, too. "She gave it, she traded it, or she sold it?"

Eileen said, "She did. I know it's crazy, but she *did*. I can prove it. Here." She set the groceries down awkwardly and pulled open the door of the truck.

Jim said sharply, "Stop," and she froze.

"I was just going to . . ." she said. "Get the registration for you."

A cruiser came down the street fast, lights and siren going, and Mike Abbott pulled up behind Henry's truck and got out with a hand on the butt of his weapon. The lights on the squad car continued to rotate, cutting the night with swaths of blue and red.

"Hang on, Mike," Jim said. "Just checking this out."

Mike nodded, took his hand off his weapon, but stayed where he was.

"I'm going to reach in your glove compartment," Jim told Eileen, "if it's all right with you, and look for that registration."

She nodded jerkily. "S-sure."

"Mommy?" the little girl said in a quavering voice.

"Shh," Eileen said. "Don't talk now." Her daughter shut up, but moved a half step closer, and Eileen took the grocery bag from her, set it down, and put an arm around each of her children.

Jim climbed into the cab, opened the glove compartment, and found the black plastic pouch sitting on top. He examined the document inside under the dome light. Great Seal of Idaho stamped on the paper, *Temporary Notice of Automobile Registration* printed on top, and Eileen's name, address, and the vehicle information handwritten on the form beneath. He put it away again, closed the glove compartment, and climbed out of the truck.

"Looks legit," he told Mike. "The registration."

"It is," Eileen said. "You can ask Hallie. Please."

Jim said, "One minute," pulled his phone out again, and made the call. Four rings. Voice mail. He hung up, waited a second, then redialed, while everybody stood and waited.

Damn it, Hallie, he thought. *Pick up. Either I'm solving about three cases, or I'm the world's biggest prick. And I'd sure like to know which it is.*

◆ ◆ ◆

Hallie was grabbing her laptop bag from the back of the car when the phone rang. She lunged across the front seat for her purse, which had slipped onto the floor, and got whacked in the hip by the car door on the way out. She swore, scrabbled in her messy purse for the phone, finally got her hand on it . . . and it stopped ringing. She dropped it back into her purse and headed for the house. Probably some parent wanting to talk about terrorism some more. Well, she didn't have to answer tonight.

The phone started ringing again, and she swore again, fumbled with her bags and pulled it out, stuck it under her chin, and said, "Hello?"

"Hallie." Not some parent, or, rather, it was. The only one who made her heart flutter.

"Hey," she said. "You forget something?" It came out a little flirtier than she'd intended.

Trying out your pool table with you would be about the finest thing I could imagine.

He said, "Did you know that Eileen Hendricks is driving your father's pickup?"

She blinked. *All righty, then. Not the pool table.* "Yes." She put her key in the lock and opened the front door to an ecstatic Cletus, who was uttering a happy cavalcade of deep-throated barks that drowned Jim out. "Hang on a second."

She dumped her laptop bag and purse on the hall table, told Cletus, "Quiet, you," went into the dining room, dropped into a chair, and struggled to get her boots off with eighty pounds of golden retriever in her face. "All right," she told Jim. "I'm back. What about Eileen and the truck?"

"Is she driving it with your permission?"

"Not exactly. It's hers. I traded her for it. Or rather, I sold it to her. I traded for her dog, but then I thought that might not make it legal, so she paid me a dollar. It's hers. She bought it for a dog and a dollar." She gave Cletus a couple thumps on the shoulder to emphasize her point, which he appreciated.

"Which is what she said," Jim said with what sounded like resignation. "I should have figured."

"Why? Because I'm . . . what? A fool?" It had been too long a day, or maybe it was being back here. She could hear her dad's voice, when she'd tried to argue politics with him at this very table.

Here's how the world really works. You get yours, and that's it. That's what everybody else is trying to do, and don't you ever forget it. You get yours, and you hold on to it, or somebody will take it away from you. They'll be a thief, but you'll be a fool. I'd rather have a thief for a daughter than a fool, so don't let me hear that fool's talk again.

"Wait, though," she said, shoving the memory away. "Are you telling me . . . You didn't pull her over or anything, did you?"

"In a way, yeah. Hang on." She heard the muffled sound of Jim's voice, another, softer one answering, and she was yelling, "Jim! Hey!"

He came back and said, "What?"

"You're kidding me. Put her on."

"It's all good," he said. "We're done. She's free to go."

"Put. Her. *On,*" she said through gritted teeth. "She's about one step from losing it completely, and you pulled her *over?* For *car theft?*"

"I was checking."

"Put her on," she said again. "Right now."

He sighed. "Right. Hang on."

Another voice, then, a tentative one. "Hello?"

"Hey, Eileen," Hallie said. "I'm sorry about that. Don't worry, though. You're all set. And Jim Lawson is an idiot."

"He was checking, I guess."

"Did you get it registered?"

"Yes."

"Good. You bring me those receipts for the registration and the first six months of insurance this weekend, and I'll give you a check."

"Are you sure?"

"I'm sure. I told you. This is helping me as much as it's helping you. Trust me."

"All right," Eileen said. "Thanks. A lot. I mean it. Thanks."

More muffled conversation, then, for a full minute or two, and Jim was on the line again. "OK," he said. "She's gone inside with her kids, and we're all good. And, yes, I apologized. Consider me officially a . . ."

He seemed to be groping for a word, so she said, "I can't wait for you to fill in the blank. I'm glad you apologized to her, but why the heck would you pull her over instead of just calling me?"

"That's forty-five thousand dollars' worth of truck. And what I've wondered about the way your dad died, then the guns . . . when I saw her driving it, too many pieces fell into place."

"Well, those pieces don't fit." She stood up, said, "Hang on" again, and pulled her top over her head, then picked up the phone and shoved it under her ear before unclipping her bra and pulling it off. "OK, I'm back."

"So you traded that primo ride for a dog and a dollar," he said, then started to laugh. "Man, I still feel like a prize jerk, those little kids and all, but I can't help seeing the look on Henry's face."

"Yep." She wriggled her leggings and underwear down her legs, struggled to get them over her feet with one hand, and dropped the phone, which bounced and skittered across the hardwood floor. Cletus ran across, his toenails making an excited *clackety-clack* noise, and barked at it, and Hallie lunged for the phone, picked it up, and said, "Shoot. Sorry. I'm trying to get into the bathtub. Long day."

"Hallie." His voice had lost the laughter. In fact, it was sounding a little strained. "Have you been getting undressed? Just now?"

She should still be upset with him, but he *had* apologized to Eileen. He'd been looking out for her, as he had been all along. And besides . . .

"Why, officer?" she asked. "Is there some law against taking your clothes off while you talk to a man on the telephone?" She bent to pick up her clothes and give Cletus a pat, then sauntered to her bedroom as if Jim were watching. She'd never been a real babe, but when he'd been talking to her tonight, she'd felt like one. And she felt like one now.

"If there isn't," he said, "there should be, because that's cruel and unusual."

She dropped her clothes in the hamper and lowered her voice to a purr. "You going to arrest me?"

She heard the sound of a truck door slamming. "You know," he said, "I've got half a mind to come on over there right now and do just that. For disturbing my peace."

"That is the cheesiest line I've ever heard. Try harder." She sat on the edge of the tub, put the plug in, then turned the faucet to full. "And that's me starting my bath. Gotta go."

"You're going to kill me," she heard, but she was pressing the End button and setting the phone on the counter.

"Cletus," she told the dog, who was sitting right outside the door, waiting politely. "You're still the only man for me, but you've got some real competition."

At the sound of his name, the dog wagged his tail and grinned. "You're right," she said. "I'm being silly. I know it. But it's the closest I've come to sex in almost a year, and it's harmless, because I can't do anything about it anyway."

Harmless or pointless. Or both. She got into the tub, lay back with a sigh, stuck her aching toes gratefully under the running water, and wiggled them. And then she thought about Eileen Hendricks driving down the hill from Henry's house, sitting tall in that big black pickup, and smiled.

DOWN IN FLAMES

Hallie stood in the driveway on Sunday afternoon with one hand on Cletus's collar and waved good-bye to Eileen and the kids while the dog whined and strained against her hold. He'd seemed happy living with Hallie—well, Cletus always seemed happy—but today, he'd wanted to go with his real family. Especially with his kids.

The little girl, Audrey, had been crying when they'd left. Quietly, so nobody would hear her, trying to wipe her tears before her mother saw them. She'd climbed into the truck, though, like she'd accepted that this was what life was going to hand her, and Hallie had wanted to cry herself.

"I know," she told Cletus now, feeling the prick of tears behind her own eyes and hearing his gentle whine. "It stinks."

It wasn't that Eileen was ungrateful. In fact, Hallie couldn't have imagined anybody more grateful. When Hallie had given her the check, Eileen had hugged her in a spontaneous outburst that had been totally unlike her tightly wound demeanor of the week before, and had told her, "I'll never forget this. Never. I'll keep you in my prayers, too. You deserve all good things, and I know you'll get them."

Hallie had wanted to tell her that people didn't necessarily get what they deserved. Eileen already knew that, though, so instead, all she'd done was hug her back and say, "Thank you. I appreciate that."

The truck turned onto the main road and disappeared from sight, and Cletus transferred his attention back to Hallie, looking up at her with his tail waving gently. She said, "Yeah, buddy. Tough stuff," and released his collar. He gave her hand a nuzzle, then leaned hard against her legs and let her thump him.

"Come on," she told him. "Let's go get the mail." She hadn't bothered to look for days. Now, she ran down the driveway with Cletus romping beside her, opened the big black old-fashioned mailbox at the bottom of the drive and pulled out a stack of envelopes and flyers, then headed back up, sorting through it along the way.

"Junk," she told the dog. "What a surprise."

There was one actual letter, though. Her address typed on the envelope, a first-class stamp, but no return address. Probably more junk, disguised to look like something else, but she ripped it open anyway and pulled out the single folded sheet inside.

No salutation, and no signature. Just anonymous typing.

Go home libtard. We dont need more of your kind in Paradise.

"Well, that's nice," she said. "Way to antagonize the local populace, Hallie." She looked at the postmark. Friday. The day after open house. That hadn't taken long.

She went back into the house with Cletus and dumped the rest of the mail into the recycling, almost sent the letter to join it, then hesitated. She'd hang on to it, just in case any of the parents really *did* start complaining to the principal.

What did she care if they did? She was making a whopping eighty-five dollars a day as a sub. She'd earn more waitressing, and it wasn't like she needed the money. And yet . . . and yet, the thought of being driven out of the job, of somebody trying to run her out of town—it stung her pride, and it stung her heart. She was a good teacher, damn it. They'd never get anyone more qualified, and she wasn't going to let somebody win in her life—*again*—just because they were meaner and more ruthless than she was.

She gave the anonymous letter writer her two-word assessment of his or her efforts, stuck the letter into the rack under the wall phone, and forgot it.

◆　◆　◆

The next day, she parked her car as usual in the teacher's lot at Paradise Middle School, opened the back door, snapped Cletus's leash to his collar, and said, "Hop down."

He jumped down and pranced around excitedly, and she said, "You're eight. I feel compelled to point that out."

He looked at her as if he were saying, *So?* She laughed and said, "You're right. Age is just a number. Let's go."

She took off, her running shoes hitting the sidewalk very satisfactorily indeed, and pushed through the initial resistance until her muscles settled into the rhythm. Then it was her usual winding route down Haynes, turning west through the modest houses at the south end of town, finally climbing the hill and heading north again. Down gravel alleys, past neatly tended yards, all quiet in the calm of six twenty in the morning, with barely a car rolling by. Past the purple house that the owners had resolutely kept the same shocking color all these years, on beyond the frame house across from the Presbyterian church that had once been her favorite, with its pointed roof like a steeple of its own. It was looking shabby now. Probably turned into a student rental. That was a shame. It was such a cozy-looking place with its lilac bushes and crabapple tree.

Her breath puffed out in a cloud of vapor, and she took in the deep autumn-blue of the sky, the crisp, spicy aroma of turning leaves, and let the contentment settle into her bones.

Autumn. Her favorite season. Some people thought it was melancholy. Hallie thought it was homey. Autumn in Paradise was red and yellow leaves blazing like flame against the blue sky, the twirling helicopters of maple seedpods drifting around you as you walked from the high school to the library. It was hot cocoa, a woolly afghan, and a fire in your fireplace. It was a cozy interlude before the bleak cold of winter. Although she liked winter, too. Really, every season was beautiful in Paradise.

There was a man stretching against a fence ahead of her. Bouncing on his toes now, facing away from her, then doing a few jumping jacks of the type she hadn't seen since high school PE. Nice shoulders. Great butt. Shorts and a sweatshirt.

Then she came closer, and he turned at the sound of her feet, and it was Jim.

She slowed, then stopped, and he said, "Well, hi."

"Um . . . hi." She hoped she wasn't turning red, and was afraid that she was. But then, it was cool out here, and she'd been running.

Cletus was wagging like crazy, of course, the big doofus, even though he'd never met Jim, and Jim said, "Ah. The trade-in," and gave him exactly the kind of thumps on the shoulder and hind end that a big dog liked best.

"Yep. Cletus. You running?" That was stupid, though. "Well, obviously. Ah . . . is this your house?" Small—tiny, in fact—and modest, but neatly painted, the lawn mowed and the leaves raked. What you'd expect from Jim.

"It is, and I am. Just starting. Want some company?"

"Sure. I'm dropping Cletus at Anthea's, and then ending up back at the school. I guess we're safe running. I mean, running isn't sexual." She was blushing again. She could tell.

All he said, though, was, "Sounds good."

She took off again with him running beside her and said, "I'm sure I'm slow."

"Nah. I don't care."

"Is Mac at home?" That was a safe topic.

He shot a quick glance at her. "Yeah. I've been doing that for a few months if I go out to exercise early. She's asleep, and we have good neighbors. She'll be twelve in a couple months. I come back by seven, and we have breakfast. What do you think?"

"I think you probably know her best."

He said, "Mm," and after a bit, "So. A dog."

"You told me to be careful, so I got a big dog. Aren't you impressed by my ability to follow directions?"

Whoops. She might be flirting again. She got another look for that, and a hint of a smile.

He said, "Now, see, if I didn't know better, I'd think saying that fell into the same category as taking your clothes off while you talked to me on the phone."

"Good thing you know better. This is my guard dog, so watch out." They'd reached Anthea's house, and Hallie ran up the driveway with Jim following, opened the kitchen door, took off Cletus's leash, and hung it over the hook.

Ben was in there, sitting at the kitchen table with a cup of coffee, and Hallie said, "Hey," while Cletus galumphed over, skidded to a stop in front of Ben, and did some wagging.

"Hey," Ben said back. He saw Jim and raised his eyebrows. "Got company?"

"Running company, that's all. Gotta go. See you later."

Ben raised his coffee cup at them, and Hallie closed the door and ran out again, then headed north again, into the classy side of town.

"Yep," Jim said. Hallie was out of breath by now, but he sounded like he was taking a walk. "That's a real killer you've got there. What's he going to do, lick the guy to death?"

"He's got a good bark, though."

"So you leave him at Anthea's during the day?"

"Only Mondays and Wednesdays, when I run out here. Other days, I take him running from the house before work."

He hesitated a moment, then said, "Long time for a dog to be in the house alone, though, isn't it?"

"I put in a dog door."

"Oh. That's good, then. How'd you get that done? I know it wasn't Ben. I love the guy like, well, a brother, but nobody could call him handy. You could've called me."

"I could have. But I did it myself."

"Really."

She looked sideways at him. "You don't have to sound so surprised. A jigsaw, a drill, and some caulk. Half an hour."

"Sorry," he said. "I didn't realize you could. Maybe because you were on that chair with the antelope. Didn't give me the finest impression of your do-it-yourself skills."

"I told you. I didn't want to go into the garage that day. I got over it. I knew how to put in a dog door because my father wanted a son. I can change my own oil, too, not that I do." She debated with herself a minute, then said, "I don't know why my father—*our* father—didn't try to get to know Cole better. It seems like Cole would've been the answer to his prayers, although it's probably just as well for Cole that Dad steered clear. I'm wondering, though, if he did try, and your mom wouldn't allow it."

A long pause, then Jim said, "I'd guess you might be right. And you know—you're so much tougher than you look. I'm realizing that more all the time."

That had her muscles tensing. "Installing a dog door isn't tough. It's just knowledge. Women doing things men have traditionally done— that's not the definition of tough."

"Whoa, there," he said calmly. "No argument from me. I've got a daughter, remember? And I know about all the ways a woman can be strong. The dog door's not what I'm talking about, or not entirely.

Going into the garage, going into teaching, and turning your back on millions of dollars and your dad and everything he stood for—*that's* what I'm talking about."

"Oh." There was that sneaky glow again, lighting her up. It was like he saw her, and admired what he saw, in the same way she kept admiring him more. That was almost harder to fight than the attraction. Almost.

"So Cletus goes to day care two days a week," Jim said after a minute. "That's one lucky dog."

"He does. After I took him, it dawned on me how much more complicated he was going to make my life. But sometimes, complicated is better, you know?"

"Yeah. I do."

"And on Thursdays," she went on, "Eileen brings her little boy out to play with him while she cleans. At least, she has twice now. I thought it would be good, but I suspect it's sad when they have to leave. For them, at least, since Cletus doesn't exactly hang on to the negative thoughts."

"Mm," he said. He was still breathing easily, even though she'd picked up the pace. "That was a good thing you did there. Eileen told me the rest of it, about the registration and insurance and all. I was impressed."

He was doing it again, with the admiration. "I did it for myself as much as for her," she tried to explain. "It made me feel better. The truck, the dog. It was about evening the scales some, that's all."

"Winning. Living in your father's house, and proving that there's another way to live."

"You remember."

He looked at her again. "I remember everything."

Maybe the glow wasn't just in her heart. She upped her speed some more, since they were headed downhill toward the school now, and after a silent block, he asked, "You done anything with that Cadillac of

Henry's yet? You might want to let me know, so I don't pull over any more unfortunate souls. I don't think my own heart can take it. I'd have said I've seen plenty, but her little girl about did me in."

"You thought that, too."

"It's the way she looks at you out of those big eyes like she's trying to be brave. The same way you always looked. Like you didn't expect anything but the worst, and you knew you'd have to take it anyway."

Something was twisting in her chest, tightening her throat. She fought her way past it and said, "That Cadillac has been sitting on the lot at Paradise Motors since Saturday, and I've got some money in my bank account I need to give away."

"Which wouldn't be you doing a good deed. You'd be doing it for yourself again." At her startled glance, he said, "Just trying to get the jump on you."

"That's how it feels. I want to do the right thing with it, though. After what my father did to Eileen and your mother, too . . . I'd like it to be something specifically for women. Something to help."

"Cal Jackson's got a foundation, all about helping underrepresented students go to school in science and engineering. Women, minority students, like that. Cal's kind of a powerhouse with that, no surprise. It's a good deal."

She considered. "Sounds great, but . . . not quite. Maybe, selfishly, because I didn't want to go into science or engineering. I want to . . . *help*. Really help."

He was silent for another half block. She let him think, and finally, he said, "Kayla Jackson—Luke's wife—got some scholarship money a while back. It was for women headed to college when they were older, I think. Single moms, especially. And I know she got help from . . ." He stopped, then went on. "I don't think this is a secret. From a shelter for battered women, when she first came to Paradise. That could be a thought. I could send you the information, if you wanted."

"Yes," she said. "Both. Perfect. Women starting over. Getting a boost to help them build their new lives. Maybe half and half?"

"I think they'd be thrilled. That shelter does important work, but they have to do it on the quiet. I've referred plenty of women to them who didn't think they had any options. I'd guess you could feel good about what you did."

"I won't have done anything. Nothing but write a check."

"No," he said. "*Choosing* to write a check, instead of all the other things you could have done with that money. That's not nothing."

"All right," she said. "Knock it off."

She put on a final sprint down the sidewalk to the pieces of fitness equipment that stood near the entrance to the gym, and he didn't pull ahead, which she appreciated. When she slowed on reaching the black-top and started to walk, he said, "Better tell me what to knock off, or I'll do it again."

"Being so *nice*. All understanding." She got to the slanted sit-up board, looked at him, and said, "Anyway, I thought the bad boys got the hot girls." Then she dropped onto the board, tucked her feet under the bar, crossed her arms over her chest, and started doing sit-ups.

Ha, she thought obscurely. *What are you going to do about that, Deputy?*

What he did was as adolescent as this place. He went over to the bar, jumped up to grab hold, and began doing chin-ups.

He must have finished more than ten when she stopped pretending she was doing sit-ups and just lay there on her board and watched him. His arms were shaking as he lowered himself, and still he hauled himself up another time, and then another and another. Going slowly, but getting there. Biceps swelling, chest heaving. And his T-shirt riding up, showing the end of a thick white scar that ran diagonally down his side.

Quite a performance. Quite a man.

Finally, he dropped to the ground and swung his arms, looking at her, but not saying a word.

She bit her lip, realized she was doing it, and said, "I've wanted to be able to do those."

He shrugged. "It just takes practice. Working up to it. Come on over, and I'll get you started."

She hesitated a second, then got to her feet and came over to stand facing him. Not too close, but then, if he wanted her closer, he knew what to do.

"Right." He put a big hand on either side of her waist and turned her around. Maybe his touch was impersonal, and maybe it wasn't. "I'm going to hoist you up, and you grab hold. Overhand will be easier."

He lifted her, and she grabbed and held on, and so did he. His hands were tight and strong on her waist, and it didn't feel like he was going to be letting go. "We'll do five for right now," he said. "I'll just give you a little boost."

He was right there behind her, lifting and lowering her, as close as he needed to be. Or maybe closer, because every time she dropped, she brushed down his body, and every time she pulled herself up, she brushed up against it again, until he said, "Last one," and lowered her to the ground.

He didn't let go, and she didn't move away.

She was in front of him, their bodies barely touching, but it was enough. His hands were still there, too. He shifted them, and she held her breath. They stopped on her rib cage, stayed there. And she leaned back.

He wrapped one arm around her waist, pulled her in closer, put the other hand under her chin, and turned her head, and all she thought was, *Yes.* And when he kissed her, she gasped again. He had her pressed up tight against him now, he was hot and hard and so solid, and his mouth was as demanding as it had been in her garage. As it had been on the hood of his car.

"We're . . ." she said when he turned her to face him. "We're outside. We can't." But she didn't move.

He looked around. At the door to the gym. "When does security start?"

"Eight." It was a breath.

"Inside." He had her hand, and she pulled her keys out of the pocket of her shorts and shoved one in the lock with a hand that insisted on shaking, and then he followed her in.

The basketball court. Site of school dances she hadn't attended, and school assemblies she had. Bleachers and pine flooring and metal rafters high overhead. And Jim Lawson pushing her up against the concrete-block wall, his hard mouth on hers, his hand inside her shirt, cupping her breast through the sports bra, like the high school dream she'd never dared to have.

He had a hand underneath her, was hauling her up higher, grinding into her, and she was whimpering.

"C-cameras," she finally managed to say. "Come on."

She led him through another door, down another echoing hallway. A push of a door. "No cameras in here," she said. The girls' locker room.

He didn't answer. He had his arm around her again, his other hand behind her head, and he was kissing her again, too. Backing her up, right through another doorway. Into the shower room. And then into a tiled cubicle.

He had her T-shirt up before she could blink, and was yanking it off before she could protest. Not that she felt capable of it. He looked at her bra, said, "How?" and she said, "Hooks. In back," and he was unfastening them, tossing it on top of the shirt.

"I'm . . . sweaty," she said weakly.

He didn't even listen to that. He was kissing her again, his mouth taking hers like it was the only thing possible, his hand on her breast, teasing, playing, pinching, and she was moaning.

"Got to . . ." he said. "Got to do this." He was wrestling her capri pants down her legs, then dropping to his knees, still fully dressed, was yanking off her shoes and socks, then pulling her pants and underwear down the rest of the way, and off.

"Oh, man," she moaned. "Oh, man. Jim."

That was when they heard it. The *swish* of a closing door. The footsteps. Jim looked up at her, and she stared back at him, frozen.

He stood and pulled the white shower curtain closed without making an effort at quiet, then put a finger to his lips. They stood still and heard the *clang* of a locker door, some rustling.

One second, two, then Jim reached around her and yanked the faucet on. When the cold water hit, she jumped and started to yelp, but Jim had a hand over her mouth. He'd moved so fast, she hadn't seen it happen, and she sucked in a breath again beneath his hard palm, her eyes widening with shock.

The water got warmer. It was soaking her pile of clothes, there on the floor. Jim dropped his palm from her mouth, and she pulled his head down and said in his ear, "You're getting wet."

He didn't answer, but his eyes were burning her up, and there was nothing nice about him now. He shoved her shoulders back against the tile with one hand, ran the other one down her body like it was his, went to the right spot, and did some hard exploring. She stiffened and squirmed in shock, and something more, too, and his lips were brushing her ear when he murmured, "So are you."

"We . . ." She started to say. There was a noise from outside again, like the person had left, maybe, but the thought was vague. It couldn't make it through the noise of the running water. Or the roaring in her head.

Jim was fully under the spray, and not even seeming to notice. He still had all his clothes on, and she tried to get his T-shirt off, but he was already dropping to his knees again, out of her reach. In another two seconds, she lost the power of thought, because his hands and mouth and tongue were on her, just like that. Demanding, and taking. Her toes were curling against the hard tile, and she had her own hand over her mouth now, just in case somebody was out there. Somebody who could hear what Jim was doing to her, and the response she couldn't hold back.

She'd never been somebody who could relax and let loose easily. Not with a man, for sure. She always started out self-conscious, worried about what he was thinking, how she looked to him, how long she was taking, whether she was doing it right.

She wasn't self-conscious now. She was standing up, leaning against the wall of a shower with her legs spread and a man on his knees in front of her, working her over fast and hard. One of her hands was frantically trying to curl into his short hair, while her other fist was stuffed into her mouth.

And still he kept on. No letup. No choice. No mercy.

She was making some noise now, trying to muffle it, hoping there wasn't anybody out there, or hoping the water would drown it out, and then forgetting to worry about that, too. Her legs were stiffening, and everything in her was tightening, drawing in, driving her higher. When he thrust two fingers inside her, she stiffened more. He started to move them, increased the tempo, was doing it all harder, just at the edge of rough, and she was yelling into her hand. Shaking, spasming, her head hitting the tile, again and again. Going over. Going fast. Going hard.

Down in flames.

FLINGING

Jim was soaking wet. He was aching hard. He was burning hot.

Hallie's body was convulsing around him, over him. He could hear the cries she was trying to suppress, and the sound was so sweet. The pounding water was trying to drown him, and so was she.

He stayed with her until she was all the way done and headed down the other side, until the spasms had turned to quivers, and then he got to his feet, put a hand against her shoulder, and bent to say in her ear, "How you doing?"

She was limp, shaking, her palms pressed against the shower wall. Her curvy, pale body stretched against the white tile, her red-gold hair in wilder ringlets than ever. It hadn't gotten wet, not the way his had. But then, she hadn't been the one kneeling under the spray.

Maybe next time. A thought that did him no good at all.

She didn't answer, just put a trembling hand on the back of his neck, pulled his head down to hers, and kissed him, long and deep. And he was falling again. Or still.

He pulled away from her with the last ounce of willpower he possessed and whispered, "Gotta go."

He didn't have a condom. He didn't have time. They didn't have privacy. It was a killer.

It took her a second, but she nodded, and he reached out and shoved the faucet closed. They both stood still, the silence echoing around them, and Jim listened hard. Heard nothing.

He shoved the shower curtain back with a rattle of rings, then listened again. Hallie whispered, "Wait," and stepped out of the shower and into the empty room.

She still looked shaky to him. She still looked great. He was looking at her from behind, and it was a view he liked just fine. Her skin was rosy from the warm water, from her orgasm, from the pressure of the tile against her back. And against her ass, which was round, pink, and terrific. And he wanted it.

She walked to the edge of the locker room, out of sight from where he waited inside the cubicle, dripping in his sweatshirt, shorts, and running shoes. Finally, she said quietly, "Nobody here."

He stepped over the sodden mass of her clothes and joined her. She turned to look at him, and he grinned. He couldn't help it. He was frustrated beyond belief. He was aching with need. And he was damn happy.

"Baby," he said, pulling her close, "you sure know how to show a man a good time."

"Shh," she said, and then spoiled it by giggling.

Yep. He had Hallie Cavanaugh in the girls' locker room, stark naked, hauled up tight against his body and giggling, all pink and relaxed and glowing from the rocking orgasm he'd just given her.

Were high school fantasies great or what?

◆ ◆ ◆

Of course, the rest of it wasn't as much fun. He was wet, and it was cold out, but he'd been wet and cold before. He did a few more chin-ups on his way out, just to work off some of the . . . adrenaline. Then he ran home, warming up some more, and tried not to think about Hallie. He walked through the back door, and Mac looked up at him from the kitchen table and said, "You're super late. And why are you *wet?*"

"Ah . . ." he said, feeling as guilty as if he'd been caught . . . well, there was really no equivalent. "Ran through a sprinkler."

"Why?"

He shook his head and said, "I don't know. Silly, huh," then bent over and kissed her on top of the head where she sat, her hair a mess, eating her cereal.

She gave him a shove on the shoulder. "*Dad.* Ew. You're *soaked.*"

"I'm going to hop in the shower," he said. "Then I'll do your hair. We'll keep it simple today."

Back to normal. Or not.

Once he had Mac out the door and himself on the road, he looked at the clock on the dash. Just after eight. Class wouldn't have started yet.

No texting. Texting left a trail.

A little late to be thinking about that, Lawson.

He voice dialed her, and as he drove and listened to the phone ringing, he was smiling. And he was nervous.

Basically, he was a mess.

She didn't even say hello. She just said, "I thought you weren't that guy anymore. That you'd changed."

"Turns out not so much. Anyway, it worked, didn't it? I got you."

"You did." He heard the sigh in her voice, and now, there was no question about it, he was smiling like a loon.

"You know," he told her, "the second I start talking to you, it's like somebody flips a switch."

"And what?"

"And I'm turned on."

"Oh." It was another sigh. "You didn't quite . . . get me, though."

239

"I noticed. I had some . . ." He had to stop and breathe. "Some ideas about that."

"We can't." She was back to that brisk voice. Her teacher voice. "That was incredibly reckless. I told you—there are cameras in the gym. And kissing like that? Outside? I can't *believe* I did that."

"Nobody was there," he pointed out. "Besides, Virgil Owens is the security officer out there, and ol' Virge never does a single thing he doesn't have to. Long as nobody tells him he has a chance of seeing a half-naked woman on that footage, he's not going to check. Couple days, and it's recorded over anyway."

"I wasn't half naked," she said. "I was dressed."

And getting kissed hard and felt up good against the wall, which Virgil would've watched without any objection at all. She was right. It had been reckless.

Too bad it had felt so good.

"What if somebody had come into the shower room, though?" she went on, sounding troubled. "I'd have lost my job. Not to mention . . ."

"Yeah. This is the problem with not actually being in high school anymore. Consequences."

"We can't do this."

"Man," he sighed, "I was afraid you'd say that." He wasn't smiling now. *Damn* it.

"It's not worth it," she said. "Not for a fling."

"And that's what it would be?"

"Wouldn't it? I know you want that fling, and so do I. It almost seems good, doesn't it, because it would have to be discreet, and it would have to be short, and that's perfect for you, I'm sure." He was going to answer that, but she was still talking. "But it's not worth it, not if anybody finds out. Not even thinking about the money—what about your mother? Your brother? Who's *my* brother. And, all right, the money. I'm pretty sure this would count as a sexual relationship, even what we've . . . done already."

"Yeah," he said. "That's what Anthea said."

"You *told* her?" No teacher voice now. She sounded pure-redhead furious. "How could you *do* that?"

"Whoa, now, Red. I asked her, that's all."

"When?" Still fired up.

"That first day. After the bear."

"You asked her *what?*"

"What a . . ." He cleared his throat. "What would be the definition of a sexual relationship. And she said oral sex counted. Ah, specifically, I think she said oral and . . . manual."

She moaned. "I cannot believe you had this conversation with my best friend."

"Well," he tried to point out, "she's my twin, you know? And it's not like she didn't know. Or like she's going to tell anybody but Ben."

"Well, it doesn't matter anyway." She was back to brisk. "We can't do it. No way. This has to stop. That fling? It's not worth it. Not for either of us."

"Henry's money," he said. "Yeah, well, guess I can't compete with that."

"Jim—" she said. "Shoot. I have to go."

"Yeah. Me, too. See you around."

He hung up and thought, *That went well.*

It almost seems good, she'd said, *because it would have to be short.*

A few months long, to be exact.

COMMIES BURN

When Jim stopped by the office to drop off some paperwork on Thursday afternoon, DeMarco looked up from his desk.

"Hey," he said. "I thought you knew that Cavanaugh girl. Daughter of that guy who drowned on the ice cube, the one who's back in town now? Didn't you have her dad's guns, or something? And somebody tried to rip them off?"

"Hallie?" Jim's antennae went up fast. "Why?"

"I heard there was something in his will, too," DeMarco said. "A whole lot in there, in fact. Not to poke into your family business. But I guess you two are keeping your distance now, since the guns and all. Selling the guns for her wasn't what you'd call discreet. I suppose that's why she didn't call you this time."

Jim was cold, but he was burning, too. "Call me about what? What happened?"

DeMarco shrugged. "She got some anonymous letters, that's all. Maybe just stuff to do with school, she thought. She called in this morning, and I took it. Didn't seem like much of a deal, but Franks is headed out to talk to her."

"No," Jim said. "I am."

"Franks is already on it."

"Yeah, well, I'm calling him right now and telling him to forget it, because I'm on it."

DeMarco leaned back in his chair and studied him. "You know," he said slowly, "when Carrie tried to set you up with her friend that time, when you came to dinner at our house, and you didn't follow it up? She said maybe it was just as well, because you'd probably be too hot for that Rebecca to handle. And I said, 'Lawson? Dudley Do-Right? Mr. Mom? Mr. By the Book?' And *she* said—"

"I don't care what she said. I'm going to check it out."

"She said she'd be at—"

"At school. I know. I'm already gone."

"If you're not supposed to be getting involved," DeMarco called after him, "looks to me like you're doing lousy. Just saying."

◆　◆　◆

Jim entered the school the right way this time. Through the front door, and then down the hall to room 115. He rapped a couple times with his knuckles on the half-open door, then poked his head around. "Hallie?"

She'd been typing furiously on her laptop, but she jerked her head up with a start, then sat back and said, "Oh. Jim. You startled me."

Her eyes slid away from his, though. *Right*, he thought. *Off-limits.*

"You called in about some letters," he said.

"Oh." A crease appeared between her eyes. "I talked to somebody else, though."

"Yep. But turns out you've got me. Which is good, because if you're getting threatening letters, I want to see them. Being familiar with the situation and all. Why didn't you tell me?"

She gave a little laugh, shoved her hair back, and pushed back from the desk in her rolling chair. "I am. I mean, I reported it. And you're right, we're both adults. We can move on. Come on. I'll show you."

He crossed the room, pulled a chair over from a nearby table, and said, "Show me."

She seemed a little distracted. She was looking at his body or something.

"Sorry," she said. "It's just so different to see you in uniform, with all the gear. Is it heavy?"

"Nah." All right, not his body. Unfortunately. "Not compared to Ranger gear. That could be thirty pounds."

"Oh." She swallowed. "I guess that's why you'd have to be so strong."

"That would be it. Are we talking . . . Hallie." He went for stern, just in case. "Are you saying you think men in uniform are hot?"

"Ah . . ." She was definitely getting pink, and then she caught that lip in her teeth, and he reminded himself that he *was* in uniform. And on duty. And that there was such a thing as 'conduct unbecoming an officer.'"

"Tell me it's the handcuffs," he said, losing the battle, "and you'll make my day."

"I didn't say it was the . . ." She swallowed. "Handcuffs." The word was a whisper.

Oh, yeah. It was the handcuffs.

Focus, Lawson. Conduct unbecoming. "Not that I'm hating talking about this," he said, "and I'd like to get back to it real soon, but I do want to know about those letters."

"Oh. Sure. Right." She swiveled around and bent to unlock her desk drawer, coming out with a stack of white envelopes. She started to hand them to him, but he said, "Hang on," reached into a pocket for some disposable gloves, then took the envelopes, handling them by the edges. "Probably won't get anything off these," he told her, "but you never know."

"I didn't even think of that."

"Well, you'll have a mail handler, then a mail carrier," he said absently, "and even an idiot has heard of prints. But just in case."

He'd pulled the first letter out, now—first by the postmark, anyway. It didn't take long to read.

Go home libtard. We dont need more of your kind in Paradise.

Hallie had come around to sit beside him, reading over his shoulder. "I thought that one was about the open house," she said, and he tried to ignore her breath, soft and warm against his neck. And her scent. Somehow, she still smelled like flowers. "It came on Saturday, postmarked Friday, that next day. But then I got this one on Monday."

She pointed to the second envelope, and he pulled that letter out. Short again.

Commies burn in hell. Sometimes before they get there. Your father died in you're house. You could too.

"That's a very weird thing to write," Hallie said. "Don't you think? Maybe it still has to do with school, the 'commie' part, but . . ."

"Mm," Jim agreed, noting the tingle at the back of his neck. That tingle was information, and it had nothing to do with how he felt about Hallie. The lurch in his gut, on the other hand, was something more primitive—and more personal. He opened the third letter. "When did this one come?"

"Yesterday. This is why I called. This seemed to really get into . . . threat territory."

You don't listen, do you? Could be well have to find another way to get thru to you. Don't worry. Well find it.

"I know they're just letters," she said. "And a couple of my students *are* hostile. Their parents could be, too. But what do you think?"

"You know what's weird about these?" he said.

"Yes, that they're being sent at all. I didn't work in what anybody would call a 'good' school in Seattle, but I've never had anything like this."

"There's that," he conceded. "But mainly . . . it's that somebody's *trying* to make you think that they're some Idaho redneck, when they're not."

"How can you tell?"

He set all three of the letters down flat on the desk, one on top of the other, so all of the simple sentences were visible.

"First letter has 'don't' without the apostrophe," he pointed out. "Second and third letter, though, you've got the apostrophe again. First one has 'your' with no apostrophe, which is right, and the second has it spelled Y-O-U-R-E. It's like they're trying to pretend they don't know how to spell it, instead of *really* not knowing how to spell it. Then the third letter leaves out the apostrophe again, in 'we'll.' You get the feeling that's their big tell of who's a redneck or not—the apostrophe. But they've forgotten which way they did it before. And they used the comma here, see? 'You don't listen, comma, do you?' That's not an . . . not uneducated punctuation."

"I never thought I'd hear Jim Lawson use the phrase 'uneducated punctuation,'" Hallie said.

His head shot up, and now, *he* was the one who was frowning. "Because I'm dumb, maybe."

"No!" She looked horrified. "No. Of course not. Obviously you aren't dumb. You noticed this, and I didn't. Something felt off, but I couldn't have said what."

"It's my job." He was studying the letters again. "I don't think of this—sending letters—as the kind of thing somebody would do if they hated what you were teaching, or how you were teaching it. They'd be getting together with the other parents, going to the principal. They'd be *talking*, not being anonymous. Why be anonymous?"

"You're right," she said. "People who are very ideological—they *want* you to know what they think. They want to engage you. They want to argue."

"So have you had anything like that? You had your phone number up there on the board the other night. Any calls? Anybody going to the principal?"

She shook her head. "No. But everyone knows that calls can be traced. If you wanted to do something threatening, you wouldn't do it on the phone, and Paradise isn't exactly full of pay phones. Same thing with e-mail. You could send one from computers at the library, maybe, but—the library's small, too. Not anonymous. And e-mail leaves a trail."

"Yep. It does." He replaced the letters in their envelopes. "You got a big envelope or something that I could put these in?"

"Sure." She rummaged around again and found a folder. "Will this do?"

"Yeah. Just don't want to smear them around any more than they have been."

He put them carefully into the folder and removed the gloves, and when he didn't say anything else, she asked, "What are you thinking?"

"That these have nothing at all to do with your teaching, whatever smoke screen the person's trying to throw out. Never heard of anything like that, and we have a lot of liberal teachers. You get that in a university town. Besides, you're a sub, here for a few months. Why would anybody get their panties in a wad? I don't think they're about that at all. I think they're about the same thing as the guns."

"The guns weren't about making me leave town, though."

"But they *were* about money. They were about somebody who knew what was in Henry's house—which wasn't hard to know—and where it was going, which was a little harder to know. Either a target of opportunity, or not. These letters . . ." He tapped the folder with a finger. "If they're trying to scare you into leaving town, and thinking that'll make you do it—well, first, they don't know you very well."

"They could think they know me fine. I never used to be anything you could call tough. I'm not that tough now, for that matter."

"No? Not what I'd say. I'd say that everything you've done so far, here in town and before you came back, shows that you know your own mind, and you don't mess around. You've been here a month, and you've sold off or given away half of Henry's house. And these things—" He tapped the folder again. "How do they make you feel? Like running?"

"No," she said. "Like staying."

"Because that's the part of your old man you *did* end up with. But sometimes, people think things like what you've done are weak, not strong. So that's how they could be looking at that. But I'd ask—who'd want you to leave? Somebody who benefits if that happens, most likely. Somebody who knows you had half a mind not to stay. Somebody who's going to get millions, maybe, if you go. And maybe who's also thinking that you don't deserve those millions. Because there's hostility in those letters. That part—that didn't feel fake."

"Which would mean . . ."

"Anybody who was in Bob Jenkins's conference room that day."

She said, speaking slowly, "The main person who would benefit if I left, of course, would be Cole."

"Trust me," he said grimly, "that's occurred to me."

"But if the guns weren't just a target of opportunity," she said, "that makes it different. One thing was as direct as it could be, and this, the letters, is so indirect. Sort of soft, really. Anyway, you wouldn't have *two* people doing . . . some kind of crimes, even for money. Not in that little group. This isn't some English mystery novel, it's normal people. Cole might be resentful, but he seemed awfully normal to me. Normal fifteen-year-old boys from strong families who do well in school—*does* he do well in school?"

"He does great, actually. In most subjects. Not too interested in English, maybe, but I'd guess he knows how to use an apostrophe."

She nodded. "Well, teenage boys like that—they don't typically have criminal connections they can call on at a moment's notice to steal major firearms, in my experience. Boys in a gang, sure, but Cole? No."

"You known lots of boys in gangs?"

"More than my share," she said, and he thought, *Yeah. Seattle.* He still tended to think of her as Henry Cavanaugh's sheltered daughter—and so did somebody else, he'd bet—but she wasn't that. Not anymore.

He said, "Which leaves, of course . . ."

"Well, your mother," she said. His head went up at that. "But—same thinking. Your mother might write a few letters to make me leave town, but she wouldn't send scary people to your house to rob her own son with her granddaughter in the house. At least the woman I remember wouldn't have done that."

"No," Jim said. "She sure wouldn't. If she wanted money that bad, she'd have gotten it out of Henry. She didn't do that, though, because it would've hurt Cole. She's not a ruthless woman. She's never been that."

"Obviously. Or she wouldn't have raised you and Anthea so well."

"I wasn't what you'd call a model citizen."

"But you are now."

"Well, could be. And maybe not. Considering, ah, recent events."

The pink was rising in her cheeks again. She was still scooted close, half turned to face him. He'd noticed what she was wearing the second he'd seen her. A long, stretchy top with skinny black and white stripes, with black leggings underneath it, and black boots this time. She looked curvy. She looked sweet. She looked good enough to eat.

So to speak.

"Know what DeMarco—the deputy you talked to—called me today?" he asked her.

"No, what?"

He smiled ruefully. "Dudley Do-Right."

"Ha. Shows how well he knows you. Dudley *Do*-Me-Right, maybe."

"Man," he said, still looking at her, because he liked doing it, "that's a nice image."

"You're staring at me that way again," she said. Her voice was husky, and he loved it.

"What way?"

"Like you want to . . ." Her cheeks were even pinker now, her breath coming fast. "Eat me up."

"Ah. Yeah. Well . . . could be." He didn't say, *Maybe because I remember how good you taste. And all that noise you have to make while I do it.* But he thought it.

"We can't." She didn't move, though, and she was breathing too hard all of a sudden.

He rubbed a hand over the back of his head and tried to get a grip on himself. He was in uniform. He was on duty. "Yeah," he said, and stood up, since she wasn't going to. "But tell you what. Let's maybe put some security cameras up at your place. Just in case. I don't like that 'commies burn' idea."

"I'll do that." *Now,* she stood up, walked around her desk again, and put space between them.

"And," he said, "think about your aunt and uncle."

She wasn't pink anymore. She was looking troubled again. "I was trying not to."

"The letters—that could be her. Faye. Seems like something she'd do. Although maybe a little sneaky for her. All that messing around with the grammar. I'm guessing she'd just be flat-out poison."

"My uncle, though? He's my *uncle.* He's always been nice to me. Not going out of his way, but still. Nice. Softer than my dad. And Faye—do you think she'd be able to arrange for the guns? I don't think she'd do that. That would seem so . . . dirty, to her, I think. Too lowlife. Too messy."

"Could be," he said. "We're guessing here, on all counts. Get those cameras. You need any help installing them—call me."

"Or not. It'd be a bad idea for me to invite you over. I think that's obvious." She was looking wary now, and that was—well, it was annoying. Or more than that.

"Let's get one thing straight," he said. "If you tell me that's it—that's it. I have a mother. I had a wife. I have a daughter. If you say yes, I'll be pushing it all the way. And the minute you say no, it's no. If you don't believe I mean that, you don't know me at all."

"Jim." She wasn't looking wary anymore. Distressed, he'd call that. "No. Of course not. It's not . . . not you I don't trust."

"Oh." His muscles relaxed, and then they didn't, once he thought over what she was saying. He had to get out of here, and he didn't want to.

Focus. It's your job. It's her safety. That tingle at the back of his neck? It was real. "I'm going," he said in order to make himself do it. "I'll let you know if we lift any prints, and you let *me* know if you get more letters. Don't open them, even if you just *think* that might be what they are. Drop them by the station with a note on them that they're for me. And if you talk to either of those two—your aunt and uncle—it might not hurt to tell them about the cameras. Just in case."

DANCING AROUND IT

Hallie did that the very next week, because her aunt and uncle had invited her to dinner again on the following Friday. Something she hadn't been looking forward to at all, but on the other hand—they *were* her aunt and uncle.

Her uncle, at least, seemed to feel the same way, because after some stilted early conversation, he finally said, "I'm sorry we got off on the wrong foot last time, Hallie. Those guns were—well, I guess I was startled, that's all. But I hope we can leave that in the past. Family's family, after all. The more I think about that, the more I know it's true."

"You're right," Hallie said, taking another bite of the tuna-noodle casserole, complete with peas and crushed cornflakes on top. "And you and my mother are all the family I have left, other than Cole, of course."

She said it from defiance, and to hear the reaction. Faye's mouth hardened some, but Dale said, "That's true. And he's *our* family now, too, isn't he? That's a strange thought."

"As much as I am," Hallie said. "Maybe we should do something about that." *You're an adult,* she'd thought the night before. *Time to act like one. You don't like the situation? Take it in two hands and change it.* "How about you two coming to my place next time for dinner? It's about time I paid you back for your hospitality, and I can show you what I've done with the house. I thought I could invite Cole, along with Anthea and her husband and the kids. That might break the ice—and maybe make it easier for Cole, too, if he had his *other* sister there. It feels pretty strange for me even to say that, but how much stranger must it be for him? At least I'm an adult, and I knew my father. And on a lighter note," she said, seeing Dale's troubled expression and Faye's intent eyes, "it could be my first dinner party. So far, the only meal I've eaten with anybody out at the house is pizza. Pretty sorry showing for a new homeowner."

"Would that be with Jim Lawson?" Faye asked, her tone nothing but sweet. "I heard you were running through town with him last week. *Very* early in the morning. You're such a big exerciser now, aren't you? I guess that's how you've gotten rid of most of that puppy fat you used to carry. I was so glad to see it. Losing weight isn't easy, I know, especially when you've always had that smidge extra. It's almost like you feel destined to stay just a teeny bit overweight. I'm so glad to see you're starting to push past that. Pizza, though—you'll want to watch what you eat, especially now that you're getting older. 'A moment on the lips, a lifetime on the hips.'" She sighed. "Isn't it the sad truth?"

Hallie's knees pressed together under the table. *Puppy fat? That smidge extra?* She had to force herself to ignore it and speak calmly. "Thank you. It hasn't been too hard, fortunately. I find I enjoy it. I did see Jim one morning, and we ran together for a ways. He's incredibly fit, but he slowed down and kept me company, which was nice of him. He had some good tips for me on my upper-body strength, too," she threw in, just in case anybody had witnessed the chinning-bar scene. "And, yes, he and Anthea had pizza at my house the day the will was read. They helped me clean up after the sheriff's department did their investigation. The house was a mess. There was fingerprint dust everywhere, for one thing."

"Goodness," Faye said. "I hadn't heard about that. We *wondered* what was taking so long, getting the . . ." She touched her napkin to her lips. "Body released. Did they find anything suspicious, then? That's the first I've heard of it. I thought Henry fell and hit his head, so why on earth would they be looking for fingerprints?"

Dale's fork jerked, and some noodles fell onto his plate.

Faye said, "I'm sorry, hon. I know it's upsetting." She took her hand out of her lap and put it on her husband's. "But there poor Hallie is, having to face it every day. No wonder if she wants some company to make her feel more . . . secure." Her round blue eyes rested on Hallie again.

"I did, that day," Hallie said. "Thank goodness Anthea and Jim were willing to come over and help me out for a few hours. And as for what the sheriff's department found—I know they had questions and weren't completely satisfied, but I guess they didn't find anything conclusive, or they wouldn't have said it was an accident. Isn't that what they told you?"

She looked inquiringly at Dale, and he shook his head and said, "That's what they told me, all right. Accident. Said he choked, then tripped and fell. I was never aware that they thought it could be anything else, but I guess they have to check every possibility, especially with a man of Henry's stature. He had enemies, no doubt about it. I suppose that's the curse of the successful man."

"I'm surprised you didn't ask Jim about it, Hallie," Faye said. "After he went to so much trouble with those guns and all. He went around checking up, too, after somebody tried to steal them, did he tell you that? He wasn't in uniform, though, which we thought was strange, didn't we, hon? Like it was personal, not official at all. And I know you have those crazy terms in the will," she told Hallie, "and that word's gotten around, so—just a tiny hint—you might want to watch that. People can be so suspicious."

"Honey," Dale protested, "he told us why. It wasn't his jurisdiction."

"There was an official report, yes," Hallie said. "To the Paradise PD. Jim told me about it." *After* she'd confronted him with the knowledge, but still. "But since it happened on his property, I suspect he *did* take it personally and put some extra time into it on his own. I know he wasn't one bit happy about it, especially coming so soon after my father's death."

"He's the quiet type," Dale said, "but I don't think he'd be a good enemy. My gosh." He shook his head. "If you're saying there might have been something suspicious about Henry's passing—that puts a new spin on things. Huh. Jim Lawson. That sure is a thought."

"What's a thought?" Hallie asked. "That Jim had something to do with my father's death? And that he arranged for somebody to steal my father's guns?"

"Whoa, now," Dale said. "I'm not making any accusations. But you do have to wonder, when you put it that way. *Did* somebody try to steal Henry's guns? I didn't get the impression that anybody but Jim saw it happen, and the Paradise PD never came by here to ask us, either. Are you sure he actually filed a report and didn't just question a couple people who'd get back to you with it? I don't want to bring up episodes from the past that might be painful, but Jim sure could have a grudge against your dad, and against you, too. I think you might want to keep that in mind. Going forward, if you want to put it that way."

He looked at Hallie, and she couldn't read his expression one bit, but—her father had told his brother what had happened? If he had, Dale would have told Faye. How much?

It was fourteen years ago, she tried to tell herself. She did her best to will her face into serenity but was sure she wasn't doing it well enough. How could she, with Faye watching her so sharply?

Faye said, "Well, since you mention it, Dale—I'll admit I was surprised, Hallie, to find that you and Jim had been so . . . *close* since you came back. I hope I'm a forgiving woman, but I'm not sure I could've forgiven all that."

All that.

Hallie groped for something—anything—to say. Her heart was beating too hard. She realized she was still holding her fork and set it down carefully across her plate, leaving her casserole unfinished, because her stomach was a lump of lead. She couldn't talk to them about this. Instead, she changed the subject. "I think that attempted burglary might have made the sheriff's department more suspicious about my father's death, yes. And then I've been getting anonymous letters, too. Four of them, now. It's like somebody wants me to leave town."

"What kind of letters?" Dale asked, looking concerned.

"You could call them threatening," Hallie said. "About how I'm a left-wing nut job, and how I'm unwelcome in town, and how I'd better get out before I get hurt like my father did. Which the sheriff's department thinks is *very* interesting, and so did Bob Jenkins when I told him, just in case I *did* have to leave town for my own safety. I know it sounds crazy, but I thought it was best to take precautions. But here's what I don't understand. It's almost like the person is *trying* to point out that there was something fishy about my father's death, which seems pretty stupid to me if something actually happened out there that night. But if that's it—I guess they don't realize that I inherited more than his house. Seems I've got his stubborn streak, too, because I'm not going anywhere. I've got his burglar alarm, and I've installed security cameras. It's pretty much a fortress over there."

"Goodness," Faye said. "That sounds like overkill to me. Haven't you got the kids talking about all sorts of things over at the school? I'm sure that's what it is. People can get so bent out of shape over politics."

"They can," Hallie said. "Like you said—it can get almost personal."

SANGRIA

It was when Hallie considered giving Cletus a bath that she faced facts.

Here she was, the day after her dinner with her aunt and uncle, looking at another Saturday night alone at home. She'd done her grading already, had taken Cletus for a brisk, late-autumn romp among the cedars on Paradise Mountain, then had come home, had a leisurely bath with a loofah scrub, and given herself a manicure and pedicure. Now she had pink cheeks, smooth skin, pretty fingers and toes, and nobody to show any of it to.

She should cook dinner, but she didn't feel like it. Another meal at the kitchen counter with a book? Not happening. Instead, she went downstairs with Cletus padding after her, turned on some music, and played a game of pool on the new table that had been delivered a few days earlier.

When she finished, she looked at Cletus, curled up in the corner of the room, and said, "You want a bath?"

His ears pricked, his tail thumped against the new gray carpeting, and she sighed. "You know what?" she told him. "I'm bored, and I'm lonely."

Perk up, she told herself. *You're an independent, successful woman. You have a career. You have friends. You have a life.*

In Seattle.

"You're right," she told Cletus. "That's feeling sorry for myself. Staying was my choice, and I still have a career of sorts. I have students who need me. I have a house, too. I even have a friend. Besides you, I mean."

She followed her newfound resolution back upstairs with Cletus once again behind her, went in search of her phone and finally found it in the kitchen, and called Anthea.

"Hey," she said when Anthea picked up. "Want to go out for a drink with me, watch me troll for hot boys, and pretend to be jealous that you're married when you're actually grateful you're not single? Which is a long way of saying I'm bored."

That sounded bright and breezy. And not desperate.

"You've never trolled for boys in your life," Anthea said. "And, shoot, I'm sorry, hon. I can't. We're about to do a family movie night. You want to come over?"

The thought of being a fifth wheel in Anthea's happy family wasn't one bit appealing, no matter how many times Hallie had done it before. She normally didn't feel so . . . *alone,* though.

It was being back here. In Paradise, Saturday night and nothing to do, convinced that everybody else was out there dancing and kissing and being a wild, reckless teenager, and only pale, geeky, redheaded Hallie Cavanaugh was in her bedroom with a book.

She wasn't seventeen anymore, though, and she didn't have to travel in a pack, even a pack of two. If she wanted company, she could go where people were. All right, maybe not a bar, but she could at least go *out.*

"Hey," Anthea prodded. "You still there? You coming over or what?"

"No. Thanks," Hallie said, adding hastily, "I'm sure it'll be super fun."

"Yeah, right. So what are you gonna do?"

"I'm going to Sangria Station," Hallie decided on the spur of the moment. "I'm going to eat something delicious that I didn't cook myself, drink sweet Spanish wine, *not* look at college students and fifty-five-year-old guys, because why bother, and convince myself all the same that they think I'm hot and mysterious and that they want me. And before you say anything—you're right, it's not the big time. I'm not walking into a cowboy bar, but, hey—you always say I'm too cautious, so this is the new me. Baby steps."

"I'm sure they *will* want you," Anthea said. "Wear a short skirt, and they'll want you in a hot minute, because men are easy. I know you'll stay safe."

Anthea knew her too well.

"Right," Hallie said. "I'm getting pretty. I'm adjusting my attitude. Watch my smoke."

◆ ◆ ◆

Jim was pouring himself a beer when the phone rang.

"Hey, Jimbo," came his twin's breezy voice. "Whatcha doing?"

"You know what I'm doing. Kicking back, since I'm not on dad duty. And no, you don't have to invite me over. I'm good." Maybe he was and maybe he wasn't. He wasn't telling Miss Manager.

"Oh," she said. "Too bad. I thought you might be company for Hallie. She's out there at Sangria Station by herself, and I don't know." Her sigh came right down the line. "I feel like she's in a dangerous mood, you know? Like she might be going to do something stupid. I know she's not supposed to get involved with you, but the will didn't say anything about anybody else. She doesn't have great judgment with guys, like I mentioned. Ben was thinking we should set her up with this new math professor. Maybe we could have a dinner party, or as close as we come. Would you be willing to babysit next Saturday?"

"No," Jim said. "I'm hanging up now."

"Nice," Anthea was saying, but Jim had already done it.

◆ ◆ ◆

When Anthea set the phone down, Ben, who was taking the popcorn out of the microwave and emptying it into a bowl, raised his eyebrows at her. "I thought that was the whole deal," he said. "That they wouldn't."

"Well . . ." Anthea pulled a couple beers out of the fridge and three chilled mugs out of the freezer. "I ask myself, what does Hallie need most, millions of dollars or a good man? And what does my twin need more, a good woman or another lonesome night on his couch watching ESPN? And I answer myself, too. Or maybe it's just a night out for both of them. Keeping each other company for a while. Keeping the ghosts away."

"Maybe you should let them decide for themselves," Ben said, "not open up a whole can of worms."

Cole, who was pouring his own Coke into one of the mugs, snorted, then said, "Or open a can of 'Welcome to Tahiti' for me, maybe. Way to invite her without asking me, too."

Anthea looked at him measuringly. "She's your sister, exactly as much as I am. And you're getting millions of dollars already. You start getting greedy, and having that money will turn out to be a *bad* thing, not a good one."

"Saying she's my sister doesn't make it true," Cole said. "It's DNA, that's all. And how could that money ever be a bad thing? Being able to do whatever I want with my life? Not owe the man?"

"First of all," Anthea said, "*you'll* be the man. There's a concept to ponder. And if you turned out to love money half as much as Henry Cavanaugh did, that would be one very big way it could be a very bad thing."

Cole took a sip of his Coke and seemed to be thinking about it, at least. "That's what Jim said. Like it would be the worst thing ever to be like him. He was *rich,* though. He was *successful.* He was—"

"He was hated," Anthea finished for him, concentrating on getting the perfect head on Ben's beer. This was exactly what she'd feared. The money was screwing Cole up already, and he didn't even have it in his hands yet. "He had two kids. One of them—that would be you—his mother wouldn't even let him know his father, because she was afraid it'd warp him. The other one, a woman with the kindest heart in the world, spent the last five years of her father's life not coming near him. She never even talked to him on the phone. Have you had to read *A Christmas Carol* in school yet?"

"What?" Cole said. "No."

"Change of movie plans," Anthea announced. "We're watching it tonight. Because I just realized—that's Henry Cavanaugh. He was Scrooge. Minus the turnaround and the turkey."

"I only came over because it was going to be *The Incredibles,*" Cole said. "I'm not watching some lame Christmas movie. It's not even Halloween."

"You came over because Mom wouldn't let you go to that party," Anthea said, "and even though she's at work and won't know, you were afraid that I—or Jimbo, more like—would drive by the house and check to make sure you hadn't gone, and a cop at a party is such a drag. And because you love your niece and nephew, and Ty thinks you're Superman."

Right on cue, Tyson came through the entryway from the dining room on a burst of four-year-old energy and said, "Cole! Come *on.* I've been *waiting* and *waiting.* For twenty *hours!*"

That got a smile out of Cole at last. "What do you want to play?" he asked.

"Mario Kart!" Ty said. "Come *on.*"

"Ten minutes," Anthea said. "Then it's movie time."

"Come *on*," Tyson said, tugging at Cole's hand.

"Geez," Cole said. "Hold your pants. I'm coming." He grabbed the popcorn and his Coke and headed into the dining room.

Anthea watched him go, then turned to Ben. He'd allowed her to do the talking, but he had the thoughtful look in his eyes that was one of the many reasons she'd married him. "We'd better make more popcorn," she said. When he didn't move, she asked, "What are you thinking?"

"Same thing you are. That it's too bad about him getting that money."

She finished pouring her own beer and sighed. "You think he'll be OK?"

"Yeah. Eventually. He's got a good family, and he's a good kid, underneath all that drama." He looked at her, and she realized she was frowning into space. "Hey," he said gently. "Come here." She went over to him, and he pulled her into his arms, then held her and rubbed her back until she hummed, until she could feel her pulse rate actually slowing.

"Your beer's getting flat," she finally said.

"Don't care. My wife's getting relaxed. That's the one that matters."

She stayed there a while longer, then said, "You ever think about us having another baby?"

"Uh . . ." He leaned back so he could look at her, but his arms were still tight around her, and he was getting the light in his eyes that always got her motor running. "Can't say I have so much. But I can't say I wouldn't be willing. I do love the babies you make me. I'm up for some practice, anyway, so if we decide to go for it, we're ready."

"Think you can hold that thought through *A Christmas Carol?*"

"Oh," he said, "I think so."

◆　◆　◆

Jim stuffed his hands into the pockets of his bomber jacket against the late-October chill and hustled across the Sangria Station parking lot, pushed through two sets of glass doors into the warmth, then pulled off his jacket and hung it on the rack by the door.

The place looked even better at night. Classier. It felt better, too, with the deep yellow walls glowing gold in the low lighting, some fairly hot music pumping just loud enough to give you ideas, and a sweet, spicy scent like cinnamon and cloves filling the air.

The crowd didn't quite match the atmosphere. Some guys at the bar, most of them still wearing their feed caps like nobody'd ever taught them manners, and couples and groups filling most of the tables and booths. Nobody too special, except one person. A lone woman sitting at a booth under the windows. A redheaded woman in a blue top that crossed over in front and showed her collarbones and some tantalizing extra, a matching skirt that revealed a few inches of thigh, and those killer gray cowboy boots with the blue roses. Her legs were crossed, showing even *more* thigh, one toe was circling to the insistent music, she was sipping something from a big pewter mug that he'd bet wasn't coffee, and she was gazing around her with a little smile on her lips.

She looked poised. She looked elegant. She looked confident. She looked like a woman ready to do something very un-Hallie-like. Something she shouldn't be doing with anybody but him.

What, that was wrong? Tough. It was true.

"Hey, Jim." A man turned from the bar, and Jim recognized Wes Allen, manager of the Safeway store in Paradise. His hair was still parted ruthlessly on the side, but he'd dressed up tonight in black jeans and a western shirt with snaps, looking like no kind of rodeo cowboy ever, and wearing enough aftershave to knock out that cowboy's horse.

"Hey," Jim said back, but he was still watching Hallie. She didn't seem to have noticed him coming in. Who had she been smiling at, then?

"I'm about to head on over there," Wes said, noticing the direction of Jim's gaze. "So you can just back the hell off. She's all by herself, and that's not right. Plus, I saw her first."

"Nope," Jim said. "You're not. The ink's not even dry on your separation papers, and I know Anthea told you to keep things on the down low until you get to court."

Wes wasn't looking at Hallie now. He was looking at Jim, and he wasn't looking friendly. "Anthea's not supposed to talk about my case. She told me it was that attorney-client thing. Besides, it's none of your business."

Jim had had a lot of practice staring other men down, and he did it now. It was working, too. It usually did. "That's not insider information, and it's not rocket science. It's basic divorce lawyer. Plus, that's one of Evan's teachers you're looking at. I saw your wife sitting in her classroom over at the middle school's open house. You'd know that yourself if you'd gone. Could get awkward as hell."

Wes squinted at him. "Why's it awkward for me and not you? If you were in her classroom, it's because she's Mac's teacher, too."

"Because she's an old friend. And because I'm single, and you're not divorced."

"Aw, man," Wes complained, like a man who knew when he was beaten, which he was. "Why do you have to rain on my parade like that? Here I am, all ready to start being a bachelor, and I can't even get started."

"Yeah, well, good luck with that. It's not everything it's cracked up to be."

"Neither is marriage," Wes said glumly.

"Speak for yourself."

The bartender, a woman in her forties, worked her way over to Jim and said, "Help you?"

"Yeah," Jim said. "Whatever the redhead over there is drinking? Send a couple more of those to her table." He pulled out his wallet and handed over a twenty.

"Mulled wine," the bartender said dubiously. Jim guessed he didn't look much like the mulled-wine type, which was true, but who cared. "And she's been turning down company so far. You could be drinking that alone."

"Trust me," Jim said, "that won't be anything new. I'll take my chances."

"Nice," Wes said. "Old friend, huh?"

"Yeah. Old friend."

Fifteen miles away from Paradise wasn't far enough. He knew it. And all the same, he was walking over to Hallie's table and saying, "Well, hey."

She looked up with a frown that changed to a smile, and then went straight back to wary. She'd be a lousy poker player.

"That's right," Jim said. "It's not just another random guy hitting on you. Or it is, but it's me. Wait," he said when she uttered a startled laugh. "That didn't come out right. Hang on. I'm trying again. You're very beautiful. Mind if I join you?"

By the time he'd finished, she was laughing harder, and looking so pretty, and he had to smile some, too.

"Sorry," he said. "Out of practice."

"Sit down," she said. "You don't look so bad yourself, by the way. Are you out on the town? I didn't know you did that."

His white button-down and good jeans had worked, he guessed. His hair was still wet from the shower, but the way she was looking at him, it didn't matter. Or maybe she was remembering that other shower they'd taken. He knew he was.

He finally processed what she'd said. "First time for everything, I guess. How good is it that it's with you?"

Her face softened, her color rose, and then her chin did. "Anthea," she breathed. "I will *kill* her. She is the most interfering . . ."

That was the moment when a waitress showed up with two more pewter mugs and took away Hallie's empty one.

Jim said, "Thanks," lifted his mug, took a sip, and considered, then told Hallie, "This actually isn't terrible. I mean, it's not what you'd call *alcohol,* but it's not too bad, in a Christmas Eve kind of way."

"It has more kick than you realize," she said, abandoning the topic of Anthea, to Jim's relief. "There's brandy in it. I'm a little buzzed after one mug, to tell you the truth."

"Mm," he said. She was taking her own sip, looking at him over the rim of her mug. Her eyes were dark again, too. He knew what that meant by now. "Good thing I'm here, then."

She set down her mug and almost visibly shook herself. "Wait a second. Where's Mac?"

"Spending the night with a friend. Girls do that a lot."

"Oh. But not at your house." She sounded distracted when she said it. One hand had gone to a little blue pendant at her throat, was stroking it in a way that was distracting him, too.

"No," he said. "It's never at my house."

"That's lucky, I guess." Her fingers were tracing her collarbone now, and he could swear he saw, out of the corner of his eye, that her nipples were hardening again.

Damn. What was he, a glutton for punishment, sitting here watching that?

"Not so much." He guessed they were supposed to be having conversation here, so he went on. "That's how it works for single dads."

"Why?" Her hand had stopped moving.

He shrugged. "When there isn't a mom at home, you find out that you're not considered safe anymore. They don't let their daughters spend the night."

If he'd wanted to stop fantasizing about Hallie, this had been a good way, because the thought was making his hand tighten around his mug. Why had he brought that up?

Hallie's eyes were snapping green again, which wasn't at all what he'd been going for. "That's terrible," she said. "How could they think that about you?"

"Protecting their girls? How can you blame them? It doesn't feel good, but hey, I'm a cop. It's not like I can be too surprised anymore about the things people can do."

"But not *you*. Especially not the man you are now, although I'll admit that I'm still surprised by how much you've changed. That you got married at all, I suppose, and then all the rest of it."

"Call it shock treatment. The changes happened pretty fast, and then they kept happening." He drank some more wine. It tasted better the more of it you drank, he discovered. Went down sweet and easy. Kind of like Hallie.

"I never heard that much about how you got married," she said. "Anthea never told me. Or maybe I never let her." Hallie must be getting a kick from those drinks. She *was* looking a little buzzed. "Maybe I was still hurting over you."

All Jim wanted to do was scoot closer and take her hand, the one that was on the table now, just asking him to hold it. But he couldn't. Instead, he said, "I'm way out of practice, but I'm pretty sure that if you're looking to get somewhere, you're not supposed to talk about your marriage."

"Mm." She looked at him from under her lashes. "Is that what you're doing?"

"You know that's what I'm doing."

There was some pink in her cheeks. She took another sip of her drink, and he watched her swallow and tried to keep his eyes up high, but it wasn't easy.

"Well . . ." She seemed to be considering. "If you're bitter, that's true. But if you were happy? I think you can tell a woman about that. I think she might want to know that you know how to . . . love somebody.

So tell me, Jim. How did that bad boy I knew end up married and with a baby at twenty-two? She must have been some woman."

This wasn't Danielle Delgado. This was nothing but a headfirst plunge into complication.

"She was," he finally said. "She was tough, like you."

"I'm not tough."

"Sure you are. Tough doesn't have to mean badass, hard-edged. Tough means you know what you're worth, and you won't settle for less. Tough means you stick to your guns and you know what's right. And that's you."

She moved her hand like she wanted to hold his, the same way he wanted to hold hers. "So what happened?" she asked.

He drained his mug, looked around for the waitress, held up two fingers, and she nodded. Then he looked back at Hallie and said, "It was almost over before it really got started, is what happened. I was that same guy I'm sure you remember. Twenty-one, just out of Ranger School, cocky as hell. I thought I was all that, and Maya didn't. I had to work hard to take her out and harder to get anywhere. And then I messed up a couple times, showed up when I'd been drinking, showed up late. She told me to go find somebody else, because she didn't need that. But I didn't want somebody else, so I talked her into giving it another shot. And I screwed up some more. One time too many, and she dumped my butt. Then I was about to deploy for the first time, and I went over to her place to try again, because I realized I didn't want to leave it like that. Knowing you're shipping out . . . that tends to put a different spin on things. I finally wised up that I wouldn't be there, some other guy might be, and my chance would be gone."

He'd said it all too fast. He wasn't used to being in this situation, but he'd been right. It was the absolute wrong topic. The waitress came over with the drinks, and Jim thanked her absently, turned the mug in his hands, then looked at Hallie again.

She hadn't said anything. She was just listening, so he went on in spite of his intentions. "That's when she told me she was pregnant, and I said, 'Let's get married before I go, then.' Who knows why I said it? Maybe because I'd never known my dad, and I'd watched my mom struggle all my life, and I didn't want that to happen all over again. I didn't want to be that guy."

"So you got married," she prompted when he stopped. "Or engaged, I guess."

"No. I didn't. She said no."

"Oh. Whoa."

"Yep. She said she didn't want a partier, and she sure didn't want a man she couldn't count on. And that was it. I shipped out on a six-month deployment, knowing she was pregnant with my baby, that I wouldn't even be back before that baby was born, and that I was no part of their lives. And then I got to Iraq and found out that being a Ranger was a whole lot different than training to be one. I saw things I'd never wanted to see, and did things that woke me up sweating afterwards. The first time you kill somebody . . . you're not spending any time at all thinking about it in the moment, but you sure do think about it afterwards. All in all, I guess you could say that I did some growing up."

It was too much to say, it was no part of what he'd come here for tonight, and it was out there anyway.

"And then what?" She wasn't drinking anymore. She was just hanging on to that mug and looking at him.

"And then I came home. Maya was living over at her folks', and Mac was six weeks old. I went over there to see her—to see both of them—and Maya said hi and was so . . . *careful* with me. All I wanted to do was hold her, and I couldn't. I got to hold Mac, though. Turned out that was enough."

She paused a minute, then said, "I guess you knew how. How to hold a baby, I mean. Because of Cole being so much younger than you."

"I did. But this was completely different. I thought I knew what to expect, and I didn't have a clue. I held Mac, and she was . . . she was mine. She smiled at me." He had to stop and take a breath, and his voice was shaky, to his dismay, when he went on. "I still thought I was a badass. I held my baby girl, she looked at me that way she still does, like she knew I was her dad, and that was it. I was done. Turned out I was no badass at all."

She put a hand out and set it on his. Public or no, she did it. "Oh," she said. "Jim."

"Yeah. And, of course, Maya still wouldn't take me back. I had to work for it again. I had to realize how much I wanted it, and prove it to her, too. So you could say," he said, looking at Hallie, her eyes and mouth so soft, but her hand gripping his with plenty of strength, "that I've had practice."

"I'd say you've been through the fire and back again," she said.

"One way and another," he said, "you could be right. So that's it. That's my story. What's yours?"

◆ ◆ ◆

Maybe it was the wine. Or maybe it was Jim. So serious and so strong. So sexy, even when he was talking about loving another woman. *After* he'd come here to find her, had sat down with her like it was the only place he wanted to be, and had looked at her like she was the only woman in the room.

She was confused. She was all upside-down. And she didn't think it was the wine.

"You know my story." She took her hand back. What was she doing, holding his hand in public? It was the last thing she should be doing, and so was this. "It's not that interesting. I was teaching, not killing people. And as you know, I've never been married. Never had kids. Nothing like you."

"Hard to believe you haven't at least come close," he said. "Looking at you tonight. That outfit . . . man, that's pretty. Or maybe I should say that *you* are, because that's true, too. Anyway, it's what I told you. My deal—that was nothing but an accident that worked out better than I had any right to hope. You made as many real choices as I did, seems like. A lot of tough choices. But no special guy, in all these years? Nobody you ever said yes to?"

"Nope." She took another sip of warm, spicy wine for courage. It was probably a mistake. It was her third. Just like that night on Paradise Mountain. Another thought she didn't need to be having right now. "I've always backed off, or chosen guys where it'd fizzle out on its own, maybe. Because I didn't have much of a model of a good man, or maybe . . ." The sneaky tendrils of desire were sliding their slow, insidious way down her body again, touching her everywhere, curling into all her secret spots exactly the same way Jim had done in that shower. Like he knew exactly where she wanted to be touched, and exactly how she needed it. And like touching her was all he wanted to do. The same way he was looking at her now. "Maybe," she heard herself saying, "the kind of guy I wanted, the tough kind, the fierce kind—maybe I didn't trust that guy. And the guys I trusted didn't turn me on. Maybe I've got a thing for the wild side, even though it scares me to death. Maybe I want a man I can trust to take me there, and to keep me safe along the way. Maybe I want that, and I've never found it."

Was it warm in here? She was burning up. It could be the way he was looking at her. Or it could be what he said next. "You're saying you want a guy who's out there on the edge. One who's going to pull you up there with him."

"No." She couldn't catch her breath. She couldn't stop looking into his eyes. "I want a guy who's going to push me *over* the edge. I want a guy I can fall with, because he'll be holding me all the way down. I want a guy who's going to pull me screaming down the other side."

She was drowning in his hard gaze, his hard body. He was leaning across the table like he wanted to take her there right now. But he *was* on the other side of the table, where he needed to stay. And the restaurant was full of people.

She realized she was fingering the little turquoise pendant at her throat, running soft fingers over her collarbone, just because she needed the touch of a hand. She'd never burned for it more. And her own hand wouldn't do.

She recognized the thought, rejected it, and dropped her hand. That was more than enough. And still, the next words out of her mouth were, "I'm a little drunk, officer. I'm not sure I'm good to drive home. What do you think? Would you arrest me?"

All right, it seemed she wasn't quite done. And it was cheesy. So what? It was just flirting. It was as close as she was getting to sex, and if fantasy fuel were all she was getting tonight, she was going to take it.

If they were done, Jim hadn't gotten the memo, because his voice was the slowest, darkest caress. "Yeah," he said. "I would. I'd arrest you in a heartbeat. We could go out to my truck and test your levels right now. Or you could do something else. The Hilltop Inn is right down the road. You could leave your car here, walk on down there, get a room, and sleep it off. All night long."

She shouldn't. She couldn't. And she was saying it anyway. "Maybe I will. I could get something by the back door where it's quiet. What do you think?"

She thought his eyes were glazing over some, but maybe it was the wine. Hers or his. He said, "I think that's a real good idea."

"I'll go, then," she said. "By myself. I'm supposed to be by myself."

"You got your phone? Just in case?"

She reached under the table for her purse, and when she came up again, he was looking down her shirt, and not even pretending he wasn't.

She hadn't been sure, when she'd put this outfit on tonight, whether it was too much. Whether the top was too clingy or the skirt too short. Now, she was sure. It was too much, and it was perfect.

She said, "Got it right here. Looks like I'm all set to be safe. All night long." Then she slid out of the booth, pulled two twenties out of her wallet and set them on the table, picked up her jacket, slid it on, zipped it slowly up and pretended she was undressing instead, and watched him watch her do it.

"Pay my check, will you?" she asked him. "I'm out of here."

THE WILD SIDE

The room was eighty-nine dollars. Plus tax. The price had given Hallie a momentary qualm, coming on top of that dinner and those expensive drinks. More than a hundred thirty dollars for one night out?

Then she'd remembered, even through the fuzziness from two and a half strong mulled wines, that she had tens of thousands of dollars in the bank. Even though she didn't want to go down that road, didn't want to feel like the money was hers to spend. Especially if she were risking the rest of the inheritance right this minute.

She wasn't a wealthy person, and she wasn't a reckless one. She wasn't impulsive. Well, she was, but she didn't want to be, because impulsivity led to heartache and regret, and she knew it. But here she was, sitting on a king-sized bed after spending full price on a motel room she didn't need, hoping that she wasn't risking millions of dollars just so a man would join her for one night of sex with no strings attached. A man she was afraid she cared about a whole lot more than that.

Teeth. She headed into the bathroom to brush them with the toiletry packet she'd requested from the bored young woman at the front desk. She contemplated a shower, too, then decided it was overkill.

She'd miss Jim's call, and besides, she'd just taken a bath. She was clean. She was pretty. She was perfumed and soft skinned and fresh and . . .

And stupid, and reckless, and alone. She'd texted Jim when she'd gotten into the room. *Good suggestion. I got a place in back. Nice and quiet.* Which had seemed ambiguous enough. Texts could be traced, but that one wasn't proof of anything. She'd never said *motel,* or *join me,* or anything, and neither of them would be parked in the motel lot. At least she figured he wouldn't.

But she hadn't heard anything back.

She came into the room again, set the phone on the bedside table, pulled the comforter back, sat on the edge of the bed, then stood up.

She should take off her boots, maybe. But that would look like she was waiting for him.

He knows you're waiting for him.

Then why didn't he come? Maybe she'd gotten it wrong. Maybe he really *had* been suggesting she sleep it off instead of driving home. He'd just spent fifteen minutes telling her how much he loved his *wife.*

Because you asked him to.

What was that he'd said? *I'm way out of practice, but I'm pretty sure that if you're looking to get somewhere, you're not supposed to talk about your first marriage.*

He *had* been looking to get somewhere, because he'd shaved tonight, too. He'd taken a shower, he'd shaved, and she'd bet he'd changed. And he'd looked at her like all he'd been thinking about was delivering the rest of everything he'd promised in that shower. He still loved his wife, but he wanted Hallie. That was enough.

Well, no, it wasn't. But she could make it be.

She went across to the lone window and pulled back the drape. Nothing but blackness out there. If it had been daylight, she'd have seen a field, and some houses behind it. She dropped the drape, went back to the silent phone, and picked it up.

Nine forty-eight. More than fifteen minutes since she'd left the restaurant.

The phone dinged, and she almost dropped it. The green balloon said, *Cold out here.* and that was all.

Key card, she thought. She picked up the white rectangle, opened the door into the empty hallway, and walked fast to the back door. Nobody visible through the glass. Nobody there.

She shoved at the handle, and the door opened into the cold air, freezing her instantly, since she was wearing nothing but the thin top and skirt. And Jim stepped out from the shadows beside the door. He was through so quickly she had to take three fast steps back, and then he was on her. The door whispered shut, and he was pressing her against the wall next to it, one of his hands behind her head, clutching tight, holding her for him. And he was kissing her. Devouring her, the same way he had every single time. And this time, she wasn't telling him no.

His lips were warm and firm and so demanding, and he tasted like cinnamon and cloves and brandy. His big hand was inside her top already, too, going straight to a peak that had sprung to attention as if he'd ordered it to. His hand was freezing, but his touch was a live wire, a jolt straight down her body. Hot and cold. He kept on touching, squeezing now, and the electricity was buzzing through her in earnest. Going straight there and sparking hard.

She heard a noise and wondered what it was, then realized she was whimpering. No, she was *mewing.* She was on her toes, her arms around Jim's broad shoulders, the wall hard against her back, and Jim hard against the rest of her, his mouth forcing hers open, his hand inside her shirt, teasing, stroking, pinching, lighting her up.

The voices took a moment to register. A woman talking and then a man's laugh.

"Whoa," she heard, and realized that Jim wasn't kissing her anymore. She opened her eyes and turned her head, the same way he was.

He'd taken his hand from her breast, but the other was still thrust through her hair, holding her tight.

A middle-aged man and woman were coming down the hallway, each trundling a suitcase behind them. The man cleared his throat and said, "Evening, folks," and then they looked away, swiped their key card, and went into a room across the hall. She heard the woman's soft laugh, a murmur from the man, and then the door shut behind them, and they were gone.

Hallie did her best to smile at Jim, but he wasn't smiling back. He hadn't let go of her, either. "Take me to your room," he said, his voice low. Dark. As sure as she wasn't. "I need to take off your clothes. I need to touch you everywhere."

She took her shaking hands from his shoulders, and finally, he stepped back.

A bad moment, then. Where was her key card? On the floor, where she'd dropped it when he'd grabbed her. Jim was already there, though, picking it up.

"Uh . . . one seventy-seven," she told him, surprised she could remember it, he had her so dazed. "Down here."

She led the way, and he followed, swiped the card, and stepped inside.

Not much to it. A motel room. A bed and not much else. And all at once, she was nervous.

He looked at her, still not smiling, pulled a box out of his jacket pocket, and tossed it onto the bed.

"Oh," she said. "Condoms." It was why he'd been gone so long. He hadn't been having second thoughts at all. He'd been doing things right this time. Making sure she was safe with him when he pulled her screaming down the other side.

"That's right," he said. "A box of them, because it's going to take a box for everything I want to do to you." She was still standing there, barely into the room, but he walked over, sat down on the bed, pulled off his jacket, then his boots and socks, and looked at her. "I suggest," he said quietly, "that you come on over here so I can get started."

She could swear her knees were wobbly and knew she was staring at him. She bent to pull off her cowboy boots, but he said, "Oh, no. That's mine to do. Come over here."

She did it. She couldn't have done anything else. A few steps, then he was pulling her onto the bed so she straddled his lap, a knee on either side of him. She would have overbalanced, but she didn't, because he had her, and he wasn't letting go.

"Oh, yeah," he said. "That's right." His hands were under her top, skimming up her ribs, and she was unbuttoning his shirt, but getting distracted along the way, because he'd tugged her close, was kissing her neck now, sucking at it, using his teeth on her, and she was moaning again.

When he finally lifted his head, it was only to pull the top over her head and toss it to the ground. "This," he said, his thumbs tracing the low, lacy cups of her bra. "Been wanting to do this for so long. Wanting to see all of this again. Wanting to touch it. So pretty. All mine."

It was the dark-blue, push-up demibra she'd been wearing that first day, when he'd come into the house and found her in it. He had his lips on her breast now, and they were taking the slow path his thumbs had traced, making every nerve ending spring to attention in their wake, and then the bra was gone, because his sneaky hands had somehow made it behind her back and unfastened the clasp.

"Ah," he said, and that was all, because his mouth and hands were busy, stroking, biting, working her hard, and she was burning up.

Somehow, he'd turned her. Her back was hitting the mattress, and then she was sprawled crosswise on the white bed. He had her boots off at last, then her socks, and she was lying there in only her little blue skirt. And she still hadn't managed to get anything off him beyond unbuttoning a couple buttons.

"Come here," she said, pulling him down by the waist, then rolling fast so he was the one on his back. She managed to get his shirt unbuttoned the rest of the way, one slow button at a time, and she was biting at his neck, beginning to kiss her way down his chest, tugging his shirttails out of his jeans, brushing her hand "accidentally" over his fly and feeling him pulse against her, hearing the intake of breath he couldn't suppress, and thrilling to it.

Unfortunately, he wasn't cooperating. He had his hands up under her skirt, was stroking her bottom, tracing the edges of the high-cut underwear, and he was distracting her.

"Stop that," she said, her mouth against his nipple now. She ran her teeth over it, then sucked hard just to feel him twitch. "I need to . . . get this done."

"Oh, no," he told her. "I need to get *this* done." He sat up and yanked his shirt off impatiently, and when she went for his belt, he let her unbuckle it, and he pulled it out of his jeans and dropped it onto his shirt. She saw that long white diagonal line of scar tissue, and then she forgot to look at it, because he was kneeling over her, pulling her skirt down over her thighs, down her calves, and off of her.

Once again, he surprised her. He had his hands under her hips, was flipping her over onto her stomach. "I have to look at this," he told her, while she pressed her cheek into the mattress and gasped, because his hand was stroking over lace trim, over warm flesh, delving and exploring. His other hand was on her lower back, holding her down, and she was squirming.

"Jim," she said. "Jim."

He toyed with her, his touch first gentle, then firmer, then back to gentle again. He touched her everywhere, his hands roaming up and down her back, down her bottom, over her thighs, then, when she couldn't stand it anymore, diving between her legs, probing, circling. Leaving again to touch her sensitive inner thighs, run over the spot at the small of her back, just before she would have gone over.

Teasing again and again, merciless, until she was boneless, until she was moaning.

She was going to combust. She needed him so badly, she ached. She began to turn over again, but he said, "No. Don't move."

He was unbuttoning his jeans, pulling them off, and she had to touch him. She *had* to. She was turning despite his words, sitting up, reaching for him.

It had been fourteen years since she'd seen Jim Lawson naked. Fourteen long years since she'd touched all of him. And fourteen years was much too long.

When she ran a hand down the length of him, he groaned, and she felt a thrill of purely feminine power.

"I said . . ." he began.

Her voice came out throaty, like it belonged to somebody else. "Yeah. You did. And now *I'm* saying. In a little while, you can do whatever you want to me. You can put me in any position you want, and I'll go there. You can have anything you want from me. But right now, I'm doing this."

◆　◆　◆

He could have objected, but he wasn't an idiot.

When she'd been seventeen, he'd been the first man she'd touched. He'd known it, and he'd loved it.

Holy hell, but she'd learned a lot since then.

She kissed her way down his scar first, stroked his abdomen, his thighs, the same way he'd done to her, teasing him with feather-light touches until he was swaying. When she stood up and pushed him to sit on the edge of the bed, he didn't exactly resist. And when he had what he'd wished for, back there in that shower, when she was the one on her knees? He lost the power of speech. His hands were in her hair, pulling, tugging, and she was doing it all. Working him over. Taking her time. Making his breath come hard. Making him want to beg.

"You need . . ." he finally said. "We need to stop, or I can't . . ."

She kept her hand on him, sat back on her heels, and looked at him, and he looked down at her and got a vision of heaven. If heaven was full breasts, white skin, pink lips, green eyes, and red-gold curls. Which, right now, it was. She still smelled like flowers, and all he wanted was for her to keep going. But all he wanted was to be inside all that softness, all that delicious heat. Both things. Right now.

It was greed. It was pure lust. It was grabbing everything he could hold and making it his.

"You going to give me some more of that good stuff?" she asked, her voice a purr.

"Yeah," he managed to say. "Going to do all that to you. Going to do you good. Got a . . . got a plan. And then I'm going to . . ." He shut his eyes and shuddered, because she'd bent her head to him again.

"Then," she said, giving him a long, slow lick and then some delicate little kisses that had his hands tightening in her hair, "we'll call this pressure relief, shall we?"

It was all that and more. It had been much too long, it was much too good, and it was just about too much to take. He was groaning, his hands fisting tight in her hair, his body jerking and shuddering and riding the wave all the way over the top. And she was staying right with him, taking it all.

It was a long few minutes before he got his breath back, and his mind along with it. He lay back across the bed, panting hard, and she went into the bathroom and came back with two glasses of water and handed him one.

He levered himself to an elbow and drank it down, and watched her doing the same. Kneeling on a white sheet, all white and pink and rose gold, about the best thing a man could possibly find to look at. And all his.

"Miss Hallie Cavanaugh," he finally said, "you've gone and grown up."

She was still wearing those tiny dark-blue panties, and he had a flash of how they'd looked from behind, curving halfway up her cheeks. He was so satisfied, and he wasn't one bit satisfied.

He didn't get around to everything he'd thought of, but he got around to enough. He took his time getting her underwear off, because rubbing her through them, kissing her through the fabric made her squirm so deliciously, and reaching his fingers stealthily under the lace band made her cry out loud, made her hips start moving and her thighs part as if his hands had been there, pushing them apart. And then he took that scrap of blue off her, and he *did* push her thighs apart, and held them there, too, and that was even better.

It wasn't like the shower this time. They had all night, so he made it last. He made her moan, and he made her cry out, and after a long, long time, he finally let her come, and then he did it all over again. And when he finally levered himself up her trembling body again, threaded his fingers through hers, held her hands down tight, and slid inside her, and her eyes opened wide with the thrill of taking him in . . . that was something else. She was so warm, so open, and so wet that he knew that if she hadn't taken that pressure off him, this would have been over much too fast.

"Jim." Nothing but a soft breath from her parted lips. "Jim."

"Yeah." It was his heart, somehow, that was aching now, hearing her say his name like that. "Yeah. It's me. I've got you, baby. I've got you."

Slow and easy, sweet and tender. Watching her eyes drift shut, her mouth open wider, her breath start to come hard again. Feeling her legs come up to wrap around his waist. Keeping hold of her hands, and feeling what that did to her. Knowing how much she wanted him there. Knowing that, whether her eyes were closed or not, she knew it was him. That no other man would have done, just like no other woman would have done for him.

She deserved his best, so that was what he gave her. *You can put me in any position you want,* she'd said, *and I'll go there.* So he did. He turned her over, and it got wilder and hotter. She was on her hands and knees, was calling out with every stroke when he found the right way, the way that worked. And when he got a hand down there and began to help her out, she was backing into him, gasping, begging.

"Please, Jim. Please. Do that. More. Oh, please."

If she was going to beg him like that, there was absolutely no choice. He did that, and then he did it some more. And when she started to spasm around him, when he heard those soft screams again, when she was biting her fist to try to stop them . . . he was nineteen again. He had Hallie Cavanaugh underneath him, and he was doing her so good, and she was letting him know it. And she pulled him right along with her. Right over the top. She took him up, and then she took him tumbling down, until they were screaming down the hill together. All the way. Straight to the wild side.

THE MIDDLEMAN

Hallie woke slowly the next morning.

The first thing she was aware of was how deliciously sleepy she was. The second thing was how deliciously *sore* she was. The gentle, throbbing ache between her thighs let her know it hadn't been a dream, and the satisfaction curling through her entire body let her know it had been good.

She opened her eyes to a room just beginning to lighten, heard soft movement, and turned her head to see Jim coming out of the bathroom, pulling on his shirt and buttoning it over his broad chest.

"Hey," she said.

"Hey yourself." A slow smile lit up his brown eyes, and then he sat down on the edge of the bed and was brushing her hair back from her face while she reached up to trace the scar at the side of his cheek, loving that she had the right to do it. When he kept touching her, she grasped his wrist and ran her hand up his forearm, just for the pleasure of feeling the bulk of it. And to hold him there so she could smell him. Clean soap, warm man. He smelled like hers. He *felt* like hers.

When they'd finally fallen asleep the night before, his arms had been around her, and her head had been on his chest. They hadn't talked, but they hadn't needed to. His hand stroking down her back had felt like everything she needed to hear.

That had been last night, though, and this was the morning after.

"I'll take off first," he said now, which *wasn't* what she wanted to hear. "I parked over at Walmart, behind a couple RVs. Even our cars weren't in a compromising position." His smile was lopsided. Rueful. "Hell of a thing, having to sneak around like this."

"It is. But I need to go home and feed Cletus anyway."

"Ah. The hellhound."

"Yeah."

"OK." He bent down and kissed her forehead, his hand cupping her cheek. Nothing but tender, but with an assurance that recalled the possessive lover of the night before. "That was one of my better nights, by the way."

"Yeah." She swallowed over the lump in her throat. "But you'd better go."

"Give it half an hour before you leave," he suggested. "Have some breakfast, maybe." He didn't let go of her, though. "This is weird," he finally said.

"I know. But . . . don't text me, right? And calling's probably not great, either."

"So we just—what? Pretend it didn't happen?"

"Yeah. We do. Don't tell anybody. Don't even tell Anthea. Please, Jim. And please go, before people get out on the roads."

Now that she was awake, she was anxious. Nervous. What had she been thinking, risking being found with him? They hadn't left the restaurant together the night before, no, but she'd been holding his hand at the table. "You need to go," she said again.

"Right." His face had hardened, and she wanted to explain, but there was nothing to say. He stood up, grabbed his jacket, and headed for the door, and he was gone.

She didn't stick around to sample the dubious delights of the Hilltop Inn's continental breakfast. It was better to keep her presence as far under the radar as possible. Instead, she walked down the side of the highway to Sangria Station in the cold, gray light of dawn, her hands shoved into the pockets of her jacket and her bare legs freezing, climbed into her car, and drove home.

She turned up the driveway thinking about Cletus, because it was easier than thinking about Jim. And then she stomped on the brake with her heart thudding in her chest.

Oh, no.

◆　◆　◆

Jim had changed, eaten breakfast, and was gearing up to head over and pick up Mac from her sleepover when his phone rang.

He glanced at the display. *DeMarco.*

"Hey," he said when he picked up. "What's up?"

"I'm out here at your girlfriend's house," the other man said. "Oh, excuse me, your *not*-girlfriend. Guess she didn't call you again."

Jim was already halfway to the door. "What happened?"

"You could call it graffiti. Pretty spectacular, I'd say, by Idaho standards. Not a popular lady, is she?"

Jim swore, and DeMarco said, "I thought you might like to know."

"She all right?"

"Oh, she's fine. Plenty tough, isn't she, considering she's a teacher, got those big eyes and all. I'm getting it, I guess. Pretty lady. What does she see in you?"

"She doesn't."

"That's right. I forgot. Not your girlfriend. That's why she didn't call you. So you coming out, or am I doing this all by my lonesome?"

"I'm—damn. I have to pick up Mac and take her . . . someplace. Be out there in fifteen."

Which was why, when Mac climbed up in the truck a few minutes later outside Danielle's house, Jim said, "Sorry, partner, but I have to take you over to Grandma's for a while. Seems that somebody messed up Ms. Cavanaugh's house last night."

She looked at him sideways in that way she had. "You're not on duty today."

"I know I'm not, but she's a friend."

"Then how come you never do stuff with her? How come I never heard of her before she came here?"

"She's an . . . *old* friend."

Mac wasn't looking one bit happy. "It's your day off. You said we were going to spend it together. You said we were going to cut firewood and then get lunch. It was going to be a special day."

He shot her a look, but he didn't start the truck. "You're trying to guilt me. I am a good father." Well, reasonably good. He did his best. "And, what, you've been looking forward to stacking all that wood in the trailer? I find that hard to believe."

"Fine," she said with a sigh. "I'll be eleven for a whole two more months. There's plenty of time for us to do things together."

He choked off the word that had risen to his lips. "Remember how I said things would change when you were fifteen? I was wrong. This right here? This is it."

Did she have some kind of female radar? He could swear she must, because she crossed her arms and said, "Dad. I'm trying to have a *discussion*. I'm trying to tell you my *feelings*."

"Right." He put the truck in gear. "Well, I'm having a discussion, too. We're going to Hallie's. You're coming with me, I guess. You can tell me your feelings on the way."

If there was one thing he knew how to do, it was to control his emotions in difficult situations. Even this one. He could do this.

"So," he said when he'd taken the turn onto Main that would lead them to Arcadia Ridge, "since you don't seem to be talking to me, I'll start. Speaking of friends, I hear you've gotten to be good friends with Eli Chambers."

She'd been twirling a lock of hair around her finger and looking out the window, but now she turned to face him. "He's in my World Geography class, that's all. With Ms. Cavanaugh. And he's not going to be Eli Chambers anymore. His stepdad's adopting him."

"Really." Jim took a second to think about that.

"He talked to me about it," Mac said, looking out her window again. "Because I don't have a mom, and he doesn't have a dad. That's why."

"He has a dad now. Luke's his dad if anybody ever was."

"That's what I *mean.* He already *had* a dad. So it was weird to get another one."

This was important, Jim had a feeling. "Maybe," he said cautiously, "you could have two. Maybe you could have both. I can't believe Luke didn't think about that. He wants them to be a family, that's all, and he wants Eli to feel like part of it. You don't have to have the same name to do that, but maybe he thought it would help. I'm sure he gave Eli the choice."

"That's what Eli said. He said Luke told him he could keep his dad's name as his middle name if he wanted to. Eli Chambers Jackson. That sounds nice, doesn't it?"

"You've given this a lot of thought."

She shrugged a little too elaborately. "You asked me about it, that's all. He's my friend. Like you said."

"So that question you asked me," Jim said. "About whether I'd want to date again. Eli's mom did, and it seems to have worked out all right for Eli in the end."

Mac didn't answer that. They were almost to the end of Ridge Road now, and she asked, "Is this where she lives? Ms. Cavanaugh?"

"This is it." Jim negotiated the final sweeping turn, and then he was pulling into the long drive on the left, heading up the hill. And then they saw it.

"Wow," Mac said on a breath.

The letters were a good two feet high, the words scrawled in black spray paint with no pretense at artistry, covering the entire width of the three-car garage.

LESBIAN BITCH

GO HOME OR DIE

He should have left Mac at his mom's. She shouldn't be seeing this.

"That's homophobia," she said.

"Yeah. It is." He was so tense, he could barely speak.

"It doesn't matter if Ms. Cavanaugh is one or not."

"You're right. Not OK."

"Dad." Mac was looking at him as he pulled up beside the sheriff's vehicle in the driveway and put the truck into Park. "You're being weird again."

How was he going to get through this with DeMarco in there and Mac watching, too, and the rage building up inside him?

Somehow, that was how. "Let's go," he said, turning the truck off and hopping down.

Mac followed him without saying anything else, and by the time he rang the doorbell, he had himself back under control.

The Hallie who opened the door couldn't have been more different from the soft, sleepy woman he'd held a few hours earlier, even though she was wearing a long-sleeved T-shirt and snug jeans that emphasized her curves. It was the tension that was new. And when Jim looked beyond her at DeMarco, standing in the living room with his notebook in his hand, the other man raised his eyebrows with an expression that didn't need any interpretation.

"Hey," Jim told Hallie, ignoring DeMarco but reaching an absent hand down to give Cletus, who'd rushed forward to say hello, a friendly thump. Some killer guard dog.

"Hey," she said, stepping back to let him and Mac into the house. She was hugging herself tight, keeping it together. *Plenty tough.* He wanted to take her in his arms and tell her it would be all right, that he'd make sure of it, but he couldn't.

"Why didn't you call me?" he asked her as she shut the door behind him and Mac.

She shrugged, not looking him in the eye. "I called the sheriff's department. It seemed like the thing to do. Hi, Mac. How are you?"

"Fine," Mac said with a smile that didn't look entirely natural to Jim. *Uh-oh.*

"Cletus," Hallie said as the dog crowded close to Mac. "Sit."

Cletus thumped his butt down onto the hardwood, but his tail was swishing across the floor like mad as he smiled at Mac. Cletus was the only one here who wasn't tense. Well, Cletus and DeMarco, who was still watching.

"Sorry," Hallie told Mac. "He loves kids."

"Can I pet him?" Mac asked, sounding shy for once. "I heard about him from my cousins."

"I'd love it if you did," Hallie said. "He's upset by all the excitement, I think."

"He doesn't *look* upset," Mac said dubiously, and it was true. Any animal less upset looking than Cletus would be hard to imagine. Now, his entire backside was wriggling as Mac petted his ears.

"He *was* upset," Hallie said. "Or maybe I was just upset, and he noticed."

Jim had had enough small talk. He told Hallie, "I thought you were getting cameras."

It came out mad, which wasn't what he'd intended, and her head jerked back before she said, an edge to her voice, "I did. And I installed them, too. The deputy was just about to go check them with me."

They moved into the living room, where DeMarco's dark eyes were more sardonic than ever. "Ms. Cavanaugh was just explaining to me," he said, "that she wasn't home last night. Interesting that this would happen on the one night she happened to be gone."

"It is," Jim said. "Let's look at that footage."

Once they pulled the cards and took a look, things got more interesting, though not at first. The camera mounted near the front door didn't show a thing.

"They didn't come to the door," DeMarco said unnecessarily. "Probably not trying to break in, just to do this. Pretty small-time stuff. Did you have any lights on, Ms. Cavanaugh? Would they have thought you were home?"

"No," Hallie said, feeding the card from the garage-mounted camera into the TV. "I wouldn't think they'd have thought so. I didn't leave any lights on. I didn't know I'd be gone for the night."

She was in an easy chair. Biting her lip, her face so troubled, sitting apart from the two men and Mac, all of whom were on the couch. DeMarco looked at Jim again, and Jim looked back, his face carefully blank. Hallie wasn't looking at either one of them.

The second camera was motion activated, too, but this time, there had been motion. A time stamp of nine thirty p.m.; not nearly as late as you'd expect. And two slight figures in hooded jackets. One of them holding back, hovering just at the fringe of the camera's range, the other one darting forward, holding something.

"Dad," Mac said urgently. "I—"

Jim put an arm around her. "Shh. Wait."

DeMarco muttered, "Well, this is about the most professional situation I've ever been in," but Jim wasn't listening. He was watching the blurry, low-resolution figures. One of them backed out of view, then appeared briefly again, as if the person were shifting from one foot to the other, or wanting to leave and changing their mind. The other figure was busy. An arm swept up, then down. The garage door was out of sight, but it was obvious what was happening. Spray-painting. A minute or two max, and then the person was turning around, joining the other one, and they were both gone and the screen went blank.

"No car," DeMarco said. "At least not in the driveway." He rewound, and they watched it again in silence, and then he asked Hallie, "What age do you teach?"

"Eleven to fourteen or so," she said, but she wasn't looking at DeMarco. She was looking at Jim.

"Could be thirteen or fourteen," DeMarco said. "Easily. I'd say those were teenagers, if they're boys. We could measure the image against the door, but I'm thinking five five to five seven. The one doing the painting is shorter, but neither of them is tall. The one holding back had longer hair, looked like. Could be a girl—can't really tell. Graffiti's more of a male thing, but maybe two teenagers. Girls grow before boys do. The girl holding back, the boy doing the work."

Jim didn't say anything, and DeMarco went on. "Those letters, though, Ms. Cavanaugh—would you say they were from teenagers? I'd guess you'd know how they write."

"I don't know," Hallie said. She jumped to her feet. "Thanks for coming out. Do you have what you need? Mainly, I just need a police report for the insurance company, if the damage is beyond the deductible. I don't know what that is, and I have no idea how much it costs to paint a garage door. I don't imagine you'll find out who did it, so I'll just focus on getting it fixed."

DeMarco persisted. "I'll take that camera card with me, but you should put another one in there, keep that going. How many of those letters have you had?"

Hallie said, "Six altogether, now. The latest one was just a few days ago. I've dropped them all off for Jim. But I'm all good."

DeMarco nodded and, finally, stood. "You're right that there isn't a whole lot we can do, realistically, even if we call that a terroristic threat, which it is. We won't get an ID off that video, though we can estimate height and weight and get closer. But if anybody says anything at school, if you hear anything that makes you think it was one of your students—let me know, and we'll follow it up."

She made a dismissive gesture. "It's just graffiti. Get me the report for the insurance, and it's done."

DeMarco put his notebook away and headed outside, with Jim following him and Mac trailing behind, and Hallie bringing up the rear.

Once they were out there, DeMarco asked Jim, "Talk to you a second?"

"Sure."

Hallie said, "Thanks again for coming out, Deputy. Mac, do you think you could do me a favor and throw a ball for Cletus for a few minutes? He hasn't had enough exercise today, and I'd like to make some coffee."

"Because you were gone all night," Mac said.

"Yes," Hallie said. "I was."

Jim waited until they'd gone into the house, then looked at DeMarco and said, "What."

"No, man. I'm asking *you* 'what.' And 'why.' Why didn't she call you, why did you bring your kid out here, and what just happened in there? I'd swear I was the only one who didn't get it. Why did she stop being worried about somebody vandalizing her house and threatening her life and want me to get lost? You tell me. Why?"

"I'm not sure why," Jim said, which wasn't exactly true. "I'll let you know if I find out."

He'd switched off the emotion and gone to autopilot. DeMarco looked at him searchingly for another minute, then said, "Paradise. My wife says it makes up in intensity what it lacks in importance."

"That's almost poetic," Jim said. "But I don't care."

DeMarco turned for his rig. "If there's any actual police work that needs to be done here, maybe you'll let me know. Next time, tell her just to call you, will you? Cut out the middleman."

SHAME

When Jim went back into the house, he found Hallie in the kitchen, making coffee.

"Sit down," she said. "And tell me what you didn't want to tell the other deputy."

He took a seat at the breakfast bar. "How do you know I didn't want to tell him something? And thanks for getting Mac out of here. I know I shouldn't have brought her. I was expecting this to be something simpler."

She ignored that for the diversion it was. "Because I just spent all night in bed with you. I spent it watching your face and your body and caring about what I was seeing. I saw the moment something changed in you, and I saw it in Mac, too. So tell me, Jim. What did you see?"

There was no choice. He'd known that from the beginning. There was loyalty, but there was also right and wrong, and there was protecting this woman. "One of those guys," he said. "The one who wasn't painting—I'm pretty sure that was Cole."

Her mouth opened, but nothing came out. Her hand jerked, and she spilled coffee on the granite countertop, and on her hand holding the cup. She jumped back, spilled more, and cried out, a sharp, anxious sound. Then she set the pot down on the counter, shoved her hand under the sink faucet, and turned it on.

"I'm sorry," she said, her voice not sounding all the way steady. "I thought it must be something. I don't know why I—"

He was up, taking her hand under the water, examining it.

"I'm fine," she said impatiently. "I was surprised, that was all. I'm just glad it wasn't Mac. I had the most horrible feeling when both of you froze up like that. All I wanted was to get him out of the house so he wouldn't notice."

Her first impulse had been to protect him, and Mac, too, when she herself was the one who'd been threatened. It was so Hallie, and it was doing painful things to his heart.

"No," he said. "That wasn't Mac. She wouldn't do that." He grabbed a rag, mopped up the spilled coffee, then poured two mugs while Hallie pulled her hand out from under the water and examined it.

"Just some redness," she said. "I'm fine. And are you sure about Cole? That's bad news."

Distress again in her voice. For Cole, and for him, and for—who knew who else. His mother, probably. Anthea. Everybody but herself. "I'm pretty sure," he said. "And let's keep a wet rag on that." He picked up her hand himself to check, but she was right. A red patch across the top, but no blistering. He kissed her knuckles, careful to avoid the burned area, and her gaze lifted to his, which let him see the tears she was trying to suppress. Pain, and not from the burn. Shock that somebody had done this to her. Hurt that somebody could hate her so much, when she'd tried so hard to do what was right.

"Hey, baby," he said helplessly. "Hey, now." He finally did what he'd wanted to do from the beginning. He pulled her into him, put his arms around her, and held her close, stroking a hand over her hair. "That was nasty to come home to. I know it." He gave in to impulse and kissed the top of her head. "You're so damn tough, and so damn . . . *good*. And we're going to fix this. I promise."

"Dad." It came from behind him, a sharp, imperious sound.

Hallie jerked back, but Jim didn't let her go for a second. He stepped back with deliberation, turned, still with an arm around Hallie, and looked at Mac, standing there, legs planted, with Cletus, oblivious, beside her. "Yeah, partner?" he asked.

Hallie moved away from his side, and he said, "Rag," rinsed it under the faucet, squeezed most of the moisture out, then wrapped it around her hand. "Hallie burned herself," he told Mac.

"Dad," Mac said again. "Can I talk to you?"

"If you want to tell me that was Cole on the tape," he said, "I already saw it, and I already told Hallie. Ms. Cavanaugh."

"'Hallie' is fine here," Hallie said. "Ms. Cavanaugh's for school."

"Oh." Mac's gaze flew to Hallie, and Jim said, "Cole's her brother, too, you know. This is all about family, even if Cole's messed up right now, so if it's all right with Hallie, we're going to talk about it like a family."

Hallie said, "It's all right with me. And I'd appreciate your help." Still shaken. Still strong.

"Are you going to tell Grandma?" Mac asked. "She's going to be so mad."

"She's not going to be madder than me," Jim said. "And, yeah. I'm going to tell Grandma. But mainly, I'm going to talk to Cole. And then Hallie will do whatever she wants about it. Including pressing charges if she decides to. That's her right."

Hallie stood there, the rag around her hand, and thought about it. Finally, she said, "I'd like you to bring Cole out here, if it turns out it really was him. Who you tell is up to you, but I'd like to talk to him."

◆ ◆ ◆

She had another two hours to think about it before that happened. She got a brief call from Jim and that was all. Meanwhile, she went out and washed the garage door with a mop and a bucket. She had to wash it before she primed it, and she wasn't waiting to hear about the insurance. She was painting this mess over herself. She wanted it gone.

When Jim finally showed up again, he didn't bring Mac. He brought Cole. The boy climbed out of the truck with his face half averted and the hood of his sweatshirt up, followed by his mother.

Vicki shut the door of the truck and said to Hallie, her voice tight, "I apologize for my son. And I apologize for myself."

The lump in Hallie's throat was so big, she could hardly speak past it. "You have nothing to apologize for. Please don't."

"I'm sure I do," Vicki said. "He must have gotten it from me. I didn't talk enough about all of this to him, because I didn't want to. I didn't make it clear enough that none of this was your fault. I probably thought it *was* your fault, somehow. I might as well say it now, when we're all here. It's no secret anymore. What happened to Jim all those years ago, which I just found out about recently, all the things your father did . . . I hope I know better, though, than to blame women for what the men in their lives do. Or to shame a woman," she said, looking Hallie straight in the eye, "because she had sex with a man, even if that man was my son. Especially if he was older than she was, and more experienced than she was. Especially if she might not have wanted it as much as he did."

Hallie was at a loss for words. Cole had backed up a couple steps and was looking absolutely miserable, and Cletus was pressed close to Hallie's side. And Jim came forward and did the same thing he'd done this morning at her sink. He put his arm around her and said, "Hey, now. It's all right. It needs to be out there. It's hurt too much keeping it in."

She took a deep breath, then said, "Would you—would you all like to come in?"

"Yes," Vicki said. "I would. Thank you."

When she walked through the door, she did it with her head high, and it was only then that Hallie realized that the last time she'd been in here, it had probably been as a cleaner. Or as Henry Cavanaugh's unwilling bed partner. Or both.

When they were sitting down in the living room, Hallie told Vicki, "Now I'm the one who's going to tell you I'm sorry."

"It's not your fault," Vicki said. "None of it."

"I know it isn't," Hallie said, "but I still have to say that I'm sorry for everything you went through, and everything you're going through today. What my father did wasn't right. Any of it. And what Cole did— it's part of my father's legacy, too. It's part of the ugliness that's still hurting all of us. All the secrecy, and all the shame."

Vicki had been stone-faced since she'd showed up. Now, her face twitched, and after a moment, she said, "You're right, and you're wrong. You can say it's part of your father's legacy, but it was Cole's choice. Cole's wrong action. And I'm . . . I'm sorry." Her throat worked hard as she swallowed, and she sobbed once, then put her hand up, trying to muffle her weakness, or to hide it.

Cole made a protesting noise from where he sat huddled in the armchair, and Jim raised his head from where he'd been studying his clasped hands, looked at his brother, and said, "Look at that, Cole. That's your mom. She's crying. She has to come back into this house and be ashamed again, and this time, it's because of what you've done. She thinks it's her fault."

Cole's mouth twisted, and he said, "I didn't . . . I didn't mean to. I didn't . . . I'm sorry. I didn't think—"

"Tell her," Jim said.

Cole took a deep, shuddering breath and said, "Mom, I'm sorry. I'm so sorry." Then he was crying, too. Trying to wipe the tears away and failing. Sitting in the chair, huddled up tight, a miserable ball of fifteen-year-old guilt.

It was ten draining minutes by the time they sorted through it all. Finally, Cole was perched on the edge of his chair, ripping a Kleenex in his hands over and over again, his eyes red, and saying to Hallie, "I told . . . I told some of my friends about the letters, after I heard Jim telling Mom you were getting them. And they said, uh . . ." His Adam's apple bobbed as he swallowed. "Wouldn't it be cool if you just left. That we should do some . . . something else, and see if you would, and then I'd get it all. So after I came home from Anthea's last night . . ." He gulped again. "I heard from Anthea that you were gone, so we rode our bikes out here, and we saw that there weren't lights on, and we . . . we did it. I didn't know there'd be cameras."

"You didn't do the painting, though," Hallie said. "You were the one standing back."

Cole shook his head, and Jim said, "What Cole's trying to say is that it doesn't matter who actually did the painting. They were both here. They were both responsible. But it does matter that the other person faces up to it, too, and that you get justice for it. Who was it, Cole?"

Cole said, "I can't . . . I can't tell. I can't do that, too. I can't get him in trouble, too."

"Let me guess," Jim said, his face hard. Grim. "Mr. Invisible Hand."

"I *can't*," Cole said, anguished. "If I tell, so somebody else is in trouble, it's worse. I just make it . . ." His breath was uneven. "I make it worse."

"I understand that," Hallie said. She knew it was a good thing for Cole to take responsibility, but it hurt to see his pain. There had been too much pain in this house, and most of it so unnecessary. "It was the wrong thing to do. You went along with it, and you shouldn't have. And now you know how bad it feels to do something so wrong. I'll bet you lay awake all night thinking about it, didn't you?" When Cole nodded miserably, she said, "That's a good thing. That's shame, and you need to remember how it feels, so you don't have to feel it again. You can see how bad you made your mom feel, and your brother. Remembering that is what's going to make you change."

"And you." The words were low. Muttered. "How I made you feel. If I . . . scared you."

"Yes," she said. "It did scare me. And now . . . it hurts my heart." She was clutching at it, she realized, because it was literally true. She ached. "It hurts me so much to know how bad you've felt about me, that you've been that jealous. And I want to tell you so much, too. I want to tell you about our dad. I want to tell you not to be sorry you didn't know him, because he wasn't a decent person, but that's my own bitterness, and I don't want to focus on that. It's not something I can figure out how to tell you in five minutes, or in a day, but I hope . . . I hope that we'll be able to talk about it, and that I can let you know."

A few tears were making their way out despite all her efforts to suppress them. Jim had his arm around her again, seeming to defy anybody to say anything about it.

"And I want to tell you," she finally went on, swallowing the tears once again, "how glad I'd be to have a brother. I always felt alone. I knew I didn't have anything to complain about, not compared to other people. I was rich, and my dad wanted me, and he paid attention to me, even though it was the . . . the wrong attention sometimes. But I've never had a whole family. And now I might, and I can't stand to think that you . . ." She took a deep breath and tried to continue. "That you hate me. If our father were here, he'd tell me that saying something like that to you was just lying down and asking to get kicked. He always said that there were winners and losers, and if you weren't a winner, you were a loser. But I don't think that's true. I know I don't want to win if it means somebody else has to lose. I don't ever want to win like that. If that's what having his money means, I don't want it. But I don't want his money to hurt you, either. I don't want to see it twist you until you can't even feel shame, the same way he couldn't. That would hurt me more than anything."

Cole wasn't saying a word. He was sitting and staring at her. Jim looked at him, not taking his arm from around Hallie, and said, "And what you just heard—that's the real invisible hand, so you know. That's the hand that pushes you in the right way. Maybe nobody's teaching it in high school, but it's real."

"That's the hand of good," his mother said quietly from his other side. "Or the hand of God, if you want to look at it like that."

"So what do you think?" Jim asked his brother. "Feel enough like an asshole yet?"

Cole gasped, then gave a laugh out of what seemed like sheer surprise. "Yeah," he said. "Yeah."

"Right," Jim said. "Then get out there and paint Hallie's garage while she decides whether she wants to press charges." He stood, and when Hallie got up, too, he said to her, "Oh, no. No way. Your part of this deal, whatever else you do, is to let Cole make up for what he did, and not let him off the hook. We bought everything we needed to do it, and it's going to come straight out of that million-dollar trust fund. Mom and I are taking Cole over to Bob Jenkins's office tomorrow and letting Cole explain why he needs it. But my main part of it is to make sure he does that painting right. He probably won't finish today, but that's all right. He'll finish tomorrow."

"No," Hallie said. "If you don't mind—I'd like to do it together. I'd like to wipe it out and let it be over."

"In that case," Vicki said, "I'd like to help."

Hallie walked over to Cole and put her arms around him. He stiffened, but she didn't respond to that. She kissed him on the cheek, stood back, and said, "No way I'm pressing charges against my brother. No way." Then she went to Jim, pulled his face down, and kissed him, too, heedless of his brother and his mother, and said, "And thank you for being such a good man. Even though you take my heart and just about tear it out."

His arms came up to hold her like he couldn't help it any more than she could. "Funny," he said, "but you do exactly the same thing to me."

She looked at Vicki and hesitated. In the end, Vicki was the one who kissed *her*, then said, "This isn't easy, but lots of things aren't easy. We'll do it. We'll get there."

THERE AND BACK AGAIN

They painted the garage in a few hours, with only one early interruption. When Hallie turned to run her roller through the pan and saw her uncle's Cadillac headed slowly up the driveway.

She set the roller down and wiped her hands on her old jeans as Dale and Faye emerged from the big black car. Cletus, who'd been lying down at the edge of the driveway, was already up, wagging his tail. He would have gone over to greet the newcomers, but Hallie said, "Sit," and held on to his collar for good measure.

Faye spoke first, of course. "Goodness," she said. "I wasn't expecting to see such a . . . family party. Whatever happened?" She was staring at the right-hand side of the garage, which Cole hadn't quite finished painting over yet. A couple words were still visible.

ITCH

DIE

"Yes," Hallie said. "Vicki and Jim and Cole came over to help me after my garage got targeted last night. As you see."

"Hello, Faye," Vicki said. "How are you?" Taking the high road and speaking first. There was a spot of color in each cheek, but nothing but assurance in her voice. She was wearing faded black yoga pants and an old white T-shirt that Hallie had loaned her, but she stood like a queen against Faye's casual-perfect slacks, long sweater, and gold jewelry.

Hallie thought, *That. That's how I want to do it.*

"Oh, I'm just fine," Faye said. "Dale took me to lunch at Sangria Station. He spoils me, I know. I'm too lucky." She looped her arm through her husband's. "Have you been there?"

"No," Vicki said. "Not yet."

"Well, it's a little pricey, isn't it, unless you can get somebody else to pay for it?" Faye's smile was sweet as sugar.

Dale said, "Hi, Vicki. Good to see you. Jim. Cole. But what exactly happened out here? Something to do with those letters you were getting, Hallie?" He looked at the scrawled black writing. "Is that what it said? That you'd die? Terrible."

"It did," she said. "And you're right, it was pretty upsetting. And as far as the letters—I don't know for sure if they're connected." She didn't look at Cole, but she could see from the corner of her eye that he was staring at the ground. "This was just some nastiness, I think. Mischief. I'm happy to have help to get rid of it."

"When did it happen?" Faye asked.

"Last night," Hallie said.

"And you didn't hear anything?" Faye said. "Goodness, I'd think that big dog would have barked or something." She eyed Cletus without much approval. Hallie had taken her hand off his collar, because for once, Cletus wasn't trying to go over and love everybody up.

"I wasn't home," Hallie said. "I was at Sangria Station myself last night, in fact."

"Really," Faye said. "What a coincidence. All by yourself? Or are you seeing somebody?" Her eyes went, reliably as clockwork, to Jim.

"I went by myself," Hallie said. "Decided I needed a night out. Tired of my own company, I suppose, not to mention my own cooking. But I ran into Jim and talked to him for a little while." She was going to put it out there before Faye could find it out. *Nothing to see here, folks.*

Move along. She channeled Vicki, who was still standing there, calm and straight. "I'm afraid I drank too much of their mulled wine and had to go sleep it off, though, so I missed the excitement of catching them in the act. Did you try that wine today?"

"No, we sure didn't," Dale said. "Give me a Budweiser any day. Guess I'm old-fashioned. These days, seems like all kinds of things are old-fashioned. Regular beer, regular coffee. Minding your parents and your teachers, and being married to one person instead of fooling around." He looked at the lettering again. "Well, we won't keep you from your job. I sure hate to see that. Probably just kids, though."

"Probably," Hallie said. "Which is actually a better thought. When an adult does hateful things, it seems more malicious, doesn't it? Teenagers don't have much impulse control. Adults, though—they have to go out of their way to be hurtful."

Dale nodded. "That's true. Well, like I said, we won't keep you. Just stopped by to check how you were. Good to see you, Vicki."

When Dale had turned the big car and they were headed down the driveway again, Hallie said, "Well, that was fun," and picked up her roller again.

"You did good," Vicki said. "Stood right up to that and gave it back like a lady." Hallie felt more than shaky, but Vicki still looked cool. But then, she'd probably had a lifetime of hearing that kind of thing.

Now, Vicki drew her brush along the groove between two panels and said to Cole, "Paint out those words. I don't want to see them anymore. I don't like hate."

◆ ◆ ◆

Hallie had her second dinner party at her house that evening. Pizza again.

They ate it in the dining room, site of so many awkward family meals featuring Hallie's father grilling her about school, ranting about politicians who wanted to give away hardworking people's money, about welfare cheats, and people who had too many children, and immigrants who prayed to the wrong God. And cutting her to miserable shreds if she dared to argue with any of it.

Tonight, it was different. The pizza was in a box on the middle of the table, she'd opened a bottle of red wine, and they were all tired and paint splattered, but the garage door was white again, and things were better.

Everything was going well except for Cletus, who'd started out in his designated spot on the living-room carpet, but was inching forward as Hallie watched.

"Cletus," she said. "Bed."

He wagged his tail like an innocent dog who didn't know what she was talking about, and Cole turned to look at him and said, "He's still lying down, though."

"Yeah," she said, "about five feet from where he started. He does this snake thing." Even as she said it, Cletus wriggled his hips and slid a little closer to Cole. "That," Hallie said. "Like he's sneaky and I won't notice. *Bed*," she said more forcefully, staring Cletus down until he hauled himself up, walked away like a dog carrying a heavy burden, and plopped down with a sigh next to the couch.

"He sure likes people," Cole said.

"He sure likes *pizza*," Hallie said. "He was living with two little kids before, and I'm pretty sure they snuck him every single thing they didn't want to eat, and he cleaned it up for them. He was Eileen Hendricks's dog," she told Vicki. "My dad's cleaner."

"How's she doing?" Vicki asked. "I heard you gave her Henry's truck. I have to say . . ." She smiled, a secret, satisfied thing, and took a sip of her wine. "That made me feel good to hear."

"It made me feel good to *do*," Hallie said. "Even better than getting rid of the bear."

"He had a *bear?*" Cole asked.

"Stuffed," Hallie said.

"Trophy," Jim explained. "Mounted on its hind legs in the entry-way. Big sucker. Had a snarl you wouldn't believe. Claws. The works."

"Wicked," Cole said.

"Well," Hallie said, "not so much. Although maybe if I'd stuck it in the driveway, we might've spared ourselves some work today."

Cole grinned. "You mean, like, the lights would've come on, and we would've run? Oh, man. Tom w—"

He cut himself off, and Jim said, "Oh, yeah? Ingeborg scared of bears? Scared of their invisible hands, maybe?"

"I didn't mean to tell you," Cole said. "Please don't tell," he begged Hallie, sounding much younger than fifteen, in that way teenage boys had of bouncing back and forth between childhood and adolescence. "He'll know it was me that busted him."

"Nope," Jim said. "The cameras busted him. You didn't tell, but too bad, so sad, he got busted anyway. Unless you're in Hollywood, don't perform on film. Words to live by. You can tell him all about it at school tomorrow. I promise you, he'll already have found out."

◆　◆　◆

He'd put a damper on the mood, Jim found. Well, tough. Actions had consequences. Painting over the graffiti was all fine and good, but no matter how forgiving Hallie was, it had still happened. And if the lesson was going to sink in for Cole, the bad feelings had to last more than a day.

After dinner, his mom walked out the door with him and Hallie. Cole was already in the truck, as if he couldn't get out fast enough, but Vicki lingered for a moment.

"If I can suggest something . . ." Hallie said.

"I guess you've earned the right to suggest," Vicki said, but she was looking wary.

"Well . . ." Hallie said. "When you take Cole to see Bob Jenkins tomorrow and tell him about paying for the paint, you might talk to him about getting the money for some counseling for Cole, too. This was so much to have dumped on him. The money—that's a huge complication, and it's going to keep on being one. I know how hard it's been for me to deal with everything it's brought up, and he's only fifteen. I can get you some names from people at the school, if you like." She paused another minute, then went on. "Doing what he did, something so reckless and out of character—as a teacher, I'd call that acting out. I'd call it a cry for help. If you get him talking, get him working out a way to deal with those feelings, though, today could be the best thing that could have happened."

Vicki nodded thoughtfully. "I guess I get that. I wouldn't have thought of it. Counseling hasn't come much my way. More like a sharp slap across the face and a twist of my ear. Which is probably why I ran away from home and got pregnant, so I'm willing to believe there's a better way."

"I could see if I could find a therapist who's a younger man, maybe," Hallie said. "One who's cool. Somebody who can gain his trust, who he can open up to, who'll understand how confused he is."

"Not like me, you mean," Jim said.

Aw, damn. He'd known he'd done it wrong. It was so hard not to react like a cop.

"It's hard for you to separate," Hallie said. "I'm guessing you were too much like him. That's why he frustrates you."

Jim couldn't help smiling. "You're a witch, you know that?" When she looked startled, he said, "You see too much."

"I'm a high school teacher. It's my job."

"Yeah, well, it's my job, too. And you still see more. Or you see differently."

Vicki said, "Probably true." She gave Hallie a quick, strong hug and said, "I'll give it a try. Good idea. Thank you for today."

"Thank *you*," Hallie said, hugging her back.

Vicki glanced at Jim, then said, "I'll be in the truck," and took off.

"It's cold out here," Hallie told him when it was just the two of them. "You should go before they freeze in the truck."

"I'm going to drop them off," he said, "then do one more errand, and then I'd like to come back. To talk to you," he added when she looked alarmed. "I can't stay anyway. I have to get Mac from Anthea's by eight thirty. But I want to come out for half an hour first."

She wasn't exactly looking welcoming. "I'm not supposed to open the garage door for two days after it's painted, though. We can't even put your truck inside."

"Half an hour. That's it. We can finish that bottle of wine."

"There's only about one more glass."

"That's OK. We had enough last night." He gave in, then, put his hands on her shoulders, bent his head, and brushed his lips over hers. His body tried to fall into her softness, and he had to force himself to step back and say, "Yeah. Be back here by seven thirty or so. Half an hour, that's all. Just because I need to."

"Because you need to what?" Her arms were wrapped around herself, and she was shivering. It *was* too cold out here.

"Because I need to talk to you. And I need to kiss you goodnight."

◆　◆　◆

When he pulled up forty-five minutes later, she was outside waiting for him, looking cold again.

"Really," she said when he hopped down from the truck. "It's not a good idea for you—"

He shouldn't feel this way, and he knew it, but the anger was bubbling up in spite of himself.

"Yeah," he said. "It's not a good idea. I can't park in your driveway for twenty minutes and talk to you about the crime that's just happened at your house because somebody will report that I'm in there banging your brains out. Would it help if I came in uniform? Or doesn't that work, either? If I brought DeMarco, would that be an orgy?"

"Jim." That was all she said. It was enough.

He took a breath, ran his hand over the back of his neck, looked up at the cold, pale sliver of moon, then exhaled and dropped his hand. "Sorry. Out of line. You're right, I'm frustrated. And you're allowed to say that you don't want to see me. I didn't give you the chance before, did I?" He tried to smile. "Never mind. I know I didn't. Guess I'll do it now."

She said, "I want to see you. And even if somebody saw your truck—I guess you're right. It's half an hour, and you were out here today with a whole bunch of chaperones. But thank you for noticing."

"Noticing what?"

"That you didn't give me the chance to say no."

"Oh. Yeah. That. It's been a while since I've been with somebody who won't let me get away with being the boss."

"You mentioned that. I guess you'd better come in."

They sat on the couch with Cletus curled up in the corner of the room, and she poured the last two half glasses of wine and said, "We've got quite the habit going here."

"We can go back on the wagon tomorrow."

"So," she said. "I'm thinking there's a reason you're here. That you were so . . . insistent. And it's not because you want to jump my bones."

"Nah. I want to jump your bones. But I know we can't. I wanted to tell you how the rest of it went, and I wanted to tell you in person. And maybe to make sure you're all right," he admitted. "Because I hate leaving you out here alone."

"Ah." It was a soft breath. She was sitting against the arm of the couch, her legs, in a clean, faded pair of jeans, curled up under her. She'd taken a shower and changed while he'd been gone. She looked pretty, she smelled like flowers again, and she was distracting. "Let me guess," she said. "You paid Cole's friend a surprise visit. You put the fear of God in him, and into his parents, too."

"His mom. And did I mention that you were a witch?"

"So how did it go?"

"All right. Cocky little ba—twerp. Tried to tell me it wasn't him. That lasted about five minutes. Then, when he was trying not to show that he was shaking and his mom was starting to cry—and, no, I didn't enjoy that part—I told him you were deciding whether to press charges. That got him going good. My advice? Take a few days to decide."

"I don't need a few days."

He sighed. "I know you *don't*. But take a few days to tell me you've decided. Make him sweat it. Although I have to tell you, he wouldn't be hurt by a trip to a courtroom."

"I believe you. But I can't do that without Cole being dragged into it, too, and it's just . . ." She shook her head. "Too ugly. My aunt and uncle knowing, and everything. Faye saying something even more poisonous to your mom. Cole feeling like everybody saw him as a delinquent. If he'd done something more than this, if *he* needed a trip to a courtroom, it'd be different. But I don't think so. I think he's . . . teetering. When seeing your mom cry made *him* cry . . . that was good. I bet—what's the other boy's name again?"

"Tom Ingeborg."

"I bet Tom didn't cry when his mom cried."

"No. But teenage boys without dads . . . they can be all kinds of screwed up. That's no news flash."

"Fortunately," she said, "lots of them turn out all right all the same, especially once they get a little help. Some of them turn out just fine."

"With a *lot* of help."

"And Cole's got a lot of help. He may not have a dad, but he's got you. And you're something special."

Approval. That was what women did that killed you. No, not *women*. One woman. The right woman. When she looked at you like that, let you know she thought that much of you . . . that was the one you couldn't fight.

"Can I ask you a question?" she said.

"You know you can."

She waited a second, and he had no idea what to expect. And then she asked, "Could you . . . would you tell me about your wife? About when she died?"

It was a U-turn for sure. It wasn't anywhere he wanted to go tonight.

"You don't have to if you don't want to," she said. "But I'd like to know. It's so much a part of you, and of Mac. I know I don't have a right to ask, but I—"

"No." He took a sip of wine just to do something. "You can ask. But I would've thought Anthea would have told you."

"I didn't want her to. She knew that. We never talked about you. All I know is that you were back here and that Maya died of breast cancer. And that the baby died, too."

WITH HER LIFE

He was still reacting to that when she said, "I'm sorry. I shouldn't have blurted it out like that. You don't owe me any explanations. What we did—I know it's not a relationship, and it doesn't obligate you." She'd swung around to sit up straight, all her earlier ease gone. "It's just this day. It's just . . . family, and seeing you with Mac, and—"

He couldn't stand seeing her working herself up like that. "It's a relationship," he said. "Some kind of one, anyway. And I can tell you."

"I don't want to make you feel worse, making you talk about it."

His mouth twisted, but it wasn't a smile this time. "Ah, yeah. People say that. What they don't realize is, you live with it every day. Every minute, at the beginning. It's not like they're bringing it up. It's already there. And there's no way it could feel worse."

She'd sunk back against the arm of the couch again, still watching him warily, and he turned the glass in his hands, looked down at the ruby-red liquid, dark and rich as blood, and said, "So—yeah. All right, here we go. It was almost three years ago. I got home from a pretty rough deployment and found out that Maya was four months pregnant. Must've happened right before I left, and she hadn't told me while I was gone, because she didn't want to distract me, or she wanted to surprise me, or both. And I was just . . ." He sighed. "Thrilled. I mean, *thrilled.* Mac was nine, and we'd kind of given up hope of another baby. Funny, because Mac was an accident, you know, but we'd been trying for a few years, and had never been able to make it happen on purpose. Until then."

"And then . . ." Hallie said softly.

The words came slowly. "I went to the next doctor's visit with her. Man, I was excited about that. I'd missed the whole thing with Mac, like I told you. Didn't get to be there to see her born or anything. But this time—we were going to get the sonogram. I was going to see my baby's heart beating on the screen, the way you do." He took a deep breath, let it out. "I couldn't wait. And then we got into the room, and it wasn't like that at all."

They'd been shown into the doctor's private office instead of an exam room, and the doctor, a tired-looking woman, had greeted them without smiling, and had said, once they sat down, "I'm afraid we have some bad news."

"What?" Maya's hand went instantly to her barely there bump. "The baby—"

"It's not the baby," the doctor said. "Or it is, in part." She folded her hands on the desk, and Jim remembered looking at those clasped hands. At the engagement band she turned endlessly with a finger, back and forth, back and forth. He looked at her hands, because he couldn't stand to look at her face. He'd clocked more missions than he could count by then, but he couldn't look at her face. "The biopsy we did of your breast," she told Maya. "The news isn't good."

"What biopsy?" Jim got out.

Maya looked at him, her pixie face stricken. "I had a lump in my breast. I didn't tell you, because I knew it was nothing. I knew it had to be nothing."

"I'm sorry," the doctor said again, and then she gave them the details, and none of them were good.

314

"I'll be referring you to an oncologist, of course," she said. "But this type of tumor is aggressive, especially in premenopausal women. Which means that the only way to combat it is aggressively."

"Let's do that, then," Jim said with relief. "We can fight it, you mean. Let's do it."

"In order to do that," the doctor said, "we'll need to terminate the pregnancy."

"No," Maya said.

Jim said nothing. He waited.

"Otherwise," the doctor went on, "all we can do is a mastectomy, which isn't enough. You won't be able to begin radiation or chemotherapy until after the baby is delivered, and even if we take it early . . ." She shook her head. "Four months' delay could be a very long time."

Maya said, "What if I do . . . delay, though? The baby would be OK, right?"

The doctor hesitated. "There are no guarantees."

"But I could get treated then?"

"Yes. If it were soon enough. I know this is a difficult decision," she went on. "I realize you'll need time to think. But I must tell you that terminating the pregnancy offers you your best chance at survival."

Survival. It had hit Jim exactly like that bullet in the side. Hit him hard, and spun him around. *He* was supposed to be the one in danger. Not Maya. Not their baby. He'd kept thinking, *This isn't how it's supposed to work. It can't be this way.* But it was.

He told Hallie the bare bones of it, but it was enough. He'd noticed that her eyes seemed to change color according to her mood. Right now, they were a mossy gray-green. "What . . ." she asked. "What did you do?"

"It wasn't what I did. It was what Maya did. She made them show her the baby, first of all. What they'd been going to do that day, the reason we went in there. The doctor said, 'If you're going to terminate the pregnancy, it's better not to see,' and Maya turned on her like a wildcat and said, 'It's *my* baby. It's mine, and it's Jim's. We need to see it before we decide.' And there I was, doing that thing I'd thought about so much. Holding her hand, seeing the tears roll down her cheeks, watching these shadows on the screen with her. Having the tech say, 'That's the heart. See that white pulse?' His arms were all close to his body, like he was hugging himself, and his legs were kicking. A boy. Our son."

Hallie was crying now. Just a few silent tears, exactly the way Maya had done that day. "And I knew," Jim said, "looking at that white pulse? I knew Maya wouldn't do it, even before she told me. She was such a good mom. All light and . . . fun, but fierce as a tiger, too. Once, I was taking Mac to kindergarten with her, and this jerk pulls up and double-parks to let his kid off, and the kid starts walking behind the car, and the guy starts *backing up*. And before I can get there, because she's closer, Maya's behind his car, pounding on the trunk. Like she's going to stop it with her body. She didn't even think. She was just there. I think that was about the most scared I'd ever been. But that day we found out . . . that was so much worse."

"But you don't have a son. It didn't work." Her face was gentle, so much compassion in it. And still, the words hurt.

"No. I don't have a son." *It can't feel worse,* he'd said. But it could still cut him to the bone. "I got a compassionate discharge, left Fort Benning, and took Maya back home to Paradise, which I guess you knew. Where my mom could help take care of her and Mac. I got the job here, and I did the job, because I didn't have a choice. And she kept saying, 'It's going to be all right, babe. You'll see.' But it wasn't. She got to thirty weeks, and that was all. Not even seven months. And then she was too . . ." He took a breath. "Too sick. They said they had to take the baby. He wasn't doing . . . great."

"And they couldn't do it in time?"

"No. They took him. I was in the room with her, holding her hand. Her body couldn't take the strain. She died right there on the table. The last thing she said to me was . . ." He had to stop and breathe again.

"'Take care of our babies.' She died thinking he would live. She gave her life so he would live. And he didn't."

"I'm glad she didn't know," Hallie said.

"So am I."

He'd buried their son in her arms. The tiny, fragile little body, his head much too big for his skeletal limbs, dressed in one of the preemie outfits Maya had ordered online, because she'd been too sick to shop. The little blue hat atop his wizened, old-man's face. Jim had had them put the baby on her chest, her arms wrapped around him, so she'd be holding him forever, the same way she'd done all along. Protecting him all the way to the end. With her life.

"And I kept thinking," he told Hallie. "When I was standing there with Mac, holding her hand, watching the casket go into the ground. I kept thinking, why didn't I try harder to get her to have the abortion? Why didn't I keep hammering until she gave in? Because God help me, I'd have made that trade. I knew it then. I knew it all along."

"Because you couldn't have," Hallie said. "Because you could never have changed her mind."

"I tried hard, but not hard enough. She said, 'There's no choice. Maybe I can get rid of my baby, and I'll survive. *Maybe*. Probably not, and you know it as well as I do. And I know it wouldn't be a wrong thing for somebody else, but it's wrong for me, and I can't make it right. If I got rid of my baby just for a better shot at saving myself, I wouldn't be able to live with myself.'"

"If she was sure," Hallie said, "then it *was* right for her. But oh, Jim. I'm so sorry."

She'd moved, somehow. She was in his arms, holding him the same way he'd wanted to hold her earlier that day, to tell her it would be all right, that he'd keep her safe. But now, she was the one doing it. And her arms around him felt so good, in a completely different way than they had the night before. He held her, and it was better.

Finally, she moved back. "That wasn't the right thing to bring up when you had half an hour," she said. "And I did it anyway."

"Chalk it up to a raw day. A rough day. And you thinking about family. The family you had, and the one you wished for."

Saying it made something twist hard in his chest, but it wasn't the raw pain it had been at the beginning. It hurt, and it always would, but it was pain he knew how to live with.

"You don't get over things like that," she said, echoing his thoughts. "Not really. You just move through."

"You're right." He left the rest of the wine, stood up, and said, "And I do have to get Mac. I wish I could stay, but seems like we've always got reasons we can't be together."

"Yes," she said. "We do."

◆ ◆ ◆

Hallie stood in the driveway for the third time that evening, watching Jim's taillights receding down the hill. He turned onto the main road and disappeared from view, and she looked at Cletus. He looked back at her, his tail gently waving, and she said, "Yeah. You're right. Sometimes you have to know."

Back inside, she rinsed out the wine glasses and put them in the dishwasher. It was almost eight thirty, and tomorrow she'd be up at five thirty to go running before school. She moved around the house mechanically, packing up, getting ready for the day. The same routine of a thousand other nights. Done alone. Always alone.

When she was finished, she pulled her nightgown out of the closet, but she didn't get undressed. She sank down on the edge of the bed, clutched the white fabric to her, and tried to hold the sorrow back, but it refused to be contained. It rose like a hot red tide, just that strong, just that insistent. The tears came despite everything, and they overtook her until she sobbed. She was rocking back and forth on the bed, crying until her chest hurt. Her chest and her heart. Until she was hollowed out.

Still holding her nightgown. Still alone.

She didn't even know who she was crying for most. For Jim, who'd had to bury his wife and his baby. For Mac, who would never feel her mother's touch again or hear her voice. Or maybe, shamefully, for herself, because she'd never had anybody she could love that hard, anybody whose loss would have torn her apart like that. And because she was afraid she never would.

The bitter truth was—asking Jim about it hadn't been for him. She'd put him through that pain just to . . . to inoculate herself. To remind herself of what he'd had, and what he'd lost, and what he missed. And to remind herself, above all, that the woman he still loved, the mother of his children, the woman who'd risked everything, who'd been so strong and so brave . . . that woman hadn't been one single bit like Hallie Cavanaugh.

IN THE FAMILY

Jim went with his mother and Cole to see Bob Jenkins on Monday, as he'd promised. Bob listened to Cole's halting explanation with his shrewd eyes traveling between the three of them, finally resting on Cole with a speculative expression.

"So you tried to push Hallie into leaving town," he said at the end. "And you're saying she's not going to press charges?"

"That's what she said," Jim said. "Of course, she could still change her mind." He didn't want Cole to get too comfortable. "So what about that money for the paint?"

"And we'd like to get Cole some counseling, too," Vicki said, "to help him adjust to all these changes. Which I imagine could get a little expensive, take a while."

Bob waved a hand. "That seems like a good idea, and it's easy enough. I just have to get Aldon Cranfield to sign off on it. I should be able to do that within the next couple days."

"Better get there early in the day," Vicki said drily. "Why Henry would appoint him as a trustee, I can't imagine. If Cole's money is tied up in that trust until he's twenty-five, who knows how far Aldon will slide by then? Everybody knows he's dipping into that bottle in his desk by two every afternoon."

"Well, never mind," Bob said. "When Henry got an idea in his head, there was no talking him out of it, but I assure you that I'm watching out for Cole's interests. I'll be reviewing the statements carefully to make sure Aldon hasn't made any mistakes. But to get back to Hallie, I have to say—she's more forgiving than her father would have been. Henry could be a bad enemy. Hallie takes after her mom more, I guess. She's probably getting pretty nervous, between what happened here and those letters, even though she knows now that the graffiti came from Cole. You sure you didn't send the letters, too?" he asked Cole.

"No," he said earnestly. "I mean, yes, I'm sure. I didn't send them, I swear."

Jim believed him. He'd hammered on his brother some more on the way over here, with his mom pitching in, had asked Cole some questions that would've tripped him up if he'd sent them. He'd done the same with Tom Ingeborg the night before, and he was satisfied that neither of them had sent the letters. The letters weren't impulsive. They were a steady campaign, a slow, insidious *drip-drip-drip* on Hallie's sense of safety.

"Kinda being hit from all sides, isn't she?" Bob said, echoing Jim's thought. "And now she's involved the sheriff's department, which tells me she's feeling mighty unsafe. If you're talking to her, you might suggest that she spend some of that money she's getting on some security measures, just for some peace of mind. Or maybe I'll drop by sometime and check on her, mention that myself."

"She's done it," Jim said. "She's bought security cameras. That's how Cole got busted."

"Hmm," Bob said. "Not a bad thought, although the letters sound like a parent to me, something to do with the school. 'Two isolated incidents,' that's what I'd call it. Why would the letters have anything to do with the money?"

"I wouldn't call it that," Jim said. "And I'd say that whoever's sending the letters is underestimating her."

Bob's gaze sharpened. "Do you have a reason for saying that?"

"Call it a cop's nose twitching."

"Ah. Well, in the law, we don't deal so much in twitches. We tend to like cold, hard facts. And the facts I have are that Hallie's got somebody mad at her, and that she wasn't home on Friday night." He gazed at Jim. "Was she hiding out, maybe? Scared about the letters after all? I saw her in here when we read the will, of course, and I've talked to her some since. I'd be happy to think she's toughened up, but I'm not so sure. Or is there some other explanation?"

Jim looked back at him. "Why do you want to know?"

"Well . . ." Bob spread out his hands. "I *am* Cole's trustee, and his interests aren't necessarily the same as Hallie's. In fact, they're diametrically opposed, aren't they? My job is to make sure the terms of the will are carried out, but as far as the individual parties . . . with a situation that's getting this complicated, Cole may want to have legal representation to ensure his interests are looked after." Bob cleared his throat, then addressed Vicki. "As you're Cole's guardian, I'm thinking that you may want to have a conversation with me about protecting his interests. And that it may be better if it's a private conversation, so I can spell it out to you a little better. Family . . . that always gets tricky, doesn't it? So many different . . . priorities."

"Not really," she said.

"Mom," Jim began.

Vicki held up a hand and said, "Mind if we take a minute, Bob?"

"Of course." He stood up. "Whatever you need. Use my conference room."

"Thanks," she said.

Bob led them to the room and said, "Just poke your head into my office when you're done."

When he closed the door, Vicki looked at Jim and said, "What?"

Jim pulled out his phone and dialed a number. When it picked up, he said, "I'm sitting in your conference room. Could you come in here, please?"

His mother looked at him, a little smile on her face, and said, "You always were a whole lot smarter than you liked to let on."

Thirty seconds later, Anthea was sliding into a chair beside Jim, saying, "I didn't hear you were coming by."

Vicki said to Jim, "You tell her. You're the best at explaining."

Jim did it, laying out the facts, quick and concise. Anthea heard him out to the end, making a few notes on a pad, nodding.

"So why am I here?" she asked when he was done.

"Because," Vicki said, "I'm not letting Bob, or anybody else, drive a wedge between Cole and Hallie. There's nothing worse than family ugliness over money, whether it's a daughter-in-law taking the good china that the daughter thought was coming to her and cutting that family in two, or a brother and a sister trying to do each other out of millions of dollars. I'm not having that in my family. I spent all night and all day thinking about it, and I'm not doing anything—*any-thing*—that's going to make that more likely to happen, including—especially—hiring somebody to help it happen. That kind of ugliness makes the person who does it ugly, too." She turned to look at Cole. "If you go after your sister's money, you'd better know that you'll be breaking my heart. You'd better know that I'd want to lie right down and die if I thought that was the son I raised."

"Mom," Cole said, "I get it. I got it yesterday. You don't have to tell me."

"That means," his mother went on, "that even if you knew for *sure* that Jim and Hallie were having sex, you wouldn't tell anybody. *Anybody.* Bob. Your friends. Anybody. You're not saying, well, here's a way I can get her money, and all I have to do is tell, and anyway, *I* didn't do it, *she* did it. You're not going to do that, because you'd be hurting her, you'd be hurting Jim, and you'd be hurting me. For *nothing.*"

Nothing that matters. For millions of dollars that you don't need. That you *want*, and then you'll want more and more and more, until nothing will ever be enough. I don't care if you walk in on the two of them stark naked and doing the wild thing in your bed. You keep your mouth *shut*, you hear? They're your family."

"Mom," Cole said. "Geez. Ick."

She ignored that. "Promise me."

"All right," he said. "I promise. Geez."

"Not enough," she said. "Sit here in front of your brother and your sister and me and *promise* us that you won't. Tell us that you love us more than your father's money."

"What do you want?" he said.

"Cross your heart," Anthea said.

"What am I, five?" he complained.

"Nope," she said. "But it still counts."

He drew the *X* on his chest. "I cross my heart that I won't go after Hallie's half of the money. I won't do anything else to try to get it. And I will always love my mother bestest of all. How's that?"

"Sarcastic," Jim said, "but not bad."

"But, dude," Cole told him. "Don't do it in my *bed.* Come *on.*"

Jim had to smile. "Nah. Cross my heart."

"Right," Anthea said. "So we done?" Managing, as always.

"No," Vicki said. She opened her purse and took out her wallet. "In the movies, somebody gives the attorney a dollar, and that makes them her client. Is that actually how it works?"

"Well, yes," Anthea said. "You have to hire the person."

Vicki pulled out a bill from her wallet. "All I have is a five. That'll have to do. You're your brother's attorney now. I'm hiring you. As his guardian, I'm telling you that from now on, we're only talking to you. We're keeping this in the family."

ALL THE WAY AROUND

It was proving a whole lot trickier than the killer had hoped. Hallie wasn't showing any signs at all of being scared off. In fact, she looked to be hunkering down. Refurnishing the house, making it hers. Settling into her job at the school like she was planning to stay there, even though her contract was only for the semester.

The graffiti incident had been in the police blotter on Monday morning, and news had gotten around pretty quickly in the days since, but even that hadn't seemed to shake her, and the letters weren't doing a thing, either. For somebody as soft as she was, she was sticking like a burr. But then, nothing had been violent yet. Could be she thought it was only words. And she'd be used to hard words after growing up with Henry.

Physically, though, she was probably still timid. That was unlikely to change in a person. She'd sold Henry's snowmobile, his Jet Ski. Probably didn't like to go fast. That was a thought to consider, if worst came to worst.

There was no need to go there yet. The will had included more than one condition she had to satisfy, after all, and in that other area, she didn't seem to be doing nearly so well, did she?

She'd been seen running through town with Jim Lawson in the early morning hours. She'd admitted that he'd been at her house a couple times. He'd helped her clean out her house and repaint her garage. And best of all, he'd been spotted at Sangria Station with her. Holding her hand. On a night when she hadn't come home.

Too bad there was no proof beyond that.

That was the tricky thing. Proof. Unless you actually got eyewitnesses to spot them having sex, how did you *prove* that two people had had a sexual relationship?

If they'd spent the night together, that was how. If only their cars had both been in a motel lot on that night when Hallie hadn't come home. A bill passed to a front-desk clerk, a look at the motel register, a talk with a maid—those might have been enough. If only their cars had been in the same place. And if only you knew in time.

A private investigator. That was a thought.

Who Jim would spot, or hear about, in a heartbeat.

The answer came a couple hours later, popped into the killer's head just like that. It was simple, and a bit of online research confirmed it. If Jim and Hallie couldn't keep their hands off each other already, even in a restaurant, *something* would happen by February. Or, better, multiple somethings. A pattern of secret meetings, simultaneous disappearances, and the records to show where they'd both been. It would be easy. No need to test Hallie's courage at all. No need to escalate. All neat and clean. They'd hang themselves, with no need even to provide the rope.

A discreet order, paying extra for fast delivery, and by Friday, everything was ready for step one.

Hallie's car was easy, too, parked as it was at the staff lot of the middle school every day. A quick trip home for a change of clothes, finishing the outfit off with a camo parka nobody would associate with the killer, even if anyone happened to notice the lone pedestrian hurrying up the street, head down and hood up, in a driving pre-Halloween storm in which rain was rapidly turning to sleet. A dash through the parking lot as if heading for the shelter of the school, a hand on the rear bumper of first one car, then the other, weaving through the rows. Hands in your pockets already, because it was nasty out here, then a rapid downward bob. A hand under the rear bumper, and turning and dashing back the way you'd come.

Easy.

The other vehicle was trickier. Garaged, which was inconvenient. And there were people you could follow to find your moment and people you couldn't. Not in a town as small as Paradise. Not with somebody who'd been trained to watch for pursuit.

There was no rush, though. It was barely November. Patience, that was all. Of course, bugs would be the best. Yeah, *that* would be proof. You'd have to get access, but that would be possible, too. It only required patience.

It was all starting. A few hiccups, but overall, playing out almost as if Henry had known this would happen. Could he have planned it this way, somehow?

Yes. Of course he could have. Henry had cared about one thing above everything and everybody else. Winning. It didn't matter who it was. Even blood ties didn't register with Henry the way they did with other people. The killer had seen that often enough.

Given all that, what could be more likely than that Henry had set Hallie up? She'd seemed to live her life to defy her father, and her last five years denying him altogether. That had galled him. It had *more* than galled him. It had infuriated him. Wouldn't it have been just like him, then, to put her into a situation where she'd fall, where she'd fail? Where she could be humiliated and exposed? Where she'd have the prize in her grasp and know that it was her own fault that she'd lost it?

Yes. That would have been *exactly* like Henry. The killer hadn't helped Henry in his last moments, maybe, but helping this situation along would surely make up for it. Or maybe you could look at it another way entirely. What would Henry have hated most? Helplessness.

Impotence. Having his wishes ignored, his anger and threats disregarded. He would've fumed in a hospital, raged in a nursing home.

On the other hand . . . a quick exit in the prime of his life, before he'd lost his eye for a big-game animal or a pretty woman, or his ability to hunt either of them down and win his trophy. While he'd still been the prince of his domain, the conqueror of his kingdom, the master of all he surveyed.

And now he could win from beyond the grave as well.

Yes. You could definitely call it a favor all the way around. One final service to a man who had lived to be served.

SURPRISE PACKAGE

Jim had the front end of the truck jacked up, switching over to his winter tires. He'd left it late, not doing it until mid-November, with the first major storm of the season blowing in the night before. But then, he'd been busier than usual, too.

He remembered what Hallie had said when she'd been telling him about Cletus, about her life being more complicated now. That sometimes complicated was better. It was true. And she could go on and complicate his life a bunch more as far as he was concerned.

Unfortunately, other than talking to her on the phone the week before about the graffiti incident, during which she'd—no surprise—told him she wasn't pressing charges, he hadn't seen her since that night at her house. When he'd told her about Maya.

There'd been something odd about her when he'd left. Like she was drawing back. She'd asked him to tell her, though, and she'd seemed to care so much. So why would she do that?

She'd felt like it was too much involvement, maybe. Or she'd worried that it was getting out of control, that he couldn't be with her without touching her. The way he'd come back that night without asking her if he could, without seeming to care that he was putting her at risk by doing it.

Damn it. All right, maybe complicated wasn't better.

He got the front tires on, then jacked up the back of the truck, got the stands in place, and was working on the left rear wheel when Mac came out to the garage.

"Hey, partner," he said. "Coming out to give me a hand?"

"Dad," she said. "I have a crisis."

He put down the wrench and swiveled on his haunches. "Oh?"

She stood there, hand on her hip, drumming her fingers, and frowned absently. "So I bought Candy a make-your-own-jewelry-box kit for her birthday party tonight, right?"

"Uh . . . I don't know. Did you?"

"Yeah. I did. And today Monique was texting me about the party, and she said *she* got that for her. And Monique's Candy's best friend."

"OK," he said cautiously.

She sighed as if he were dense. "So if she's her best friend, I have to let *her* give it to Candy. Because it's what Candy really wants. I guess I could give it to *Monique* next month, when it's *her* birthday, if she invites me to her party, and then they could match. She and Candy could match, I mean. But I'd have to tell Candy first, so Candy doesn't buy her that."

Jim was working on the lug nuts again. This didn't seem like a crisis so much as a long, girl-logic talk of the type he never understood. "Or you could just go on and give Candy the box and let her return the extra one and buy something else," he said, even though he was pretty sure that would turn out to be wrong. "Give her the receipt. That's like—free present, get what you want."

"*Dad*. No." As he'd figured, he'd been wrong. "She wouldn't do that. She'd have to pretend she was excited about getting two. She'd have to say, 'Oh, that's great! Now I can have one for earrings and one for everything else!' or something like that."

"Right," he said. "Sounds like you had a problem, but you know the answer. Not sure why it's a crisis."

"Because I have to buy a new present before the party."

"So we swing by the mall on the way."

She sighed again. "I have to *wrap* it. I can't just *hand* it to her in the *bag*. And I have to think of something good."

He was wrestling the wheel off now, rolling it to the side of the garage and then rolling the snow tire over. Mac was talking more, something about him giving her a ride, but he wasn't listening. He was pulling something out from behind the wheel well, something his work light had picked up. Something that definitely shouldn't have been there.

He was still on his haunches, turning it in his hand, and Mac said, "Dad?"

"Huh?" He looked up.

"What's wrong? What's that?"

He considered not telling her. He didn't want her to know.

"If you don't tell me," she said, suddenly not sounding like an eleven-year-old diva, but like his responsible daughter again, "I'll worry about you. It's not like a . . . a bomb, is it?"

"No," he said slowly. "I'm guessing it's a GPS. A tracking device."

Mac crouched beside him, and touched the shiny metal disk on the top. "Is this a magnet?"

"Yep. Somebody reached right up under the truck and slapped this sucker on there. Could've happened anytime."

"But why? Who would want to track you?"

"I don't know." But he was getting a pretty good idea.

"What are you going to do about it?"

"I'm going to log it in at work. And then I'm going to . . ." He turned the black box in his hand. About three inches long and two wide. "I'm going to figure out what's going on."

"You know what you should do?" She was looking excited. "You should fool them. If somebody's trying to track you, you should put it on some *other* car. Except if somebody was trying to hurt you," she seemed to realize, "you couldn't do that. If they were trying to find out when you were someplace so they could get you—that would make somebody else be in danger. But you could put it on a—a train, or something. A train that was going to New York City, maybe, and then the person would be driving all the way to New York City, following it. Or not a train, because then the GPS would show the railroad tracks, right? A semi. How about that? That would just be on the highway."

He smiled, put a hand out, and tugged her braid. "You know," he said, "whatever you talk about—you're pretty darn smart."

She smiled, then was serious again. "*Do* you think they're trying to follow you to hurt you?"

"No. Why would they? They know where I live." That probably hadn't been the best thing to say, so he went on quickly. "I think I know what this is about."

"I only have you, you know." She wasn't looking at him anymore. "And you're a cop."

Mac was always confident, but now, the vulnerability was right there. This was the nine-year-old who'd slept with her battered old stuffed rabbit for months after her mother had died, then had put it back on her shelf every morning so he wouldn't know.

"You *don't* only have me," he said. "You have Grandma, and you have Aunt Anthea and Uncle Ben and Cole. You've got a whole bunch of family, and they all love you like crazy."

"I don't want you to die, though." Her voice was small, and it tore at his heart.

"And I don't want to die. That's why I'm smart, and I'm careful."

"Mom was smart. Mom was careful."

"Yes. She was. Mom got unlucky, and so did we. But I'm a lucky guy, mostly. I know that, because I got your mom, and then I got you. And besides," he said, putting an arm around her, "I have to stick around to do your hair. I have to go to your college graduation and cheer too loud and embarrass you. I have to check out your first car before I let you buy it, and hang the shelves in your first apartment, and walk you down the aisle when you get married, and tell you you're beautiful and pretend I'm not choking up when I give you away, and be there for you any other time in your life that you need a dad. And I intend to be around to do every bit of that. You bet I do." He held her a little closer, squeezed her a little tighter, and pretended he wasn't choked up right now. "OK, partner?"

She nodded, still not looking at him. "OK. But be careful."

"Always. And I'll think about what you said. About tricking them. That was a good one. I liked the semi idea."

She looked up and smiled at last, and he smiled back and thought, *Yeah, Lawson. You got pretty damn lucky.*

"But I do need a ride to the mall," she said. "Please."

◆ ◆ ◆

After thinking about it some, he put the device back where he'd found it, got the tires on the truck, dropped Mac at the mall, then paid a visit to Vern's Auto, catching them right before they closed. And then he drove back to the mall, sat in the parking lot waiting for Mac to text him, and called Hallie.

When he explained it to her, she sounded scared. Of course she did. It was scary stuff.

"The motel . . ." she said.

"It wasn't on my truck then," he said. "I had it in for some work on the transmission a little over a week ago, and Vern says, no way that was on there. He would've seen it when it was on the rack. So it's recent. My guess is, they couldn't get you with the letters, they heard about the garage being graffitied, and they went for this."

"You mean," she said, "that they've moved on. Escalated. That there's something like this on my car, too."

"I'm betting. I'd like to come over and check it out."

"Uh . . ." she said.

"Mac's got a birthday party thing tonight. If I were to come over after dark . . . the snow's supposed to get worse after seven. Most people will stay indoors." And it was just about checking out her car.

Yeah, right.

"But—" she said. "The tracker."

"I'll deal with that. I've got a couple ideas."

There was a long pause on the other end, and he tried to tell himself that this was just about her safety, and knew it was a lie.

Finally, she said, "If you get rid of it tonight . . . nobody would catch on to that instantly, would they? It would take them a while to figure out it wasn't working. So they couldn't find out if you came to my house for an hour . . . or two, especially if your truck were in the garage."

"You're right. They couldn't. If I traded cars with Anthea for the evening and it was snowing, it wouldn't even matter if there were a camera set up on your mailbox or someplace like that. Not if I drove straight into your garage and went back to Anthea's afterwards, switched cars again, and drove mine into *my* garage. Just in case anybody was watching."

"Do you think there's a camera set up at my mailbox?"

"No. But I'd like to check and make sure."

"It'll be dark, though."

"I can check in the dark. There'd only be a few places to look. I've got a powerful flashlight. I can take care of it."

Another pause. "OK," she finally said, and he let go of the breath he'd been holding. "That'd be good. And you could . . . if you wanted, you could come over and play pool. You know how we said . . ." She sounded like she was stopping to catch her breath herself. "That you wanted to play on my pool table. We could do that. If you wanted."

"You been a badass with it yet?"

"I haven't been a badass at all."

"Then," he said, "I guess I'd better come over."

Then he hung up, Mac texted him that she was ready, and he got a strong dose of reality.

"All set?" he asked when they were back in the truck. The snow was still drifting down in fat white flakes, and he turned the defroster up and the windshield wipers on, glad he'd changed out the tires.

"Yeah. Except I have to wrap it." She held up the bag.

"What did you get?"

"A really cool coloring book and new colored pencils. And lip balm."

"Uh . . . isn't that a little . . . young?"

"*Dad.* No. That's what *everybody* does."

"Oh. I guess it's a girl thing."

"Boys color, too. Didn't you?"

He had to smile. "Well, no. I did not color. Not after I was, you know, five."

"It's very good for concentrating. You should try it."

"I'll probably give that a pass. I'm reasonably good at concentrating." He pulled up at the house again. "Right, then. You can get that wrapped up, and I'll take you over there."

She didn't get out of the truck, though. "What are you going to do while I'm gone?"

He hesitated. How was he supposed to answer that? This single-dad thing was getting trickier all the time.

"I'll probably go out," he finally said.

She was giving him the side-eye again. "With Ms. Cavanaugh?"

"I might."

"I thought you weren't supposed to go out with her."

"I told you. She's a friend." Which wasn't honest communication, but there was no way Mac needed more information than that. Or that she should be carrying his secrets for him.

"When we were over there before, you were hugging her. You kissed her, too. You called her 'baby.' That's not 'friends.'"

"I thought you liked her." All right, he was weaseling out.

"I like her *dog*. She's a good *teacher*. I didn't say I wanted you to *marry* her."

"I didn't say I was marrying her. I said she's a friend. I like her very much, and I was trying to make her feel better about her garage. And come on." He opened the door. He was out of ideas, so he punted. "Go wrap your present so I can drive you to this birthday party before everybody hands out all the jewelry-box kits."

PLAYING GAMES

After Jim had called, the first thing Hallie had done was to go out to the garage and walk around her car, then look under it with a flashlight. She hadn't known what she was looking for, though, and she hadn't seen anything.

The thought of driving around with somebody virtually watching her movements—it was more than creepy. She walked down to the mailbox in the fading light with Cletus beside her and checked it over, but there was nothing. She ran her flashlight down the light pole beside the driveway, too. If there were a camera there, surely she'd see it.

And anyway . . . even if there *were* a secret camera recording here, what would anybody see tonight? Anthea's car coming over for a couple hours. And Anthea wouldn't say anything if Jim asked her not to.

He'd said he'd be there at seven. "I could bring another pizza," he'd said, "but it might be better not to show my face anywhere public tonight. Just in case."

"That's fine," she'd said. "Besides, maybe we should, ah . . . use our time for the pool game. And checking my car, of course," she'd added hastily. Now, she went back up to the house, ate a quick salad and some cheese on bread, and then . . . *didn't* take a shower. She took a bath, instead. A long one.

Whatever he said, she knew it wasn't a relationship. It sure wasn't a romance. Tonight, it was Jim checking her car out, helping her with her problem. Playing a game of pool with her and helping her with her *other* problem. One more time. Just once more. Last chance, because they had to be even more careful now. Surely she deserved one last time.

At seven o'clock, Cletus barked, and she went out to the garage with the dog following behind, opened the huge rolling door, and watched headlights coming up the winding driveway through the snow, which was falling faster now, and blowing so hard that nobody would have been able to identify those headlights, or the car, even if there *had* been a camera. Jim pulled in beside her own car and turned the engine off, and she punched the button and watched the garage door roll closed.

Cletus barked once but stayed beside Hallie, his tail whipping a mile a minute while Jim got out of the car, came around it, and said, "You know, I've never felt more like I'm having an affair. I shouldn't like it. Too bad I do."

He bent and gave Cletus a thump, then said, "Sit," and the dog did. "He doesn't mind me as well as he does you," she said. "Unfair."

"Because I say it like I mean it."

"That's probably it, Sergeant."

He smiled a little, her heart gave a skip, and the rest of her got busy waiting to get kissed.

He wasn't doing it, though. Why not?

"I've never had an affair, either," she said, for something to say. "You're right, it shouldn't be exciting, but it is anyway. Sort of—forbidden fruit, I guess."

His face changed. He reached down, threaded his hand through her curls, tipped her face up, pulled her close with his other hand, and finally gave her the long, slow kiss she needed.

By the time he was done, she was hanging on hard. "It is," he said. "Because you're my forbidden fruit for sure. I'm hating this, and, man— I'm loving it. Tonight—I couldn't wait. I'm all messed up, and you're the one doing it to me. Leaving you feels bad every time, and so does seeing you and not getting to touch you. And here I am, back for more anyway, because there's no way in hell I can stay away."

"Better make it good, then," she murmured against the faintly rough texture of his neck. It felt good, so she nuzzled under his ear some more, wrapped her arms around the very satisfactory breadth of his back, and snuggled in. He was wearing a blue plaid flannel shirt and jeans tonight, and he was so wonderfully warm and solid.

"Guess I'd better," he said. "And I should've shaved. I didn't want Mac to notice, though. She's a little suspicious."

"Mm." She should care about that, and she would. Later. "I like it a little rough. Exciting again."

It wasn't a smile she got from him. It was just a lightening of his eyes. A gleam. Something like that. "Well, damn, girl. Let's go inside, then."

She realized what she'd said and could feel the warmth stealing up her cheeks. She thought about saying that wasn't what she'd meant, then abandoned the idea. One thing she was sure of—Jim wouldn't hurt her. "Uh—yeah," she said, instead. "You came over to show me how to be a badass. Shouldn't you check out my car first, though?"

"I thought I would. But I just changed my mind. Hang on one second." He opened the passenger door of Anthea's car, pulled out a paper bag, and said, "Have to have the right drink to be a badass."

"Oh." She swallowed. "Right. Well, uh, come inside."

Now that he was here, she was nervous again, and she didn't have two and a half drinks in her this time to quiet the voice of caution. She opened the door to the house, and Jim followed her inside with Cletus bringing up the rear, then took him into the family room.

"What do you think?" she asked.

He looked around. Soft blue walls, chalk-white trim, squishy couch in pale-blue velvet, and a row of three velvet cubes in front of it serving as a coffee table, thanks to a tray on one of them. A mahogany bar with its shelves empty, because only the wine fridge had anything in it. Pale-blue drapes behind the couch pulled tight against the winter dark. And the pool table, all soft green felt, leather bumpers, and rich mahogany legs that matched the bar, complete with a rack of cues against the wall.

"That's one sweet table," he said, running a hand over the felt. "That's solid. And the rest of the room isn't half bad, either."

"Yep." She pulled the bottle out of his paper bag. "Single-malt scotch, huh?" Two-thirds full, coming out of his liquor cabinet, she guessed. Avoiding a telltale trip to the liquor store before their clandestine meeting. "Am I worth it?"

"Oh, yeah. You're going to be. How about I pour the drinks and you go on up and change out of those jeans into a skirt, so we can get started with this game of ours?"

"What, my jeans aren't good enough for you?" She wanted to play pool with him. She did. But not if he was going to tell her what to wear. She'd had enough of that in this house.

He looked at her, his gaze measuring. "The kind of pool I had in mind," he said, "was strip pool. You could say that I've been thinking about that for, oh, about two months now. I'll play with you either way. Any way. But if you changed into a skirt and kept that pretty sweater on, let's just say that it would give me one hell of a head start."

"Oh," she said weakly.

He didn't say anything else, just stood there, leaning up against the bar, big and patient, and waited, his dark gaze on her face.

"I'll be back," she finally said. "Cletus, come." Maybe she could be a badass if she didn't have an audience. Even a canine one.

◆　◆　◆

He'd thought, for a minute there, that he'd pushed her too hard. The problem was, he *had* been thinking about this pool table for months, and since the locker room and the motel, he'd thought about it more.

"Thought about it more" sounded better than "had nonstop fantasies about it," anyway.

Then Hallie came back downstairs in the same little buttoned-up, pale-pink sweater with a wide V-neck and not much under it that he could see, a silky gray skirt that didn't reach her knees, and her cowboy boots.

"Oh, yeah," he said. "That's good."

She shut the door and said, "I left Cletus upstairs. In case we, um . . ."

He handed her a tumbler of ice, scotch, and water. "Good. Because we're definitely going to 'um.'"

She gave him a little smile that might have meant anything or nothing, picked up a remote, and turned on some music. A little bit loud, and plenty hot, right from the start, all guitars, fiddles, and slow, insistent drumbeats.

Then she took a drink, racked the balls, chalked up her cue, and it was on.

She was a decent pool player. Unfortunately—or fortunately—he was better.

"No fair," she said after he sank four in a row. "You didn't tell me you were a shark."

"I was a soldier." He watched her lean over to take her shot in that short gray skirt, and that was a very nice view. "It's a pretty fair bet that any soldier's going to be a good pool player. Too many hours in too many bars too far from home."

She missed her shot and stood up, her cheeks tinged with pink. "Shoot."

"Thanks. Believe I will." He took care of the last two balls and said, "Guess what. You lose."

"Huh," she said. "How come I have the feeling that this is going to end up with me naked and you still completely dressed?"

Because that's my plan, he didn't say. Instead, he said, "Ground rules. Winner gets to say what you take off."

She was even pinker now. "Ground rules get decided on before you start. For your information."

"Well, see," he said, "that's the other thing about me. When you're in the survival business, there's no such thing as a fair fight. And you could figure you'll be getting an advantage. You're going to be even more distracting this way."

Over the speakers, some guy was singing about a woman taking down her hair, and about buttons that weren't staying buttoned. "What is this?" he asked. "105.5 Make Out Tonight?"

"It could be called mood music." She was distracted herself, he could tell. She bit her lip, then took another gulp of scotch and said, "OK, then. What?"

He took a sip of his own, watching her nibble at that lip some more. The single malt went down strong and sweet, giving him ideas, like he didn't have them already. He said, "Bra."

"Uh . . . not in order."

"Didn't we establish some ground rules? Winner decides, and I'm the winner." He gestured at her with his glass. "Go on."

She sighed, laid her cue down across the table, and took a final sip of scotch before handing him her glass. She told him, "Hold this." And then she started to unbutton.

There were six pale-pink buttons on that little sweater, and she worked the hell out of every one of them. Underneath them, she was wearing a pale-pink bra. Lace. And nothing else.

He sighed. "You have some truly great underwear. I ever mention that?"

She tossed her head and said, "I don't like padded bras." Which made two of them. Then she reached behind her, unhooked it, and took off both it and the sweater, one slow side at a time, and he may have forgotten to breathe. Her breasts were as white and round as he remembered, and as deliciously pink tipped. Her nipples pebbled under his gaze, right on cue. He could've looked at that all night. Unless he'd had the chance to touch.

She handed him the bra and said, "Guess that's yours," and started to put the sweater back on.

"No," he said, still watching. "*That's* mine. And leave the top two buttons undone for me."

"You get to say?" She was still going for badass, and not doing too badly at all.

"Yeah. I do."

She sighed and did up four slow buttons, bottom to top, and said, "Notice, though, that I'm covered up again. I don't think this was your brightest idea."

He barely heard her. The cleavage she'd exposed was too distracting, and so were the two hard little points showing clearly under the thin, soft fabric, letting him know how aware she was of his gaze.

"Just going to . . ." he said, setting the glasses down on the bar. Before she could reach for her cue, he grabbed her at the waist and hoisted her up on the wide, padded leather bumper of the table.

"But this *was* my brightest idea," he said. "I'm pretty sure." And then he kissed her.

Soft, sweet mouth opening under his, taste of smooth scotch and warm honey, one of her arms coming around his back, her other hand fisting in his hair. He kept one of his own hands behind her head, and with the other, he gently shoved one of her knees away from the other so he could get closer. He needed to be closer. He needed to be right there.

He didn't rush. He stood there and held her head tight and kissed her pretty mouth, nibbling and sucking and licking at it, into it, until she was soft and sighing against him. Only then did he trail a string of delicate kisses along to her throat.

He got a little more demanding, then. But how could he resist, when her hands had tightened on him and her head had tilted to the side to ask him to kiss her neck some more? To kiss it better?

When his fingers began to trace the edge of that unbuttoned sweater, gliding over soft wool and silky skin, she sighed. And when he reached the sensitive spot on her breastbone and stroked her there, she moaned.

He let go of her and stepped back, and her eyes flew open, unfocused and dreamy. "What?" she asked.

He smiled. "Next game."

"Oh." She still looked confused. He traced a gentle hand over the red abrasions he'd left on the soft skin of her neck and said, "I've marked you all up."

"Well, if you're going to kiss me that much," she said, "you're going to mark me."

"Mm," he said. "Beard burn." And teeth, and hard, demanding lips. He'd done all that. He was going to do so much more, too. For right now, he put two hands around her waist, lifted her down, and went to the bar for the ice bucket and the scotch, then handed her a glass and said, "Ready?"

She took a drink, gave him back the glass, and said, "Ready and waiting." And then she set out to smoke him.

"All right," he said when she was two shots ahead with four balls still on the table. "Explain why you didn't show me that from the beginning."

She walked around the table, and he might have gotten a little distracted when she leaned over opposite him to take her shot and he looked down that unbuttoned sweater. Maybe his plan had its drawbacks. "Why do you think I bought a pool table?" she asked, looking up from where she was still bent over, catching the direction of his gaze, and smiling, a slow, wicked thing that was all soft pink lips, sparkling green eyes, and female sorcery. "Because I'm very, very . . . good." She took her shot, straightened up, watched the ball roll right into the corner pocket, then walked around the table again, leaned over right in front of him, and lined up her next shot.

"By the way," she said, looking over her shoulder and reading his mind, "no touching during the game. Those are *my* ground rules." Then she sank another one.

When the table was cleared, she was standing there, leaning on her cue, with that smile playing over her lips again. "Shirt," she said, gesturing with her cue. "Both of them."

"It's strip pool," he said, starting to unbutton the flannel shirt and revealing the white tee underneath. "One at a time."

"Nope. No such thing as a fair fight. Both of them, soldier. Get them off. Right now."

He gave her his best hard-ass stare, even though everything inside him was saying, *Hell, yeah,* pulled the flannel shirt out of his jeans, yanked it off, and tossed it on a velvet cube on top of her bra, his own pale-pink trophy, then started to pull up the tee.

She stepped closer. "Changed my mind. I'm doing this part."

He could have told her that that wasn't how it worked, but he wasn't crazy. Her hands moved slowly, just like they had when she'd been unbuttoning her own sweater. They brushed over his sides, his ribs, traced the raised edge of his scar, then stroked over his chest as she pulled the soft material up his body. She felt him like she meant it. Like she wanted it.

"Mm," she said, when his shirt was most of the way off, his hands tangled up in cotton. She dropped her hands, leaving him to deal with the shirt, bent, and licked over one of his nipples, then gave it a soft bite. Her hands were still stroking, too, and he was sucking in a breath and forgetting about taking his shirt off. He stood there, arms over his head, and let her feel him.

Eventually, he remembered the shirt and tossed it. But when he got a hand under her own sweater and started to slide it up her body, she raised her head from his chest and said severely, "No. Winner does the touching. You get to hold my head. And that's all."

This was a new Hallie. Damn, but he liked her. He didn't need telling twice, either. He got a hand around her head, burrowed into her soft curls the way he loved to do, and held on. And she tortured him. Touching, stroking, licking, biting, over his neck and his chest and his belly, tracing all the way down to his belt buckle and back again, until he was groaning, and he would've done anything—*anything*—if she'd just kept going. If she'd moved on down.

She didn't. She stood up and said, "The other rule. The part of the body we uncover is the part we get to touch. So if you want those jeans off . . ." She took a long, slow look down his body. "You'd better lose." Then she brushed two fingers down his fly, smiled as he leaped into her hand, and said, "Whoops. Slipped."

He didn't lose. He won. Maybe it was the second drink she swallowed down during the next game, maybe it was the pulsing music, and maybe it was the way he stood behind her every time she took a shot, but she wasn't focusing as hard this time. Or fighting as hard, either. And he was. He needed to win.

When the last ball had fallen into its pocket, he took her cue from her hand and said, "Underwear. Let's go."

She didn't even argue. And she didn't look one bit like a loser. She looked him in the eye, got her hands up under that skirt, lifting it high enough to show him just about every inch of creamy, curvy thigh, and then she was wriggling her way out of a pale-pink scrap of lacy fabric and handing it to him draped over one finger.

It was a sight he could have taken a picture of, and he drank it in before he crushed the filmy little things in one hand and said, "These aren't as dry as I bet they were an hour ago."

She gave his body a long, slow scan and said, "Your jeans look a whole lot tighter than they were an hour ago, too. Guess I'm not the only one."

He tossed the bit of lace into the pile on the coffee table and said, "You could be right. I'm going to put you up on that table again, too. And we're going to try a little experiment. If I'm not going to win every time, I'm going to have to maximize the impact."

He had the satisfaction of seeing her eyes widen, but all she said was, "Well, it's your call."

He sighed. "Now, those are some truly special words." He hoisted her up on the bumper again, picked up his drink from the bar and took the last swallow, then plucked a cube from the glass. He came over to her where she sat perched, watching him, half aroused, half wary, and in one swift move, pulled the neckline of the sweater right down under her breasts, baring and lifting them for him. Then he took one in each hand, closed his mouth over one hardened peak, and sucked hard as he touched the other one with the ice.

She jumped. She gasped. And then she cried out as he kept doing it. He went to work. Hot and cold, hard and soft. The ice circling before it touched her where she was so sensitive. Teasing her the same way she'd teased him, while he pinched and played and drove her crazy.

She was making some noise. Panting breaths, little moans, until she couldn't hold still anymore. Until she was squirming on the bumper.

Finally, he raised his head, looked her in the eye, and said, "Game's over."

"Oh?" she said. He could see her trying to rally. "Who says?"

"I say."

He was shoving her skirt up now, inch by inch, revealing her thighs, and then more, his hands following the material, and she was panting hard.

"Jim," she moaned. "Please. I know I should be undoing you. But please. Touch me."

If there were three better words for a man to hear than "Please touch me," he couldn't think what they would be. "Where?" he asked.

His thumbs were moving up the insides of her thighs now, ever closer. "Here?"

"More," she said. "More. Please."

He came close, then skirted the area and traced the crease where her thighs met her hips. "Here?"

"No. *Please. Touch* me."

By the time he finally ran a slow hand down the smooth slickness of her, painted her with it, and began to explore, he could tell she was already halfway there. While he did it, he was kissing her again, taking her pleasure sounds into his mouth.

"You like that?" he murmured into her.

In answer, she was reaching for his belt, starting to unbuckle it, and he shoved her hand away.

"Gotta win it," he told her. "I won. So I get to do this."

"Jim—"

"My game. My rules. And the one I'm going to tell you now is this. Lie down on that table."

"I'll mess up . . . the felt."

"I'll replace it." He meant it, too. "Come on, baby. Lie down for me."

She did it. Her hips were high in the air, he got a hand on each knee and shoved her legs farther apart, and then he just looked.

Pink. Open. Vulnerable. All his.

The power was running as fast and hard in him as the desire was running through her. He drank down the last of his scotch, took an ice cube in his hand, and ran it all the way down her belly while she jumped and gasped.

"Jim—" she started to say.

"Shh, baby," he said. "You might want to save your strength. Because this is where it gets really fun."

ALL THE WAY DOWN

She'd said she wanted to be a badass. She'd said she wanted wild. But she'd never expected anything like this.

The ice was so cold. So very cold. And it was moving down her belly, coming closer and closer. She tried to close her thighs, but Jim's hand was there, holding them open, and he told her, "No. Don't move. We're going to do this."

She knew she could tell him to stop, and he would. But she didn't want to tell him to stop. She wanted to feel him pushing her to that edge. Pushing her over it, screaming all the way. So she let the cold come closer. And then the freezing touch was circling her outer lips, and she was squirming.

She couldn't see him anymore. He must be on his knees, but there was no question who was in control here.

When he finally touched her where she needed him most, it wasn't with ice, but with cold liquid. His fingers were wet, they were finally there, and she was leaping into his hand. It felt so good. So *good.*

Then he set his mouth to her and started to work. Hot, hard sensation, after all that cold. She was crying out, her breath coming in sobs. And when he lifted his mouth from her, she reached to pull him back.

"No," he said. "Hands back behind you."

"Wh-what?"

"Go on, Hallie. Stretch them out behind you. Show me how you hold still for me."

It was the hottest thing she'd ever heard. Slowly, she stretched her arms overhead, feeling the fuzz of soft felt against her skin, and he sighed and said, "That's it. That's so nice, baby. That's what I want to see." She could hear him moving around, but she couldn't see him, and she didn't want to. She looked up at the beamed ceiling, and she waited. She couldn't stand it, and she couldn't stand not to do it.

After that, he went on and on. Burning cold and icy hot. Little flicks of his tongue, blissful moments of gentle suction, teasing probes with his fingers that didn't go far enough, that circled and, when she tensed, waiting for them to dive, needing to feel them stretching her . . . didn't.

She was completely out of control now. But every time she squirmed, every time she lifted her hands, he stopped what he was doing and said, "Hold still. Or I won't let you." Again and again, driving her up one careful step at a time, never giving her quite enough.

One second, he was teasing again. The next, his mouth and hands were gone, and she saw him rising to his feet.

"Jim," she moaned. "Don't stop. Please. Oh, please." She was nearly sobbing. "I need it so much. Please. Let me . . . please."

"You're going to do it," he said, and his voice didn't sound like Jim anymore. No patience at all now. Nothing but command. "When I say."

In one swift thrust, he was inside her. Hot, and hard, and deep. And she screamed.

He was moving hard. Fast. No gentleness at all this time, but she didn't need gentleness. She needed this.

She pulled her arms down to hold him, and he stopped again and pulled all the way out of her. "What did I say about holding still?" he asked.

"I can't . . ." she said. "I can't."

"If you can't, you don't get it. Come on, Hallie. Arms over your head. Hold still, baby. Hold still."

She gasped, and she did it, and he started again. But he'd slowed down. A hard thrust, an achingly patient withdrawal, while she felt every inch of him and wanted more. *Needed* more.

When he finally got his hand there, he did it differently. Instead of the circling motion she was used to, he was pinching and releasing in time with his thrusts.

It was too intense. It was too much. It was all she needed.

"Now," he said. "Now. Come on, Hallie. Hold still and come for me."

He was the one holding still now. He was all the way inside her, nothing but his hand moving on her, his other hand hard around a hip, and she was finally set free from the torturously almost-there plateau where she'd been stuck. From one moment to the next, she was hurtling up, and nothing could stop her. Everything in her body was tensing, squeezing him inside her in the same way he was squeezing that little button where everything was centered. The pleasure came in tightening, concentric circles, drawing closer and closer, pulling her up and up, until with a long, low wail, she was there.

It was more than an orgasm. It was an earthquake. It was a full-body seizure. Her arms stretched out farther, her fingers tried to reach the back wall, her legs shuddered as she shook and spasmed, as she rocked and rolled through the waves that took her over and tumbled her senseless. And Jim was moving again, too. Slamming into her, exactly like that night on his car. Keeping the pleasure going, so she was barely down from the peak before she was climbing up again. Up and over the edge. Spinning and twisting and falling free.

With Jim holding her hard all the way down. All the way to the bottom. All the way to the end.

TESTING THE POSSIBILITIES

It took her a while to come back to earth. And when Jim lifted her off the table, she still wasn't steady.

"Whoa," she said, leaning up against him, letting him hold her. He was still wearing his jeans. They were both still dressed. "Guess I won't go for four out of five."

His smile was just a warming of his eyes. He was still feeling fierce, she could tell. And she loved him fierce.

"Might be the best game of pool I've ever played," he said. He adjusted her sweater, covering her breasts. "But right now, I think we should take a shower and climb into your bed for a while."

"We need to check my car, though." She had to get it together. She was shattered. Destroyed.

"And we will." He ran the back of his hand down her cheek, the gesture so tender it nearly brought tears to her eyes. "But I'd sure like to hold you first."

After that, she couldn't refuse. She took him upstairs, and they took a shower, and she soaped him up, and he did the same to her and kissed her a little more, too. When they'd dried off again, they climbed into her bed, pulled the covers up over themselves, and lay together, listening to the cold wind whistling in the pines outside.

Jim didn't talk, and neither did she. He seemed satisfied to hold her close in the dark, and she lay with him, one hand on his broad chest, her bare legs intertwined with his. She felt his heart beating under her cheek and thought, *Memorize this moment. Hold it forever.* If memories were the only thing that lasted, this was one she needed.

After a while, she must have fallen asleep, because she woke to find him gone. It didn't feel as warm without him, somehow.

She was sitting up in bed when he came back into the room, said, "Turning the light on. Look out," and switched on the lamp by the bed. He was dressed again, and he handed over her underwear and bra, which he must have picked up from the family room.

"Since I can't spend the night with you," he said, "we should probably go look at your car now."

"Right." She still felt flustered and sleepy and much too vulnerable. She realized that he was looking at her breasts, since she was sitting up naked with the sheet over her lap, so she got busy putting something on.

He said, "Remember that thing I said about how hard it was to leave you?"

She smiled with an effort, fastened her bra, reached for her underwear, and said, "Just because I'm putting out."

His face hardened. "Don't say that. It isn't true."

"Joking."

"No. You're not."

She'd felt so good before, but now, she didn't know what to say. Instead, she got out of bed, pulled her jeans from the drawer and pulled them on, added a thicker sweater and warm socks, and said, "OK. I'm ready to look at the car."

He sighed. "Hallie—"

"It's OK." Too much vulnerability tonight, in every way. Her feelings were too exposed right now, too tender. She couldn't bear to look at them too closely, much less have them touched. "Let's go."

He didn't pursue it, to her relief, just went out to the garage with her. While she pulled on her coat and hat, he grabbed his from his car, together with a Maglite a good foot long.

It didn't take him long to find the device under her car. He pulled it out, examined it, and said, "Same as mine. Got to be a tracking device."

"And there'd only be one reason for that," she said, trying to be as cool and professional as he was. "To catch us being in the same places, hopefully someplace where we'd rented a room by the hour. But even that might not be enough evidence, I'd think."

"No. What they'd really want would be a camera—in your house or maybe even mine—or a bug. Cameras would be a tricky proposition to install, though, and anyway—my house wouldn't make sense. I wouldn't be likely to take you there, not with Mac living with me. And here, they'd have to know which room you were sleeping in, and they'd have to hide them. Bugs, on the other hand—that'd be easy."

"Oh." She remembered everything they'd said in her family room, and shivered.

"Who's been in the house these past weeks?" he asked.

"You. Your mom and Cole. Eileen. And Anthea. That's all. And I've got the security cameras and the alarm."

"You been checking the footage?"

"Every night. Nobody's come."

"Eileen . . ." he said slowly.

"No. She wouldn't."

"Not even for money? Good money just to do something simple, like dropping a pen behind a bed and picking it up again a month later?"

Hallie was already shaking her head. "She *wouldn't*. I have her dog. I've seen her with her son sometimes when she brings him to visit Cletus on Thursdays, and she's . . . getting stronger. All she wants to do is raise her kids. I've taken some of the money pressure off, and she's doing better. She's a good person. I'm sure of it."

"Even good people can do bad things under enough pressure."

"But she'd be nervous with me. She'd feel guilty, and she'd show it. Instead, she's more relaxed."

"We'll ask her anyway," he said. "You can go with me. That'd be better. She'd have a hard time lying to me with you there."

"All right," she said reluctantly.

He sighed. "Hallie. This is what you do. It's police work. You check things off. You think—this probably isn't it, but you check anyway. And it's still a possibility, it's just a five-percent possibility instead of a fifty-percent one. And then you keep narrowing down, keep testing until you've knocked out more of those possibilities and you're left with one. Then you figure out how to catch that one. And right now, I'm going to check over the car for that listening device, too. Just in case."

He did that, going under the dash, into the glove compartment, under the seats, examining every pen, every seemingly innocuous item. "I'd say no," he said when he was done. "Not without a whole lot of time to hide something, to sew it into the upholstery or wire it behind the dash. Which, if your car's in your garage and then in the teacher's lot at the school, he probably wouldn't have. And anyway, you haven't talked to me on the phone from your car, have you?"

"No. This conversation we're having right now—this is the closest."

"And we're not saying anything other than—" He cleared his throat and spoke louder. "That whoever is doing this is a scumbag, and I'm going to track him down and make him wish he'd never been born."

She had to smile at that. "Good job."

"Thanks. I liked it." He hit the switch for the garage door. "Let's go check out your mailbox."

The storm had worsened, and they had to walk through four inches of snow. "Not sure we're going to see much," he said when they were standing in the blowing white fury at the bottom of the drive, and he was shining his flashlight in vain up the light pole, and then into the pines on one side of the drive. "I should've done it when I got here, but I'll admit, I got sidetracked. Mailbox is clear, but that's about all I can tell."

"I came down and looked earlier," she said. "Before it got dark. I didn't see anything."

"Well, good work. I'll swing by when I'm back on duty on Monday and check it out better."

"Without coming in," she cautioned.

"I get it. But right now—let's go back up and talk this over. And then I'll leave."

When they got back into the house, she asked, "Do you want something to eat?"

"Cup of coffee would be good."

"Will you be able to sleep?"

"After two scotches and some of the most smokin' sex I've ever had? Yeah, I probably will."

That was nice to hear, anyway. She made him coffee, and tea for herself, while he went back to her bedroom and bathroom and down to the family room again, too. "To check behind the bed and the couch," he said. "Just in case."

He came back a few minutes later and reported an all clear. "Eileen's been vacuuming under your bed, so you know. Not so much as a dust bunny under there." They sat at the breakfast bar with their mugs then, and he said, "Right. I can bring out a bug detector and look for audio bugs or more GPS trackers, just in case that wasn't the only one. So we know what we're dealing with. Or better yet, get DeMarco to come out with me and do it. Make it official, and give me a good reason to be here, one nobody can question. But—obviously, this has to be about the will. You're not allowed to leave town, and you're not allowed to have sex with me. They tried to make you leave town and you didn't, and now they're trying to catch us having sex."

"Obviously."

"First question. Who could benefit by cutting you out? Cole. My mother. Your aunt. Your uncle."

"I can't believe it's Cole or your mother."

"Neither can I. Especially after what happened in Bob Jenkins's office." He described the scene to her, and after he'd finished, she sat a minute, drumming her fingers on the counter and thinking.

"So not your mother," she said at last. "Absolutely no way, not that I ever thought there was. And the letters, the tracking devices—those don't seem like Cole, not with what I saw from him. Which leaves my aunt and uncle."

"Either of them," Jim said. "Or both of them together. We have to consider—doesn't have to be them together. Which could explain some things."

She looked at him more sharply. "Like what?"

"OK." He set his coffee cup down and ticked off on his fingers. "When I went over there to talk to them about somebody trying to steal the guns, Dale pretended at first like he'd forgotten that I was going to sell them for you, and then he said, 'Well, they're gone, so no point.' *Both* of those things couldn't have been real. Either he remembered that I was selling them and when I was picking them up and taking them up to Spokane, or he didn't. Faye, though—she thought I was saying that you'd changed your mind and you hadn't sold them at all. She really *didn't* know they were gone, I'd swear. And then Dale was real quick to suggest that the theft must have been random. He said he didn't know that somebody'd tried to steal them, but he was mighty interested in knowing if I'd gotten a look at the people. And he said *them,* too. He knew there was more than one. So—from that, I'd say it could've been him, and it couldn't have been her. I'd say she didn't know."

"But the letters," Hallie said. "That sounds more like her than him. And unless it's the two of them together, it can't be *two* separate people doing the letters and going after the guns and leaving the tracking devices."

"No," Jim said. "It can't. Not realistic. But if they're in it together, why wouldn't he tell her about the guns?"

"Because she's got a big mouth?" Hallie suggested. "And he doesn't. But another thing about Faye that makes it less likely she's in on it— she's been so quick to tell me, over and over, that I've been seen with you. Like she's pointing it out, warning me. Which is nasty, but counterproductive. If it *was* her—especially if she was sneaky enough to pretend she didn't know about the guns—she'd want me to be seen with you, and she sure wouldn't be warning me that I'd been noticed. She'd be offering her house for a rendezvous or something, and filming it. She's about as subtle as a wrecking ball. And Dale—he suggested to me that nobody really tried to steal the guns. That you made that up. After I told him you suspected my father's death wasn't an accident. He was trying to say that you did it. Which makes it sound like him again."

Jim's face went still. "You told him that. And that's what he said?"

She shifted a little on her stool. "Yes. I did. It seemed like a good idea at the time. Letting them know that I was telling people about the letters and that I was being careful. That I knew everything."

She recounted what she could remember of her conversation with her uncle, and Jim said, "That makes it sound even more like Faye isn't much of a possibility, and Dale is. And if you're talking about some-body crawling under a car, figuring out where to put a GPS, tailing me enough to put it on my truck this past week, finding some lowlife guys on pretty short notice willing to earn a hundred bucks for some late-night burglary—that sounds like Dale, too. Sure doesn't sound like her."

"So how do we prove that?"

He sighed. "We don't. Not officially. I can report this—the devices under our cars—but none of it adds up to much, other than a pattern.

Not enough has actually happened to warrant a full-scale investigation, though I'm sure I'll get some help."

"So what do we do?"

"Well, Mac had a suggestion. We could put the devices on another rig. I could put mine on my service vehicle, since I drive it home at night, and you could put yours on . . . I don't know. How about a school bus? Goes to the school every day. Might fool them for a little while. But on the other hand—if we know they're watching, but they don't *know* we know—that gives us the upper hand. You'd have to be OK with that, though. With knowing they're watching. Could feel bad."

"And we'd have to make sure we didn't both drive to the same place. Which rules out this affair of ours, unless we took off the devices and left them in our garages for a couple hours. We could do that."

"Mm. I'm still a little leery about that possible listening device, too. Be careful. Check your purse and your laptop bag every day, especially if you've been with your aunt and uncle. Keep them cleaned out. It can be a pen, a key fob—anything."

"Oh, man," she complained, "you don't know what you're asking."

He smiled, but persisted. "And don't let anybody into the house."

What if there *had* been a bug in the family room? She trembled, thinking about it, realized what she was doing and couldn't believe herself. "You remember when you told me how most people feel when they find money in your jacket pocket?" she asked him. "That it's theirs?"

"Sure."

"Well, I think that's me. I wasn't sure I wanted to stay, even for millions of dollars, and now I'm worrying that somebody's going to bust me and I'm not going to get it. I'm falling into my father's trap."

He didn't say anything right away. He took his time and thought about it. "Or maybe that's not it at all," he finally said. "How much of the money have you spent?"

"Well . . . the family room."

"Uh-huh." He took a sip of coffee. "Ten grand?"

"Seven. Seven *thousand* dollars." She shifted uncomfortably on her stool. "And I bought those cowboy boots you like, too. Just like my dad. They weren't cheap. And some more clothes."

"Uh-huh. You bought some furniture and a few clothes. And how much have you saved or given away?"

"Not enough." That was the problem. "Given away, I mean. I gave away the money for the car. You know that. That was more than thirty thousand. The rest of the money for the guns, the money for staying . . . I haven't done anything with that yet. I get another thirty thousand at the end of November. Almost eighty thousand in all. I'm trying to decide."

"Uh-huh. Decide what?"

"Where it goes. I don't know. Maybe I'm holding on to it because I want it. I can't tell. But I can't tell what I'd *do* with it. It'd be nice to feel financially secure—*really* secure, I won't lie, but—the only thing I'd really like is a house. A different one. A more . . . homey one. I'd like to trade this house for a real house."

And a real family to live in it with me, she didn't say. *A baby.* She wasn't confessing *that.*

"Sounds to me," he said, "like you aren't staying because you want to be a multimillionaire. Sounds to me like you're staying because you're sick of the bad guys winning just because they're more ruthless and they have no limits. Sounds to me like you've decided good girls can fight, too. Nothing wrong with that. All that makes you—" He smiled at her from over the rim of his cup, and his eyes were so warm. "Is a badass."

She laughed, although it was unsteady. "Some badass."

"Oh, I don't know. Smoked me at pool, took off my clothes, teased the hell out of me? Yeah, that's some badass stuff. Surprised me, I'll tell you that. So—you watch, you're careful, and *we're* careful. But the good news is—whoever this is, they haven't done much so far, have they? You're almost three months into this deal, and everything they've done has been pretty tame. Pretty *lame,* actually. Which makes me think that, if it really is somebody who stood and watched your dad die, they didn't give him that push I was thinking. Nothing's been violent. More like—trying to nudge things along. Cautious. Wussy. Which would be your uncle all the way."

She sighed, suddenly feeling so tired. "My uncle. You know—I don't have that much family."

He set his hand on hers on the counter, then threaded his fingers through hers and held on. "You've got Cole now. You may have lost one, but you've gained one."

She looked up at him. "You think I've gained one?"

"I think you'll find that you have."

"So we just—leave this?"

"Yep. We do. We investigate around the edges, and that's all we do. If they think they've got us marked, and all they have to do is wait for us to make our mistake? They can relax, and they won't be doing anything else in the meantime. Which means they won't escalate."

NARROWING IT DOWN

When Jim told DeMarco his plan on Monday, the detective wasn't exactly ecstatic.

"I don't like this," DeMarco said when Jim showed him the device and told him about the one on Hallie's car. "You're too mixed up in it, and sounds like your brother's a suspect. Having you be part of the investigation—that's coloring outside the lines all the way around."

"I won't be investigating," Jim said. "You will be."

"Yeah, right. You aren't going to lean on anybody. And you want her to come, too? That's all-the-way irregular."

"But more effective," Jim argued. "Anyway, it's not like we're going to get somebody into court for putting a GPS device on a car. I'll let you lead, and she won't say anything."

That earned him another skeptical glance.

"Call it friendship," Jim said. "Call it Army strong." DeMarco had been an MP. "Or is loyalty just for Marines?"

DeMarco sighed. "You had to go there."

"Seems I did."

"All right, then," DeMarco said in resignation. "I liked the lady. Seems like a raw deal, and this whole thing is starting to smell like yesterday's fish."

Which is why he was here now with Jim at four thirty on Monday afternoon, searching Hallie's house for the telltale pinholes of cameras while Jim carried the portable bug detector and swept the place as he'd swept her car earlier, and Hallie followed behind and didn't say anything.

Once again, Jim came up with nothing. He went over the family room extra thoroughly, cursing the recklessness that had had him ignoring this possibility, just because he'd needed Hallie stretched out on that felt.

She wasn't looking at him as he ran the detector over the walls, behind the bar, around the legs and pockets of the pool table.

"Clean," he said.

"Nice table," DeMarco said, running a hand over the surface, exactly where Hallie had been lying, her hands behind her, holding still for Jim. Her mouth open, her breath coming hard, her sweater pulled down, her skirt up around her waist, and her legs spread, while he'd played with her. While she'd made the kinds of noises and said the kinds of things that would've been gold on any recording device.

"This is solid," DeMarco said. "Wasn't here before, or I'd have remembered. New?" he asked Hallie.

"Um . . . yes." There was some pink in her cheeks now, and she was nibbling at that lower lip, had her arms wrapped over her chest, and Jim was having major professionalism issues.

"You played much on it?" DeMarco asked.

"Some."

"Good times," he said, and Hallie shot a look at Jim that he met with a shake of his head. *No. I didn't.*

"Right," DeMarco said. "Looks like you're clean."

Jim handed Hallie the bug sweeper. "I'm leaving this with you for a while." He'd given her a demo of it at the beginning and had her run over the living room to make sure she understood how to use it. "You can sweep with it as often as you need to, make sure nobody's dropped anything, that you stay clean. So you don't have to worry."

"Thanks," she said, and put it in her purse.

DeMarco said, "I guess you're coming along on the next part of this, too, Ms. Cavanaugh. But I have to emphasize—you'll be there as an observer, only because Jim thinks our subjects will be less comfortable lying to us if you're there. That doesn't mean you're questioning them, or talking at all."

"I understand," she said.

DeMarco glanced at Jim, and Jim could read the thought. *Yeah, right.*

"Well," DeMarco said, "let's go, then. Get it over with."

"Did you call ahead?" Hallie asked on the ride over to Eileen's. She was in the backseat, which Jim didn't like. He'd offered her the front, but she'd said, "I've never sat in the back of a cop car before," and looked at him, and he'd shut up.

"No," DeMarco answered her. "We didn't call. It works better if you catch people off guard, before they've had a chance to rehearse, or to get advice. If she didn't do anything wrong, she's got nothing to worry about."

"That's a nice thing to say," Hallie said, "but not true."

That earned a quick look in the rearview mirror and another glance at Jim, which Jim answered with a raised eyebrow of his own. Then DeMarco pulled up in front of Eileen's apartment house in Frogtown, and the three of them climbed out.

Jim and DeMarco walked up the steps, with Hallie waiting below, and DeMarco rang the doorbell. After a minute, Eileen answered, wearing old jeans and a faded blue T-shirt.

"Oh," she said on a breath. Her eyes had widened, and her face paled. Jim guessed two deputies in uniform could do that. "My daughter? Is it—is she—"

"No, ma'am," DeMarco said. "It's nothing to do with your daughter. We just have a couple questions for you."

"Oh." She sagged a little and put a hand to her chest. "Sorry. She went to a friend's after school, and I thought for a minute—but never mind."

"May we come in?" DeMarco asked.

"Uh—sure, I guess." She opened the door. When she saw Hallie, she said, "Oh."

"I just came along," Hallie said, which was lame, but seemed to reassure Eileen.

They sat on a faded couch with Eileen perched on a kitchen chair that she pulled over from the dinette. Her little boy, who'd been playing with some trucks on the floor, came over, and Eileen pulled him into her lap, wrapping her arms around him as if for comfort. She still looked tense as hell, which could mean anything or nothing.

DeMarco said, "We have reason to think that somebody may have planted a device in Ms. Cavanaugh's vehicle. We're wondering if you know anything about that."

"Oh, no," she said. "And how would I— Like what? Like a . . . a bomb?"

Jim could tell Hallie was about to jump in, but DeMarco beat her to it.

"Did you leave anything at her house?" he asked. "Take anything from it? Or did anybody approach you to do that?"

"No!" she said. "I wouldn't. I'd *never*—you mean, did I put something in her car? Or steal something from her house? I wouldn't do that." She was leaning forward in her chair, clasping her little boy tight, her face intent. "I wouldn't. Not to anybody, but to *Hallie?* How could I do that to her?"

"Mommy," her son complained, "you're hurting."

"Oh. Sorry, sweetie." She let go of him, and he climbed down and went back to his trucks.

Jim stepped in, then. "We're not trying to get you in trouble here, Ms. Hendricks. This is for Ms. Cavanaugh's safety. Maybe somebody asked you to pick up something they'd left there. Something small. A pen, a bunch of keys."

"No," she insisted. "I would've told Hallie if I'd done that."

"You're sure?" Jim pressed. "It might've seemed completely innocent. We're not interested in going after you for it. All we need is the name and to know what happened."

"No," she said again. "I *didn't.* Don't you *see?* I was in—I was at the bottom. I didn't know how I'd ever get out. I was . . . if it hadn't been for my kids, I'd have . . ." She glanced at her son and didn't finish the sentence. She looked at Hallie now. "You know. You *must* know. How grateful I am. I'd never—"

"And nobody's even approached you," DeMarco cut in. "Asked any questions about cleaning her house. Offered you money, maybe. A hundred dollars to pick something up that they dropped, because Hallie was annoyed with them, and they didn't want to ask her. It wouldn't be stealing. It would have been their property. Nothing valuable. All we need is a name. Even if you said no—we need a name."

Eileen was shaking now, the tears coming to her eyes. "I don't know how to prove it," she said, and Jim thought, as he often did, that this job was sometimes harder than the one he'd used to do. "I don't know how to make you believe that I didn't. That if anything like that happened, I'd have told Hallie. Or I'd tell you now. It would be . . . it would be against everything I believe in."

Hallie made a choked noise in the back of her throat, and Jim said, "Well, thanks. We had to check. And if anybody *does* talk to you, asks you anything at all about cleaning for her, even somebody you think can't possibly have anything to do with any of this—you'll call us?" He handed over his card. "And please don't talk about this. We'd rather it not get back to the person that we're investigating, if possible."

"Yes," she said, clutching it. "And no. I promise."

DeMarco stood, and the others did, too. Eileen asked Hallie, "But you're all right? Nothing happened? It wasn't a bomb?"

"No," Hallie said. "It's fine. But please—really—don't tell anybody. Jim thinks that'll be safer for me."

Eileen nodded. "Sure. I won't say. I don't want to talk about your house anyway." Her face twisted. "Believe me."

Hallie'd clearly totally forgot about not talking or interfering, because she'd wrapped her arms around Eileen and was patting her on the back and saying, "I know. It's all right. Really. Nobody thought you'd done anything wrong."

Jim cleared his throat, and Hallie stepped back. "We won't take up any more of your time," Jim said. "Thanks again for your help."

When they were in the car again, DeMarco said, "I have to say, since Jim here probably won't—that's not what we call, in technical terms, 'being an observer.' That's more what we call 'talking.'"

"Well, I couldn't just let you *browbeat* her," Hallie said, buckling herself in. "I waited as long as I could. But she was *crying.*"

"Yeah," DeMarco said with a sigh, starting up the rig again. "Which is why we take civilians along on all our investigations. Because they're so helpful."

"Oh, I don't know," Jim said. "I thought we got a pretty strong reaction. That's always helpful."

"Don't tell me you *do* think she did it," Hallie said. "If you do, I don't think much of your detection abilities."

"Nice," DeMarco said. "But, no. I'm satisfied. You satisfied?" he asked Jim.

"Yeah. Always an outside chance, but good to know that nobody's approached her."

"Right," DeMarco said. "And off we go to the next stop. At which," he told Hallie, "you don't talk. And I mean it. Or I take you home right now."

"Are all cops this dictatorial?" she asked. "Or is it just you and Jim?"

Jim caught the lift at the side of DeMarco's mouth. "What? Dudley Do-Right? He's always the good cop. Didn't you notice?"

"Ha," she muttered, and DeMarco smiled some more.

"Right," Jim said with relief. "Here we are." Done with this conversation and at his mom's house. A pretty weird place to be showing up in an official role.

Another trip up the walk, but this time, Jim stood back with Hallie while DeMarco did the honors at the doorbell.

"Dictatorial?" Jim asked out of the side of his mouth.

"I could've said 'alpha,'" Hallie answered sweetly. "But I thought it might embarrass you."

He was still digesting that when the door opened to reveal his mom. Oh, yeah. This wasn't awkward. Much.

"Ma'am," DeMarco said. "I'm here to talk to your son Cole."

His mom, of course, looked right past DeMarco to Jim, because that was one of a mom's gifts: the ability to find you anywhere. "Jim?" she asked. "What's this about?"

Jim came up the steps. "Something else happened out at Hallie's," he said, "and we'd like to talk to Cole about it. Make sure he doesn't know anything."

Her eyes were sharp, and now they went to Hallie. "You're all right, though?" she asked her.

"I'm fine," she said. "And, uh—hi."

"Well," Vicki said, opening the door wider, "you'd better come in and ask whatever it is. Take them into the living room, Jim. I'll go get Cole."

When Cole came out, he was slicking his hair down with both hands, looking completely nervous and awkward.

Uh-oh. Jim sure hoped he hadn't been wrong.

"Should I get Anthea?" Vicki asked. "Since she's Cole's lawyer?"

"If you want to do that," DeMarco said, "you're free to. We just have a few questions, though."

"Well," Vicki said, "Jim's here. So go ahead."

DeMarco shot Jim a look that didn't require any interpreting. *This is why you shouldn't be here.*

They went through the whole thing again, and Cole seemed genuinely confused. He, too, thought "device" must mean "bomb," which was a good sign.

"Seriously?" he asked Hallie. "Somebody put a *bomb* in your car? How did you find out?"

This time, she didn't answer, at least. DeMarco answered for her. "No. It wasn't a bomb. And you don't know anything about this? Anybody who'd want to check where your . . ." He cleared his throat. "Your sister had been, or where she was going?"

"No," Cole said. "Why would I?" His face changed, then. Nothing wrong with Cole's processing speed. "Wait," he said. "They're trying to find out that you went the same place as Jim. But to do that . . ." He looked at his brother. "Did they put something on your car, too? Were they *tracking* you? You mean, for, uh . . ." He stopped himself, turned red, and said, "Man, that's messed up."

"Would you mind," DeMarco asked, "if we took a look at your computer? At your online purchases?"

"Ah . . . I guess," Cole said.

"We'd like to rule you out, that's all," DeMarco said. "We're talking to lots of people."

"Go get him your computer," Vicki said quietly. She was sitting tall. Sitting like a queen.

"Mom—" Cole said.

She turned on him, fierce as a tiger. "If you've done this, *tell* them. Tell them *now.* Show them. Get it over with. Tell your sister. Tell your brother. Tell me. Let us know it was you, so Hallie doesn't have to be scared anymore. And if you haven't, prove it, so they can find out who it was. *Help your sister.*"

"Vicki—" Hallie began, sounding helpless, but when DeMarco turned his head and stared at her, she subsided.

"I'll get my computer," Cole said. "Because I didn't. I'll prove it."

They sat in silence while he was gone. Jim couldn't think of what to say, and his mother didn't say anything.

Cole came back into the room about thirty seconds later, holding a laptop. "This is my computer for, uh, school and everything. I'll need to borrow Mom's computer, so, uh . . ."

"We'll get it back to you as soon as possible," DeMarco said. "Couple days. Just have to run it through a few programs."

Cole was shuffling from foot to foot, looking miserable and uneasy, and Jim said, "It wasn't somebody else, was it? If we need to go over to Ingeborg's house and look at *his* shopping history—Mom's right. Tell us. Help Hallie. How do you think it felt for her to know she was being tracked?" His hands were fisting despite all his efforts at self-control. "Maybe it wasn't your idea. Tell us anyway. Help her."

"I *didn't*," Cole said. "I *swear*." He looked completely anguished now, and Jim studied him for long moments during which Cole didn't shift his eyes away, and decided he was telling the truth. Cole wasn't a good liar. Fortunately.

"I heard what you guys said," Cole went on. "I *heard* what Mom said, with Anthea. I don't . . ." He was gulping now. "I don't want to make everybody . . . disappointed with me again. I know I . . . I know I did that. I don't want to do it anymore."

"Felt crappy," Jim said.

"Y-yeah," Cole said.

"Right," Jim said. "We'll check this."

"But you believe me," Cole appealed. He looked at Hallie. "*You* believe me, don't you? Because I didn't."

"I believe you," she said. Strong and true. She did the same thing she'd done two weeks earlier. She stepped forward, took him in her arms, and held on. "Because you're my brother."

Cole grabbed hold of her, a convulsive movement, and held her for a second before he pulled away and turned his head, clearly embarrassed by the emotion he'd betrayed.

Hallie, meanwhile, looked at DeMarco, and said, "So I talked. Sue me."

"Well," he said, "it's not exactly by the book, but we'll let it slide."

"We'll head out, then," Jim said. He wrote out a receipt for the laptop, handed it to his brother, and said, "Quick as we can."

"Uh . . ." Cole was looking nervous again, and Jim thought, *Oh, no.*

"What?" Jim asked.

DeMarco was already heading to the door, with Hallie following, and now, Cole's eyes *were* darting side to side. Jim said, "In here," and led the way into the kitchen, where he turned to face his brother. "OK," he said. "Shoot. If there's anything to tell, it's a whole lot better if you tell me now."

"Uh . . . there might be some, uh . . . Will they look at everything? Or just for, you know . . . um, shopping?"

Jim hardened his heart. "What's on there? What are we going to see? Tell me now."

"Well . . ." Cole swallowed. "Maybe some . . . videos."

Jim wanted to laugh, but he didn't. "Right. You got some porn on there."

"I tried to remember to clear my history every time," Cole said, "but, uh . . ."

"They can see," Jim said. "Wiping isn't really wiping. OK. What kind of thing?"

"What . . . *kind?*" Cole was looking wild-eyed now.

"Anything illegal?" Jim pressed. "Any kids?"

Cole gaped at him. "*Kids?* No. I mean . . . no. I like, uh . . ."

"What?" Jim pressed.

"Uh . . ." Cole muttered the words. "Sort of . . . MILFs. And," he added hastily, "regular stuff. I mean, normal."

"Ah." Jim forced himself not to smile. "Well, I don't think mature ladies would be a problem."

"Are you going to tell Mom?" Cole asked.

"Nope. I'm not. And if I did, I doubt she'd be real surprised. She's already raised one teenage boy, remember."

"Yeah, but you didn't . . . you're so straight."

"Sometime," Jim said, "we'll have a talk about how straight I wasn't, except that I don't want to give you or Mac the idea that it's OK. Tricky business. But—no. I wasn't. And I need to go. They're waiting."

"Tell Hallie," Cole said. "Tell her I said—that I hope she's OK. That stinks, if somebody's following her. Tell her I'll help, if I can."

Jim did what he'd so rarely done. He grabbed Cole, hugged him hard, thumped him on the back, and said, "You bet, bud. And that's a stand-up thing to say. That's the real deal."

UNCOMFORTABLE MOMENTS

Cole's laptop came back clean, not that Hallie had thought it could be either him or Eileen. As uncomfortable as the confrontations had been for everybody, at least it was what Jim had said. Narrowed down.

Her aunt and uncle—that was trickier. And when another week went by without anything happening, and Hallie getting more and more jittery, Jim said, "Time to go proactive."

He told her over the phone, of course, which was the only way she'd talked to him. With Hallie walking circles around her driveway, bundled up against the cold, not talking in the house just in case the bug detector didn't work. "We'll see if we can catch them off guard," Jim said. "Scare them out of it, since they've been so wussy about it so far. It's one thing to wait and hope it means they won't escalate, but— doesn't feel too good, does it?"

"No," she agreed. "So what do you think?" And he told her.

Hallie knew it wouldn't be Vicki's idea of a good time, but when Jim called to tell her his mother had agreed, Hallie wasn't too surprised.

"Mom said it's better for Cole to get used to facing them anyway," Jim said. "And if he has to do that, she'd rather be there."

Which was why, on the Saturday night before Thanksgiving, Vicki, Cole, Anthea, Ben, and the kids were at Hallie's house, along with Jim and Mac. The entire Lawson family, at Hallie's first non-pizza-centric dinner party.

The doorbell rang, and Hallie took a breath, wiped her hands on her skirt, and went to open the door, rehearsing the sequence in her mind.

"Hi," she told Dale and Faye. "Come in, please. Let me take your coats."

When she got back from the bedroom where she'd dumped them, Jim was saying, "I'm bartending for Hallie tonight. What can I get you? Wine, beer, something stronger?"

They'd talked this out beforehand. Making it appear normal that Jim was in her house, together with the rest of his family. Taking any sting out of his familiarity.

The group exchanged some stilted conversation for a couple minutes, with Anthea introducing her kids and Mac to Faye and Dale, and Faye managing to convey that she wasn't impressed, until Hallie finally said, "Well, maybe it's unfashionable, but—how about if we just sit down and eat?"

She'd had a conference with Anthea about what to make for eleven people, a daunting prospect at the best of times, and had settled on enchiladas and salads. Simple, and she'd been able to make it all ahead of time.

But first, she had to do this. She directed people to their spots at the table, into which she'd put leaves that had never been used. When she was seating Faye, she said, "Now, how did that get there?" and snatched away a folded newspaper sitting on the table.

The black box with its heavy magnet fell on the hardwood with a crash, bounced, and landed on Faye's foot in its spike-heeled pump, and Faye jumped and shrieked.

"Oh, my gosh," Hallie said. Her heart was beating a mile a minute. "Let me get that." She bent down and snatched it up. "Are you all right?" she asked Faye.

"Fine," Faye said through gritted teeth. "I'm sure the mark will come out of my shoe."

"Oh, dear," Hallie said. "I'm sorry." She held the box out and turned it in her hand. "This fell off my car today. I was afraid it was something important. Is this some kind of . . . auto part, Uncle Dale, do you think?"

He glanced at it and said, "Looks like something electronic to me."

Hallie looked around the table. Jim had briefed his family, and nobody said anything, even though Mac appeared to be bursting at the seams and kept sending her father significant looks. "Jim?" Hallie asked. "What do you think?"

"Hmm," he said, putting on his serious face. "I don't know. If you give it to me, I'll take a look at it."

She handed it over, then didn't look at him again. She'd sat him far down the table from her, and she spent the evening *not* talking to him. Until Mac, who'd been nearly silent through dinner, remarked into a pause in the conversation, "So I have an announcement. I decided what I want to do when I grow up."

"Oh?" Vicki asked. "What's that?"

"I'm going to be a Ranger," she said. "Like Dad."

Jim set down his fork and looked at her without saying anything.

"You're dreaming," Cole said. "Girls can't be Rangers."

"They can, too," she said. "Two women just did. The first ones."

"You're too shrimpy," Cole said.

"I am *not*."

"Cole," his mother said.

"Dad," Mac said, leaning into her father, "women can *too* be Rangers, can't they? Anyway, you always say women should be strong.

Not just have girl careers, like nurses and teachers and things." She didn't look at Hallie when she said it.

"I thought you wanted to be a doctor," Jim said.

"That was before," she said. "Because of Mom." She turned to Faye and said, "My mother died of cancer. My dad loved her a lot. He always says he'll love her forever."

"I'm sure he did," Faye said with a glance at Hallie. "Some women are like that. The kind a man just can't forget."

"I know *you* are, hon," Dale said, closing a hand over his wife's. "I'm going to spoil you your whole life. That's our deal."

Jim said, "Mac's right. Women can be Rangers. And being small isn't necessarily as much a handicap as you might think. When you're doing extreme things, a bigger frame can be a handicap, truth to tell. You get tired faster, need more calories. Women have more endurance than men. Better pain tolerance, too. As long as she can build up her upper-body strength enough—which isn't easy for anybody, but harder for women—a woman can do it."

"See, Cole," Mac said. "I *told* you."

Dale shook his head. "I don't want to discourage you, honey," he said to Mac, "even though I'd sure be sorry to see a daughter of mine do something like that, but if they let girls in—that's because they've made different standards for them, since they're not really strong enough. Every time I see some petite little girl who's a policewoman, a firefighter—well, even though I'm sure it's wonderful to be politically correct, makes everybody feel all happy—I think, how about if there's actually a fire, or she's trying to get the cuffs on some two-hundred-pounder? I don't feel near as safe as I ought to, thinking about that. And if a man has to be worrying about taking care of the woman next to him out there in combat—I don't think that'd be good for either one of them."

"Did you serve?" Jim asked him. Nothing challenging about it. Level. Calm. But Dale stiffened all the same. As, Hallie was sure, Jim had meant him to do.

"No," Dale said. "But I wouldn't think you'd have to serve to know that."

"Oh," Jim said, "I think you might. As a matter of fact, Ranger standards are the same for men and women, because, yes, you have to be physically up to the job, and trust me, the Army's going to make sure you are. But who you can count on when the chips are down—I think any soldier or any cop would tell you that that doesn't have much to do with how big the person is. I've known plenty of big, tough guys who found they couldn't handle combat after all, and plenty of little guys with hearts like lions. It's about mental toughness, too. It's about keeping your nerve under fire, about making the hard decisions and staying calm in the tight spots. And I'd bet there are teachers and nurses out there who could teach most men a thing or two about that."

That shut everybody up for a minute. "And what I want to know," Vicki said into the silence, "is whoever in the world told you, Mackenzie, that a nurse or a teacher couldn't be strong? I know you didn't hear that from your dad. I have friends who do those jobs, and I'd call them strong. Strong enough to go back in there every day and fight the good fight, anyway, for not enough money and not enough respect, exactly the way your dad does. If they don't get respected because they're women—well, that's no reason for *women* to go around disrespecting them, too. That'd be a pretty sorry state of affairs."

"Hear, hear," Anthea said softly.

"And hey," Ben said. "I'm a teacher. I'm insulted."

"You're a *professor*," Mac said.

"Same difference."

"So what do you think, Dad?" Mac demanded.

"About what?" He didn't look at Hallie.

Mac sighed. "About whether I should be a Ranger, of course."

"I think it'd scare me to death," he said. "The last thing I'd want for you would be to go into the Army. And I'd also like to remind you that your mom was a bookkeeper, and most of those are women. If you don't think your mom was strong enough, we can have a talk when we get home."

"That's sexism," Mac said. "If you say it would scare you to death."

"No," he said, "that's being a parent."

"But, honey," Faye said, "you wouldn't want to have those big muscles and be all dirty and sweaty all the time, would you? Or not to be able to keep your hair nice? I can tell that would bother you, after you spent all that time on those pretty braids tonight." Mac's hair was pulled back from either side of her face in French braids that had been gathered into a single braid down her back, with the rest of her glossy dark hair falling free. "Ah—" Faye said with a twinkling smile when Mac would have answered. "Caught you, didn't I? And I'll tell you a little secret. Boys don't like girls who think they're stronger or smarter than they are. You go around trying to outdo them, and you'll never have a boyfriend. And I *know* you wouldn't want that."

"My dad does my hair," Mac said frostily. "So I guess soldiers can like pretty hair sometimes, too."

"And I don't know about the rest of that, either," Ben said into the ensuing silence. "I found a woman like that, who was smarter than me. Stronger than me, too, if you twist my arm and make me admit it. I'm still here. I guess it just depends how secure the man is."

"Well, if you want to put it that way," Faye murmured into her napkin.

Mac's eyes were too bright, Jim looked like he wanted to say about six things at once but they were choking him, so he wasn't saying anything, and Anthea looked like she wanted to lunge across the table and stab Faye in the eye with her fork.

Vicki caught Hallie's eye, and Hallie read the message as if Vicki had said it aloud. *You're the hostess. Take charge.*

Stand your ground, Anthea had said, what felt like a year ago, in the September heat in the parking lot of the funeral chapel. *Take up your space in the world.*

Hallie channeled every bit of professionalism she had. She didn't need to channel anybody else, because she was enough. She wasn't seventeen anymore, and she didn't need to cower when somebody said objectionable things at this dining-room table. "Well, that's a very interesting topic," she said in her best classroom voice. "And one you could spend hours talking about, I'm sure, although I think I'd need my ground rules of discussion up on the wall for it, because we aren't doing as well as we could be, are we? Some topics are just like that. It just makes me look forward to Thanksgiving dinner more and more. Vicki's invited me," she told Faye. "It gives 'extended family' a whole new meaning." She stood up. "But you know—I actually baked brownies for this thing. It may be too feminine, but there you go, I did it anyway. And I could debate sexual politics, or I could eat chocolate, and right now—I choose chocolate."

Now she was just babbling. Time to wrap it up. "I've got ice cream, too. Cole, do you want to help me dish up?"

"Uh—sure," he said, standing up.

Anthea jumped to her feet. "Ben and I will clear the table," she said. "Mac, give us a hand."

The evening didn't last much longer, to Hallie's relief. It had felt like a lifetime.

"Thank you so much, hon," Faye said at the door. She and Dale left first, which was just as well. "You did fine, considering that you probably haven't had much practice entertaining. It gets easier, I promise. And the conversation was so . . . educational, too, wasn't it, Dale?"

Dale shook his head. "Well, if I didn't want to hear left-wing ideas, guess I wouldn't live in a nest of liberals like Paradise. You have to take what you get in a college town, I suppose. But thanks, Hallie. You take care of yourself. I don't like hearing that you're having car trouble. Idaho roads can be dangerous in winter. Watch yourself."

"Oh, I expect Jim will take care of her," Faye said. "Seems like he already is."

"I'll take it into the shop if I need to," Hallie said. "To figure out what that . . . part is. At least I know about it now."

"Well, we'll get on," Dale said. "Thanks again. Nice to have a chance to meet Cole, and all. I have a nephew. Imagine that."

On that note, they left. Hallie shut the door after them and went into the living room, where the rest of the party was still sitting.

Anthea said, "We'll take off, too. Getting to be the kids' bedtimes. I just wanted to stay till the end. See if there was a big climax. A grand finale."

"Ha," Hallie said, sinking down into a chair.

"You did good," Vicki said, standing up herself. "Come on, Cole." She reached down a hand, and Hallie raised hers and accepted Vicki's squeeze.

"Thanks for playing along on the . . . thing," Hallie said. "Especially you, Cole. Not giving it away. I just want to show it to as many people as possible and see if anybody knows anything."

"Yeah, right," Cole said. "That wasn't why. I'm not stupid."

"Cole," his mother said, her voice sharp, and he glanced at Mac and shut up. Hallie got up to walk them to the door, but Vicki said, "No. You sit. See you on Thursday for that Thanksgiving dinner. You can put up the rules for . . . what was that?"

Hallie smiled. "Ground rules for discussion. And thanks. I'm looking forward to it. I'm guessing it'll be easier with the, ah, smaller group."

They left, and then Jim and Mac were the only ones there. Jim said, "We're only staying because I'm thinking Mackenzie might have something to say to you."

He'd disappeared with her for a few minutes between dessert and coffee, supposedly to "say hello to Cletus," who'd been banished to the family room for the evening. Now, Mac said, her face tight and closed, "I apologize for being rude about teachers."

Hallie thought a moment before she spoke. "That did hurt my feelings a little," she said. "But I think I understand why you said it."

That made Mac look apprehensive, but Hallie wasn't sure there'd be much point in pursuing the topic. Mac was bound to resent anybody who came between herself and her father. Hallie was the first, that was all.

"I'll call you," Jim said. "Later on. Or we can stay and help you do the dishes."

"No," she said. "Go on. I'd like the quiet time." Mac didn't need Hallie rubbed in her face anymore tonight, either. It would serve no purpose.

Whatever Jim had thought about the results of her performance with the tracker—that would have to wait.

FULL TILT

Once again, Hallie was out on the driveway talking to Jim on the phone, walking around to keep warm. They weren't supposed to get snow again until after Thanksgiving, but that just meant it was *cold*, especially at nine thirty at night.

"So," she asked him, "when I dropped the GPS, what did you see?" That had been their deal. She'd drop it, and Jim would watch. Since that was, as he'd reminded her, his job.

"Your aunt was upset about her shoe," Jim said. "Or scoring a point on you. That was about it. And your uncle—I'd call that no reaction. He got more steamed up about being called on his fossilized worldview than he did about the GPS. If he recognized it, he must be one hell of a poker player."

Hallie thought a minute about that. "Well, he worked with my dad all those years, and never reacted when my dad was nasty to him— which was all the time. I always just thought he was nice, growing up, but now I think . . . he holds it in. Though he did tell me something about the roads being dangerous, about being careful when they were leaving, which sounded like a warning. But again—why would he warn me?" She sighed. "I don't know. Seems like we went through a lot of tension for nothing. Especially what happened with Mac."

"Sorry about that."

"Yeah, well . . ." She walked another circle, and Cletus, as always, followed her. "It's natural. If I really am the first woman you've shown interest in, she's not going to like it. It doesn't matter."

"What do you mean, if you really are? I wouldn't say that if it wasn't true. But you'll be there for Thanksgiving dinner, and we'll give it another try. And after that—Anthea and Ben are taking the kids right after dinner and driving to Seattle to visit Ben's folks. You and I could meet up at her place. I could walk over there. No motel clerks, my rig in my garage, and Mac at her grandma's for the night. I could work that out with Anthea, I know. What do you say? I'd sure like to spend the night with you again."

"No." She realized that this was the reason she'd dreaded his call tonight as much as she'd looked forward to it. Because this had to be said, and he wasn't going to say it. Of course he wasn't. It wasn't the same thing to him as it was to her. "We can't do that. Why wouldn't somebody—all right, my uncle—be watching, somehow, or listening, if he's done all this already? Especially now that they know we've found my tracker." They'd decided to leave Jim's on his truck for now, but to leave Hallie's in her garage. It might still fool somebody into thinking Jim wasn't aware that he was being watched. Meanwhile, Hallie could move around unseen. Maybe.

"It's too risky," she went on, "and you know it, and there's no point anyway beyond . . . adventure seeking, or something. We got it out of our systems, and that's got to be enough."

When he didn't answer, she hurried on. "Don't get me wrong. It was great, and I'm glad we did it, and I appreciate all your help. With everything, but especially with . . . with that. It settled some things for me, and it's going to help me move on. You moved on with your life a long time ago, and in some ways, I didn't. What we've done, connecting with you again—it'll help me close that door. I can see you as part of your family, and I can be part of it, too, in a sort of . . . fringe way. The way it needs to be now, with Cole. But if I keep up with this, it's going to be so much harder to do that. I'm not *going* to be able to move on. I'm going to be wishing again, stuck between my past and my future, hu—" She stopped, breathed, and finished it. "Hung up on you. And I can't do that. I need to move forward."

Silence on the other end, then he said, "I need to talk to you."

"You *are* talking to me. You're doing it right now."

"No, I mean *talk*. I need to see your face when you say that. Cops are like dogs. We get ten percent of our information from what somebody says, and ninety percent from how they look when they say it."

Men didn't talk over relationship problems. Not willingly. They walked away. She knew that. But now, he wanted to talk, and she didn't, because there was nothing to talk about. "We can't do anything anymore," she said. "I mean it. It's been too risky already. You know it as well as I do."

"Did I ask you to? No, I didn't. I said I wanted to *talk* to you. I'm saying I want to look you in the eye when you tell me that I was some kind of transition person for you, or a bad part of your past that you needed to put behind you, and that now we've done that and can both move on, because it's too hard anyway to figure out how it'd work out for us."

"But . . ." She began to pace faster. She was too antsy to stand still.

He didn't wait for whatever she would have said. "I want to see the expression on your face," he said, "when you tell me you're going to find somebody that you can go out to dinner with on Saturday night like a normal woman with a normal life, and then take home afterwards so you can try him out. That being with me and giving me your heart and facing up to what that means feels too hard and too scary, so you're going to find somebody who's happy to be your Mr. Right Now, who can't believe his luck that you don't want anything more. And I want to see your face when I tell *you*, the hell with that. If I'm not just another guy, the same way you aren't just another woman—then get some guts and go for it. Cowboy up and take what you have to take to get where we need to get, the same way I will be."

He was stealing her breath, and he was taking her heart with it. He was making her flinch, too. What he was saying was impossible. She didn't want to remind him, but she had to. "I'm leaving after February, remember? I can't live in this town again. There's too much hurt here for me. On February twenty-eighth, my time is up. On March first, I'll be in Seattle."

Now, she wanted to see *his* face, because he was saying, "So everything we've done so far, everything we've said—you *were* just getting me out of your system. That's all that was."

"Yes. No. I don't know." She started to move again, because somehow, she'd stopped. Cletus walked with her, looking up into her face as she said, "Maybe it's easier for me to think of you like that, since I can't afford to think of you the way I wish I could. Can't this be it, since it's not realistic to think we can have anything else? Can't we just be glad we're friends now, that the bad feelings are gone? Or maybe . . . all right, even if it's just having that affair after all. Can't we get together sometimes, when I'm back in Seattle, and we can be open about it and enjoy it for what it is?"

"No." His voice was flat, and he was right about the phone. Not seeing his face—it was terrible. "That's not how it works. You don't get the right person when things fall your way, when everything's perfect. And you don't get to say that there's too much hurt in it, so you'll go do something easier. You get the right person when you're ready to work for it and you're willing to sacrifice for it, and you show each other you're willing. When you show him he's more to you than a convenience, and he knows he can believe it, that you're ready to be his steady place in a hard world just like he'll be that for you. When you can tell him and mean it that even if he's halfway around the world, getting shot at—hell, getting *shot*—and you're lying alone in bed every night for six months, crying because you're so lonely and so scared of what could happen, and because your little girl's forgotten what her daddy looks like—you're willing to keep doing that anyway. You're going to *keep* lying alone in bed and waiting for him to come home."

There was a pause, and she tried to think of something to say and couldn't. Her hand was shaking on the phone. She didn't want to hear this. And then he went on.

"You can't do anything else," he said, "because he's your man, and that's it. And you know that he's out there himself, halfway around the world, running and sweating and hurting and bleeding, with your picture in the pocket next to his heart. That he wrote a letter for his best buddy to send you in case he doesn't make it, telling you that you're the one he was thinking about when the end came. That the only thing he died regretting was having to leave you. And you know that he can be in some bar after all that's over, and it doesn't matter how many women are in there or how pretty they are or how much they let him know that they're willing to be his right-now comfort spot. It doesn't matter how lonely he is and how glad he is to still be alive. He doesn't care, because he's holding out for the best. He's holding out for you."

She didn't answer. She couldn't.

"That's life," he finally went on. "And that's what it means to live it all the way, full tilt. It's too short even when it's long, and sometimes it isn't long at all, because life can be pretty damn brutal. If being alive in the world means anything, it's got to mean finding what you want—a man, a woman, a family, a job, whatever it is—and fighting to keep it. It's got to mean holding on to it with everything you've got. It's got to mean giving it everything, or what's the point?"

When she still didn't say anything, he said, "Yeah. Well. I guess that's what I get for saying all that into a metal box. Everything you didn't want to hear. Tell you what. If you see me? You could wave."

And he hung up.

FACING THE MONSTER

She'd been right. She wasn't enough, and she never would be. She'd opened up, she'd taken the risk, and she'd fallen short. Again. Always.

She barely slept, and she spent too much of Sunday crying. Every time she thought she'd stopped, there the tears and sadness came again, along with the same unwelcome thoughts.

Finally, though, she'd had enough. "This is not going to work," she told Cletus, who'd been following her around the house all day. If a golden retriever could have a worried look, he had it. "We need to do something else," she said, and since he seemed to be nodding, she took him for a run on the mountain, and then she came back and forced herself to do her planning for the week.

No matter what, you kept going. The alternative was to give up, and that wasn't an option. So she shoved Jim Lawson and her own inadequacies and the aching sadness into the back of her mind and got it done.

On Monday, she woke up mad.

She'd had a horrible dream that she couldn't remember very well, except that it had been full of flames and shouting and running and a shadowy figure behind her, chasing her, gaining on her. She'd turned, and it was Jim, and she'd started to laugh with relief, and then she'd started to scream, because it wasn't Jim anymore. It was a monster.

He wasn't a monster, she told her pounding heart when she was sitting up in bed, gasping for breath. But he was wrong. Or at least—he wasn't all the way right. He hadn't been fair, for sure. And she needed to tell him so.

She got up in the predawn chill, the light just beginning to turn gray over the hills. She fed Cletus, ate a piece of toast and drank a cup of coffee, then put him in the car with her school clothes and drove into town and thought some more.

At the school, she fastened Cletus's leash on, but she didn't take her usual route. She ran straight to the little house on the roughly paved street, the house that was neatly painted and had all its leaves raked. She ran up to the kitchen door with Cletus and knocked. And when nobody answered, she knocked again.

The door opened, and it was Jim. In a T-shirt and sweatpants, his feet bare, his face unshaven.

"Hallie." His face was empty of expression, but his eyes weren't. They were searching her face. Getting that ninety percent of his information.

"Get dressed," she said. "Come for a run."

He opened the door. "Come in."

"Cletus—"

"Bring the damn dog." Well, *that* was conciliatory. Not. She stepped inside with Cletus, and Jim pointed at the kitchen table and said, "Sit."

Cletus sat, but Hallie didn't. She crossed her arms over her chest and said, "No, thanks. I'll stand. Hurry up."

He walked out of the room and toward the back of the house. After a minute, Hallie heard the sound of a door opening down the hall, and Mac came out. She stopped halfway through the living room and said, "Oh."

"Hi," Hallie said, doing her best to shift gears. "Your dad's going to go for a run with me before work."

Mac said, "No, he isn't. He doesn't have to work today."

"Oh," Hallie said, trying not to feel foolish. "I don't know his schedule, I guess."

"I guess not. I do, though. It's his day off. He's supposed to get to sleep in. Except that you woke him up, so he can't." She reached down and gave Cletus a pat. He'd crossed the room to say hello to her, of course. For Cletus, "tension in the air" meant, "Time to start loving people up!"

Mac said, "I'm going back to bed," and turned around and went.

"Cletus," Hallie told the dog when she heard the sound of a door closing, "I have the feeling we aren't welcome here."

Cletus, of course, just wagged.

Jim came back in about three minutes. Same clothes, but he'd added a sweatshirt and running shoes.

"One sec," he said. "I'll leave a note for Mac."

"She knows where you're going. She came out to say hello. Or maybe that was, 'What are you doing with my dad, you slutty home-wrecker.' Or something similar."

As a joke, it fell flat, because Jim just shot a glance at her and said, "Let's go."

When they hit the sidewalk, Hallie took off running hard, and Jim, of course, kept pace with her. She ran that way for two blocks, then slowed to a jog and said, trying to keep her voice level and failing at that, too, "I am not Maya. I am not the perfect woman. I never will be. And expecting me to be that isn't fair."

There was a long pause, and then Jim said, "I didn't say she was the perfect woman."

"Oh, yeah? I'd say you said just exactly that. I'd say you made your point. And I agree." She blinked the tears back and tried to pretend it was the cold. "But how do you think it feels to know I'll never measure up to that, and to have you tell me so? I can tell you how, because it isn't the first time somebody's told me that kind of thing. I spent most of my life hearing that. So why have I put myself in a spot to be told that again? And why is it fair for you to do it?"

"I didn't do that." He was still running. He looked like he wanted to run *away*, judging by the strain on his face and the set of his shoulders, but he didn't.

"Yes," she said, "you did. You've got this set of rules that *you've* made up, that I'm supposed to follow, or I'm not good enough. Well, I'm not going to give somebody my heart and know even as I'm doing it that no matter what I do, I'll never be enough. That I'm not strong enough and brave enough and tough enough for him. For *you*. I'll tell you right now, I'm none of those things, and I know it. I'm scared all the time. When people get mad at me, I shrivel up inside and want to hide, because I know I've failed. The same way I felt yesterday. The same way I cried until I didn't have anything left, because I was failing at *life*. That you couldn't love me, because you'd already loved somebody who could do life the way you needed her to. The way I *know* I should be doing it. I get it, all right? But—you say that loving somebody means being brave? I say it means being honest. I say it's saying—this is who I am. I'm scared. I'm trying my hardest and knowing that sometimes, that isn't enough. I'm never sure. I'm doing my best, and if my best isn't good enough for you? Then s-s-screw you."

That last part had come out on a puff of air, and she was hauling breath into her lungs, trying to run past it. To run through it.

"Hallie." Jim had stopped running, and she didn't realize it until Cletus started dragging at the leash, holding her back.

She circled around, came back to him, and said, "I've never said that to anybody before. Do you realize that? And right now, I'm trying not to cry. I'm not brave, and I'm not tough. I love you, and I'm scared to love you. That's never worked for me, and I'm scared to try. There you go. I'm scared. I know you think I'm living on the surface, and I'm sure you're right. But I don't know how to love a man and make it last. I don't think I can. My aunt was right. I'm not the kind of woman that men—"

She *wouldn't* cry, she told herself fiercely. She *wouldn't*. "That men love no matter what. That they're crazy about. I'm the kind of woman where men say, 'Oh, Hallie. She's nice. She's sweet.' And then they leave and fall in *love* with somebody else. Somebody exciting. Somebody who can live full tilt, no limits. That's why I can't tell you to go away until you can do better, the way Maya could. If I said that, you'd do the leaving part, and that would be it. I know what you want from a woman, and I know I'm not it. If I don't hang on hard, the way you want? That's because I know I couldn't really hold you. I know I *am* your transition woman. You need somebody to help you get out in the world again, and here I am. I need your help, and I'm crazy about you. You know I am, because you've always known it. And I'm willing to be that person for you and then to . . . to leave afterwards, to have my real life, and to let you have yours with that woman who's strong and brave and tough, the one you can fall in love with and stay in love with."

"Hallie," Jim said again. "Wait."

She didn't. She had to finish this. "So if that's weak?" she said. "Maybe it is, but it's my best. What you said—it isn't fair. It hurt too much, and you didn't need to hurt me like that. You could just have said something . . . something nicer, to let me know it wasn't going to be me. And I had to—to tell you so."

"Oh, God." Jim dropped his head and scrubbed at his still-unshaven jaw. "Damn it to *hell*."

She started walking, and then she started running. She had to move. Cletus was coming, and then Jim was, too. He said, "I never said Maya was perfect."

"No, you didn't. You didn't have to. You just told me all the ways she was."

"She wasn't perfect. She got mad at me plenty. The same exact way you just did. You say you're not able to tell me to go away until I can do better? What do you think you just did? And I wasn't perfect either. *That*, I know for sure. All she did—all either of us did—was stick."

"Yes," Hallie said. "That's what she did. She held on to you, and she held on to Mac, and she held on to her baby. No matter what, she held on."

"Yeah. She did. And I told you what that did. It killed her. She might've been too stubborn. She might've been a lot of things. I loved her with all my heart, but she wasn't perfect, and I'm not holding her up as some saint that no other woman can measure up to. You're completely different from her, and you're pretty damn terrific. But you're wrong, too. I see you. I know you're scared and that sometimes you're fighting yourself all the way to do what you have to do. You're so sure that it's right to put that hand out for somebody else, so you're going to do it no matter what. You're here in the first place, and it's not because you want the money. It's because you don't. You want to give it away."

"But I bought a pool table."

"So you bought a damn pool table!" It came out in almost a shout, and she flinched, and he said, "All I want to do right now is to stop right here and hold on to you and tell you I'm sorry, and I can't. So let me tell you this. Yeah, you bought a pool table, and you bought a little furniture, too. You could buy yourself a brand-new car, and there'd be nothing wrong with that, either. You deserve good things as much as anybody else."

"No," she said. "I don't. I had it easy. So much easier than Cole. So much easier than you."

"You did not have it easy. Why did Maya have so much confidence at twenty-two that she could toss my butt out until I got it together? How did she know she was worth more than that? Because she had two parents who thought she'd hung the moon. They kept their kids' pictures on the mantel, and every one of them knew that, no matter how bad he screwed up, he could come home and his mom and dad would give him a hug and tell him they loved him and they were behind him no matter what. I had that, too, at least with my mom. And my sister, too. And you didn't."

"My mom's all right."

"Where was she that night, then, when some redneck punk with no future who'd never even taken you out drove off with you and put you on the hood of his car and took your virginity like he had a right to it? Where was she any night? Where has she been since you got back here?"

"I'm an adult."

"So was I when Maya got sick. So was she. And her folks helped me take care of her and Mac, and then my mom did. They all jumped in there, because that's what loving parents do. And look at what you've done, all by yourself. You've taken what was worst in your dad, all the bad he'd done, and turned it around and made it good. Eileen Hendricks is driving his truck, and I saw a guy at the Quik Mart the other day wearing what I swear were his alligator boots. Henry spent his life in this town trying to be better than everybody else, trying to shove them down so he could climb on top of them, and you're spending yours pulling them up. You're teaching kids and taking Eileen's dog and being a stand-up woman. That first night, you didn't want to stay in that house, and you did. Because you've got guts, and you've got heart."

"If that's true," she said, "why were you so hard on me?"

"I'll tell you why. Because I'm in love with you, and I want you, and you don't want me as bad, not enough to sacrifice for it. It hurts, so I tried to hurt you instead, and all it did was make me feel worse."

"You don't know me, though," she said miserably. "You don't know about when I didn't have guts. I haven't told you about it, even though I've wanted to. I thought, it's over. It doesn't matter. It's so long ago. But it just keeps . . . *hanging* there."

The seconds passed, and he stared at her, and she had to look away.

"Hallie," he finally said. "Tell me what you're talking about. Tell me now."

She took a breath, and she said it. "I got pregnant. That night. And I had an abortion. My dad said I had to, and I did it."

LETTING GO

She had to tell him. After all those things he'd said about her, about how she was strong, even though she knew she hadn't been strong enough . . . the secret was there, the thing that only her mother had known.

Her mother. And her father.

"Tell me," Jim said again. His face was hard, but now, she knew why. Because that was what he did with the tough things. He stuffed them down deep and covered them up.

"After we were caught," she said. She was walking again, and he was walking with her. "After that night. I didn't tell you, but my dad made them run a whole rape kit on me, and I thought that was the worst. Lying there in that cubicle in the ER . . . I thought it was the lowest I could feel. And then I found out that it wasn't. He took me to his doctor, even before I missed a period. The day I saw you in the grocery store . . . that was where I'd been. My dad told the doctor to check me over and do all the tests. To make sure I didn't have a . . . disease." She closed her eyes against the shame of it. "He came into the room to hear what the doctor said. While I was still lying there under the paper, not dressed. He was there when the doctor said I was pregnant."

She remembered what he'd said, too.

"Get rid of it," Henry had said instantly, before Hallie had even taken it in.

"It can't be done yet," Dr. Ivey said. Hallie had never liked him. Big, serious, and remote, he'd scared her as a child. And now, with her insides still feeling the unfamiliar touch of cold metal, he terrified her. "Not for two more weeks, until the embryo's more developed."

Embryo, Hallie thought.

"Good," her father said. "That works. Get rid of it before school starts."

Dr. Ivey said, "I don't do this procedure."

Henry's only response to that was an impatient gesture. "You know how, right?"

"Technically. But I don't have the best equipment to make it comfortable for her." Her father started to say something, probably, *Who the hell cares if she's comfortable,* but Dr. Ivey didn't let him. He said firmly, "I don't do this procedure. You'll need to take her to the clinic in Spokane. My girl will give you the referral."

Hallie said, "Wait."

Her father said, "You don't talk. You get yourself dressed and get off that table and get in the car."

"But—" she said.

"You *don't talk.*" He was standing over her, his lips pulled back from his teeth in a snarl. "You get your ass in the car. I don't want to hear from you. I don't want to look at you. You disgust me."

It was too much remembering. Too much pain. She started to run again, only because she couldn't stand still. She told Jim, who was keeping pace with her, "He wouldn't talk to me. Anytime I tried, he said, 'If you want to go to college, you'll do what I say. If you want to be on the street, you do what you want. Your choice.' And I . . . ." She closed her eyes against the memory. "I chose."

"You were seventeen," Jim said.

She nodded jerkily. "And who knows what the right thing was anyway. It isn't that I thought it was wrong in itself. Just like Maya. That's not it." It was so hard to explain. Or it was impossible. "Maybe it was better after all, even though it didn't feel that way. I'd love to think I'd have been able to carry the baby and give it up for adoption, have chosen some couple that was made to have kids and couldn't. That I would have had that kind of strength. But I never put myself to the test, so I don't know. And I would have been a terrible mother. That wasn't an option. At least I knew that. I was so scared, and so stupid, and so . . . *young.*"

"What about your mom?"

She shook her head. "I didn't tell her, not until later. She was living in Arizona by then, you know. So busy with her new life. That's what I told myself, but really, that was cowardice again. Selfishness, because I didn't want to face it, didn't want to have a choice. I'd look at this University of Washington postcard, you know? It was my dream. And I'd think, I can't lose my dream. I *can't.* So I went along with my dad. That felt like a . . . like a dream, too. Like maybe it wouldn't happen after all. Like maybe it would all go away." She smiled, even though there was no smile at all in her heart. "They call it 'magical thinking.' Very common in adolescents. You think if you wish hard enough, it'll go away, or it won't have happened, or it'll magically just get . . . fixed. But it doesn't."

"So you didn't have anybody with you."

"My dad. In the waiting room. He said that when you did things you were ashamed of, you paid for them alone. That was the price, he said. It was a very simple procedure, they said, but it hurt, and I was cold. I cried. I was so scared. So sad. When it was happening . . ."

She was crying now. She tried not to remember this. It was so very long ago. Fourteen years. Half a lifetime. "When it was happening, it was real. And I wanted to say, 'Wait. Stop. Wait.' But it was too late. There was this tube, and it was . . . gone."

"Hallie." They'd reached the school parking lot, and she slowed. He had his arm around her, was pulling her close, his other hand going to her hair, smoothing it again and again. "I'm sorry, baby. I'm sorry."

She shook her head violently against his chest, and then she gave into the tears. She cried for her lost chances, and for his. For all the things life had taken from both of them. He held her and murmured something she could barely hear, and his arms and his chest were rock-solid comfort.

Finally, she stood back. She knew she was a mess and that anybody driving by could see them, but she couldn't care. Her chest ached, her throat hurt, her eyes were puffy, and her nose was running. She was empty. "I'm sorry," she said, not looking at him. "Sorry to tell you this way. Sorry I didn't tell you before."

"I'm sorry, too," he said. "Guess we're both sorry."

She wiped her face on her sleeve and knew it was disgusting, and he didn't seem to notice. After a minute, she said, her voice still husky with tears, "You know, if I were talking to a student, to a friend's daughter, to any girl in my situation, I'd never judge her. There's no good answer, and I know it. There may be women who think, 'Oh, yay, today I get my abortion,' but I doubt there are many. I think it's always a horrible choice to have to make, no matter what, and when you're seventeen?" She sighed. "I don't know."

"It feels different when it's you," he said, and she nodded, because it did. It felt terrible. It always had.

"You could think, instead," he said, "that it was my fault. I know that's what I'm thinking. You don't have sex if you don't have a condom. There *is* one right answer for that, and that's the one."

She shrugged tiredly and said, "Girls have a responsibility, too."

"I had the responsibility for that. I let you down. And I'm sorry."

She looked at him, and he looked straight back at her, so solid and so strong, and she had to swallow. "I'm sorry, too," she said. "I'm so sorry. About my dad. About everything. It was all one big mess, wasn't it?"

"It was. But it started with me."

"No. It started with us."

He sighed, and she did, too. They stood there a minute longer, and then she said, "Anyway. It's over. It's a long time ago, and it's over."

"No, it's not. Because it still hurts your heart."

"How do you know?"

"Because it's hurting mine."

He had his arm around her again, and she let him hold her. And somehow, sharing it with him had helped. Some of the dragging sadness she'd carried for so long gave a flap of its wings, then flew away into the quiet, frosty morning like a giant black moth. And she opened her aching heart and let it go.

STEP IT UP

On Monday evening, the killer sat and drummed angry fingers on the desk, thinking it through.

Jim and Hallie *had* to be getting it on. Why else would he be so concerned with her welfare, so eager to help her out? Men didn't do that unless they were getting something out of it.

Or, more likely, if they were hoping to. Once Jim had had her, once he'd overcome her resistance—surely he'd lose interest. It had to be partly about getting revenge against her father, anyway. Hallie Cavanaugh wasn't the face that launched a thousand ships. She'd been a mousy, timid little girl, and she'd turned into an overly curvy, redheaded teacher who cared too much that everybody liked her. Soft in all ways. A pleaser. An easy mark. Not a woman that a man like Jim Lawson, with those kinds of hard edges, would go to the mat for.

The GPS devices should have worked, but they hadn't. Jim clearly hadn't discovered his, since he was still driving around with it. Hallie's, though, had been stationary in her garage since Saturday. It was stupid of both of them not to put two and two together and realize what the point of tracking Hallie would be. But then, whoever said cops were smart? Jim had barely graduated from high school. Giving out speeding tickets didn't make anybody a rocket scientist.

But Hallie would be on her guard now. Which *also* meant she'd be nervous. *More* nervous.

Time to step it up.

The plan wasn't hard to figure out. It would take a few days to put into place, but that was fine. There were still three months to go. Hallie would be anticipating receiving her first big payment, her thirty thousand dollars for staying three months, which was up on Thanksgiving. She'd be feeling safe. Feeling smug. Spending the money in her head already. If you pulled that rug out from under her feet now? She'd be that much more rocked. The price of her inheritance would be too high.

Especially if things got physical. She was a mouse. What did mice do when they saw danger? They ran.

Danger, that was all. *Not* injury. Nothing to feel guilty about. Just giving her a good nudge. And carrying out Henry's wishes. The more the killer had thought about that, the more likely it had seemed. Henry had wanted to humiliate her, to show her she couldn't win.

She had insurance, too. It wouldn't even cost her.

It was clear and cold all week, the temperature hovering near zero, as the plan took shape. A thin layer of snow still covered the ground in patches from the storm a couple weeks earlier, with the next storm not due until Friday morning. Perfect conditions.

Thanksgiving dawned gray, with a heaviness in the air that spoke of snow to come. Wind would be perfect. Snow wouldn't. The killer sweated the day, and did everything possible not to show it. Thanksgiving dinner had never seemed longer or more tedious. Chat-chat-chatter as you plowed through a plate of food with no appetite for any of it. The excruciating delay while dishes were done and dessert was served, and then, finally, waiting to see if the two crushed Ambien tablets could really go undetected in sweetened whipped cream.

A long half hour, then, for the result the killer had been waiting for. The yawn, the exclamation.

"I'm so tired, I can barely keep my eyes open. Too much Thanksgiving. I'm going to bed."

"Go on. It's been a long day." Which was true.

It was only six o'clock. Two tablets on somebody who almost never took them? The Internet had been clear on that. Those would last all night.

The hours until one o'clock dragged by, but they did pass. The killer crept to a bedroom and checked for activity, but heard only deep, rhythmic breathing. A shove at a shoulder, a whispered name, and . . . nothing. No movement. No reaction. Out like a light.

Into the back of the storage closet, then, pulling out the three paper bags that held supplies purchased at the Goodwill store in Union City two days earlier, a safe thirty miles from Paradise. Two heavy sweatshirts, oversized cargo pants, a shabby parka, a baseball cap to shade the face from those cameras. Two pairs of extra socks, and the best part. The shoes. Two sizes too big, which would make it hard to walk even with the extra padding, but the shoes were necessary, just in case. And the gloves, which would come later.

The final item. The most important one. The battered backpack that was already filled with the key supplies for tonight's adventure. Also purchased in Union City, and nothing unusual about any of it.

It was hard to breathe evenly, to stay cool with the adrenaline running high, but it was all planned. All rehearsed.

Simple. Logical. Perfect.

A quiet exit from the sleeping house and into the car that had been left by the curb instead of the garage, on an excuse that had sounded nothing but plausible. Hard snow by morning. Drifts, maybe, and not being able to get out of the driveway without shoveling. Who wanted that on the Friday after Thanksgiving?

The drive wasn't long, but it was long enough to run through the elements of the plan one last time before the killer was parking around the bend from the target, then climbing out of the car, stashing the keys carefully in a cargo pocket for quick recovery, shouldering the backpack, putting up the hood of the parka over the baseball cap, and heading up the street to the driveway.

The walk up the hill in darkness, because a flashlight was too risky. Clouds covering moon and stars, and the wind was picking up now. Snow by morning for sure, but that was all right. Snow would mean covered-up footprints, which was too bad, but those were the breaks. You had to be flexible. Wind, though? Wind was nothing short of wonderful.

Cautiously now. Quietly. Creeping the final thirty feet to the house, along the side of the garage, shrugging the backpack off. And then the preparations. Quick, but not hasty. Rehearsed. All going to plan.

Until it went wrong.

THROUGH THE TUNNEL

When Cletus began to bark, Hallie swore, rolled over, and shoved her pillow over her head.

"Shut *up*," she moaned as the deep-throated barks continued from the other side of the house. From outside, clearly. Coyotes getting too close and being warned off. "All *right*," she muttered when Cletus *didn't* shut up. "We *get* it. You're the baddest dog in the west."

Ugh. She'd eaten too much at Vicki's this afternoon, and now, she had heartburn. Probably because it had been easier to stuff her face than to look at Jim. She still felt raw, like she was missing a layer of skin. He'd been so caring, so—loving—on Monday, and it had torn her to bits, even as it had healed her. Both things couldn't be true, but they were. And they'd had to say everything they'd said standing on the blacktop outside the gym of the middle school, unable to hold each other again, even as she'd ached to have his arms around her.

They'd left it with nothing settled. No time for it, and no opportunity. And since then—it wasn't the kind of thing you could talk about on the phone. *Thanksgiving,* she'd thought, but Thanksgiving hadn't turned out to be the answer at all. Too many eyes. Too many unanswered questions.

What was she willing to do? What was he? Those kinds of questions took time and talking and walking and thinking to sort out. They took evenings of lying together, arms and legs tangled up together, hands stroking over backs, soft confessions and wishes and dreams you could only express in darkness. Words offered tentatively, received tenderly, held safely in cupped hands and loving hearts.

At least she imagined that was how it would work.

And all that—it was everything she and Jim couldn't have. Not now. And afterward? She'd be in Seattle, or—

Or she'd be taking the biggest risk of her life, *without* those confessions and those evenings in the dark to give her strength, to make her believe.

She'd always thought she couldn't live in Paradise again. But really, maybe she'd just been thinking that she couldn't stand to be the person she'd been in Paradise. But living in the same place—did that mean you had to be the same person?

No. Surely not. If Jim had changed—maybe she had, too. That had been the whole point of accepting this challenge, because that's what it had been. That was why she'd done it.

Maybe I just want to live here on my terms, she'd said that first night. *Maybe I want to say that there's another way to live, right here with his . . . ghost watching. Maybe I want to win.*

But then there was Mac, whose watchful gaze had been on Hallie and her dad all afternoon. Hallie got it; of course she did. It still didn't feel good, though. Or hopeful. She had a long way to go with Mac.

She pulled herself up against the pillows to ease the heartburn and thought about it some more, and Cletus kept barking.

Finally, she'd heard enough. Thought enough, too. She needed to call Cletus into the house and shut his dog door so he *stayed* in, however much she didn't want to get out of her warm, cozy bed and go down into the cold. And then she needed to set all of this aside and go to sleep. She sighed, sat up, turned on the bedside light, and was reaching for her slippers when Cletus came bounding into the room.

Oh, good. She wouldn't have to get up. "Cletus. Quiet. Shut *up*."

He wasn't listening. He was galloping around to her side of the bed, still barking.

It was a racket to raise the dead. Cletus *never* barked in her face. She put her hands over her ears and said, "Stop. I mean it. STOP."

He barked again, and something in the sharpness of it finally made it through the fog in her brain, the result of too much turkey and too many uncomfortable thoughts. She shoved her feet into her slippers while Cletus dashed for the door and came back again, still barking his head off. After a quick moment's thought, she went to the closet, took the shotgun and box of shells down from the shelf for the first time since she'd bought them, set the ammo on the bed, and forced herself to stay calm as she cracked the gun and loaded it.

Overkill. Maybe.

She grabbed her fleece robe from the hook on the back of the door, pulled it on, and tied the belt. Then she picked up the shotgun and, after another moment's thought, pumped the handle to chamber the shell.

If you need it, you'll need it now. If you don't, you unload.

Out into the hallway, then, switching on lights as she went. Out the front door, with Cletus running ahead of her, then circling back.

She flipped the porch light on, took a firm hold on the gun, opened the door, draped the gun over one forearm in the way she'd been taught, respecting its power, and followed her dog.

That was when she smelled it. Smoke.

The smoke alarm hadn't gone off, though. Brushfire?

Even as she had the thought, the shriek began overhead. She hurried after the dog, forgetting to shiver in the cold. Her heart was beating hard, her breath coming out in icy puffs.

Around the side of the house, to a view of flickering orange. Yellow. Red.

Fire.

Fire in the bushes to the right side of the path. Fire on the other side, starting to lick up the side of the house. A wall of fire.

No. A tunnel through fire. But it was a *wide* tunnel. It had barely started. She could get through it. Right now.

She ran, the heat warming her on either side, smelling smoldering wood and resinous pine. On her right, a small tree caught and went up like a torch, sending up a shower of sparks that landed around her. And on her, too. She smelled something worse, felt her hair sizzling, was beating at it with one hand as she kept her feet going, her slippers sliding on the icy concrete, her breath coming hard.

She was out. Through the fire, around the corner. She was *out*, and it wasn't that bad. She could get the hose and put it out.

She was headed around the garage for it when something hit her. A flash in her peripheral vision, and a sharp starburst of pain blooming in her forehead. She stumbled, and the shotgun went flying from her hand as first her knee and then her palm hit the ground. Then she was crawling. Getting away from the fire, and the pain.

One second, she was moving. The next, something hard crashed into her upper back and her forehead hit the concrete. And that was all.

◆ ◆ ◆

The killer ran.

Running hadn't been in the plan. Neither had hitting Hallie. There wasn't supposed to be violence. It was supposed to be scaring her, that was all.

The stupid *dog.* All that careful planning, and the dog had messed it up.

No time now. *Get away.*

Skidding down the driveway, the too-large shoes cumbersome, still holding the gas can, because there hadn't been time to put it into the backpack. Which was just as well. The can had been necessary. Regrettable, but necessary.

Along the empty road to the car, wrenching off a glove and grabbing the keys from the right-hand pocket of the cargo pants. Diving into the car, taking precious seconds to shove the gas can into the backpack again, so it would leave no trace in the car. And then, finally, stabbing the key into the ignition and driving.

Not too fast. No squeal of tires, nothing noticeable. Almost two o'clock on the Friday morning after Thanksgiving. Nobody awake, every oversized house, up its discreet driveway, dark and silent.

Not taking the fastest route to town, because it was also the fastest route from the fire station. Instead, the longer route around the winding curves that spelled "exclusive real estate," and finally coming out on the highway that led to Union City in one direction, into Paradise on the other. Meeting not a soul along the way.

No relaxing. Not yet. Instead, driving all the way out to the mall on the opposite side of town, the streets still weirdly empty. And this was farther away, surely, than anybody would expect anyone to drive before dumping the gear. They couldn't search every trash container in town.

Pulling around behind a deserted ShopCo, the parking lot as empty as the streets on this quietest of nights, turning off the car and killing the lights, and struggling out of the layers of heavy clothes in the awkward confines of the driver's seat. Getting rid of everything that would hold any residue of gasoline, of smoke. The hat. The parka. The sweatshirts, the pants, the shoes, the socks. Until it was a turtleneck and jeans and bare feet.

Putting on the gloves, then, groping for the big black trash bag from the floor of the passenger seat, stuffing everything into it, first the gas can, and the shoes and clothes on top, and tying it shut. No prints on anything. Even if they found it all, somehow—no prints.

Tugging the gloves off again, shoving feet into regular shoes. Moving fast, trying to be calm, while the sound of labored breathing belied the attempt. And then, with gloves on again, looking into the rearview mirror one last time and seeing only darkness, then hauling in a deep breath and leaving the safety of the car. Moving fast to the dumpster and hauling it open, leaning into it, digging through stinking piles of trash to make a hole, and finally stuffing the black bag down, as deep as possible, dragging other refuse over it to cover it.

Finally—*finally*—back in the car, trying to calm a racing heart, to keep steady hands on the wheel. Back home, down deserted streets, with the wind starting to blow the first icy particles of snow across the windshield.

Just in time. There would be no tire tracks through that snow, and nothing to show the car hadn't been there all night, not it if was parked in exactly the same spot, which it was.

Back into the house, leaving nothing behind. Stripping off every stitch of clothing along the way, tossing it all into the washing machine and turning it on. Just in case. And, finally, a soft creep through the house, a quick, thorough scrub in the shower of the second bathroom, until every trace had to have been removed.

Back to the storage closet, dressing again, underwear and pajamas like every night, back to normal.

A slow, stealthy slide down the hallway. A rustle from a bed, and the worst moment since the dog had come running out of the flames with Hallie behind him.

"Wha—?" The voice sleepy, confused. "What happened?"

"Shh. Indigestion. Go back to sleep."

"Oh." It had been a sigh, and that was all. Two Ambien.

And Hallie would be fine. Of course she would. A knock on the head, that was all. Which was probably better anyway. If you wanted to scare her out of town? It was *much* better.

Anyway, it was done.

REAL-DEAL INVESTIGATION

Once again, Jim heard it from DeMarco first.

When your phone rang in the middle of the night on Thanksgiving, you picked up.

"Lawson," he said.

"Hallie's place is burning," DeMarco said.

Jim was already on his feet. "Hallie—"

"Ambulance just got here," DeMarco said. "I came in right behind the first fire engine. She was on the driveway, just out of the flames, barely crawling, with that big dog of hers trying to pull her along. Damnedest thing I ever saw. Dragging her by the collar of her robe."

"Is she all right?" Jim was moving on autopilot now. He had his jeans on, was pulling a sweatshirt over his head and grabbing his socks.

"Groggy. I can't tell. Her forehead was messed up when they turned her over. Scraped from the dog dragging her, and from something else. Quite a bit of blood, and a lump like she'd been hit, or she'd fallen. Exactly like her dad, which is hinky. But she's awake."

Your dad died in that house, the letter had said. *You could too.*

"I'll head to the hospital," Jim decided. "I'll meet them there." He had to get off the phone and call his mom to come over. He couldn't leave Mac alone, not with something—*somebody*—out there.

"You do that," DeMarco said.

"I'm on duty in the morning, though. Shit."

"I'll take care of that," DeMarco said.

"Thanks. That fire—where? Sounds like it was set?"

"Side of the house, and I'd say, yeah, it was set. Burning from the outside, not the inside, no source that anyone could see. They'll have it under control fast. Not a way you'd kill a person, because they'd be able to get out. Unless you were planning to smoke them out and then whack them on the head. But it didn't look to me like they whacked hard enough for that to be the plan."

"A way you'd scare somebody." Jim had his boots on now. "Scare them enough to leave, since nothing else they've done has worked. *Damn* it. I shouldn't have let her aunt and uncle know we saw the GPS."

It had been too big a risk after all. He'd thought the person doing this was wussy. Lame. But they'd upped their game.

"Whoever it was might not have meant to hit her," DeMarco said. "They probably meant to set the fire and leave. I'm guessing the dog woke her up, and she ran out and interrupted the perp before they could get out. And another thing about that."

He hesitated, and Jim said, "What?"

"There was a shotgun on the driveway," DeMarco said. "Loaded."

"But she hasn't been shot," Jim managed to say.

"No," DeMarco said, and Jim took a couple deep breaths and thought, *No. Not shot,* and talked himself back under control.

He hung up and called his mom, and fifteen minutes later, he was on his way to the hospital. And trying not to think about the last time he'd been there with a woman he loved.

◆ ◆ ◆

It was more than an hour before he got to see her, and only after she'd been transferred to a room.

When he walked in to the sight of the narrow bed with its privacy curtains, the white face against the pillow, the blinking lights of an IV—it wasn't his most wonderful moment. But at least he was walking in with DeMarco, and the two of them were going to take care of this.

Hallie was going to get better, too. That would be the other difference.

She was lying there with her eyes closed, her curls the only spot of color. Well, her curls, and the red abrasions on her cheekbones, her nose, her chin, and the palm that lay turned up on the white blanket. Her face was all scraped up, a bandage only a fraction paler than her skin covered most of her forehead, and a sharp, acrid stench lingered in the air.

Burned hair. The sickening smell made Jim's own hair rise on the back of his neck. He'd smelled that often enough. Burned hair. Burned flesh.

He pulled a chair from the other side of the room up to the head of the bed and sat down on the side of her bed where her uninjured hand lay, leaving DeMarco to find his own chair and sit beside him, so Hallie wouldn't have to turn her head.

Her eyes opened at the movement. They were unfocused at first, which made Jim's gut clench, but then they cleared. She'd been asleep, that was all. No wonder.

"Hey," she said, her voice a little hoarse. That would be the smoke. Her eyes slid past Jim to DeMarco, and even that movement, Jim saw, made her face tighten with pain.

"Hey." Jim smiled at her, which wasn't easy. "Detective DeMarco's here to question you. I'm here to hold your hand." Which he did—the uninjured one. Gently. "How you doing?"

"Not too bad."

"Yeah, right," he said, and she managed to raise a smile herself that reached right into his chest and squeezed his heart.

"You guys . . . can you tell me?" she said. "Cletus. Did somebody get him?"

"Yes, ma'am," DeMarco said. "I took him over to Jim's place and dropped him off."

"Oh." She closed her eyes again for a moment. "Thank you. I've been so worried about him running around loose, trying to find me."

"No way," DeMarco said. "He's a canine hero. Dragging you out of the fire like that? You bet we took care of him."

"I remember . . . moving on the driveway," she said. "Trying to get out. Was that him? Mostly, I remember him barking. It's why I went downstairs."

"With your shotgun?" Jim guessed. "Was that yours?"

"Yeah. But I was so stupid." She coughed. "Could you get me some water?"

Jim picked up a plastic container from the swivel table and held the straw for her. Something else he'd done a hundred times. Something he'd have given anything not to have to do again.

She drank thirstily, in gulps, and when she stopped, he set the container down.

"My head . . . hurts," she said. "I hit it. How did that happen?"

"Somebody hit it," DeMarco said, with a glance at Jim that told him, *You're the boyfriend. I'm the investigator. Shut up.* "Did you see who it was?"

"No," she said. "Sorry."

"You've got a few stitches in there," Jim told her. "And after they hit you, they shoved you in the back, or kicked you, maybe, so your forehead hit the pavement hard. You've got some good bruising in a different place from the cut, plus what they're calling a moderate concussion."

"OK," she said. "Thanks." And Jim thought again how much braver she was than she realized.

"They pushed me, and I fell and hit my head, like my dad," she said after a minute. "Like the letter said, and like you thought. Somebody pushed him, too, I'll bet anything now."

"Yeah," DeMarco said. "Like Jim thought."

"But I was stupid," she said.

"How?" DeMarco asked.

"Why did I run through the fire? I followed Cletus, but why? I should have gone through the house. Downstairs, and out the door from the family room. Why didn't I do that? I've kept wondering."

"Because you reacted automatically," Jim said. Forget not being the investigator. This was boyfriend territory. He couldn't resist stroking a gentle hand over her hair, and she sighed and closed her eyes, so maybe it helped. "If you're trained in emergency situations, the training takes over in a crisis. It's automatic. If you're not trained, you do what's automatic for *you*. You followed the dog and ran out the front door. Never mind. You got out."

DeMarco asked a few more questions, most of which Hallie couldn't answer. She was clearly flagging, so DeMarco put his notebook away and said, "We'll be in touch when we know more, or if we need to ask you anything else. Where will you be?"

"Uh—I don't know," she said. "I guess I can't go home."

"Not until the fire department clears it," DeMarco said. "They aren't going to let you back in right away."

"Anyway," Jim said, "you don't want to go back there alone."

"I don't," she said with a sigh. "But I have to."

"No," he said. "We'll call Bob Jenkins and talk about it. I can't believe you'd have to live there after something like this happened. But don't think about it tonight." He told DeMarco, "She'll go to my mom's."

"Oh—" Hallie said.

"Because," Jim said, "I don't have a spare bedroom, and neither does Anthea, and anyway, my place would be out for obvious reasons, and Anthea's out of town. But my mom *does* have a spare bedroom. You need to be someplace where you're safe, and where somebody can look after you for a couple days."

DeMarco looked at him for a long moment, then said, "Talk to you outside a second?"

"Yeah." Jim squeezed Hallie's hand again and said, "Be right back."

"Will you stay for a while?" she asked. "I'm a little—" Her throat worked, and her eyes were shadowed with fatigue and pain.

"A little scared," he finished. "You bet. I'll be here. It's OK, baby. You're safe." To hell with DeMarco. He needed to say it, because she needed to hear it.

She tried to smile, but a couple tears leaked out and trailed down her cheeks.

This time, Jim thought, *I'm here for you.* "Hey, now," he said. "Hey." He grabbed a tissue, blotted the tears gently, and said, "I'll be right back. And in the meantime, I'm right outside the door. Nobody's getting in here. I promise."

He got up. He didn't want to, but he had to talk to DeMarco. It was a hell of a choice.

The second they were out the door and out of earshot, he asked the other man, "You check out the aunt and uncle yet?"

"As soon as the fire investigator confirms what you and I already know," DeMarco said. "That this was arson. But we'll also be checking out your mom and Cole."

Jim wanted to protest, but he couldn't.

"And you're off the case," DeMarco said. "Already talked to the lieutenant about it. Or rather, you were never *on* the case. This is a real-deal investigation now, and having you be part of it would be the dictionary definition of 'personal involvement.' I hate to ask this, but—are you absolutely positive about taking her to your mom's? I'm not necessarily talking about your mom," he hurried to add, "although we'll have to check her out. But your brother?"

Jim had told him about the graffiti. No choice on that, either. He'd seen how much an investigation could be messed up by people withholding information out of a misguided attempt to protect somebody else.

"I'm sure," Jim said.

DeMarco nodded, though he didn't look entirely convinced. "It's not exactly unheard-of for a fifteen-year-old to set a fire—or any of the rest of it. But kids who are that twisted haven't hidden it their whole lives. They've hurt other kids, pets. Set fires, for that matter. Their parents know it, even if they don't want to admit it. Their brother would know it for sure."

"I would," Jim said. "I do. It's not him. If it could have been him, I'd tell you. I wouldn't leave Hallie in this much danger. Focus on the aunt and uncle. And tell me what you find out."

"You're off the case."

"I know. Tell me anyway."

When he went back into the room, Hallie was asleep, and he spent what was left of the night sleeping in the chair, his legs stretched out in front of him. He'd done that before, too. And in the morning, he took her to his mother's house.

Hallie didn't even object. She was quiet. Hurting. When they got to Vicki's, she patted an ecstatic Cletus, then told Vicki, who'd brought Mac over to her place for the day, "I'd love to take a shower. I stink."

"That's your hair," Vicki said. "You go ahead. And after that, I'll trim those burned pieces for you so you don't have to lie there with that scorched-hair stench."

"Thanks," Hallie said. "That'd be great."

When she disappeared into the bathroom, Vicki looked at Jim and said, "You'd better find out who did this."

"Don't worry," Jim said. "I will."

Hallie was in bed again, her curls a few inches shorter, by the time the doorbell rang. DeMarco.

As hard as it had been not to do it, Jim hadn't warned his mother they were coming. He wasn't worried that she'd incriminate herself, and her answers would be more obviously genuine if it was apparent that she hadn't been prepped. Besides, he'd had a chance to think it through.

She looked startled and then resigned when DeMarco explained the reason for their visit.

"We'd like to talk to your son first," DeMarco said. "And we'd like to talk to him separately from you."

Vicki said, "I'd rather his sister were here. She's his attorney."

DeMarco's eyebrows rose. "He has an attorney?"

"Because of the trust."

DeMarco nodded. "Well, that's your right. Want to call her up, then, please?"

"She's in Seattle," Vicki said. "I can ask her to come home, but— no. I don't want to wait." She looked at Jim. "Can you sit with him?"

Jim said, "Sure," then cocked his head at DeMarco.

DeMarco sighed. "You're not investigating."

"Nope. I'm his brother, that's all. You can talk to him with me sit- ting in, or I'll tell him to lawyer up and you can wait for my sister to get home. Your choice."

DeMarco chose to talk now, of course. They did it in the kitchen, and Cole didn't have much to say. He'd eaten Thanksgiving dinner, and before and after that, had played board games and video games with Mac and his cousins. Anthea and Ben and the kids had left right after dinner, Jim and Mac had taken off around six, and his mom had gone to her room to read.

"And what did you do?" DeMarco asked. "Go out?"

Cole's mouth twisted. "Go out *where?* Almost all my friends were all having Thanksgiving dinner, too. I watched a couple movies and fell asleep on the couch."

"How about your mom?" DeMarco asked. "She go out anytime?"

"No," Cole said. "I'd have noticed. I was up until about eleven, and even then, I was still on the couch. I sleep out there sometimes, because that's where the TV is. Except she went out later," he added. "After she got the phone call."

"Her cell phone?" DeMarco asked sharply. "When was that? And how could you hear it from the living room, when you were asleep?"

"No. The landline. It's loud. No chance I wouldn't hear it. I don't know when. She came out and told me she was leaving to stay with Mac, because Jim had to leave. She was in a hurry. She didn't tell me it was Hallie. That was all I knew."

"What did she smell like?"

Cole stared at him. "*Smell* like? I don't know. I didn't notice. I don't go around smelling my mom."

"Did you smell anything unusual after that, or before?"

"Well, turkey," Cole said. "That turkey smell." He looked completely baffled. "Why?"

"How about cars?" DeMarco asked. "Hear any stopping outside, or starting up?"

"Uh . . . no, not that I remember. My mom's car was in the garage, if that's what you mean. I would've heard that. The garage door is pretty loud."

DeMarco gave it one more try. "Did you see your mom at all before the phone call? Hear her? Going out or coming in? Moving around the house?"

"No. I'd have woken up. I mean, I was on the *couch*. It's, like, about five steps from the front door. I'd have heard the door. It squeaks."

"Right. How about the back door? Would you have heard that?"

"I don't know," Cole said. "Probably. My stomach kind of hurt. I kept waking up."

DeMarco sat a minute, and Cole sat, too.

"Can I see your phone?" the detective finally asked.

Cole looked at Jim. "Is it OK to show him?"

"Depends," Jim said. "If you haven't told the truth about any of that—the next words out of your mouth are, 'I'd like to talk to my lawyer.'"

Cole said, "I don't need to do that," then reached into his pocket and handed over his phone.

DeMarco scrolled through the text messages for a couple minutes in silence while Cole sat and looked a little tense, but not horribly so.

Finally, DeMarco handed the phone back. "Before you look at it, what did I see on there?"

"Uh . . ." Cole stared into space. "Some texts with Aaron Clayborn about the game I was playing. *Halo.* I was at level fifteen. And some about a band I was listening to, I think. How lame Thanksgiving was. Pie. Like that."

"Pie?"

"You know. What kind of pie they had. They had mince at his house, and it was gross. He's got this really weird aunt who brought dessert, and it was only mince, plus a fruit salad, which is lame. He was asking me if I'd save him some pumpkin."

"Anybody else?"

"One from Tom Ingeborg, asking if I wanted to come over."

"But you didn't."

"Nah." Cole looked down and rubbed a thumb along the wood grain of the table. "I haven't been hanging out with him much."

"Thanks." DeMarco stood up. "If we have more questions, we'll check back with you." He looked at Jim. "And in case you're wondering—I'm talking to your mom now. And no, you're not invited."

He left the room, and Cole said, "I did stay here. I swear."

Jim said, "They'll check your phone records. If those texts came from here, you'll be good. And, yeah," he said when Cole looked startled, "another good reason to stay out of a life of crime. It's tricky business if you're not used to it."

He sat with Cole another ten minutes, watching his brother jiggle his leg under the table and unable to think of anything to talk about. When DeMarco appeared in the kitchen doorway again, he told Cole, "Give us some time here, OK?"

"Sure," Cole said, and left the room, clearly glad to escape.

Jim eyed DeMarco. "You coming in to tell me what you've got?"

DeMarco sat down with a barely repressed sigh. "Maybe I'm just hoping you'll offer me a cup of coffee. I'm on overtime, and I'm not acclimated anymore. Can't take all this crime. If you pick my brain while I'm in a defenseless fatigued state, I'll deny it."

The corner of Jim's mouth twitched, and he got up and poured a mug of coffee from the pot and handed it to DeMarco. Strong and black, the kind that saw you through the long nights. "Let me guess," he said, grabbing a cup himself and sitting down again. "My mom passed the test, too."

"Yeah. She took a bath and read until nine thirty or so. Tired from all the Thanksgiving stuff, she said. She went to bed, but she says she woke up around eleven, maybe, and went to check on Cole, make sure he was there." He shook his head. "Man, I'm not looking forward to my kid being a teenager. And after that, she went back to bed, but she swears she would've heard if he'd gone out, 'because I'm a mother.' Whatever that means. She said the thing about the garage door, too. And of course, that you called her. On the landline."

"Yeah. She turns her ringer off at night on her cell."

"You could've told me that from the beginning and saved me some trouble. If Cole and your mom both heard the landline when you called here at two fifteen, and your mom picked up and then talked to Cole right afterwards, it's hard to see how either of them could've been walloping Hallie on the head half an hour earlier, even in a town as small as this. Not without stinking of smoke and with the car in the garage."

"Maybe I didn't tell you because I'm distracted," Jim said. "Or maybe because I thought it'd be more convincing if you found out yourself."

"Or maybe you just like to waste department resources."

"That's it. You've detected it." Jim got serious again. "What about Dale and Faye?"

"This would be the investigation fatigue loosening my lips."

"No, it wouldn't. Not if you've crossed off my mom and brother, or come close, at least. Unless you're thinking they were in it together. What did you get?"

"Not much, is what. They had Thanksgiving dinner. Alone. Cozy little pair, aren't they? She was tired and went to bed early, like your mom, but nobody called *her*. Both of them swear the other one didn't go out, and unfortunately, I've got zero probable cause for a warrant. We can all see they're the ones with a motive and no alibi, and we can all see that's not enough."

"What about the scene? Anything there?"

DeMarco eyed him sardonically. "After the fire department had stomped all over it, soaked it down with water? And then it started snowing? That would be a no. Fire department says accelerant, probably gasoline, though they'll test. Rags. Pine trees. Gasoline splashed over those and probably along the wall. Wood-frame house. And Hallie maybe got hit with a mostly empty gas can. Hit hard, but no way that's going to kill you. I'd say the person didn't *want* to kill her, or even to burn the house down. They shoved her head into the concrete, yeah, because she hit too hard for anything else, but that probably wasn't going to be enough to kill her, either. It was all small potatoes. Plus, she came out with a fully loaded shotgun on her, and she dropped it. They could've shot her—*and* the dog—or they could've beaten her head in with it. Easy murder weapon either way, and you can bet they had gloves on." He must have seen Jim flinch, because he softened his voice. "But they didn't, right? So they're still just trying to scare her out of town, I'd say. Still keeping it lame."

"How about the cameras?" Jim asked. "The neighbors?"

"Fire and water. Not good for electronics. The camera on the garage—that's toast. And nobody saw a damn thing or heard anything, either. Who'd hear a car driving down the road at two in the morning? That house is too isolated. As far as Dale and Faye's neighbors—they didn't see a car leave or one come back. They were all asleep. And, no," he said, anticipating Jim's next question, "they haven't seen anything like Dale conveniently carrying a gas can into his house. Of course, I'm sure there'd be plenty of gas cans at his construction office. Easiest thing in the world for him to get hold of anything he needed. I'll keep working on that—ask him for access to the security cameras out there, poke around some, ask questions—but it's a little hard when the guy in charge of the place is your chief suspect."

Jim sat for a minute and thought. "The main thing I'm coming up with besides that? It's one hell of an escalation."

"Yeah. It is." DeMarco levered himself up from the table. "I'm going home and getting some sleep, and then I'll think about it some more. Meanwhile, I'd say—keep Hallie here, if you can. I don't think small towns are good for her health."

IN LIMBO

For the next two days, Hallie hung around Vicki's house and felt terrible.

"Face it," Vicki said at dinner on Saturday night. "You're going to have to call in sick for a few days. You look awful."

Hallie sighed. She'd faced it. It wasn't the bandage, which would have been fine. It was the dizziness, the headaches, and the fuzziness in her brain. She couldn't concentrate to save her life.

So to speak.

"The doctor said I shouldn't drive for a week or so," she admitted. "Until I can focus better. And unless we watch movies for a week, you're right. My kids are going to have a sub for their sub for a few days, anyway. Probably this whole week."

"Which is fine," Jim put in. He and Mac were having dinner with them.

"How do you know?" Hallie asked him. She was feeling restless and grouchy. Her head was tender, her heart hurt, and her future looked way too questionable in every way.

"Well, let's ask Mac," Jim said. "Is it all right to have a sub for a sub?"

She shrugged. "Hallie isn't like a sub. She's like a regular teacher. She gives homework, and she's strict."

"Doomed," Hallie said. Mac actually laughed, and Hallie smiled at her and felt a little better.

"So what are they doing?" Cole asked. "About Hallie's . . . case?"

"Still investigating," Jim said.

Cole rolled his eyes. "Yeah, right."

"You know I can't tell you," Jim said.

"What about your house, Hallie?" Mac asked, for once sounding a little shy. "What are you going to do?"

Jim had taken them all out to look at the house earlier that day. The garage wall had burned through, the floor above it damaged by water to the point where that entire section of the house would have to be torn down and rebuilt. Hallie's car had survived, parked as it had been on the end of the garage closest to the house, but her father's tools, his workbench—those were history. Above that—her father's bedroom and bathroom had been empty. Now, they would be gone, replaced with something new. Which wasn't necessarily a bad thing.

Hallie put a hand to her aching head and pushed her sweet potatoes, the final remnants of Thanksgiving, around her plate with her fork. "Get it fixed, I guess. Rebuilt. I called the main insurance number yesterday and left a message."

"You could do something fancy when you redo it," Mac said. "Like have a giant fish tank in the bathroom. Something happy like that."

Cole snorted. "That's lame. She should have a giant *Jacuzzi* in her bathroom. *That* would be happy. And get her garage wired for an electric car, maybe, with a recharging station. That'd be cool. It would be the first one in Paradise, I bet."

"Seattle on the Palouse," Vicki said.

"You could do a swimming pool, Hallie," Mac suggested. "Instead of the fish tank. Since you're going to be rich."

Hallie laughed, even though it hurt her head and her back, which was aching, too. "I don't think so."

"Cletus would like it," Mac argued. "Golden retrievers like to swim."

"I'll take him to the river this summer, then," Hallie said. "I have no idea if he's ever swum or not. We could see."

She stopped in confusion. Where had *that* come from?

"Whoops," Jim said. "Kinda sneaks up on you, doesn't it?"

"What does?" Cole asked.

"Paradise," Jim answered.

Cole gave him a sardonic look for that. "Really? I can't wait to get out of here. Is living in Seattle really cool?" he asked Hallie.

"Pretty much. Lots of coffee. Lots of rain. Lots of bookstores. Lots of traffic, too. Are you thinking about going to school there?"

"UW," he said. "It's big, it's far away from home, and it's got tech. That's good enough for me. I don't even have to worry about paying for it anymore, I guess, which is awesome."

She said, "That was my school, as a matter of fact. If you come out to visit, I'll give you a tour."

"Wicked," he sighed.

Jim must have noticed Hallie's loss of interest in her sweet potatoes, because he asked her, "How you doing?"

"OK."

"Right. I'd say, time for bed."

"And I'd say you're being dictatorial again," she said. "Except that in this *one* instance only, you're probably right." She saw Mac smile into her own plate, which was a good sign, too.

"One question," Jim said, "before you head off. Were you able to reach Bob Jenkins this afternoon?"

"No." Hallie sobered again. "Anthea got hold of his wife, though. They're down in Boise for the weekend, coming back tomorrow, and I've got a meeting with him on Monday."

"So did she talk to him about you being out of the house?"

"Yeah. Obviously, I can't be in there until the house is habitable. He agreed to that." She felt more tired than ever at the thought. "And by the way—Dale called me today and offered to have some of his guys come over on Monday and seal it off, which was nice of him." Protecting it against the elements, which would be necessary no matter what she decided to do about the rest of the rebuild, aquarium or no.

"What did you tell him?"

"I told him thanks, but I already had Kevin Yost coming to do it." Which Jim had arranged on Friday, and thank goodness for that. You might be able to find a worse time to have your house burn than Thanksgiving night, but she couldn't think what it would be.

"Good," Jim said. He didn't offer anything more, but from the look on Cole's and Vicki's faces, he didn't have to. They got it. Dale wasn't her first choice to keep her house safe, from the elements or anything else.

"And now," Hallie said, standing up and picking up her plate, "I *will* head off to bed, if you all don't mind. And tomorrow, I'll see if my feeble brain is up to lesson planning for that sub."

"Or we could watch movies," Mac said.

"Maybe for the first day, anyway," Hallie agreed. "Goodnight, everybody."

Staying away from Jim, which had once seemed so impossible, was now depressingly easy. She sure didn't want to kiss anybody right now. Not even him.

Everything was on hold right now, and it felt lousy. Her job. Her living situation. Her future. All because somebody wanted more money.

Once, she might have walked away and let them have it. Once.

◆　◆　◆

On Monday, it took everything she had to remember that resolve.

"Are you sure?" she asked Bob Jenkins. She'd walked to his office for her appointment, had refused Jim and Anthea's offers to go with her. She wasn't eighteen. She was a professional woman with good judgment, concussion or no. She had to be able to stand on her own two feet. She had all kinds of decisions to make here. She had to know she was making them independently.

Now, though, she wished she had somebody else with her, because this wasn't going the way she'd hoped.

"I'm sorry," Bob said. "Despite what happened to you, the will is perfectly clear. You have to live in the house to inherit. The house is habitable, or at least it will be after today. You're already a day past your three-day-a-month limit."

"No," Hallie said. "I'm not. The will said three days a month. It's December first."

He smiled faintly. "You should have been a lawyer. You're right. I'd forgotten that. I concede your point."

"And there's water damage. Smoke damage."

"It's habitable," Bob repeated. "You have two more days, and then you have to go back there. If you want to inherit, that is." He leaned across the desk, his tone softening. "The alternative is, you can take the forty thousand dollars you've already received, sell the house as is—most of the value is in the land anyway—take the insurance payment, and go back to Seattle a million dollars richer."

"I'd think that there could be leeway with the will, since somebody tried to *kill* me in the house."

"It's terrible, but 'leeway' isn't a legal concept. It is, or it isn't."

"Well, thanks." She got up, grabbed for her purse, and headed for the door.

"Hallie," Bob said. "I'm sorry. I wish the answer could be different. Think about what you want to do and let me know. Nobody would blame you."

She turned and faced him. "My father would blame me. Or he'd be laughing. I don't even know which. This was a test, and I don't care about his tests anymore, but I'm tired of him winning." She shook her head and wished she hadn't. "That makes no sense. But I'm not letting him win."

She didn't wait for Bob to answer. She just left.

She set out to walk through the cold back to Vicki's house. She'd be there two more days, and then she'd be stuck out at the house. Without even being able to drive, which was going to be ridiculously inconvenient.

The thoughts whirled as she made her way up the hill past the courthouse, then turned right at the Presbyterian church. And past "her" house again, the one with the peaked roof, looking shabbier than ever with its dingy paint contrasted against fresh white snow.

She could do what Bob had said. Sell the house and buy something like this one. There were some neighborhoods like this in Seattle, homey places with kids playing in the neighbors' yards, places where you could ride your bike to work, where you could have a dog and didn't have to lock your door.

Well, maybe she wouldn't go *that* far. Seattle wasn't Paradise. And when somebody might be trying to kill you, you locked your door, wherever you lived.

She was always a slow reactor, and she was even slower now. Her footsteps dragged as she reached the corner beyond the white house, and then she turned and walked past it again, stood staring at it without really seeing it.

Bob had said that there was no choice. The will was clear.

But *was* it? Who said? Who decided? Didn't it say something about "exceptional circumstances?" She thought she remembered that.

If somebody had told her she had a rare disease, and she wasn't convinced, what would she do? She'd get a second opinion.

She started walking again, turned left at the Presbyterian church this time, and headed back down the hill.

NEW POSSIBILITIES

When she got back to the office, she didn't ask to see Bob. She walked into the waiting room and told Pam Garrett, the receptionist, "I'd like to see Anthea."

"I'll check and see if she's available," Pam said.

For once, Hallie didn't go along. "Tell her it's urgent. If she's sitting back there, unless she's got somebody in her office, I need to see her."

Pam spoke into the phone, and thirty seconds later, Anthea came out from the back. "What's going on?" she asked. "Weren't you here to talk to Bob?"

"Yeah. Let's go to your office."

Anthea studied her. "Your head OK?"

"My head's fine." It wasn't, but oh, well.

When she was seated in Anthea's office, she said, "I need legal advice."

"Well, sure."

"I need to know if I can go to court and tell a judge that somebody tried to burn down my house and tried to kill me, so living in it isn't reasonable, because it's putting my life in danger. I need to see if I can get a . . . dispensation, I guess."

"It'd be worth a try," Anthea said. "But surely you can't live in it anyway until the damage is repaired."

"Bob says I have to. As long as it's not . . . red tagged or whatever. So I want to hire you to go to court and argue that. I've got almost eighty thousand dollars," Hallie tried to joke when she saw Anthea looking thoughtful. "That's probably enough."

"That's not it," Anthea said. "It's that I represent Cole. That could be seen as a conflict of interest if I asked for a change that would benefit you at Cole's expense. But Bob could do it."

"Ah," Hallie said. "But he's got a conflict of interest, too, doesn't he?"

"How?"

"Isn't he Cole's trustee? *And* my aunt and uncle's lawyer? And—wait."

Anthea said, "Yes, but—"

Hallie put up a hand to stop her. "I think I want to talk to Jim about this, too. And I want to do it somewhere else." She stood up. "Come on. We're going to the coffee shop. I'll call Jim along the way."

Anthea raised her hands, then dropped them again. "Where's the Hallie Cavanaugh I know and love?"

"Taking up my space in the world, that's where. Standing my ground."

◆ ◆ ◆

She and Anthea sat in Brewster's for half an hour. Hallie had had two cups of coffee, and her head was buzzing with more than just concussion and caffeine. She'd refused to explain to Anthea, saying, "I want to wait. I want to talk it out all together."

Finally, she saw Jim. Coming through the door, his stride purposeful and quick. He looked around, saw her, and headed straight over, then sat down beside her and said, "What happened?"

Hallie said, "Hi," and smiled. "I'm so glad to see you." Because she was.

His eyes softened. "Me too, baby. You OK? You about gave me a heart attack when you called. I was all the way out at the edge of the county. Had to put the siren and lights on."

Anthea said, "I do not need to know this. Don't call her 'baby' in front of me."

Hallie said, "Unless we actually have sex in front of you, or I tell you we are, or Jim tells you, you don't know. So back off."

Anthea's mouth opened, then shut. "What did that knock do? Transplant your personality?"

"You can get grumpy," Hallie said, "when somebody's trying to kill you. But never mind. OK. Here's what I wanted to say. I met with Bob Jenkins this morning about the house, you know, Jim, and he seemed . . . pretty unreasonable about it to me." She explained in a few quick sentences. "And I started thinking about getting a second opinion. So I asked Anthea, and she said she couldn't represent me, because she represented Cole. And *that* made me think about conflicts of interest."

"Explain," Jim said.

"Bob is the executor of my father's will. But he's also Cole's trustee. And he's not the only one."

"Aldon Cranfield," Anthea said.

"Didn't you say something," Hallie asked Jim, "about that meeting in Bob's office, when your mom hired Anthea?"

"My mom said Aldon Cranfield had a drinking problem," Jim said. "Which he does. Misses a few days every few months, and more than that at other times. When he's 'on vacation.' But he's been there forever, and sharp as a tack anyway. Shrewd. That's why he's still got the job."

"He was one of my dad's big pals," Hallie said. "A hunting buddy of my dad's, at least when I was still talking to my dad. I'm betting he knew my dad's gun collection. And if he's been talking to Bob—I'd told Bob I was selling the guns."

"And Bob said something about looking after Cole's money," Anthea said. "That he'd be checking the statements, which made it sound like Aldon was handling the investments."

"You think Cranfield could be cooking the books?" Jim said. "Could be. It'd be tempting, especially once Cole gets the rest of the money."

Hallie nodded, then wished she hadn't. "It's in trust until he's twenty-five. Ten years. All along, we've been thinking about who has a financial motive, and the answers are, obviously—Cole and my uncle and, once removed, my aunt and your mom. It isn't Cole, and it isn't your mom, at least whoever burned my house and hit me on the head, which has to be the same person. And the same person who planted those devices on our cars."

"Right," Jim said.

"But there are two other people with a vested interest. I've never heard exactly how much money is in the estate. We won't really know until the six months are up. But say it's—six million, maybe eight million, after the million to Cole and the half million to Dale."

"Say it is," Anthea said. "So?"

"So what if Cole's share isn't forty-five percent? Say it's seventy-five percent? Trustees get paid, right? How much?"

"One percent annually is typical," Anthea said.

Hallie tried to do the math in her head and failed. "Stupid concussion. So what kind of difference would that be?"

Anthea cocked her head and said after a minute, "Maybe thirty to fifty thousand more a year. That's nice money, but it's not hit-you-over-the-head money."

"But if somebody was skimming," Jim said, "it could be *great* money. Almost twice as much to play with? That could be an honest-to-God motive for anything. And thirty thousand a year? Hate to tell you, but some people will kill for a hundred dollars in somebody's pocket."

"Not lawyers," Anthea said. "Not bankers."

"Depends on their habits," Jim said. "Depends what they're trying to hide from their wives, or their boss. Thirty thousand could cover up a gambling problem, for example. But we're not talking about that anyway. We're talking about *big* money. That one of them could be going after, or even both of them. That'd be easiest, if it were both of them, and if they kept it small. Five percent skimmed off the top, say? How would you even know?"

Anthea said, "I just got the first statement for Cole's trust today, because it's quarterly. I only glanced at it. It's complicated—a big portfolio—and I'd say to really know, I'd have to run it by a forensic accountant. It could take some digging, though. Some time, too, for me to find the right person and get it done. Could get expensive. Normally, I'd take it out of the trust itself, but—"

"But if Bob's the trustee," Jim finished for her, "that's a problem. In case it *is* him, or if it's Cranfield, or both of them, we wouldn't want them to know we were checking. Especially if we widen the investigation on the fire to include them."

"I'll pay for it," Hallie said. "It's my money, too, right?"

"Not my preference," Anthea said. "Gets murky, with that conflict of interest and all, but—all right. It's your safety, and Cole's, ultimately. Who says where they'd stop? Who knows when the milk wouldn't be enough, and they'd want the whole cow? Especially if it's Faye or Dale. Say they chase you out of town, Hallie. Then Cole's sitting there, the only thing between them and eight million dollars."

They all stopped to think about that. It wasn't a happy thought. Then Anthea went on. "But I want to address a point you made," she told her brother. "*Could* isn't *is*. Suspicion, possibility—that isn't anything like proof. Bob's my law partner. He's never been accused of mishandling client funds. Aldon—I don't know. He's sketchier. But still."

Jim sighed. "I know that *could* isn't *is*. That's why we try to make damn sure, before we arrest somebody, that the charge will stick. And how much of the time doesn't it anyway? But an investigation isn't a court of law. An investigation is all about *could.*" He told Hallie, "I'll share this with DeMarco. We'll widen the scope."

"*He'll* widen the scope, you mean," Anthea said.

"Yes. He'll widen the scope. It's not clean. It's still a lot of risk, considering that the person could just sit back, wait for Cole to inherit, and skim the money."

"But it could explain," Hallie said, "why the things that have happened so far *have* been low risk. What did you call them? Wussy. Sending letters. Putting tracking devices on our cars to see if we both went to the No-Tell Motel. You'd better take yours off, by the way. No point anymore. And even that fire, except for hitting me—it was small."

"All of it planned out ahead of time, too," Jim said. "Except the hitting. If they'd wanted to smoke you out and kill you, they could've done it easy. Instead, what did they do? Hit you with an empty gas can. Almost a knee-jerk reaction. This isn't somebody who solves things by violence. This is somebody who sits behind a desk."

"Somebody who's getting desperate," Anthea pointed out. "Because they thought it would be easy money, and because Hallie's alerted, and the police are asking questions."

"It's what you said," Hallie told Jim. "It's the money in their jacket pocket. If it was either of them—they had to know the terms of my father's will. Well, Bob, obviously, but I'll bet Aldon, too, or he wouldn't have agreed to be a trustee for Cole. They probably thought I wouldn't do it. Heck, *I* didn't think I'd do it. So when my father died, they thought they had that money in their pocket. And now, it feels like theirs, and they don't want to give it up."

"Especially," Jim said, "if they helped your father out of the world in the first place, then saw that money coming to them. Maybe needing it. And something Bob said, about the guns, after that little incident we had. He mentioned a gun safe sitting in the bed of a pickup. Now, of course he *could* have figured out that I'd have taken the whole safe, and that it would've been in the bed of my truck. But it struck me kinda funny all the same at the time."

He stood up. "Anyway—good to check. It's a thought. But your aunt and uncle are still a better thought. If you hear hoofbeats, look for horses, not for zebras. You go for the obvious answer, not the least likely answer. Six million, eight million in his estate? I already did the math on *that*. Ten percent of it is six hundred thousand, eight hundred thousand. Twenty-five percent is two-point-five times that much. And if people will kill for a hundred dollars—what will they do for a couple million?" He looked at Hallie. "We'll figure it out. We'll get there. Good job thinking it through. And probably enough hard thinking for one day, wouldn't you say?"

"Yeah." She rubbed a hand over the unbandaged part of her forehead. "I would."

"Mac and I are coming over tonight," he said. "We'll have dinner, and I'll let you know what DeMarco says. What we find out. And, yes, I've already taken the GPS off my truck. No point in trying to keep whoever it is from escalating at this point. Unfortunately. They've already done it."

He looked like he wanted to kiss her good-bye, but instead, he just left, and Hallie watched him go.

Anthea said, "He's right. You look beat. Come on, walk me back to the office."

"No," Hallie said. "I'm going to sit here awhile." She felt shaky, suddenly. Lousy. "But first—give me an honest-lawyer name. Whatever Jim does or doesn't find out, he's right. Bob or Aldon—they're both unlikely compared to my aunt and uncle. But meanwhile, I want that second opinion."

◆   ◆   ◆

She moved back into her house two days later. No choice. But she didn't move in alone.

"Phew," Cole said when he walked through the front door behind Hallie and his mother, after eyeing the plastic-wrapped outer wall with some awe. "Stinks in here."

Cletus, who was running around the kitchen, sniffing his way, seemed to agree.

"We'll open the windows," Hallie said. "Air it out. And it isn't as bad as it was. It was way worse yesterday, before the carpet and drapery cleaning people came."

"It's freezing outside," Cole pointed out helpfully. "If we open the windows, it'll be freezing *inside*."

"So we'll turn on the heat, too," Hallie said.

"Expensive," Vicki commented.

"Luckily," Hallie said, "I'm rich."

Cole laughed. "Wicked."

"Go check out my family room, Cole," Hallie said. "Downstairs. Big-screen TV, couch, pool table. There's a bedroom down there, too. You may never move out."

He took off down the stairs with Cletus following him, the two of them sounding like a herd of elephants, an extremely comforting reminder that Hallie wasn't alone. Vicki said, "Show me where I'll be sleeping, and then let's get the car unloaded."

Cole had been the first to volunteer to move in with Hallie. "Since I'm her brother," he'd said at dinner two nights earlier, "it should be me. Somebody has to, and it can't be Jim. She needs a man out there."

"You're not a man," Mac had said.

"Who says?" Cole had answered.

"You're *fifteen*."

"So? In lots of places, fifteen-year-olds are considered adults."

"In *what* places?"

Hallie had put a hand to her head and laughed. "Guys. Stop. And Cole—that's very sweet, but I don't think your mom would be excited about my putting you in danger."

"Well, no," Vicki had answered. "But if I'm there, too, somebody might think twice about trying anything else. Not to mention Cletus. I'm guessing Cletus came as an unpleasant surprise the other night. Besides, I'm home during the day a lot, and I can drive Cole to school. I can drive you, too, Hallie, until you're able to do it yourself again."

"I couldn't . . ." Hallie had had to swallow past the lump in her throat. "I couldn't ask you. Not in that house."

"Oh," Vicki had said, "I think you could. The worst parts are gone. Somebody did both of us a favor, didn't they?" She'd looked at Hallie, and Hallie had known exactly what she was thinking. *Sayonara, bedroom.* "Anyway, it's only for three months."

"There'll be construction going on." Hallie had made a last-ditch effort despite her gratitude.

"And somebody will need to supervise that," Vicki had said. "You never know what kinds of shortcuts those guys will try to pull."

"It's Kevin Yost," Jim had said.

"And Kevin Yost used to run up his bar tab and 'forget' to pay it," Vicki had answered. "Don't tell *me* about Kevin Yost."

Hallie had had to laugh. "All right. That would be wonderful. That would be great. And I'd back you against Kevin any day, Vicki. Glad to have you on my side."

So now, she was back in her house. And the next day, she called Bob Jenkins to tell him she was.

"My three days for December are used up," she said, "and here I still am, with three roommates. Hopefully whoever's trying to scare me off will get the message." *Even if it's you.*

"Well," he said, "I'm real glad to hear that. I'm sorry I couldn't be more accommodating about your staying there, but the law's the law, I'm afraid."

"Ah," she said. "Yes. I'm getting a second opinion on that. So you know. I wouldn't want you to be surprised."

"Oh?"

"Yes. I'm going to see Sage Christiansen down in Union City next week, to see if she thinks we can challenge it in court."

Bob sighed. "Well, it's your money, if you want to waste it. Sage is—well, she's eager. But she can have a chip on her shoulder."

"Perfect. Because so do I."

After that, she hung up and called her uncle and filled him in.

"I've sure been thinking about you," he said when she finished. "Glad to know you'll have company over there in the meantime. That was mighty worrisome. The sooner they figure out who's behind all this, the better. I don't know what the sheriff's department is doing, though, messing around the way they are. Do you know they were over here asking us about what we were doing that night? Like I'd hurt my own niece, the only family I've got left, just to get a little more money."

"You've got Cole, too," Hallie said.

"You're right. I keep forgetting. That's going to take a while to sink in. So you doing all right?"

"I am." Which was when she told him about her second opinion. Whoever was doing this, she wanted to telegraph the message loud and clear: *Be satisfied with what you're getting, because you aren't getting mine.*

"Well," Dale said slowly, "asking you to stay in that house when you've been attacked out there—I have to agree, that's too much. Your dad wouldn't have wanted that. But going to court? Are you sure you want to rock the boat like that? Could be risky."

"Yes," Hallie said. "Dead sure."

STEPS ONE TO THREE

It had started out so simply, the killer thought. So—*cleanly.* Just a matter of inaction when Henry had choked. And, all right, a slip instead of the Heimlich. A *slip,* that was all. An accident.

Which was what had happened with Hallie, too. An accident. If only the dog hadn't barked so much, it would have ended up as a small fire, easily extinguished, covered by insurance, and hardly any harm done. Which is what it *had* been. The smoke detectors would have woken Hallie up eventually, and she'd have called 911, gotten out of the house, and waited for the fire department like anybody would have expected her to do.

Even with the dog barking—it had still been an accident. She should have run down the driveway, away from the flames. Instead, she'd turned back toward the house. Toward the figure in the shadows. After that, it had been reflexive. A swing of an arm, warding her off. And then—keeping her quiet, that was all. Keeping her from seeing. She hadn't been hurt, not really. A bump on the head, that was all.

And what had happened since? A whole hornet's nest worth of trouble, that was what.

The question was—what to do now? Now that Hallie was going to another attorney, and maybe going to court. Now that she had Vicki and Cole—*and* the dog—out there at the house with her. She wasn't giving up. She was doubling down.

And why? *Because* it had all been an accident. *Because* it had all been too soft. Because she knew that nobody was really trying to kill her, or even to hurt her.

You couldn't scare somebody who knew you wouldn't follow through. You couldn't win the pot if your opponent knew you were bluffing.

So what was the answer?

Stop bluffing.

◆　◆　◆

The first step on that journey was the hardest, oddly enough: calling down to Sage Christiansen's office. The secretary couldn't possibly know Hallie's voice, but the call was nerve-wracking all the same.

"This is Hallie Cavanaugh." A pause to cough. "I can't remember when I made my appointment for next week. I haven't been feeling well. Can you remind me?"

"Next Monday," the secretary said helpfully. "December eighth."

"Thank you." Another cough. "See you then."

Hanging up, wiping the sweat off nervous hands. Right. Step two, then. Which was still nonviolent. As was step three. Well, not *directly* violent. Not unless it was absolutely necessary. At some point, Hallie had to believe it wasn't worth it. Her courage would crumble.

A long wait for Sunday evening and another stint with the Ambien. In mashed potatoes this time, and it worked just as well as it had before. And at eleven o'clock, the killer drove down the grade to Union City.

A rental car would have been better, but podunk Paradise didn't have any rental car places. But never mind. After this, there would be all the money in the world to go any *place* in the world. To go to the one that was best of all. It was a thought to firm the resolve and stiffen the spine.

The parking lot was behind the building, but the killer already knew that. Beyond the sign that read *Atkinson, Buchanan, and Christiansen, Attorneys at Law.*

In a commercial district. No houses. No neighbors. All quiet, near midnight on a frosty winter Sunday night.

The killer parked in the lot, popped the trunk, and pulled out the air rifle purchased from North Idaho Sports on a frantically busy Saturday, after a long wait at the firearms counter while wives bought Christmas presents for their hunter hubbies, clutching newspaper ads circled with black pen. In other words, a purchase the bored clerk couldn't possibly remember.

There were two lights in the parking lot, hanging low. Nothing you had to be a hunter to hit.

You have all the time in the world. Nice and easy.

The first shot went wild, the report sounding shockingly loud in the silent, frozen air, and the killer flinched and almost dropped the gun.

It's just an air rifle. Calm down. It isn't that loud. There's nobody here.

Aiming again, taking a deep breath and holding it, and pulling the trigger.

A tinkle of glass, and the light had gone dark.

Success.

On to the second one. One shot. One hit. All dark.

Yes.

Henry had always been so smug about his hunting prowess. He always got the most. He always got the best.

Who's winning now, Henry? the killer asked silently as the air rifle went into the trunk, destined for the ShopCo dumpster. *You sat there and laughed at me. You said you'd tell. You said you'd take me down just for the fun of it. But who died that night? And who's winning now?*

The surge of excitement, the delicious power—they made the killer's hands shake on the wheel. Everything up to now felt like small potatoes, even the fire. This had been *real.* Shots fired. That was real.

This is yours. Take it.

Down the driveway and nobody coming. No alarms. No shouts. No sirens.

Step two.

Done.

◆　◆　◆

Step three, now . . . Step three.

Step three was everything the other steps hadn't been. Public. Risky. And potentially deadly.

"Your appointment is on Monday at four fifteen," the secretary had said. "We'll see you then." That was where the idea had come from.

At four fifteen, it would be dusk. At four thirty, it would be full dark, and now the lights in the parking lot were out.

Hallie's appointment would take at least half an hour, and all the job required was five minutes. Practice made perfect, and the killer had practiced on a sheet of metal all week, every time the house—and the garage—had been empty. Which hadn't been often enough.

After this, though—after this, the sky would be the limit. Divorce, even. Divorce wouldn't matter if you had this much money coming in. Community property only applied to money the other person—and the IRS—knew about.

"Independently wealthy." The killer said the words aloud, relishing them, then pulled to a stop a cautious half block from the law building's driveway. A grab for a small duffel, out of the car, and walking. Not hurrying. Wearing two sweatshirts again, another parka, another pair of baggy pants, and another pair of too-large shoes. Thank God for thrift stores.

Up the driveway again, too, but on foot this time, skirting the fence at the far edge of the driveway, the camo parka and green cargo pants blending perfectly into the shadows.

Two cars in the lot. The attorney's, presumably, a neat, older-model Lexus, and Hallie's, a piece-of-junk Ford Focus with one very interesting feature on its undercarriage, noticed during the stealthy placement of a GPS device.

Rust.

She'd parked in the outermost spot in the lot, nearest the driveway. Which was perfect. That meant doing it on the passenger's side, because that was the side that was hidden from view. Maybe that was better anyway. You wouldn't want it to happen too fast. Not until she was up the hill.

The killer crouched between the car and the back wall and pulled a headlamp from the duffel. The riskiest part, but necessary. The lamp was switched to the red setting, which was the subtlest possible, especially on a head that was under the car before you switched it on, with the cordless drill in hand. And five quick holes, punched one after the other into the rear floorboards, where they'd be hidden by the mat.

Would it work? Maybe. Downhill would have been best. Uphill was better than nothing.

Even if didn't work today as well as it might—it would make her sick. And even if somebody found the holes, eventually . . . it would make Hallie think. It would make her *leave.*

Or else the killer would go to step four.

UP THE GRADE

"So that should do it," Hallie's brand-new attorney, Sage Christiansen, told her. "I'll request an emergency hearing and see if we can get in there in the next week or so to revisit the terms of the will."

"Do you think it'll work?" Hallie asked.

"Well, it's up to the judge, so you never know, but with the concussion and everything? I think we've got a great case." Sage reminded Hallie of Anthea. Brisk, no-nonsense, and frighteningly competent. It must be an Idaho-woman-lawyer thing. "I'd say if somebody tries to burn you out of the house and hits you in the head, you could call that an emergency, and reasonable grounds to contest Bob's interpretation."

"Well, they didn't try to burn me *out,* exactly," Hallie said. "It was a pretty small fire, in the end."

"Now you're spoiling my story," Sage said, and Hallie laughed.

Sage stood up. "I'll walk you out. And I'll call you when I know anything."

When she held the back door open, though, she frowned. "Huh. That's weird. Something must be funky with the lights. Can you see your way to your car?"

"No problem." It was bitterly cold, but the stars were out. "I'm fine."

"Right, then. See you." Sage went back inside, and Hallie headed for the car, climbed inside, and cranked up the heater first thing. She had to sit a minute while the defrosters worked, but that was all right.

Her phone rang, and she pulled it from her purse. Jim. That was all right, too.

◆　◆　◆

Jim was swearing. To himself, because Mac was there.

They'd been at the orthodontist in Union City all afternoon, getting Mac's brand-new braces put on. Jim was out five grand, which put that new truck even further into his future, but that was the parenting deal for you.

Unfortunately, in the face of Mac's nervousness, he *hadn't* noticed that she'd shut her seatbelt in the door of the truck, leaving the dome light on.

Well, it *had* been on. Now, it was off, and his battery was stone-cold dead. And his *daughter* was just stone cold, with a mouth that was already starting to hurt and that would be hurting more in a half hour.

"I'm sorry, Dad," she said for the fifth time, the words coming out mumbled around the alien hardware as she tried not to shiver.

"No problem, partner," he said. "I'll call for a jump. But hang on a second." He pulled out his phone.

It had upset him more than he'd like to admit that Hallie had refused to take the afternoon off so he could have driven her down here and taken her to her lawyer's appointment.

"I'm fine," she'd said. "I've been driving again all weekend. All I have left is a mild headache. I was gone all last week, and the kids have finals coming up. I can do it, and I'm going to."

"If you don't want me to take you, for some reason," he'd said, "ask my mom."

"She's got a shift. I'm *fine*, Jim. I appreciate that you feel protective of me, and I get that this has to do with Maya. I know that's triggering things for you, but as we've discussed, I'm *not* Maya. I'm not sick. I had a knock on the head, but I'm perfectly healthy, and now I'm much better. And most of all—I can't see myself as some weak flower who needs to rely on a man. That's what being here has been all about—me standing on my own feet and being strong, here in this town where my dad made me feel so weak. I made this appointment so I could start taking my life back, and that's what I'm going to do."

Jim guessed he got it, but he didn't like it. Just like Maya, Hallie was pushing back hard against his protectiveness. *Damn* it. Didn't she see that it was just . . . just love?

No. *Not* just like Maya. He had to stop thinking that, even when he was right, or it was going to slip out and Hallie was going to decide again that all he wanted was a substitute.

Anyway, Hallie *wasn't* Maya, and she was most definitely feeling better. She'd had her stitches out on Friday and had only a thin red scar and some fading yellow bruising to show for her troubles. And she had all her redhead stubbornness back, too. Unfortunately.

Now, though, he was grateful she'd driven, if only he could catch her. He dialed, and she picked up.

"Hey," she said. "And before you ask—Sage is awesome, and she thinks we've got a shot. Much as I enjoy my new roommates."

"That's great, baby. But—hey, are you driving yet?"

"Nope. Just got in the car. How's Mac?"

"Fine, but my truck's got a dead battery."

"Oh, no. Well, I'm still in town. Can I give you a jump?"

"I don't think so. It's *good* and dead, and your car's tiny to jump this monster. Besides, I wouldn't put a lot of faith in your battery itself. I'll wait for the truck. But could you swing by here and get Mac, take her home? If you were OK doing the drive down," he added. "If not, come by here, keep her warm in your car while I wait for the truck, and then

I can drive you all home and come back with you for your car another day. That's even better."

"I don't need you to drive me home," she said. "I'm fine. And of course I'll come get her. Coming right now."

◆　◆　◆

Waiting, the killer found, had been one more nerve-wracking ordeal in a whole series of them. Hallie hadn't come out of the driveway until after five o'clock.

After that, she went the wrong way. Through town.

The killer couldn't risk losing her, had to stay right behind her, and was sweating again, but she never noticed. At least, she kept driving until she reached another parking lot. A professional building, doctors and dentists.

The killer released an unsteady breath, pulled to the curb, and waited. Some kind of specialist appointment for the head knock, maybe. It was just a matter of waiting.

The killer almost missed her, because she came down the driveway again less than five minutes later. The streetlight—*not* shot out here—showed somebody else in her car. Somebody short.

Following her again, then, back through all those same red lights, all of which should help the carbon monoxide build up. Sitting in traffic with the odorless gas filtering in through the floorboards, from everybody else's car, not just hers. And not just cars. Semis, once they were on the highway, hitting those last few red lights before the grade.

The killer dropped back now. He didn't need to follow her so closely. He knew where she was going.

His heart was hammering a mile a minute, and he had to turn the heat down, he was sweating so badly.

He shouldn't be following her. He should be far away for this part. But he had to see if it would work. If it didn't . . . he needed to do something else. He needed to *act.* He'd come too far already, and he needed to go so much farther. And with Hallie out of the picture, the spotlight off, and everything settled down, he'd be able to. He could take as many trips as he wanted to that place he only got to go once a year now. Australia, for the deep-sea fishing.

Australia, which was only a flight to Thailand.

Thailand, where you didn't have to worry about stings and searches. Where anything in the world was for sale, and you weren't confined to looking. You could touch. You could get it as young as you wanted, as much as you were willing to pay for. Including that perfect blend of innocence and skill, of big eyes, soft skin, barely there curves, and thrillingly tiny, expert hands and mouths and bodies that only wanted to please you, that would do anything you asked.

Henry hadn't known about Thailand, but he'd known enough. Henry hadn't had any limits, ever. So when he'd seen a too-hasty click of the mouse after walking in unexpectedly? He'd sat down across the desk, stretched his legs out in front of him in those expensive boots he'd loved to wear, flaunting the fact that he had more money than you did, and said, "Man, I'm thirsty. Get me a glass of water, will you?" And then—he'd *looked.*

The killer couldn't forget that moment. Coming back in with the bottle of water and seeing Henry sitting behind *his* desk, clicking the mouse and *laughing.*

"God *damn* it," he'd said. "Who knew? Mr. Buttoned-Down? Mr. We Can't Do That? Mr. Conservative? With a thing for the little Lolitas?"

"Shh," the killer had hissed, shutting the office door. "For God's sake."

"For God's sake?" Henry had laughed some more. "For *God's* sake? I don't think so." He'd gotten up then, had started to walk out of the office. "I thought I had something to say, but damned if I didn't forget it. You chased it right out of my head, because now I've got something better to think about. Going to take me a while to digest this."

"What are you going to do?" the killer had asked. He'd heard himself beg and had raged at hearing it.

"I don't know," Henry had said. "I haven't decided."

Which was why, that night, after the worst day of his life, the killer had parked down the street and waited on one side of the garage for Henry to come home. Why he'd followed him inside and confronted him. Had reminded him that he knew what Henry had done, too. He knew Henry had a son, and he knew—well, he suspected—how that son had been conceived. And he'd threatened to share it.

Henry had laughed again. Had laughed at the threats, and had threatened himself. Threatened so much worse.

"Hell, I'd do it just for the entertainment value. Know what? I think I will do it. Thanks for the idea."

"But who had the last laugh?" the killer said aloud now. "Who?"

He'd dropped back, lost in his thoughts. He was halfway up the grade, and he had no idea where Hallie was. Not behind him, anyway, on the four-lane road. He'd have noticed passing her, at least.

Pay attention, he thought, even as he rounded a corner and saw oncoming headlights swerve, heard a horn blare, caught the flash of taillights going sideways across the highway.

He'd caught up. And it was working.

◆ ◆ ◆

"How bad is that mouth?" Hallie asked when she got Mac in the car and swung out into traffic.

"It's OK." Mac's voice was listless.

Hallie looked across at her for an instant before concentrating on the traffic again. "I had braces," she said. "You don't have to be brave for me. It hurts after you get them on. It's all right to admit that it hurts."

448

"How long did it hurt for?" Mac asked.

"First couple days are pretty achy," Hallie admitted. "And then it hurts less, and by a week, it doesn't hurt at all." She believed in telling the truth to children. If you didn't, all that happened was that they didn't trust you. Besides—if you told them it wasn't that bad, and then it *was* that bad, what did that do? Made them think they were babies, that they were weak. Better to admit that it hurt and let them feel strong for enduring it.

"Did they give you some ibuprofen?" she asked Mac.

"Yeah."

Hallie could have used some herself, as a matter of fact. As if Mac had picked up on it, she asked, "Is your head still feeling bad?"

"Yes," Hallie admitted. "It is. It's been a long day, I guess, being back at school, and then my appointment. How could you tell?"

"You're rubbing your head," Mac said, and Hallie dropped her hand hastily.

"My dad said he wanted to drive you," Mac went on after a moment, "but you wouldn't let him."

"Nope." Hallie pulled onto the highway, putting her foot on the gas with relief. She wanted to get home. She wanted to lie down and sleep for about a day. "I would've had to skip sixth and seventh period again."

"I had to skip anyway," Mac said. "It would've been better if we'd had a sub. Then there wouldn't have been homework."

"Well, yes," Hallie said, "it would've been better for *you*. But your class deserved to have their teacher back, don't you think?"

"Besides," Mac said, "you wanted to be independent."

That earned her another look from Hallie. "I did. How do you know?"

"I heard my dad tell my grandma on the phone. Anyway, it's important for women to be independent. My mom was independent. She always said that an Army wife had to be able to stand on her own two feet, and that was good, because everybody ought to be able to do that anyway."

Hallie chose her words with care. "Your mom sounds like a smart woman."

"She was. My mom was awesome. When she got sick, though, she didn't like that my dad had to do everything. Especially because she was pregnant."

Hallie had to concentrate to hear Mac's words. They were mumbled around the braces, and the girl's voice was fading some anyway. She was sleepy, worn out from her day, just like Hallie herself.

She cracked the window a tiny bit, letting the cold air rush in. There. That was better, and her head even cleared enough to think about what Mac had said. "Your dad told me about losing your brother," she finally said. "And how hard it was when your mom was sick, and when she died."

She heard only silence for a long moment and wondered if Mac had fallen asleep. "I thought she was going to be coming home," Mac finally said. "I knew she was very sick, but I thought she was coming *home*. With my brother. I thought I was going to get to be his big sister. But they didn't come home."

Hallie's head was pounding with pain, but so was her heart. She lowered the window a little more, focused on the red taillights from the semi ahead of her, on staying in her lane around a wide curve, which took too much focus, and said, "I'm so sorry. That must have hurt so much."

"She made my dad laugh," Mac said. "He used to smile all the time. When he came home after his deployments—I remember he was always smiling. And after she died, he stopped. I tried to get him to smile, but he stopped." She sighed. "My head really hurts. It *really* hurts."

Hallie didn't stop to think if it was all right. She took a hand off the wheel and squeezed Mac's. And then a wave of dizziness overtook her, and she had her hand on the wheel again. A blare beside her startled her, and her hands jerked, and the car swerved to the right. Toward the hill that rose steeply on one side.

"Whoa," she said shakily when she had it under control again. "I'm sorry."

Mac didn't answer, and Hallie wanted to look at her, but she didn't dare take her eyes off the road.

Slow down. She was in the right lane. She could go slower. She lifted her foot from the accelerator, watched fuzzily as the speedometer needle dropped from sixty to fifty.

There. That was better. *Fresh air.* She opened the window halfway, gulped in great lungsful of air, shook her head, and then was sorry she had. Her head hurt as if a hammer were pounding into her skull.

Another blare from a horn as a car went past her. She looked at the speedometer again. Forty-five.

No hurry. Slower is safer.

She was so tired. So tired. She'd pull off for a while, maybe. She'd sleep.

Wait. Mac was in the car. She couldn't do that. She'd pull off, and then she'd call Jim to come get them. That was it. She should have let Jim drive. She wished he were driving now.

There was no place to pull off, though. She was still on the grade.

The thought was still in her head when she registered the sign. *Slow Vehicle Turnout.* Registered it as it was going by, that is.

Watch for it. There'd be another one. Wouldn't there? She couldn't remember.

The cars were passing her in the other lane as if she were standing still. One horn blare after another, and the sound, the white lights—they hurt her head.

Speed up. Get to the top. The speedometer said forty now. She pressed her foot down, watched it go to fifty. To fifty-five.

It was too cold. She was shivering. She pressed on the window switch, and the air got warmer. But there were white lights coming at her. *Right* at her. She took her hand off the window switch and heard a screech of tires from somewhere far away.

Following the white line. Focusing. Following it.

She woke up to a horrible, shuddering impact. And then she was headed the other way, trying to turn the wheel. Seeing the white lights coming at her. Stomping with her foot for the brake, spinning the wheel, trying to get away from the white lights. The tires were screeching, horns were blowing, and she was going the wrong way.

A long moment when they were jolting over something rough, then another impact. A hard hit, and everything was swinging around, and they were flying. Flying, and spinning, and tumbling. Over and over.

The car was full of crashing noise. Like a ride. Like a roller coaster. Like being in the ocean, in a wave.

She didn't like roller coasters. She didn't like waves. She didn't like this. She wanted it to stop.

And then it did.

◆　◆　◆

She woke up. Her head hurt. Her ankle hurt more. Everything hurt. But it was quiet.

Mac. She tried to look to the side, but there was something in the way. Something white and soft, right in her face.

Noise on the other side. A voice. Scared. Thin.

"Hallie? Hallie! Are you OK?"

Mac, Hallie thought again. *Mac's in here. Get Mac out.* "I'm OK," she said. She did turn her head, then, even though it hurt. And there was Mac. It was dark in the car, so dark, but Mac was there, and she was talking.

"We have to get out," Mac said. "In case the car explodes. Dad says . . . you have to get out if you smell gas."

"Right." Hallie pushed past the pain in her head, her ankle. Her fumbling fingers reached for the door handle, and she tugged at it, but nothing happened. And she wasn't sitting right. She was pulled all the way to the right. Why was that?

"The doors are locked," Mac said. "My door's locked. And it's the ground outside. There's snow. I'm on the ground. I'm on the *snow.*"

She sounded panicked, and Hallie forced herself to concentrate. It was cold. *Really* cold. And the car was on its side. "My window's broken," she realized. "We can climb out of that. Get your seatbelt off." She fumbled for hers, but couldn't find it. Panic for a moment, then she figured it out. "Feel down your chest," she told Mac. "Trace it down. Then punch the button."

"I did," Mac said after long seconds. "I got it off."

Hallie did it, too, but the moment she did, she was falling down. Falling into Mac, the pain in her ankle blossoming like a starburst as her foot hit the center console.

Mac cried out, and Hallie said, "Sorry. I'm sorry." She was losing it. The pain . . . *Focus.*

"I'm going to try to climb around you," Mac said. "I can push past the air bags."

There was something else, now, though. A voice from outside the car. "Hallie. Hallie. My God. Are you all right?"

A face in the window. Someone she knew, looking down at them.

"Get us out," Hallie said.

The face was smiling. Holding something. Something that was in the car now, coming at her.

"No! Daddy!"

Mac, Hallie thought, and swiveled fast toward her as an iron fist hit her shoulder. Hit her hard. Broke her.

◆　◆　◆

Jim was running down the hill, his boots eating up the ground, faster than he'd gone since he'd been running through desert sand.

This wasn't sand. It was snow, and it was deep. He was running as fast as he could, but he wasn't getting there. Like being in a nightmare, but this wasn't a nightmare. It was real.

He'd gotten a jump on the rig fast, as it had turned out. A guy coming out after his own appointment, climbing into a Dodge Ram of his own. A quick battery charge, and Jim had been on the road, wishing he'd insisted on driving both Mac and Hallie home, no matter what Hallie had said.

Never mind, he'd thought. He'd catch up to them. And he had.

He'd seen the brake lights flashing red, heard the horns blaring from three curves below on the grade.

Somebody in trouble up there. He'd reached for the emergency light beneath his seat on the thought, had punched the window down, slapped the light on the hood, and turned on the siren.

He had a light and siren on his personal vehicle because he headed up the SWAT team, and he might need to get somewhere fast. He'd never had to do that yet, but he'd needed to do it now. He'd inched out to the left, had forced the cars over, and had been seven or eight cars back when it had happened.

A small sedan in the left lane, swerving into the curb lane and clipping another car, then swinging around across oncoming traffic. Narrowly missing cars that braked hard to avoid it, and headed straight for the edge. Straight for the guardrail.

The *end* of the guardrail. Nothing to hold it on the road. The car had clipped that, too, and then it had been gone.

Within ten seconds, Jim was on the shoulder, grabbing a flashlight and a fire extinguisher, diving from his vehicle and running across oncoming traffic to the guardrail, leaping it and powering down the steep slope, eating up the ground.

The car had rolled. He could see it down there, tilted up on one side. The passenger side. And he'd recognized it as it had gone over.

Hallie. Mac.

That was when he heard a sound to freeze a father's bones.

"DAAAADDDDYYYYY!"

He hadn't thought he could go faster. He did.

Somebody else was there ahead of him, and there were others behind him, too. He could hear the exclamations, the curses as they slipped in the snow.

He was close now. Somebody was leaning into the car as Jim slid down the final four feet.

Mac's voice again from inside. *"No! No!"*

"Mac! Wait!" Jim was shouting, and the figure at the window turned, and Jim saw his face in the moonlight.

Bob Jenkins. Holding something in his hand.

"Oh, thank God," Bob said. "Help me get them out."

"Daddy!" It was Mac's voice again. Panicked. Sobbing. *"Weapon!"*

Bob stepped back, and Jim saw the hand with the tire iron swinging back.

"You son of a *bitch.*" Jim's hand, the one carrying the fire extinguisher, swung out and clipped Bob on the side of the head. The other man went down like a felled tree, but Jim didn't even watch him fall. He was already at the car window, dropping the extinguisher, shoving the flashlight into his pocket.

He almost bumped heads with Mac. She was pushing herself up, scrambling through white pillows. *Air bags.* Jim got her under the arms and was lifting her free, right out the window.

"Hallie," Mac sobbed as she came. "He hit her. He *hit* her. Get her out, Dad. *Gas.*"

He'd already smelled it. The distinctive odor of leaking gasoline.

"Give her to me," a voice said at his back. "I got her, man."

Jim turned with Mac in his arms. The first would-be rescuer had reached the wreck, a big guy in a feed cap and a jacket. Now, he held his arms out. "Give her to me," he said again, and Jim passed Mac over.

"Get her up the slope," Jim said. "Up to the road. Get *back*. This thing could blow."

There were others coming, too, but he forgot about them as he looked down into the vehicle. Hallie was wedged down into the passenger side, and she was moaning.

"Hallie," Jim said. "Climb up to me. Come on, baby."

"I . . . can't," she gasped. "I can't. He hit me."

Jim was already half into the car. Wedging his shoulders through the window, pushing off. He felt a fellow rescuer's hands gripping his lower legs and giving him a shove downward, and he was reaching for Hallie.

"Give me your hands, baby," he said. "Give me your hands."

He got one of them. He had to feel around for the other arm, and when he grabbed it, she screamed in agony.

He yelled over her screams, "Pull us up! *Pull!*" and felt himself rising, taking Hallie with him. He banged his head on the window coming out and barely felt it. His feet were hitting something soft—the person who'd been pulling him—and he was tumbling, bringing Hallie with him. And they were free of the car.

"Help me with her," Jim said. "Everybody else—" His voice rose to a shout. "Out of here! Get out! Up the hill!" A few dark figures were still headed down the hill, visible against the snow, but the smell of gas was all around him, hanging in the cold air. Too dangerous. He'd come back for Jenkins once he got Hallie clear.

He got to his feet and picked up Hallie's shoulders, and she was still screaming. "Get her feet," he snapped to the guy who'd been pulling him. "Run!"

He and the other guy—a young man, and strong—were kicking their way up the slope fast, taking Hallie with them. Almost high enough.

Get her clear, Jim was thinking in one instant. *Go back for Jenkins.* The next moment, the pressure wave hit him, and the heat.

"Down!" he started to shout to the other man. *Explosion.*

The words weren't necessary. They were knocked down anyway. Him. The other guy. And Hallie.

LOVE HARD

Jim climbed to his feet. Thirty feet below him, the car was a fireball, orange flames shooting high into the night.

"Holy shit," the guy beside him said. He was on his feet now, too. "That's gone. Jesus H. Christ."

Maybe so, Jim thought, but he'd already bent down to get Hallie again. She'd stopped screaming. All she was doing now was moaning, and it was so faint. Too faint.

"I've got you, baby," he said, even though he had no idea if she could understand him. "I've got you. It's going to hurt some more now. We have to carry you. Hang on. Just a little bit more." He told the guy, "Grab her feet."

Halfway up, the paramedics came to meet them with a Stokes litter. They loaded Hallie into the basket, strapped her down, and Jim and the other man helped them carry it up. Hallie was barely moaning now, though, and he didn't waste his breath talking to her. He just planted his boots and carried her up. Got her out.

At last, they were at the guardrail, lifting her over it. A sea of flashing red and blue lights. Familiar faces, deputies and paramedics and firefighters, but Jim acknowledged none of them.

"My daughter," he said. "Where's my daughter?"

"Got her in the first ambulance," a firefighter told him. "About to roll."

The paramedics had Hallie in another truck, were slapping an oxygen mask on her, attaching an IV. Jim hesitated for a fraction of a second, but he had to see Mac. He had to find his baby girl.

The other ambulance was parked ahead, past an idle fire engine with nothing to do—nothing but to let it burn out—and a sheriff's vehicle. Other cars were stopped to the front and back, and the headlights and taillights stretched out in a long snake up and down the valley. But Jim didn't look. He climbed up into the back of the ambulance, to the small form stretched out, a blanket over her.

"Dad," she said.

He took her hand and said, "Yeah, partner. I'm here. How you doing?"

"I'm OK," she said, her voice so tiny. "I'm OK. But Hallie . . ." She was crying. "That guy *hit* her. And I think she was already . . . hurt. Is she OK?"

"I don't know," he said honestly. "They're working on her. They'll take her to the hospital, which is where they're taking you. Don't be scared, honey. You're going to be all right."

"I know," she said. "I can talk, and I can move everything. It just hurts, that's all. My head hurts. But Dad. You have to go ride with Hallie. She's hurt worse. She'll be scared."

"No, baby girl." His heart was going to rip in two. He was going to shatter. "I need to stay with you."

"No," she said. "You *don't.* Mom said . . ." She was crying harder now, and the words weren't coming out too clearly, because she'd gotten braces on her teeth today. Braces, so her teeth would be straight when she was grown up. When he cheered too loud at her college graduation, and hung her shelves in her first apartment, and walked her down the aisle. "Mom said," she kept on, "that you have to be strong. That you have to be independent. But if you're really hurt, you need help anyway. You need to help Hallie. I'm OK. She's *hurt.* Go help her."

He could feel the wetness on his cheeks. He knew he was crying, and he didn't care. "I'm going," he said. "I'm doing it. I'll see you at the hospital, partner. I love you."

"I'll see you, Dad," she said. "I love you."

◆ ◆ ◆

It hurt so much. Hallie couldn't stand it. It hurt so *much*.

The voices were talking, but her eyes were closed. She was trying to breathe, but it *hurt*.

Then they put something on her mouth, and she wanted to struggle, but she couldn't. And things were slipping away. She was floating. The pain was still there at the edges, but she wasn't *in* it anymore. She could see it, but she couldn't feel it.

She wanted to tell them "thank you," but she couldn't talk.

But Mac. What about Mac? Mac had been in the car. She remembered Jim's arms pulling her out, and that was all she remembered. Where was Mac?

The voices kept talking, and then there was another one. One she needed.

"Hey, Hallie. Hey, baby."

She opened her eyes, and his face swam into her vision, then blurred.

Jim, she tried to say, but she couldn't, because there was something on her mouth. *Mac,* she tried to tell him with her eyes.

"Mac's OK," he said. "She's in the other ambulance. She's going to be OK."

She shut her eyes, then, because it was too hard to keep them open. Jim had a hand on her arm, over the blanket. She knew, because she felt it. She knew it was his.

She woke up later, but it was different. She wasn't looking at the ceiling of the ambulance anymore, and there was nothing on her mouth.

She was on her side, and there were tubes coming out of her hand, which was lying flat on a white sheet beneath her chin. The pain was still there, just beneath the surface. She opened her eyes and saw him. Jim.

"Hey, there," he said. "How you doing?"

"Weird," she said, her voice not sounding like her own.

He laughed, and that *did* sound like him. More or less.

"What . . . happened?" she asked.

"Your car went off the road. It rolled, but it was lucky the snow was deep. That probably helped. You broke your ankle in the fall, probably because your foot was wedged under the brake pedal. That's in a cast. You didn't do your concussion any good, either. And you got hit on the shoulder with an iron bar that cracked your shoulder blade. Which is going to hurt like hell, but you're going to heal up fine. It's just not going to be too much fun doing it, that's all."

"Mac," she said.

"Mac's all good. Mac's already been released. My mom's got her." Jim's hand was on her head, now, stroking over her hair, so tender, and a few tears were leaking from her eyes. It felt so good to have him here and to hear that.

"I'm glad," she said. "I'm so glad. But I'm so . . . sorry. I was driving, and I . . . I got all fuzzy. I should have let you take us. I should . . . I should . . ."

She couldn't go on. She didn't have to.

"No," he said. "That wasn't your fault. It was carbon-monoxide poisoning. They can't tell—your car burned up—but we're sure it was deliberate. Bob Jenkins was following you, and there was a drill in a bag in the trunk of his car. It wasn't your fault."

The tears were coming a little faster now. The relief was trying to overwhelm her. "He came," she said. "He . . . hit me. I tried . . . to get Mac out, but . . ."

"I know. Mac told us."

"Where . . . is he?"

461

"He's dead," Jim said bluntly, and it took a second for that to sink in. "He burned to death beside the car."

"Oh." She should feel bad, but she didn't.

"And before you start feeling bad about that," he said, as if he'd read her mind, "you should know that they found a whole mess of child porn on his computer. Little girls." She could hear the anger in his voice, the sick disgust. "He would have killed you, too. He'd escalated further and further. I'd guess the fire was the tipping point, and once he wrecked your car, he was ready to go the rest of the way. I didn't kill him, I'm pretty sure. I just knocked him out. But now that I know everything— I'd have killed him."

"I'm glad . . . you didn't. I'm glad you . . . didn't have to." She was so tired, so she shut her eyes, and Jim kept his hand on her head, and that felt better. "Maya wouldn't have . . . wanted you to."

"No. She wouldn't have. And neither would you. That's the only reason I'm glad I didn't."

"Good." It was only a breath. She wanted to sleep, but she wanted him to stay. She wanted to stay with *him*. She wanted to tell him so, but she didn't have to. Jim wasn't going to leave her. As long as she needed him, he'd be there.

"My mom and Cole are outside waiting for you. Your aunt and uncle, too. And Anthea called your mom."

"Oh." She should say more, but she couldn't. *That's good, though,* she thought vaguely. *That my uncle didn't try to kill me. That's nice.*

"They can all keep waiting, though," he said. "And they will. You go to sleep." It was like he knew. Again. "I'll be right here when you wake up, I promise."

"Thanks." It was a whisper. *I love you,* she wanted to say, but she was going to have to say it later. That was all right, though. He'd be here. She could say it then.

"And so you know," he said, his voice rough. Choked. "Because I need to say it. I love the hell out of you."

EPILOGUE

Seventeen months later

The soft air of May was blowing through the open window of the white house across from the Presbyterian church, carrying the scent of lilacs with it. A few petals fell from the crab apple blossoms in the glass vase and drifted, gentle as snow, onto the dining-room table.

At Hallie's house. *Their* house. The only thing, other than Jim's new truck, her new car, and their education and emergency fund, that she'd kept from the millions she'd inherited a year and a half earlier.

She and Jim had been able to keep their hands off each other after all for the final few months of the waiting period. That was a lot easier, she'd found, when you had a fractured shoulder blade and ankle. She'd inherited her share—and had promptly given everything away except what she'd earned from the sale of Henry's house. All of the three-point-five million dollars from the sale of the company and Henry's portfolio was gone. A half million had made it to the women's shelter, with the rest to the scholarship fund helping nontraditional students go to college. A decision that had seemed to cause Faye almost physical pain. If Hallie had referred to her scholarship recipients a time or two when she and Jim had dinner with Faye and Dale, just to see Faye struggle with her expression and watch Jim hide a smile? Well, she was only human.

Had there been a little less in her inheritance? Yes, because Bob Jenkins had been dipping into it. The damage had been minor, though, amounting mostly to a testing of the waters for future raids, checking whether anybody would notice the discrepancies.

If he'd been willing to settle for his management fee, he'd have gotten away with it. All in all, Hallie was glad he hadn't been willing to settle. The world was a better place without him in it.

And without her father, too. Which was why the first thing she'd done on the way home from the meeting with the scholarship foundation had been to stop by Eileen Hendricks' house and give her a brochure.

"Really?" Eileen had asked, staring at the printed words as if they were meant for somebody else. "You think I could?"

"Well, let's see," Hallie had answered. "You're running your own household. You're running your own business. You're raising two children. Yeah, I'd say that gives me some faith."

Eileen had laughed like the sun was coming out, had hugged Hallie, and had even cried a little. She might not go for it, but at least she'd know she had a chance.

Of course, Jim had asked Hallie if she were sure, but that answer hadn't been hard at all.

"Financial security," she'd told him. "That's plenty. Otherwise—I want to keep doing my job, and you want to keep doing yours. A big wide safety net would be great, but everything else is just window dressing. And besides," she'd added, "we're setting an example for our brother. I inherited a family. All right, it's your family, but I'm claiming my share. And that's the most important inheritance of all."

He hadn't argued. She'd known that, deep down, he'd been relieved. That didn't stop him from being almost as excited as she was, though, when they'd gone to the Ford dealership on his last birthday and bought him a brand-new crew-cab Ford F-150. Black.

"I guess I've got a sugar mama," he'd sighed when they'd taken their first family drive in it. "Too bad I can't resist her."

Hallie had exchanged a smile with Mac, who'd been sitting between them. "Except that selling your house got us half the money for the new one, and you've put in about five hundred hours of sweat equity on it since. And except that Idaho is a community property state. Face it, buddy. From here on out, what's mine is yours, and more importantly—what's yours is mine."

Now, she sat in the recliner in the living room of the best house ever, all the way from the peaked roof to the pool table in its basement rec room, and looked at her watch. It was seven in the morning, but that wasn't why she was looking.

She waited another ten minutes to make sure, then pulled the lever to return the recliner to its upright position, heaved herself out of it, and went to the bedroom.

She'd been sleeping in the recliner for the past two weeks, ever since lying flat had grown too uncomfortable. "Practice," she'd joked to Jim. "In case he's fussy. He and I may be sleeping out there all the time, who knows."

He'd been lying across the bed at the time, his hand resting on her belly, feeling their son kick. "Nope," he'd said. "If somebody's got to walk him or sit up with him, that's going to be me. Or at least I'm going to fight you for it."

Now, she paused in the doorway and looked at him. Lying fast asleep on his side, a pillow pulled close to him as if it were Hallie, because he didn't like to sleep without her.

Her husband of a year, and the father of her son.

She went and sat on the edge of the bed, then put a hand on his shoulder. "Hey," she said softly.

He sat straight up. "What? Is it time?"

She laughed, heard the shakiness of it, and forgave herself. He'd been asking the same question every time he'd woken up for weeks now. This time, the answer was different.

"Getting close," she said. "Moving along. I think you'd better get up, and we'd better wake Mac up, too."

He was already out of bed, grabbing for his jeans and pulling them on.

"You don't have to rush," she said. "It's a first baby. For me."

He seemed to hear her nerves, because he paused in the act of dragging his T-shirt over his head, came over to her, pulled her close, and said, "It's going to be fine. You'll see. We're going to have a baby."

She leaned into him, knowing that he was reassuring himself as much as her. "Then get dressed, Dad," she said. "And get ready to help him get born."

◆　◆　◆

She wasn't laughing, though, four hours later, when he *was* helping her. Along with Mac.

"You're doing great, Hallie," Mac said from her spot near Hallie's head. "You're doing awesome."

Hallie wanted to argue, but Jim was on her other side, holding her hand. She could look right inside his heart and see the fear he was trying to hide. And when the doctor said, "Get ready to push," she looked at Jim and thought, *You need a baby, and I'm going to give you one.* So she pushed, and then she pushed some more. She pushed until she thought she'd split in two. But she'd been hurt before and pushed through, and she could do it again. So she did.

One moment, she was calling out, unable to keep the anguished cry from escaping, and the doctor was saying, "We've got a head coming. Here he comes." And the next instant, she was giving it more effort than anything she'd ever done, thinking, *Come on, baby. Come on.* And it *hurt.*

"Dad," Mac was saying beside her, her voice shaking. "*Dad.* He's coming."

Jim was still with Hallie, though. He still had her hand. He was saying, "Come on, Hallie. Come on. You're doing so good, sweetheart. Come on."

"One more push," the doctor said. "A gentle one. And you'll have a baby."

One last time, when she thought she couldn't and she did anyway. And there was a sound. A *sound.* Like a kitten, and then something else. Like a baby. An angry one.

"Well, hello, Mom and Dad," the doctor said. "Hello, big sister. We've got a boy."

◆　◆　◆

Jim knew he was crying, and he couldn't care.

He'd told Hallie it would be all right. He'd told Mac. And he hadn't believed, until this moment, that it could actually be true.

But it was. His son was here.

Thomas James Lawson. Lying on his mother's stomach, his eyes scrunched closed, his face screwed up in concentration, like he was trying to figure out whether the world out here was going to work out for him.

Jim put a hand out, then hesitated.

"Go on," the doctor said. "Go on and touch him. He's yours."

When Jim's hand covered the tiny back, though, he lost it. His hand was shaking, and the tears were coming.

And just like that, there was Hallie's hand on top of his. There was her sweet, exhausted voice telling him, "It's OK, Jim. It's OK, honey. We have a son. And he's fine."

"Dad?" Mac asked, and he shook his head, tried to speak, failed, and laughed through his tears.

"Just . . . too much," he got out. "Sorry. Give me a second."

"You've got a second," Hallie said. "You've got forever." And that made him lose it some more.

◆　◆　◆

Hallie still had her hand over Jim's. Over their son. She was so tired, but she was all good.

She turned her head to look at Mac. "Hey, big sister. Want to touch your brother?"

Mac's eyes were big and round. "Can I?"

"You bet," Hallie said.

Having Mac here had been an open question right up to the end. Mac had come to every childbirth class, though, had made a bulletin board with a diagram of the baby at each week's gestation, had researched until she knew more than Hallie did herself. And in the end, she'd been a trooper.

"Time to cut the cord," the doctor said. "You doing this, Dad?"

"Yep," Jim said. He'd pulled himself together. Of course he had. He stepped down there, took the scissors the doctor handed him, and did it.

"There you go," he said. "Now he's his own person."

"He can't do it himself, Dad," Mac said. "He's a *baby.*"

"Nope," Hallie said, smiling at her. There was so much love in her, it couldn't be contained. It was spilling out all around her. "He's going to need a whole lot of help. A mom and a dad and a big sister to love him and help him grow up strong. Think you're up to it?"

"Yeah," Mac said, sounding shy for once. "I can do that."

Hallie took her hand but left the other one on her son, cradling his body. Jim's was there again already, because Jim would never let go of either of them. Any of them.

"We need to take this little guy to the nursery to do a few things," the nurse said. "We'll bring him right back, though. You coming, Dad?"

"I'm there," Jim said.

First though, he put a hand on Hallie's shoulder, bent, and gave her a kiss. So soft, and so sweet.

"Thank you," he said. "You're amazing. And I love you." Then he was gone, and Thomas was, too, but that was all right. They'd be back. Jim would bring their baby back to her. The doctor was down there doing some stitching now, and it was uncomfortable, but that didn't matter, either.

Mac moved at Hallie's side, and Hallie took her hand. "Stay with me?" she asked Mac. "Please? It feels a little . . . lonesome." She tried to laugh. Slow reactor again. Now, at last, the tears were threatening. "You know," she told the girl, "less than two years ago, I didn't have anybody. And now I've got everything. A husband, and a son, and I hope I've got a daughter too."

"Stepdaughter," Mac said.

"To me," Hallie said, putting all the conviction she had into it, "daughter. I couldn't have a better one. I know you had a mom, and that she was an awesome mom. I'm just learning how. But I want you to know one thing. You're my daughter. That's all. I have a family. And I'm so . . ." She was crying now, and she couldn't care. "I'm so grateful."

ACKNOWLEDGMENTS

Thanks to my awesome critique team: Barbara Buchanan, Carol Chappell, Anne Forell, Mary Guidry, Leslie Harlib, Kathy Harward, and Bob Pryor.

And to my editors at Montlake Romance, Maria Gomez and Charlotte Herscher.

Finally, to my husband, Rick Nolting, for putting up with my absentmindedness during the Australian summer and the North American winter that I spent writing this book. Especially for learning to cook.

ABOUT THE AUTHOR

Rosalind James, a publishing industry veteran and former marketing executive, is the author of contemporary romance and romantic suspense novels published both independently and through Montlake Romance. She started writing down one of the stories in her head on a whim four years ago while living in Auckland, New Zealand. Within six weeks, she'd finished the book, thrown a lifetime of caution to the wind, and quit her day job. She and her husband live in Berkeley, California, with a Labrador retriever named Charlie.